The lights in Andi's house went out, leaving only the glow of the fire.

Bryce reached for Andi, tension spiking through him. "Stay here."

He pulled his flashlight from his pocket and clicked it on. There were no storms in the area. He'd stepped from his car under a clear sky, an almost half-moon casting its soft glow over the landscape. No reason for the power to go out.

"What happened?" Andi's voice was paper-thin, with an underlying quiver.

"I'm going to look out and see if there's light in my direction."

Bryce darted down the hall to the master bedroom. When he swept aside the curtains, his uneasiness ratcheted up several notches. A soft glow shone through the trees: his own porch light. His power was on.

So what happened to Andi's?

Out front, glass shattered, followed by an almost simultaneous scream. He dropped the curtains into place and ran from the room, panic pounding at his heels. At the end of the hall, flames engulfed the love seat that separated the living room from the dining area.

DEADLY MOUNTAIN PURSUIT

CAROL J. POST

&

USA TODAY BESTSELLING AUTHOR

MARY ALFORD

Previously published as *Lethal Legacy* and *Grave Peril*

LOVE INSPIRED
INSPIRATIONAL ROMANCE

LOVE INSPIRED®
INSPIRATIONAL ROMANCE

ISBN-13: 978-1-335-23091-1

Deadly Mountain Pursuit

Copyright © 2020 by Harlequin Books S.A.

Lethal Legacy
First published in 2018. This edition published in 2020.
Copyright © 2018 by Carol J. Post

Grave Peril
First published in 2018. This edition published in 2020.
Copyright © 2018 by Mary Eason

This edition published by arrangement with Harlequin Books S.A.

For questions and comments about the quality of this book, please contact us at CustomerService@Harlequin.com.

Love Inspired
22 Adelaide St. West, 40th Floor
Toronto, Ontario M5H 4E3, Canada
www.Harlequin.com

Printed in U.S.A.

CONTENTS

Carol J. Post writes fun and fast-paced inspirational romantic suspense stories and lives in sunshiny central Florida. She sings and plays the piano for her church and also enjoys sailing, hiking and camping—almost anything outdoors. Her daughters and grandkids live too far away for her liking, so she now pours all that nurturing into taking care of two fat and sassy cats and one highly spoiled dachshund.

Books by Carol J. Post

Love Inspired Suspense

Visit the Author Profile page
at Harlequin.com for more titles.

LETHAL LEGACY

Carol J. Post

Fear thou not; for I am with thee: be not dismayed;
for I am thy God: I will strengthen thee;
yea, I will help thee; yea, I will uphold thee
with the right hand of my righteousness.
—*Isaiah* 41:10

Writing is a solitary activity, but a lot of support goes into writing and publishing a book. A huge thank you to my "team":

My sister, Kim Wolff, for all your help with my Murphy research.

The rest of my family for your unending encouragement.

My critique partners, Karen Fleming and Sabrina Jarema, for making my stories the best they can be.

My beta reader/proofreader, Martha "Mom" Post, for catching the things the rest of us miss.

My amazing editor, Dina Davis, and lovely agent, Nalini Akolekar, for all your hard work.

And my wonderful husband, Chris, for thirty-seven amazing years.

ONE

Trees lined both sides of the gravel drive. Their half-bare limbs framed the old house at its end and lent a spooky edge to the air of abandonment that hung over the property. A branch dangled from an oak, curled leaves barely visible against the moonlit sky.

Andrea Wheaton slowed her Escalade to a crawl. It didn't help. The long screech against the roof set her teeth on edge and sent a shiver down her spine.

At the end of the drive, she released a sigh as childhood memories bombarded her. The old Wheaton place projected a rustic hominess that had always called to her. It didn't hold a candle to their place in Atlanta, with its soaring columns and manicured grounds, but she'd always loved it. It had represented freedom, the one place she could let down her guard and simply be Andi.

Now it was hers. Six days later, and she was still reeling from the news.

She retrieved her small suitcase from the back seat and carried it to a porch covered with a three-inch-deep blanket of dead leaves. A swing hung from one end, and two Adirondack rockers sat side by side in the center.

Judging from the layer of debris on each, neither the swing nor the rockers had been used for some time.

She laid the bag down and then pulled a wooden key chain from her purse. It was cut into the shape of North Carolina, the word *Murphy* burned onto its face. For twelve years, the key had lain in the bottom of her jewelry box, untouched. Partly because she'd been busy, first with college, and then with marriage and job responsibilities. Partly because she'd wanted to avoid the neighbors on both sides.

One she'd never cared for. The other she'd cared for too much.

When she slid the key into the lock, it turned without resistance. She frowned. Had her father forgotten to lock the dead bolt? A quick check of the doorknob told her it was unlocked, too.

A wave of uneasiness swept over her, and she shook it off. This wasn't the city. This was Murphy, North Carolina, where neighbors helped one another out and it wasn't uncommon to see a car parked in front of the Daily Grind downtown, keys still in the ignition.

She opened the door and swiped the double switch inside. Light flooded the porch and living room. When she stepped over the threshold, a sense of grief cut a wide swath through her heart. This had been her and her father's retreat, the opportunity for them to escape the incessant demands of her mother.

Less than a week ago, she'd been sitting at the huge table in her aunt and uncle's lodge near Asheville, enjoying turkey dinner, her parents across from her. Now they were gone. After leaving the lodge, they'd apparently taken a curve too fast and plunged down an embankment to their deaths. Driving fast wasn't in her dad's nature. Neither was carelessness.

But neither was moodiness. Or brooding. Or several other behaviors she'd seen over the past months. Lately, her fun-loving father had become someone else entirely.

Something had been bothering him. Now she'd never know what.

After locking the door, she lowered her carry-on and extended the handle. The wheels rumbled against the hardwood floor as she made her way to the first bedroom. It had always been hers. When her grandparents were alive, the second one had been her dad's. He'd long since taken the master bedroom and reallocated the middle one as an office.

She laid the bag on her bed and transferred the contents to the chest of drawers. She hadn't brought much. The purpose of the trip was to scout out the place, see how much it had deteriorated over the past twelve years and decide what to do with it.

The decision about the Atlanta place was a no-brainer. As marketing director for a large sporting goods manufacturer, she spent more hours at work than at home. Her two-bedroom condo was plenty of house for her. She'd already contacted a Realtor, and her parents' seven-thousand-square-foot spread was going on the market next week.

This one was harder to let go. It had been in her dad's family for three generations. Four, if she counted her own.

After shutting the last drawer, she picked up her toiletry case and headed for the bathroom. As she stepped into the hall, something moved in her peripheral vision. She snapped her gaze in that direction.

A huge man barreled toward her. Except for two eyeholes, a knit mask hid his face. He slammed into her, knocking her hard against the wall. Her head hit the doorjamb. Pain shot through her temple and stars exploded across her vision.

Another figure ran past, this one much smaller. As retreating footsteps grew softer, blackness encroached. She gripped the jamb, willing herself to remain conscious, but strength drained from her limbs. She slid to the floor, landing on her hands and knees.

The front door creaked open but didn't slam shut. They'd left it ajar. She needed to secure the house. And she needed to call the police. The front door seemed miles away. The bedroom was just across the hall, and her purse was on the bed. If she could crawl there...

She moved her right knee forward, followed by her right hand. The darkness spread, seeping in from all sides. The walls tipped ninety degrees, and the cold floor met her right side.

She lifted one lead-filled arm, trying to grasp the last threads of consciousness.

Her hand fell.

And even that small circle of light faded and disappeared.

Bryce Caldwell flipped on the cruiser's right signal and made his turn onto Ranger Road. As he accelerated up the steep incline, his headlights spilled over the tombstones dotting the landscape. The street cut right through Ranger United Methodist's cemetery.

He rounded a series of curves, following Ranger as it snaked its way upward. His gaze shifted left, the same as it always did. Since night had fallen some time ago, there was nothing to see. But that didn't stop him from looking. He'd been doing it as long as he could remember.

Many years ago, his reasons had been romantic. Now they were entirely practical. His neighbor spent most of his time in Atlanta and had asked him to keep an eye on the place.

Bryce tapped the brakes. Lights were on at the old house, and a vehicle was parked out front. There wasn't enough light to identify the make, but it was too large to be Dennis Wheaton's Mercedes.

He pulled into his own driveway a couple hundred yards down. As he approached his house, a black face nudged aside the vertical blinds hanging at the living room window. Cooper greeted him with a single bark. The dog would have to wait a few minutes longer. Since lights were on next door, the visitor was likely there with Wheaton's knowledge and permission. But it would take only a few minutes to check.

He turned around and retraced his route. As he crept up the drive next door, his jaw tightened. The front door was wide-open, and no one was outside. He stopped behind the vehicle, a newer Cadillac Escalade, and stepped from the cruiser.

"Hello?"

Silence met his call. He moved past the SUV, and a chilly gust swept through, sending the leaves at his feet into a frantic dance. When he stepped onto the porch, he called again. Still silence. Who would leave the front door open and not be somewhere nearby?

"Hello?" Now he was at the doorway, half in and half out. "Anybody home?"

A moan came from the hallway. His senses shot to

full alert, and he drew his weapon. When he stepped into the hall, a woman was working her way onto her hands and knees. Strawberry blond hair had fallen forward to hide her face.

He rushed toward her, still scanning the area. He wasn't about to let down his guard.

"Are you alone?"

She lifted her head. Blue eyes met his, sending a jolt all the way to his toes. *Andi.* Years fell away, each one a punch to his gut. She'd left just before he started college, after he'd made the biggest mistake of his life. And she'd managed to stay away for twelve long years.

Her gaze slid from his face, down his uniform and back up again. Instead of recognition, her eyes held confusion. "Did I call? I didn't think I…" She sat back, one leg curled beneath her, the other in front. "I tried, but…" She fell silent, shaking her head.

He knelt in front of her. "Tell me what happened."

"Someone was inside, knocked me into the doorjamb." She pressed a palm to her left temple. "I hit my head."

Her assailant must have run out the front, leaving the door wide-open. Bryce slid his pistol back into its holster. "He's probably gone, but we need to call it in."

The furrows between her brows deepened. "Who are you?"

Bryce Caldwell. It was right on the tip of his tongue. But considering how they'd parted, he'd better save specifics for later. "I'm with Cherokee County, but I'm not on duty. I just happened to be driving by. We'll get this reported officially. Then you need to go to the hospital and get checked out."

"I'm fine." She gripped the bedroom doorjamb and

pulled herself to her feet. Even holding on, she swayed. If she thought standing would convince him she didn't need medical attention, she was sadly mistaken.

"You probably have a concussion. You need to be seen."

She shook her head. "I've got too much to do to spend several hours in a hospital emergency room."

He frowned. If she let go of that wall, she'd be flat on her face. But it was no use arguing. She'd developed a stubborn streak that hadn't been there before.

"Let me at least get you to the couch. You need to sit before you fall down."

When she took the hand he offered, he led her into the living room, where the sofa, love seat and recliner formed a U-shape around a stone fireplace. He and Andi had spent countless winter weekends sitting on that hearth, roasting s'mores.

After he'd seated her on the love seat, he pulled out his phone. One bar. He wasn't surprised. He always lost service at the bridge shortly before turning onto Ranger, and then didn't pick it up again until somewhere between the Wheaton property and his own.

Without touching the open door, he stepped onto the porch for a clearer signal. When he introduced himself to the dispatcher, he smiled at the sharp intake of air behind him.

He wasn't surprised she didn't recognize him. Even if she hadn't conked her head, it wouldn't have been easy. Through his teen years, he'd been tall and lanky and had worn his hair on the long side. Now it could almost be classified as a buzz cut. Though he was still six-two, he'd packed on fifty pounds of muscle since his teenage years.

Once finished with dispatch, he sat on the couch opposite her. "Do you know who accosted you?"

"No. They were both wearing ski masks."

"Both?"

"After the larger guy hit me, another one ran out behind him."

He nodded. The confusion she'd displayed earlier had left, and stiffness had settled in, leaving the air thick with tension. Maybe she'd stay long enough for him to try to rebuild some bridges. Probably not. He didn't even know why she'd come. But it wasn't important. There were more pressing matters.

Bryce glanced around the room. "Any idea what they were after?"

Nothing appeared disturbed. Of course, the house had never held the usual items that attracted thieves. Other than a telescope that had been top-of-the-line twenty years ago, there wasn't any equipment, electronic or otherwise. As far as he knew, the Wheatons had never had TVs or computers.

That wasn't why they came to Murphy. Weekends here were for family time, outdoor activities, hanging with friends. Usually it was just Andi and her dad. Bryce had met Andi's mother twice and hadn't been impressed either time. She'd seemed cold and hard. And quite haughty.

Fortunately, Andi took after her father.

She shrugged. "Probably the usual things. Cash, jewelry, anything that can be pawned quickly. Empty houses make easy targets."

She pushed herself to her feet. When he hurried to help her, she waved away his hand. She seemed steadier than when she'd let him lead her into the room. She also knew who he was.

She moved away from him, arms extended for balance. "I think I walked in on them before they got very far. Nothing's disturbed here or in my room. I haven't checked the others."

He followed her down the hall. "Your dad didn't come with you?"

The glance she cast over her shoulder was brief, but the pain on her face shot straight to his heart.

"My dad—"

Her words ended in a gasp. She'd stopped at an open doorway and stood staring into the room, mouth agape.

"What is it?" He rushed up next to her and stifled his own gasp.

It was Dennis Wheaton's office. Someone had trashed it.

Every book had been pulled from the shelves. The empty bookcase lay on top. Desk drawers added to the mess, their contents strewn about, the drawers themselves upside down on the mound. The telescope that had occupied the corner of the room lay on its side. The closet had been ransacked, too. Years' worth of Christmas decorations lay in a heap, the empty boxes tossed aside.

Andi slumped against the doorjamb, and he resisted the urge to pull her into his arms. Twelve years ago, she'd have appreciated it. Not now.

"This was uncalled for." She swept one arm toward the mess. "They obviously weren't happy to find nothing more valuable than an old telescope."

Bryce frowned. She was probably right. What house

in the twenty-first century didn't have an array of tele-
visions, laptops, iPads and game consoles?

He looked around the office and shook his head.
Hobby room would have been a more appropriate name.
The space had never held Dennis's accounting, finan-
cial-planning or business books. Instead, the items that
littered the floor bore titles such as *Astronomy 101*, *The
Elegant Universe* and *Earth, Space and Beyond*, along
with numerous art-related books.

Art had been Andi's passion, astronomy all of theirs.
Many nights, her dad had set up the telescope on the
back deck, and the three of them had studied the sky.
Stargazing had been one of many activities he'd shared
with Dennis Wheaton. Andi's dad was the father he'd
never had.

Well, he *had* a father. Bryce just hadn't seen him
often enough for it to count. On those rare occasions
when the old man *did* pop in, the visits had done more
harm than good. If it weren't for Dennis Wheaton's in-
fluence, Bryce's life would have taken a different turn.

"I need to call your dad."

She looked at him, eyes glistening with unshed tears.
"You can't. He was killed in a car accident on Thanksgiving Day."

His breath whooshed out and he slumped against the
wall. A sense of emptiness swept through him, as cold
and dark as space itself. "How?"

"I don't know. He missed a curve and drove off a
cliff."

Bryce slid down the wall until he came to a seated
position against it. Dennis Wheaton was gone. He
couldn't be. This had to be a bad dream.

But it *was* real, just like the woman standing in front of him, looking as broken as he felt.

He shook his head. "That's why he didn't come."

"What?"

Sirens sounded in the distance. The police would be there shortly. He crossed his arms, trying to stave off a sudden chill.

"Your dad was here the Tuesday night before Thanksgiving. The next day, he called and said he wanted to meet with me that weekend. When he didn't show up, I figured he'd gotten busy."

Andi righted the desk chair and lowered herself into it. "Did he say why he wanted to meet?"

"Just that he wanted to talk with me. He sounded like a man ready to unload a heavy burden. I asked him if everything was okay. He said, 'It will be soon.'"

Her eyebrows lifted and her jaw dropped as the color drained from her face.

"Andi?" He rose to put a hand on her shoulder.

"Living with my mother wasn't easy, but he always seemed to not let her criticism bother him. For the past few months, though, things were different."

"Different how?"

"Something had been weighing him down. He seemed preoccupied, even depressed. I tried to talk to him, but he kept denying anything was wrong." She crossed her arms over her stomach. "The signs were there, and I didn't recognize them."

"What signs? What are you talking about?"

"Depression, withdrawal. Losing interest in activities he'd always enjoyed, like coming up here." She lifted her head, and her gaze locked with his. "The comment he made to you—that everything was going to be okay soon. It's all clear now. I should have seen it."

Now he knew where her thoughts had gone. And how much sense they made. Maybe Dennis had called him to talk about his struggles, guy-to-guy, not wanting to unload on Andi, then hadn't been able to hold out any longer. Or maybe he'd gotten involved in something he regretted and wanted to clear his conscience but hadn't had what it took to face the consequences.

No, not Dennis. He had too much integrity. And he loved life too much.

Andi's brows drew together, and her eyes filled with pain. "When I add it all together, I'm afraid my dad drove off that mountain intentionally. And he took my mother with him."

TWO

Andrea tipped back her head and stared into the endless expanse. Stars were strewn across the sky from horizon to horizon, like rhinestones against black velvet. She tightened her hands around the steaming mug of herbal tea, soaking in the heat.

She'd gotten enough accomplished today to feel good about sitting on the back deck and doing nothing. She'd given the place a deep cleaning and put everything back in its proper place. Then she'd made a list of repairs to be done, whether she sold the house or kept it. Most important, she'd had a handyman replace the broken pane in the living room window. It was how the assailants had gained access. Though the missing piece of glass was obvious in the daylight, she hadn't noticed it last night.

She'd hoped her cleaning would uncover some clue about what had been going on in her dad's life. The only thing she'd found raised more questions than it answered. It was a simple two-line poem, scrawled on a sheet of yellow paper torn from a legal pad—"When a secret is too heavy to keep, it's always best to bury it deep."

What was that supposed to mean? Was the secret

what he'd wanted to talk to Bryce about? Was the weight of what he'd carried so heavy he'd felt he had no way out?

She sipped the tea, relishing the heat as it traveled down her throat. The temperature had dipped as soon as the sun went down. But there was something soothing about sitting under the stars, holding the hot cup, with peaceful silence all around her.

There was a party going on right next door. Bryce and his two best friends had had a cookout and were now watching a movie. He'd invited her, even assured her she wouldn't be the only woman. One of his friends was married, the other engaged. She'd passed.

When he'd told the dispatcher his name last night, she'd almost fallen off the couch. She'd known if she spent much time at the Murphy place, she'd eventually run into him. But she hadn't thought it would be so soon. And she hadn't planned to greet him in a fog, on her hands and knees.

And she hadn't expected him to look like he did, all buff and mature. Though common sense told her he would've changed, she'd somehow held on to the image of the smiling teenager she'd fallen in love with at age fourteen.

Last night, he hadn't been smiling. And he wasn't a teenager anymore. He'd radiated confidence, maturity and a sense of power that was mesmerizing, standing above her, a pistol at his hip.

What was it about a man in uniform that women found so irresistible? Whatever it was, Bryce definitely did the Cherokee County garb justice.

Andrea swallowed the last of her tea and held the empty cup, drawing the heat from the porcelain. A wind gust swept along the back of the house, and a shiver shook her shoulders.

She stood to go back inside, then hesitated. Had she seen a glow deep in her woods? She waited for several more moments.

There, near the left-hand edge of her property. Or maybe it was coming from the Langman place and wasn't even in her woods.

The glow moved rightward in an erratic path, as if someone was walking with a flashlight. Whoever was prowling the woods was definitely on her property now. Was it the men who'd been in the house last night, coming back to finish their search?

She pulled her phone from her rear pocket and stared at the screen. If she called the police, it would take a unit twenty minutes to arrive. If the prowler was still there, he'd take off as soon as he heard sirens.

There was another option. Bryce had said to call if she needed anything. He was right next door. And he was law enforcement. Based on what he'd told her, so was one of his friends. They could be there in less than a minute, both armed.

She went back in to retrieve the business card Bryce had left on the rolltop desk and punched the number into her phone. The decision was a no-brainer. Looked like she was going to meet Bryce's friend after all. If she had cell service.

Though the phone showed one bar, the call wouldn't connect. She returned to the deck and squinted into the woods. The light was still there. When she checked the phone, the screen showed "dialing."

"Come on, connect already."

She moved across the back of the house toward

Bryce's property. If the signal didn't get strong enough soon, she might as well go knock on his door.

She'd just reached the corner of her house when she heard the first ring. Bryce answered two rings later. There was no background noise on his end of the line. He'd either paused the movie or left the room. She told him the reason for her call. His next words were obviously not for her.

"Grab your weapon. The neighbor I told you about has another prowler."

The neighbor I told you about? What did he tell them?

Probably that someone had broken into the house next door. Even if he'd said more, what did it matter? Tomorrow she was heading back to Atlanta to be ready for Saturday's funeral. She had no intention of hanging out with Bryce and his friends, even if she kept the place and used it as an occasional retreat.

She disconnected the call, then made her way to the back door. She'd stay locked inside until Bryce and his friend arrived.

When she swung the screen door open, the outer edge dropped a half inch. The hinges needed longer screws. Something else that would have to be done.

The property wasn't in total disrepair, but since her dad had inherited the place, he'd done the bare minimum to keep it from crumbling to the ground. That was easier than listening to her mother carry on about how he was spending their hard-earned money on something he should have unloaded long ago.

Andrea frowned. *Their* hard-earned money was a misnomer, since her mother hadn't done the actual earning. With a father who was a senior partner in a huge personal-injury law firm, Margaret Cunningham-Wheaton had grown up spending money without having to worry about where it came from. And her family had made sure she could continue the habit. Going to college and falling in love with an accounting major hadn't been in anybody's plans.

Andrea paced the floor while she waited. Her one-minute estimate was overly optimistic. One minute stretched into two, then three and eventually ten. What were they doing, waiting till the movie was over?

When someone finally knocked on the back door, she flipped the exterior light on and looked out the dining room window. Instead of two men on her deck, three were lined up side by side. She swung open the door.

Bryce and a man she didn't know kept a tight grip on the one in the center. Although she hadn't recognized Bryce, Matt Langman, her other neighbor, was easily identifiable.

His face had aged, more than it should have in the past twelve years. He'd lived a rough life. According to her father, he spent half his time in jail and the other half hatching up new ways to get into trouble. There was likely plenty of drug use involved, too.

But a lot hadn't changed. He still wore his hair in the same shaggy style and maintained that signature air of indifference. The cockiness hadn't lessened one iota. He was too thin to be the one who'd slammed her into the doorjamb. But the accomplice could have been Matt. Their sizes were similar.

"What are you doing on my property?"

"Being held against my will by your boyfriend and his goon." His eyes narrowed in the same malicious glare he'd always given her.

She crossed her arms. She'd never done anything to him, had hardly spoken to him over the years. But he'd always hated her. He despised her for her privileged upbringing and the fact that Bryce's relationship with her and her father had ended his friendship with Matt.

But the bad blood went back further than that. Three generations, actually. Their great-grandfathers had been in business together and ended up with some irresolvable differences. Her great-grandfather had bought Matt's out at a price the Wheaton clan insisted was generous and the Langman clan swore was highway robbery. The Langmans were still holding a grudge.

"What *were* you doing on my property?"

He tried to jerk away, but Bryce and his friend tightened their hold. "Going for a walk."

"At nine thirty at night?"

He lifted his chin. "Cherokee County doesn't have a curfew."

"Doesn't matter. You're trespassing."

"Not if there aren't any signs."

Maybe he had her there. Before heading back to Atlanta, she'd stop by Tractor Supply and pick up a couple, along with a handheld staple gun. "I'll have that remedied tomorrow." Whatever Matt's reasons, he was up to no good. "In the meantime, I'm giving you verbal warning. Stay off my property, or I'll have you arrested."

"It's not yours. It's your dad's."

"Since my dad's dead, it's mine."

For a brief moment, the cockiness fell away and his eyes widened. "Are you going to live here?"

"I haven't decided what I'm doing with the place yet."

His lips curled back in a sneer. "You need to take that

snooty car of yours and go back to your fancy place in Atlanta. You don't belong here."

Fire sparked inside and spread. Before she could formulate a response, Bryce gave him a shake.

"That's not for you to decide. You heard what Andi said. If you step foot on this property again, I'll arrest you myself."

Matt opened his mouth but then apparently thought better of it. Instead, he shook off the hands that held him and sauntered toward the trees separating their two properties.

Before leaving the circle of light emanating from the deck, he cast a glance over his shoulder. Even with the shadows, the hatred Andrea saw there sent a chill down her spine.

When listing the pros and cons of keeping the property, Matt definitely belonged on the con side. She wasn't about to let him push her around. But having to deal with an antagonistic neighbor needed to be a consideration in her decision. Especially when her safety was at stake.

As for Bryce, she hadn't decided whether his presence was a pro or a con.

"Stay."

Bryce extended his arm, palm angled toward Cooper. "You can't go with me this time."

He moved down the porch steps, leaving behind a pouting dog, then headed across the yard under a steel-gray sky. A cold front was moving their direction. It probably wouldn't bring snow. Murphy saw snow only a handful of times each year. November was a little early.

Today Andrea was returning to Atlanta. She'd finished the funeral arrangements before coming to Murphy but still had a lot of paperwork to get through in the Wheatons' Atlanta house.

Tomorrow he'd make the two-hour drive himself. No way was he going to pass up the opportunity to pay his final respects to the man who'd made more difference in his life than anyone else on the planet.

He stepped onto the trail that separated his property from Andi's. He'd see if Andi needed help with anything before she headed out. After the funeral tomorrow, he had no idea when he'd see her again. If ever.

Disappointment settled over him. Two days hadn't been enough time to iron out everything that was wrong between them. He wasn't sure what changes he'd expected in so short a time, but they hadn't happened.

When he reached her yard, movement drew his attention to the right. He looked that way as Andi disappeared into the woods. Where was she going?

He jogged along the side of her house and to the back. The small yard sloped down toward woods that stretched all the way to a creek at the rear edge of the ten acres. Ahead, patches of red flashed between almost bare trees. He followed, now knowing her destination.

When he reached her, she stood outside a small circular stone wall. Four posts held up a weathered roof. The crank that had at one time wound the rope to raise the bucket had frozen up years ago. He'd been there with her before. Many times.

She glanced over one shoulder before turning back to stare into the dark depths. "This was one of his favorite places." Her tone held wistfulness. "He used to say that most wells collect wishes, but this one collects burdens. Anytime something was bothering me, we would pretend to ball it up and throw it into the well."

The sadness radiating from her was almost palpable. But there was something else, too. She seemed tormented in more than a grieving sense. Her turmoil wove a path straight to his heart.

He put a hand on her shoulder, and she tensed. He dropped his arm. Would he ever be able to offer comfort as a friend and have her accept it?

"I'm sorry." So much more than two words could convey. He was sorry for the way her life had been turned upside down, sorry for the grief she felt and sorry that he'd killed any chance of a friendship with one stupid decision.

And friendship was all he hoped for. Dennis had told him about Andi's divorce, but other than a brief reference to her husband cheating on her, he hadn't given any details. All Bryce knew was she'd taken it hard. And she had walls around her heart a mile thick.

Dennis hadn't had to tell him the last part. He'd felt them for the past two days. And he didn't have what it took to break them down. A few months ago, maybe. Before he'd expended every bit of emotional energy he had on a relationship, only to have it crash and burn in the end.

A rain-scented gust whipped through, sending a shower of dried leaves down around them. Andi turned away from the well. "If I want to make my trip on dry roads, I'd better get going."

"Can I help you with anything?"

"I'm already loaded and locked up. I just wanted to come out here before I left."

He fell into step beside her. "Any idea when you'll be back?"

"Not for a while."

They crossed the small yard, then continued along the side of the house. A piece of fascia on the gable end had worked its way loose, and the wood siding needed a fresh finish. If Andi wanted to sell the place, she'd need to have some work done. Or maybe she'd keep it as a weekend getaway.

Not likely. If she'd "gotten away" anytime over the past twelve years, it hadn't been to Murphy.

He stopped in the driveway to stand next to the Escalade. "Until you decide whether to sell, I'm happy to continue keeping an eye on things. I'm sure it'll take time to settle the estate."

"Settling the estate will be the easy part." She leaned against the SUV, her brows dipping to form creases above her nose. "My dad added me to all their assets just two months ago. I didn't question it at the time. He's always been a planner. My parents have had wills as long as I can remember. But maybe this was more than good planning. Maybe he was putting his affairs in order for a reason."

She opened the driver's door and slid into the seat, shoulders hunched. "I should have asked him some questions."

"You tried. He wouldn't talk."

"He was going to talk to you."

"Then apparently changed his mind."

She nodded. "He buried it deep."

He lifted a brow.

"Last night, I picked up a book he had sitting on his nightstand. A piece of paper was sticking out of it. He'd written, 'When a secret is too heavy to keep, it's always best to bury it deep.'"

He frowned. "That secret is probably what he was going to talk to me about."

"Instead, he decided to stuff it down and hold it inside. Whatever his secret was, he took it with him when he drove off the mountain." She put the key into the ignition and cranked the engine.

He stepped back, ready to close her door. "I'll see you tomorrow."

Actually, he probably wouldn't. He'd be there, but so would half of Atlanta. He'd never been to their home church, but according to Andi, it was huge. As well connected as they'd been, it would be packed.

He'd never been crazy about big churches. Actually, he'd never been crazy about church, period. Not that he was a stranger. His mom and grandparents were what some called "Chreasters"—they attended on Christmas and Easter.

Andi's family had gone every Sunday, even while in Murphy. The church here was different from what they were used to, with a congregation of less than a hundred that met in a small building off the four-lane highway.

Bryce had usually gone with them. At that time, he'd needed it. He'd had lots of mischievousness to atone for. Now he was a law-abiding citizen, serving the people of Cherokee County. At thirty years old, his good deeds far outweighed the bad he'd done as an adolescent and young teen.

He closed Andi's door, then watched her head up the drive. If she kept the property, she'd have to visit occasionally, even with him checking on the place. It wouldn't make sense to keep up the taxes, insurance and utilities otherwise.

Of course, she could afford it. For the Wheaton family, money had never been an issue. Between her parents' wealth and what her husband made, Mrs. Wheaton had never had to work. Bryce's own mother had held a nine-to-five job in a local insurance company.

While Andi had lived in the Wheaton mansion in an exclusive Atlanta neighborhood, he and his mom had stayed with his grandparents. And during Andi's vacations to places like Switzerland, Ireland and Paris, his family had visited relatives or camped at Deep Creek.

But Andi had never let the difference in social status get in the way of their relationship. Ultimately, he had. He'd let his own insecurities push him into throwing away something special and had regretted it ever since.

He wasn't holding out unrealistic hopes of reclaiming what they'd had so long ago. There was too much water under the bridge. They were both different people now.

But if she had plans to keep the property, he hoped they could develop an amicable friendship.

Judging from her coolness toward him, maybe even that was out of reach.

The large canopy cast a shadow over those sitting beneath. Andrea occupied a chair in the front row, back straight and stiff and hands clutched in her lap. An aunt and uncle sat on either side of her. More relatives occupied the dozen or so other chairs, and numerous mourners hovered around in a loosely packed semicircle. Metal framework suspended two caskets over freshly dug graves, the pastor standing between. The

sun shone from a cloudless blue sky, and nearby, squirrels chased one another up a tree.

Andrea released a sigh. The perfection of the weather
mocked her own dark mood. The sad, angry skies she'd
driven home under yesterday would have been more
appropriate.

The pastor finished reading the twenty-third Psalm,
and Andrea's uncle squeezed her shoulder. He'd kept his
arm over the back of her chair, offering silent gestures
of comfort. She appreciated it but didn't need it. She'd
managed to sit stoically throughout the entire funeral
and graveside service. She'd do her grieving in private.

After a final prayer, Andrea stood, pulling her coat
more tightly around her. Yesterday's rain had brought
colder temperatures, and she was having difficulty
shaking the chill. As she stepped into the sunshine, a
man in a suit made his way through the crowd toward
her. His hairline had receded, and the salt had overtaken
the pepper, but other than that, he looked the same as
he had twelve years ago. He'd pastored the church all
through her teenage years.

"Pastor Pierce." She shook his hand, a wave of guilt
passing through her. Did he know she hadn't darkened
the door of a church since she left for college?

It wasn't that she had anything against attending.
Her mother had always stressed the importance of reg-
ularly attending church. But it had to be the right kind
of church—large, impressive, full of quality people. It
was good for the image, she'd said. With the advice always came the admonition to not get carried away with
the emotionalism that went on in some of the smaller
country churches, where people were poor and uned-
ucated. Large or small, it hadn't mattered to Andrea.

Since reaching adulthood, too many other things in her life had qualified as important.

She offered him a weak smile. "Thank you for coming."

"Of course." He wrapped her hand in both of his. "You and your family are in my prayers. May the Lord comfort you during this difficult time."

After accepting dozens more handshakes and hugs, Andrea made her way to one of the two limos that had transported her and the other immediate family members from the church to the cemetery. She'd take the ride back to the church and attend the dinner the hospitality committee had prepared for the family and close friends. Then she'd get to be alone. She'd survived the past nine days. She could get through the next two hours.

Her aunt Louise reached her as the limo driver opened the door. Andrea paused for the hug she knew her aunt needed. When finished, her aunt shook her head.

"I still can't believe they're gone." Fresh tears gathered on her lower lashes. "When we watched your mom get behind the wheel in our driveway, we never imagined that would be the last time we'd see either of them alive."

"My mom was driving?" There had to be a mistake. Her mom never drove if her dad was with her.

"After you left, Dennis started feeling ill. Although the offer seemed a little begrudging, your mom said she'd drive them home. Margaret has never been crazy about driving." She pursed her lips. "I can't help but think that if your dad had been the one behind the wheel, we wouldn't be here today."

Andrea sank into the seat, her feet still planted outside the car. Her mind spun, leaving her feeling lightheaded.

Her father hadn't been driving. Her mother had. Whatever had been weighing on her father's mind for the past several months, he hadn't decided to take his own life.

Her aunt climbed into the car, unaware of the bombshell she'd just dropped. The news eliminated the possibility of suicide but raised a whole slew of unanswered questions. If Andrea's dad was unlikely to take a curve too fast, her mom was even more so. They'd always ribbed her about being a turtle.

Besides, the area was familiar to both of them. They were a mile from the lodge, on a winding road they'd traveled dozens of times. The brakes had to have failed. Monday, she was going to ask to have the car checked, if that wasn't already part of the investigation.

For the next hour, Andrea engaged in polite conversation and forced down food she had no desire to eat. After a socially acceptable amount of time, she said her farewells, climbed into the Escalade and pulled out of the parking lot. Since leaving home that morning, she'd looked forward to the end of the day's activities, when she could again be alone with her grief.

But now that she was headed there, home was the last place she wanted to be. Maybe she should do some more sorting at her parents' house. Keeping busy would be good for her. Throwing herself into activity had always been her default.

She cruised through an intersection on a yellow light and swiveled her head to the right. A few blocks down was a café, one of those cute places decorated with flowers and lace that served lunch on antique china. Her mom loved it.

Andrea hated it.

Nothing against the café. It was lunches with her mom in general. No matter how they started out, eventually they evolved into battles, with Andrea on the losing side every time. Her mom was the queen of unwanted advice, usually given in the form of some pithy proverb. She was also the queen of criticism.

Andrea drew in a constricted breath. As a child, she'd gone to desperate lengths to please her mother. As a teenager, she'd clung to every word of praise from her father while still trying to gain her mother's approval. As an adult, she'd given up.

She flipped on her signal and got into the left-turn lane. As her route took her within a block of Neurology and Neurosurgical Associates, the familiar tightness returned. At two o'clock in the afternoon, her ex was either there or at the hospital.

Or home enjoying her replacement.

Her divorce had been another sore spot between her and her mother. While Andrea had been reeling with betrayal, her mother's focus had been on how it was going to affect her relationship with her friends, since the Morrisons were one of the elite families of Atlanta and Phil's mother was one of her closest friends. She'd insisted that Andrea should have tried harder.

Maybe she should have. If she hadn't been so focused on climbing the corporate ladder, maybe she'd have noticed the warning signs in time to save her marriage.

Then she'd have fallen short of her mother's expectations some other way. Her dreams of mending that relationship had never materialized. Now it was too late.

She slammed her hand against the steering wheel, palm open. She'd expected the agonizing grief over losing her father. He'd been the center of her world her entire life.

What she *hadn't* expected was the guilt she felt over the poor relationship she'd always had with her mother. No matter what distractions she'd attempted, she hadn't been able to run from it.

Maybe activity wasn't what she needed. Maybe she needed the opposite. Time to decompress and let the frayed edges of her heart begin to heal.

She knew the perfect place to do it.

Everything in Atlanta reminded her of her mother or her ex, but Murphy connected her with her father. By tonight, she could be there, tucked away in the house that had been her refuge since she was old enough to appreciate the need for escape.

She was supposed to return to work on Monday. But she still had another six weeks of vacation time banked. She frowned. That in itself was a pretty good commentary on her life.

She hit the brakes and headed toward downtown. If she was going to be gone for an indefinite amount of time, she had some work to do. After being out a week and a half, her desk would be a mess. But she'd get everything whipped into shape by the end of the day, and any loose ends she couldn't tie up, she'd deal with remotely.

When she stepped from the building hours later, it was dusk. She laid her laptop case on the passenger seat. She'd use public internet until she decided whether to have it installed at the house.

For the next few weeks, she'd be right next door to

Bryce. But she'd deal with that, too. She was a mature adult, not a love-struck teenager. Back then, Bryce had promised to love her with a love as big as the sky, always and forever. And she'd believed it. At the time, the words were cheesy. In hindsight, they were meaningless. In the intervening years, she'd learned there was no such thing as *always and forever*.

Thirty minutes after arriving home, she was ready to hit the road. She did enough traveling on business to know how to pack quickly. She tossed the two small bags into the back seat of the Escalade.

As she drove north on 75, then took the 575 ramp, the weight that had been pressing down on her lifted. Taking additional time off had been a good idea. So had getting out of Atlanta. She wasn't running away; she was just… Okay, maybe she *was*.

But it was about time. She'd never run from anything. She was always forging ahead, accepting the next challenge, whether in school or work or life in general. Now she was just tired.

She made the left turn onto 60 and arched her back, working out some of the stiffness. It was the final leg of her trip. Mineral Bluff was a short distance ahead. Then she'd make her right onto Spur 60, which would take her across the state line. Ten minutes after that, she'd be lugging her bags inside and preparing for what she hoped would be a good night's sleep.

As she tapped the brakes for the first curve, headlights shone in her rearview mirror. The vehicle drew closer, and she squinted, waiting for the driver to dim his lights. He didn't. Soon he was on her tail. She rounded the curve and accelerated. The other driver did the same, maintaining a distance of one car length.

Judging from the height of the headlights and distance between them, the other vehicle was a larger pickup truck.

Her heart pounded and her palms grew slick against the wheel. She was driving fifteen miles over the speed limit and approaching another curve.

She tapped her brakes and the gap closed. A second later, a bump from behind thrust her vehicle forward. Her tires squealed and she struggled to keep the SUV on the road.

Coming out of the curve, she straightened the wheel but didn't loosen her grip. If she could hang on until after the last curve, she could pull out her phone and call 911.

She floored the pedal, but the distance she gained quickly evaporated. The vehicle behind her slammed into her, snapping her head backward against the seat. She pressed the brake, but the truck pushed her into the next curve. After a prolonged squeal, her tires gave up their traction and the Escalade slid sideways. She bounced several times, her head snapping side to side.

Then the world started a slow spin. Her seat belt tightened against her legs and the airbag slammed into her. Pain shot through her face and one arm. A high-pitched scream filled the car. A terrifying moment passed before she realized it was hers.

The SUV came to rest at a sharp sideways angle. She pushed the airbag out of the way, her seat belt the only thing keeping her from tumbling to the passenger side of the vehicle.

She looked around in the darkness. Had her attacker fled, or was he making his way down the slope to finish what he'd started?

She wasn't going to wait to find out. After a quick check for broken bones, she pulled the handle and gave the door a hard shove. Small bits of window glass tumbled downward, but the door didn't budge. Using her shoulder didn't work, either.

After killing the headlights, she stared into the night. No one was approaching. The darkness wasn't complete, but it was close. She needed to get out of the vehicle. And she needed to call for help.

With her feet pressed into the floorboard and one hand gripping the wheel, she released the belt and eased into the passenger seat. She wasn't getting out that way, either. Her SUV rested against a large tree. It was what had kept her from continuing her tumble all the way to the bottom of the slope.

Where was her purse? She turned on the map lights, then crawled between the bucket seats. Both her purse and laptop were lying on the rear floorboard.

Her hands shook as she fished out her phone. After punching in the numbers, she pressed the phone to her ear.

As she relayed what had happened, she reached over the console to turn off the lights. She'd be safer sitting in the dark. With mobile locate, emergency personnel would find her. To make their job a little easier, she'd click on the headlights once she heard sirens.

When the dispatcher asked, she passed on the ambulance. She'd be sore tomorrow. But nothing was broken or dislocated. The airbag had even protected her from the shattered glass. She'd be free to leave after the police report. She'd take a cab to Murphy, and tomorrow morning, a wrecker would retrieve her car and tow it to a shop.

Meanwhile, she had time to think.

Why had someone gone after her? Was it a case of road rage? Maybe she'd cut someone off without realizing it, and they'd followed her from the interstate, irrational anger building with every passing mile.

If she had, she hadn't noticed. And who would wait more than an hour to react to someone cutting them off in traffic?

Another scenario was more likely. But it was one she didn't want to consider—that the attack might be personal.

A little more than a week ago, her parents had tumbled down a mountain to their deaths.

Tonight, she'd missed a curve, too, with a little help. Had her parents' brakes failed? Or had they gotten the same kind of nudge?

As much as she didn't want to think about it, the question wouldn't leave her alone.

THREE

Cooper darted to the next tree, while Bryce stood on his porch, flashlight beam pointed into the front yard. The dog wasn't in any hurry to take care of business.

A shiver shook Bryce's shoulders. He should have donned a jacket instead of stepping outside in the light sweater he wore. Friday's storm hadn't just brought hours of rain. It had also left some colder temperatures. And a tree down in Andi's front yard. During the next day or two, he'd get it cut up and hauled away.

"Hurry up, Cooper. I'm not standing here all night."

Cooper didn't acknowledge the command. Whatever smells he'd discovered were much too intriguing.

Bryce clapped his hands, and the dog's head swiveled toward him. A half second later, he was back to sniffing a browning clump of day lilies at the base of the tree.

With a sigh, Bryce stepped off the porch. "Come on, Cooper. Do your business."

The dog was much better behaved now than he'd been six months ago. Bryce had adopted him through Logan's Run, one of the rescue organizations in Murphy.

After spending the first two years of his life chained

in someone's backyard, he'd needed a lot of love and care. Bryce had given it, and Cooper was now a different dog. He no longer moped around, head lowered. Instead of listlessness and disinterest, his eyes held enthusiasm.

Bryce glanced around the yard. Early that morning, a fat crescent had sat low on the eastern horizon. Now at 10:00 p.m., stars were scattered across a moonless night sky. Beyond the beam of his flashlight, everything was black. Except…

He drew his brows together as he stared into the woods that separated his property from Andi's. Light was coming from somewhere on the other side of the trees.

Was Matt snooping around again? Or had someone come back into her house?

Bryce stalked toward the dog. Cooper was finished, whether he thought he was or not. Apparently sensing his time to dally was over, the dog lifted a leg.

After leading him into the house, Bryce put on a jacket, then retrieved his weapon and phone. Moments later, he was on the trail connecting the two properties. It had gotten a lot of use when he and Andi were teenagers—summers and weekends, anyway. Since then, he'd maintained it so he could check on the property and visit with Dennis Wheaton.

Before he reached the end of the trail, he had no doubt. Someone was inside the house. Or *had* been. Last night, everything had been dark. Now the porch light was on, and light came from both the living room and her bedroom.

People up to no good usually didn't turn on lights. But whoever was there, it wasn't Andi. Her car wasn't in the driveway. Besides, he'd seen her a few hours ago. He hadn't made it to the graveside service, but he'd attended the funeral. It had been as packed as he'd expected. He'd sought her out afterward, weaving his way through the crowd. The conversation was like all her interactions with him—brief and polite, but lacking warmth.

He'd learned she was returning to work on Monday and had no idea when she'd make it back to Murphy. Her plans wouldn't have changed that fast. Andi wasn't the impulsive type. And knowing he was watching the place, if she was allowing someone to stay there, she would have mentioned it.

He jogged past the downed poplar, then slipped behind a hemlock. Drapes hung at the windows, a minuscule gap around their edges releasing slivers of light. A shadow moved past, and he pulled his phone from his pocket.

The intruder was still there, and Bryce wasn't reckless enough to confront him alone.

He called 911 and waited, keeping watch from behind the hemlock. Ten minutes later, the living room light went off. Maybe the intruder was preparing to leave.

His hand shifted to his weapon. He hadn't planned to confront anyone alone. But if someone emerged before backup arrived, he wouldn't hesitate.

The bedroom light was still on when sirens sounded a short distance away. He drew his weapon, covering the front door. As soon as the intruder realized police were coming, he'd probably take off. Out the back.

Bryce cast a glance over his shoulder, where a unit moved up the drive toward him, red and blue lights reflecting against the trees.

He stepped into the headlight beams and motioned his intentions. The bedroom curtains shifted to the side, then dropped back into place. The intruder was likely preparing to make a run for it. If he ran out the back, Bryce would be ready. If he chose the front, the others would nab him.

Bryce had just settled into position when a loud knock reverberated through the night. He tightened his grip on the pistol. With the others in front, the intruder would surely use the back.

A deep male voice boomed. "Police. Open the door."

Bryce smiled. Sounded like Gary, one of his fellow deputies. Besides being armed, the man was two hundred and eighty pounds of solid muscle.

For the next minute, Bryce kept his ears peeled and his weapon trained on the back door. Finally, a soft female voice reached him from somewhere in front.

Wait, he recognized that voice. What was Andi doing there?

He lowered his weapon and jogged around the house. Gary was at the bottom of the porch steps, his partner Jason at his side. Andi stood above them, light from the outdoor fixture spilling over her. She'd already gotten ready for bed and was wearing flannel pajamas in a multicolored pattern.

He drew closer. Acrobatic cats? Yes, she was wearing images of cats doing cartwheels and back bends. He stifled a smile. The design was relaxed and playful. And surprisingly attractive on her. Andi was probably the only woman alive who could rock a pair of flannel pj's.

Her eyes shifted to him, then back to Gary. "What's going on?"

Bryce stopped next to his colleagues. "What are you doing here?"

Her brows rose. "This is my house."

"When I talked to you after the funeral, you hadn't planned to come back anytime soon."

"I changed my mind. And I didn't think about the fact you're watching the place. I should have called."

Gary cut in. "If everything's all right, we'll leave you two to your business."

Bryce nodded. "Sorry about the false alarm. She's already had one break-in."

"Not a problem."

He watched the men walk to the cruiser, then turned back to Andi. "How long are you staying?"

"A week or two, maybe longer. I don't know yet."

A week or two. Still too short of a time to restore any kind of friendship. But maybe it would be a start.

"If you need anything, let me know." Not that she would. He'd probably be the last one she'd ask for help.

She gave him a stiff nod. The porch light was behind her, casting her face in shadow, but something didn't look right. A bruise seemed to be forming on one cheek, abrasions on the other.

He climbed the two steps and turned her to face him. Yeah, something definitely wasn't right.

"What happened to your face?"

"I got slapped by the airbag."

His chest clenched. "You were in an accident?" That explained her car not being in the driveway. "What happened?"

She turned and walked inside. Since she didn't shut the door in his face, he assumed it was all right to follow. By the time he closed and locked the door, she was sitting on the couch, feet tucked under her.

He eased into the recliner adjacent to her. "I'm guessing your car's not drivable, since it's not here."

"I don't know yet. It's still sitting somewhat sideways, propped up by a tree. It rolled at least once. In the morning, some tow-truck driver is going to have to figure out how to get it back up onto the road."

His gut tightened. "You ran off the road?"

"With a little help. I was on the winding part of 60 before Mineral Bluff. Someone rammed me from behind and pushed me off the road at the next curve."

He clenched his fists. He didn't have to ask if she thought it was intentional. "Any idea who or why?"

"Not a clue. I'm director of marketing for a sporting goods manufacturer, hardly a position that makes lethal enemies. My ex doesn't even have it in for me." She fell silent, brows drawn together. Her mind was probably following the same track his was.

He pushed himself to his feet and began to pace. "There are too many similarities between your parents' accident and what happened to you tonight. I don't think it's a coincidence."

What if Dennis Wheaton had gotten involved in something he regretted and created enemies, ones who were prepared to come after his daughter now that he was out of reach?

He stopped pacing. "How about staying with me until we get this figured out?"

She looked up at him through her lashes.

"Come on, you'd have your own space. It's a three-bedroom house." Of course, she knew that. She'd been there enough times. Back then, it had been his grandparents' place. Now they were living in one of those over-fifty-five communities with daily activities, his mother had remarried and the house belonged to him. And his mortgage company.

"I'll be all right here." She pursed her lips. "If someone is after me, how did they know I was coming? Until a few hours ago, I didn't know myself."

"Maybe someone followed you from Atlanta." It wasn't a comforting thought. He'd feel a whole lot better if she'd agree to stay with him.

He crossed his arms and leaned against the bookcase. "How did you get here?"

"A cab."

"I told you to call me if you needed anything."

She shrugged. "Why bother you when I could just as easily call a cab?"

"Your dad would have called me."

"I'm not my dad."

No, she wasn't. Formerly a straight-A student and a member of several clubs, she'd always been driven to succeed. But now she had a hard edge, a steely strength that probably served her well in the business world but kept people at arm's length. He'd always thought she took after her dad rather than her mother. Now he wasn't so sure.

He picked up a piece of paper that had been lying on the coffee table. "Your dad's note."

"I've been carrying it around in my purse and pulled it back out tonight, hoping everything would somehow come together." She rose to stand next to him, looking down at what he held.

"And did it?"

"The words are just as cryptic as when I first read

them." Frowning, she took the paper from him. "He had a secret, something he kept buried deep inside. But there's no hint of what that secret might have been."

She laid the paper back on the table. "Whatever it was, he didn't take his life over it."

Bryce lifted his brows. Had she learned something new?

"My dad wasn't driving. When they were ready to leave the lodge, he wasn't feeling well. So my mom agreed to drive."

"He didn't kill himself." A burden Bryce had carried for the past several days slowly lifted, and a smile climbed up his cheeks.

"He didn't." A matching smile tugged at her own lips.

Bryce took her hands and squeezed, and for several moments, the tension between them dissolved. Then she pulled away, turning her back to him.

He heaved a sigh. If he hoped to restore any kind of amicable friendship with Andi, he'd have to find a way to atone for his past mistakes. But where could he start?

"I'm sorry," he said. "For everything. I know I messed up. I knew it the moment you walked up and saw—"

She raised a hand, cutting him off. She hadn't given him an opportunity to explain then and wasn't going to now, either. "It's over. All of that was a lifetime ago."

She was right. Going back to what they had was impossible. It wasn't even what he wanted. If she knew that, would it make a difference? Maybe he needed to just lay out his expectations.

He took a seat on the couch. "I don't know the details, but I know you've recently been burned. I've been

through the wringer myself, and frankly, I don't have
the energy to put into a relationship. So you can rest
assured that I won't be pushing you toward anything
that would make you uncomfortable."

She sat on the love seat and he continued.

"If we're going to live next door to one another,
even on a temporary basis, I hope you'll let me be your
friend. At least a concerned neighbor."

Some of the tension fled her features, and she dipped
her head. "Sounds fair."

Relief flooded him. "I've gotten so used to watching this place and doing odd jobs that it's going to be
a hard habit to break. I hope you'll let me continue."

"That's not necessary. Anything I don't want to do
myself, I can hire someone."

The stiffness that had characterized their interactions the past several days was gone. But she projected
a self-sufficiency and determination he didn't remember being there twelve years earlier.

She crossed one leg over the other and began swinging it in circles. The movement drew his gaze downward.

Andi had cute feet, small enough to fit into the size
shoe stores always displayed. When she was younger,
her toenails were a work of art, sometimes with lines,
curves and geometric shapes in varying colors, sometimes painted to resemble some kind of fruit or other
object.

Tonight, they were a single shade of pink. That carefree fancy she'd displayed as a teenager seemed to be
buried deep. If it was still there at all.

Andi had changed. It wasn't just that she'd grown up.
Life had knocked her around. Whatever damage living

with her mother had done, her ex-husband had added to it. Dennis had had nothing good to say about the man.

Knowing how badly he'd hurt Andi, Bryce didn't, either. In fact, he wouldn't mind throwing a few punches.

He inwardly flinched at the hypocritical thought.

Sure, the other man had added to the wall around Andi's heart.

But his own thoughtless actions had laid the foundation.

Andrea's eyes shot open. She lay stock-still, muscles drawn tight. Five seconds ago, she'd been dead to the world. Now she was wide-awake, every sense on alert. Had she heard something?

No, it was just stress, lingering effects from having been run off the road. She released a breath she hadn't realized she'd been holding and tried to slow her racing heart.

A crash came from somewhere inside the house and she stifled a gasp.

"Keep it down." The raspy whisper set her teeth on edge.

She threw back the covers and sprang from the bed. If she could close and lock the door, maybe she could escape through the window before they charged into the room.

The response came in the same hushed tone. "Why? Nobody's here."

Andrea stopped in her tracks. They didn't know she was there. If she didn't alert them to her presence, maybe she could hide till they left.

"We don't know that."

"You saw what happened. She's still back there on that slope. Or in a hospital bed."

"Just shut up and check the bedrooms."

Panic shot through her. She bounded back toward the bed, bare feet silent against the rugs covering the hardwood floor.

Heavy footsteps pounded closer, and she flipped the bedspread up over the pillow. It wasn't neat, but maybe the bed wouldn't look recently slept in.

As she snatched her purse from the nightstand, she cast a glance over her shoulder. Light seeped in through the door opening, moving erratically. Someone was approaching with a flashlight.

She dropped to the floor and slid under the bed. Two seconds later, the door swung fully open.

"You check this room. I'll check the others. Then we'll start our search. Or pick up where we left off."

She held her breath while her pulse pounded in her ears. Had she left any hint that the house was occupied? Her purse and phone were under the bed with her. The two small suitcases were sitting in the corner.

But they were empty. As late as she'd gotten in, she hadn't planned to unpack until morning. But after Bryce's visit, trying to go immediately to sleep would have been pointless.

So she'd tucked her clothes away in the closet and dresser drawers and put her toiletries in the bathroom medicine cabinet. Nothing she'd brought with her was out.

Except her father's note. Where had she left it?

Before getting ready for bed, she'd picked it up from the coffee table and carried it into the bathroom. She'd never retrieved it after brushing her teeth. But that by itself wouldn't give away her presence.

Wood scraped against wood as a drawer slid open. A moment later, the clothes she'd put away tumbled to the floor. Contents of a second drawer followed, and then a third.

Andrea watched from her hiding place, pulling in silent breaths. The men in her house were the same ones who'd run her off the road. And the same ones she'd walked in on Wednesday night. This time, they'd tried to make sure she wouldn't be there to interfere with their search. What were they looking for? And why hadn't they come for it right after attacking her on 60?

Maybe they'd needed to swap vehicles. It would make sense. Driving around Murphy with a smashed front end would be risky, especially when the damage matched hers.

More clothing joined that already on the floor. Soon the entire contents of her dresser were strewn across her room. The closet door slid back on its track, and more items followed.

"Finding anything?" The question came from down the hall, no longer a whisper.

"Not a thing."

What were they looking for? Money? Jewelry? Were they simply opportunists, hitting vacant houses? Not likely, considering they'd run her off the road to keep her away. They were after something specific.

If only she could call for help. Her phone was inside her purse. But it wouldn't be safe to use it until the men left.

Her eyes widened. She couldn't make a call, but she

could send a text. She could even receive one silently. She'd never turned the volume back up after the funeral.

Something crashed to the floor, and she flinched. That was her piggy bank.

"I said to keep it down. She's not here, but you don't want to alert that neighbor." The reprimand wasn't delivered in a whisper, but it was guaranteed to not carry outside the house. The man in the back seemed to be the one in charge.

She didn't recognize the voice. Not that she expected to. The words she'd heard so far seemed devoid of an accent. Definitely not Matt. Her antagonistic neighbor spoke in a lazy Southern drawl, infused with a hefty dose of arrogance.

"Whatevuh."

Definitely New England—Boston or maybe New York. Not much to go on, but every little bit helped.

A porcelain doll came down next. The intruder was clearing the top shelf of the closet, which meant he had his back to her.

She started to touch her phone, then hesitated. She couldn't risk it. With only the beam of his flashlight, he might notice the screen's glow.

More items hit the floor. Finally, he walked to the other side of the bed, and she turned her head. He'd stopped in front of the upholstered chair that sat in the corner. After tossing the seat cushion onto the floor, he flipped the chair onto its side. The nightstand followed.

He circled back around and kicked several items out of the way. Some of the tension seeped out of her. He was finally finished. As soon as he left the room, she'd text Bryce.

Instead, he approached where she lay. Her heart

pounded harder with every step. *Please don't look under the bed.*

He stopped, his feet inches away. A glove-covered hand reached down. The flashlight shone in her face. Her heart stopped. She closed her eyes and waited. Was he going to call the other guy or kill her himself?

He didn't do either. Instead, he stepped backward with a grunt. There was a long *shhhh* and a thud as he dragged her mattress off the box spring and tossed it to the floor. The flashlight beam swung around, and she tried to blink away the blind spot in the middle of her field of vision.

For the next minute or so, the light swept back and forth, illuminating the piles of stuff on the floor. Then he walked from the room.

Andrea emitted an almost audible sigh of relief. He hadn't looked under the bed. Now she could text Bryce. He probably wouldn't see it till morning, but it was worth a shot.

The screen lit up. She scrolled to their last call and pressed the text icon. Flat on her stomach, with her head turned at a sharp angle, she had only one hand available. But she'd make it work.

Her thumb slid over the digital keypad as she typed out a short message.

Someone's in my house.

The man retreated down the hall, toward the master bedroom, and she pressed the send icon.

The footsteps stopped. "Done in that room."

"You checked everything?"

"I did. The dresser drawers, the closet."

"The underside of the drawers? Inside the dresser itself, behind the drawers?"

"Yeah, the dresser and nightstand. Nothing taped there."

"What about under the bed?"

Sirens blared in her head, drowning out the man's response. He *didn't* look under the bed, or he would've found her.

And within moments, he'd do just that.

Her heart pounded, sending blood roaring through her ears. She belly-crawled toward the other side of the bed. Heavy footsteps moved closer. She scurried to the overturned chair and ducked behind it as the flashlight beam swept the room.

The man emitted a series of grunts. He'd apparently lowered himself to the floor. The beam of light illuminated the area to her right. She expelled the air in her lungs and hugged her legs more tightly.

Then the light shifted to her left. For several tense moments, it didn't move. Had he seen her? Was she not completely hidden by the chair?

He rose with another long grunt, leaving the flashlight on the floor. There were more sounds of exertion, some scrapes and clunks and groans. What was he doing?

The direct light disappeared, becoming a distant glow. Finally, he walked from the room, once again leaving her in total darkness.

"Under the bed is clear." He was moving away, his footsteps and voice growing softer. "I even checked the bottom of the box spring. Nothing."

The response was a soft murmur. If both men were

occupied in the master bedroom, maybe she could make it to the front door without being seen.

No, it was too risky. The one man might still be in the hallway. He'd already thoroughly searched her room and had no reason to go back in. As badly as she wanted to call for help, she was safest staying right where she was.

She peeked around the chair and craned her neck to look at the clock on the nightstand. It was 2:34 a.m. If the men planned to search the entire house as thoroughly as the one had searched her room, it was going to be a long night. Her muscles were already protesting the cramped position. She arched her back, then twisted side to side. It didn't help. Neither did leaning against the wall.

Finally, they moved back down the hall and stopped outside her door.

"You do this bathroom. I'll work on the kitchen. He hid it here somewhere. We're not giving up till we find it."

Who hid something? And why hide it in the house?

Because it was essentially abandoned. The weekly visits she and her dad had made years ago had turned semimonthly and monthly after she'd stopped coming. In the past two years, her dad's visits were even less frequent than that. If not for Bryce's diligence, the place would probably have had the windows broken out and become a hangout for the Matts of the area to get high.

Whatever the men were looking for, it couldn't be related to her father. He'd always lived an uneventful, straightforward life. He was an accountant and financial planner. One couldn't get much more boring than that.

"Hey, check this out." The voice belonged to the

New Englander. He'd probably found the paper. "He buried it."

The other man joined him. "'When a secret is too heavy to keep, it's always best to bury it deep.'" He paused. "Keep looking. The boss is going to expect us to eliminate every possibility that it's hidden inside first."

Andrea frowned. They had it all wrong. That was her dad's handwriting. Nothing was physically buried. The meaning was figurative. Surely they didn't plan to do to the yard what they were doing to the house.

One of the men tromped back toward the kitchen, while the other resumed his work in the bathroom. As bottles of makeup, cleansers and other items hit the Formica countertop, Andrea cringed. The glass door on the medicine cabinet banged shut, and the wooden one below the sink creaked open. Cleaners tumbled out while the clink and clatter of dishes came from the kitchen. At least the one out there wasn't throwing everything to the floor like this guy had.

A plastic bottle tumbled into the hall, likely kicked. "Nothing in here."

"Check the living room. We've got to find it before his kid gets her hands on it."

Andrea gasped. *His kid.* Were they talking about her father after all? That didn't make sense. There had to be another explanation.

The New Englander continued, "There's a shed out back. You want me to search that while you finish inside?"

"I wouldn't think he'd hide something this important outside, but Dennis Wheaton was a smart man. What better hiding place than where no one would think to look?"

Andrea's stomach clenched. Her dad had hidden something, and the men were determined to find it before she did. Had he taken something that belonged to someone else, something valuable? That didn't sound like him at all.

Maybe he found something incriminating during one of his audits. If that were the case, he'd call the authorities and turn over what he had. He'd never hold on to something for blackmail. And what other purpose could there be?

Soon thuds came from the living room. For what seemed like the twentieth time, Andrea looked at the clock. It was a little after three thirty. Time *was* moving. Just barely.

By the time she heard the back door open and close, it was almost four o'clock. Had the guy checking the shed come back in, or had the other one finished and joined him outside?

She crawled from her hiding place and tiptoed toward the hall. Everything was quiet. Now she could phone for help. She placed the call and returned to her room to wait.

Had the men found what they were looking for?

If not, did they think she had it? How desperate were they to get it? They'd sounded pretty determined. Based on what she'd heard, they weren't likely to give up their search. Which meant they'd probably be back.

Or maybe they *had* found it. Maybe her dad had hidden it in the shed, or the living room, and that was why they'd left when they had.

What could her father have hidden? Something had been weighing on him. She'd known that for a long time.

Then he'd contacted Bryce. How had Bryce put it?

He'd sounded like a man ready to unload a heavy burden. That burden he'd carried, the object he'd hidden and the situation he'd wanted to talk to Bryce about, were they all related?

She'd probably never know. Her heart twisted at the thought of anything tarnishing the memory of her sweet, loving father. If she didn't learn the truth, the unanswered questions would forever torment her.

She'd always been inquisitive. Her dad had encouraged it. Her mother hadn't.

But maybe her mother had been right. In this case, knowing wouldn't change a thing. It certainly wouldn't bring them back. Sometimes it was better to leave well enough alone, no matter how badly she wanted to do otherwise.

One of her mother's favorite sayings rang in her ears—

Curiosity killed the cat.

FOUR

A shrill whining sounded in the distance, and Bryce pulled the spare pillow over his head. It didn't help. If anything, the annoying noise grew louder.

Tossing the pillow aside, he opened one eye. Darkness shrouded his room; the only thing visible was the glowing red numerals on his digital alarm clock. It was 4:23 a.m. What was going on?

He bolted upright in bed. That was a siren. And it wasn't out on the four-lane. It was right there on Ranger Road.

His pulse jumped to double time as he swiped his phone from the nightstand. He had one text message, from Andi, sent at 2:21 a.m. Someone was in her house.

He sprang from the bed. Sixty seconds later, he was running out the door, fully dressed and armed. The siren died mid-screech, leaving an oppressive silence blanketing the night.

The red-and-blue glow dancing through the trees dimly lit the trail, and he stumbled forward at a half jog. Andi had to be safe. She'd been able to call for help, so she wasn't incapacitated.

But first she'd tried to contact *him*. Just as he'd encouraged her to do. And he hadn't responded. If she was hurt, he'd never forgive himself. As soon as he got back home, he was going to assign a different alert for notifications, something much more obnoxious than the single short buzz he currently had.

He broke from the tree line in time to see Gary disappear around the side of Andi's house. His partner, Jason, stepped onto the porch and rang the bell. Bryce crossed the yard at a full run and greeted his fellow deputy as the door swung inward.

Andrea stood in the opening, still wearing the cat pajamas. But this time fuzzy slippers adorned her feet, and her hair had obviously not seen a brush since sometime yesterday. It was flat on one side and poufy on the other. Her usually feathery bangs jutted upward at all kinds of interesting angles.

And he wanted nothing more than to wrap her in his arms and kiss her.

Jason stepped toward her. "Deputy Vining. We met briefly last night. You had—" he paused as his gaze flicked past her "—a home invasion?"

Andi moved back, swinging the door wider. Bryce's jaw dropped along with his heart. Someone hadn't just come inside. He'd completely trashed the place.

Jason walked into the living room and looked around. "Tell me what happened."

"I woke up to two men inside the house, ransacking everything."

"Any idea who they were?"

She shook her head. "One had a New England accent. The other didn't have any accent at all. I didn't know either of them."

Bryce listened as Jason continued with his questions.

As before, Andi had no idea who had broken in or what they were after. But any hopes he'd had that the first break-in was random died a quick and sure death. Dennis had something someone wanted. He'd apparently hidden it, and the intruders were determined to get their hands on it before Andi did.

"Would you like us to dust for prints?" The question came from Gary.

"It's not necessary in the first bedroom or the bathroom. The man who searched those rooms was wearing gloves."

Jason lifted a brow. "You saw his hands?"

"I was hiding under the bed. He bent down and laid the flashlight on the floor, inches from my face. I thought for sure he was going to check under there and find me."

She looked past Jason and met Bryce's gaze, the terror of that moment still lingering in her eyes. His chest clenched.

But the hug he longed to give her would be pushing the boundaries of the tentative friendship she'd agreed to. She'd likely stiffen and turn away. Not a scene he wanted to play out in front of Gary and Jason. He considered both men his friends. Having lived in Murphy all his life, he had dozens.

But there were friends, and there were *friends*, that small handful of people one connected with on a deeper level. For him that was Colton and Tanner. He hadn't shared all the details, but his friends knew there'd once been someone special and that he still kicked himself for having been young and stupid. Almost a decade of bonding during wilderness hikes, white-water rafting trips and rock climbing expeditions had a way of peeling away the barriers guys usually held on to.

By the time Jason and Gary left, they had a pad full of notes and a whole slew of prints that Bryce hoped belonged to someone other than Andi and Dennis. He wasn't counting on it, though. If the New Englander was wearing gloves, the other man probably was, too.

Bryce closed the front door and stood the bookcase back up, returning it to its place against the wall. Andi sank onto the couch. She didn't just look tired. She looked defeated.

He eased down next to her. "I'm sorry I didn't call someone for you. I didn't hear your text. I woke up to the sirens."

"Don't apologize. I couldn't risk the intruders hearing me call 911, so I tried shooting off a quick text. I knew it was a long shot." She released a slow breath, her body seeming to deflate with the action.

He lifted a hand to squeeze her shoulder. "I'll help you put all this back."

She didn't shrug off his touch. "I can handle it. I need to do some sorting anyway. If I decide to sell the place, I'll need to figure out what to do with everything."

If I decide to sell the place. Those words bothered him more now than the first time he'd heard them. A few hours ago, he'd assured her he wanted nothing more than friendship. Maybe *he* was the one who needed convincing. Through one casual relationship after another, he'd never been able to forget her. Even throughout his time with Pam, Andi had still held a piece of his heart.

Now she'd unexpectedly come back into his life. He'd treat it as the gift that it was and simply enjoy her friendship. He'd be insane to consider anything more.

If her ex came to his senses and decided he wanted her back, he hoped Andi would tell him to take a hike. But he couldn't count on it. After all, the last thing he'd expected was for Pam to return to her abusive ex-boyfriend. People did foolish things in the name of love.

Andi released a sigh. "The men who broke in are the same ones who ran me off the road. They think my dad physically buried something."

"Is that what you think?"

"I don't know. Something was bothering him. That note he left confirms it. Between that and his conversation with you right before he died, I can't help thinking he was in some kind of trouble."

"I'm thinking the same thing." Whatever the trouble, the man had tried to enlist his help. Unfortunately, the accident had happened before he'd had a chance to tell anyone what was going on.

"What if he was involved in something illegal?"

"That doesn't sound like the Dennis Wheaton I know." When Bryce had been headed toward a life of crime alongside Matt, Dennis was the one who'd guided him onto the right path. "As well as I knew your dad, thinking he'd done something illegal is too much of a stretch."

She wanted to believe him. It was there in her eyes. "If anyone had suggested it two weeks ago, I'd have defended him with my dying breath. Now I have too many unanswered questions."

Her gaze dropped to the mound of stuff covering the floor. "My dad has always been successful, by most people's standards. But it was never good enough for my mother. Most of the money that supported our high standard of living came from her family. And she never let my dad forget it. I'm sure she loved him at one point, maybe still did at the end of her life. But it always seemed like he was a disappointment to her."

She rested her head against the back of the couch and closed her eyes. "When I was young, she was always pushing him to run for public office. Her grandfather and both brothers were politicians, and she had high aspirations for my dad. But he didn't want any part of it. Maybe if he'd agreed to be a public figure, the rest wouldn't have been so important."

She continued, fatigue creeping into her voice. "A year ago, things started to change. My dad seemed to have a lot more money. He and two partners started a financial planning business a few years ago. He attributed his success to the fact that the business was finally taking off, that they'd gained some high-profile clients."

She lifted her head and turned pain-filled eyes on him. "I never questioned it. I was just glad that my mother had finally stopped berating him. But what if the allure of making the kind of money she demanded finally overpowered his own honesty and integrity?"

Bryce tightened his fingers into a fist, his heart breaking for the man who'd had such an impact on his life. Continually criticized and made to feel like a failure. If he'd gotten involved in something shady, Bryce could almost understand. But not Dennis Wheaton. There had to be another explanation.

"We'll get to the bottom of this. When we do, we'll find out that your father died the same honorable man we've always loved and respected." He'd cling to that conviction with everything he had, unless they uncovered irrefutable evidence to the contrary. Even then, he'd be searching for an alternative explanation.

"I hope you're right." She pursed her lips. "I need to get into my dad's office. His partners have probably divvied up his clients, but no one will have a problem with me gathering up his personal items."

His chest tightened. "How about if I go with you?"

"That's not necessary."

"How well do you know his partners?"

"Somewhat. I've met them. Talked to them several times. Why?"

"Your dad had something. You don't know what or where he got it. So you don't know who you can trust. At this point, it would be safest to trust no one."

Worry wove through her features, leaving fine creases between her eyebrows. "That's going to make it hard to find out what my dad might have been involved in."

"Just be careful who you talk to and what you say. You're not supposed to know that your dad hid something. You certainly don't want anyone to know you were there when the two men broke in and could possibly identify them by their voices. All you know is that someone ransacked the house."

She nodded. "I'll be careful. I won't say anything, and if anyone asks, I'll play dumb. I need to go through my dad's office at home, too. Maybe I'll box everything up and bring it here."

"Which leads us to something else." He geared himself for a fight. She wasn't going to like what he had to say. "You shouldn't stay here alone."

She cast him the same doubt-filled glance she'd given him when he first suggested she stay at his place. "You're not moving in here. Those guys already overturned every square inch of this house. Why would they come back? I seriously doubt they'll be digging up my yard, even if they think something's buried here. Besides, they may have already found what they were looking for."

"You can't count on that. Let me sleep on your couch. I won't bother you. If these guys come back, hiding under the bed hoping they don't find you isn't a good plan."

"I'll get an alarm and have it monitored."

That was better. But it would still take the police fifteen or twenty minutes to get there. "If you won't let me stay, then at least let me loan you Cooper."

"Who's Cooper?"

"My dog."

"Oh, no. I'm not a dog person. I wasn't raised with them. You know what my mom always said? 'A dog is a man's best friend. A fur-free house is a woman's best friend.'"

Yeah, from his brief introduction to Mrs. Wheaton, that sounded like something she'd say. Her "fur-free house" principle probably extended to cats, too. As far as he knew, Andi had never had a pet, even a goldfish.

"Cooper's short-haired. He doesn't shed much, and certainly not this time of year. I'll get him in the morning and bring him back in the evening. You won't even have to feed him. He'd at least alert you if someone was prowling around outside."

She pursed her lips. Maybe she was considering the proposal. "He's not one of those yippy ankle biters, is he?"

"No, he's a black Lab. And he's got a pretty deep bark. He'd make a good guard dog." At least Bryce hoped he would.

"And he sleeps the night through? Doesn't ask to go out at 3:00 a.m.?"

"He never bothers me."

"He's not going to expect to sleep with me, right?"

"He has his own bed. I have it in my room, but I'm sure he'll be fine wherever you put him."

"All right. I'll give it a shot. You can bring him over tonight." She rose from the couch. "This afternoon, I'll see about getting a rental car, then pick up some groceries. But right now, I need more sleep than the little I've had so far."

"Not here. You can't even secure the place." The intruders had gained entry through the back door. According to Gary and Jason, screwdriver gouges marred the jamb, and the knob looked like it had tangled with the business end of a pipe wrench. "You can finish the night in my spare bedroom. I've even got clean sheets on the bed."

"Sounds good."

He lifted a brow. That was easier than expected. But Andi seemed to no longer have the energy to fight him. Now that the immediate crisis was over, fatigue was setting in fast. Her shoulders drooped and her eyelids grew heavier with every passing moment.

At least for the next few hours, she'd be safe. He'd make sure that her house was secure before nightfall. And he'd contact Tri-State Life Safety about the security system. Or see that Andi did.

Cooper would be standing guard at night. And within an hour, his cell phone was going to be programmed with the most obnoxious text alert he could find. By the end of today, he would've done everything he could.

As Andi said, maybe the intruders found what they

wanted and wouldn't be back. But she wouldn't be willing to leave it at that.

As long as he'd known her, she'd been inquisitive. It was one of the things that had made her such a good student and fueled her love of astronomy.

What she was after now wasn't some interesting piece of knowledge. It was personal. Her father's memory was at stake.

If he knew Andi, she wasn't going to give up until she'd overturned every stone. She'd learn what had weighed so heavily on her father.

Regardless of who tried to sway her otherwise.

Andrea pushed the cart through the produce section at Ingles. Lettuce, tomatoes and cucumbers were stacked in one end. Since she was going to be staying in Murphy for some time, she needed to stock the fridge and pantry with more than milk, a box of cereal and some soup.

After adding carrots, apples and avocados, she wheeled her cart away from produce. In another twenty minutes, she'd be through her shopping. She glanced at a woman moving toward her, then turned to head down a canned goods aisle.

"Andi, is that you?"

Her cart screeched to a halt. She didn't get a good enough look at the woman to recognize her, but she'd know that sweet Southern drawl anywhere.

"Angie." They'd been casual friends but lost touch once Andrea stopped coming to Murphy.

Angie parked her cart against the end cap and stepped around it to give Andrea a hug, both of them bending to accommodate a large baby bump.

Angie stepped back, holding her at arm's length. "You look great. I haven't seen you guys in forever. Is your dad with you?"

Andrea winced. If she was going to go through this with every person she ran into, she might just lock herself inside the house and never come out.

"My parents were killed in a car accident. I'm here figuring out what to do with the house."

Angie's eyes widened. "I'm so sorry. I really liked your dad. He was always so nice."

Yeah, that seemed to be everyone's sentiment. Was there a side of him no one saw, including herself?

She redirected her thoughts. "You look like you're doing well." Angie had always been cute, but six or seven months pregnant, she radiated joy. Life had apparently turned out well for her.

"I'm married, expecting our second child." She rested a hand on her stomach. "I've got a party supply store and do special-events decorating. But I'm trying to sell my business so I can be a full-time mom."

"I hope it works out."

After chatting for a few more minutes, Angie returned to her cart. "I'll let you get back to your shopping. If you were planning to stay, I'd try to talk you into taking over my business. With your artistic ability, you'd be really good at it." She laughed. "You'd hardly even have to change the name. It could be Designs by Andi instead of Designs by Angie."

Andrea waved away the compliment. Whatever artistic ability she'd once had had lain dormant for so many years it was well past the point of resurrection. Her mom had never encouraged anything that didn't further Andrea's climb up the social or corporate ladder.

Phil hadn't expressed an opinion one way or the other. But most of their married life, she'd been too busy putting him through medical school to pursue anything more frivolous than sleep. Once he finished his residency, she'd kept up the pace. Giving 140 percent was a hard habit to break.

Andrea finished her shopping and headed out the automatic doors. Her rental car waited in the parking lot, a dark blue Honda Accord. She'd agreed to let Bryce take her to pick it up. Her own vehicle was at a body shop, where the wrecker had towed it. Her insurance adjuster would look at it sometime this week.

Though she'd let Bryce give her a ride to town, she'd turned him down when he'd insisted on helping put the house back in order. He didn't need to spend his day off working at her place. She'd rather be alone for the task, anyway. Sorting through her dad's possessions wasn't going to be easy. Too many things in that house had memories attached.

After leaving her empty cart in one of the corrals, she climbed into the Accord. A stack of mail sat in the seat next to her, the first of many thank-you notes she'd be writing for flowers and donations made to her parents' favorite charities. They wouldn't leave the post office till tomorrow, but she may as well deposit them while she was out.

Then she could head for home. She'd managed to tackle the kitchen and part of the living room before picking up the rental car. This afternoon and evening, she'd see how far she could get on the rest of it. She also needed to call a tree company tomorrow to take care of the downed poplar. She was surprised Bryce hadn't insisted on doing it.

Finding out he had no interest in renewing a romantic relationship had been a relief. She couldn't deny that the spark was still there. But it didn't matter. Anything deeper than friendship was out of the question.

It wasn't because he'd broken up with her years ago, saying he thought they should date other people. It was because she'd found him less than two hours later making out with a friend of theirs. Based on what she'd seen, it hadn't been the first time. So much for *always and forever.*

She drove from the parking lot and stopped at the traffic light, waiting to cross the four-lane. Next to her, an array of Christmas trees occupied the field at the corner, for sale by the Rotary Club.

The light changed, and she stepped on the gas, her chest tightening. Christmas was three and a half weeks away. She'd been dreading this one, her first holiday season as a divorcée. It was also going to be her first holiday season without her parents. A double whammy. If she could figure out a way to go to sleep on December 23 and not wake up until December 26, she'd do it.

But that wasn't an option. She'd face the upcoming holiday the same way she'd faced everything else life had thrown at her the past several months. She squared her shoulders and then let them fall. All the determination in the world wasn't going to fill the emptiness that had taken up residence inside.

She crossed a bridge and pressed the brake. On the left stood a small church with white stucco walls and a steeple topped by a cross. The post office was just past it. She dropped her mail into the box, then pulled back onto Andrews.

As she passed the church again, she looked at it more

closely. A small sign on the side said Free Methodist Church. At twelve thirty, the service was probably over, but several cars still occupied the parking lot. Small and simple, it looked like just the kind of place her mother had warned her about.

And exactly where she needed to be.

Something tugged at her, a longing she couldn't identify. Maybe she could find it inside. Maybe her church back home had had it, too, and she'd just been too preoccupied to see it.

She glanced in her right-side mirror, which framed the image of the little white church. Next week she'd go. She'd even see if Bryce wanted to attend, if not this one, the one they'd gone to years ago. That church had been small, too, filled with people who were warm and friendly, without pretense.

She traveled back to the four-lane and headed for home. As she snaked her way up Ranger Road some time later, she glanced left, then wished she hadn't. Matt was out front, blowing leaves from the Langman drive. He stopped to stare at her as she passed, eyes narrowed.

She'd gotten the same glare from him when she'd ridden by a couple of hours earlier in the front passenger seat of Bryce's Sorento. Matt's dad had apparently put him to work doing chores and he wasn't happy about it.

Or maybe he just wasn't happy to see that she'd come back.

Ignoring her neighbor, she rounded the next curve and turned onto her own property, stopping at the mailbox. After arriving so late last night, she hadn't thought to check it.

She shifted her gaze toward the house and heaved a frustrated sigh. If there *was* any mail, it would wait.

Bryce stood in profile, gripping a chain saw, safety glasses shielding his eyes. As she made her way up the gravel drive, a high-pitched whine seeped through the car's closed windows, growing louder as she approached.

When she stepped from the car, he killed the saw's motor and pulled a foam plug from one ear, letting it dangle from a plastic string.

She planted one hand on her hip. "What do you think you're doing?"

"Cutting up your tree."

"My trees are my responsibility."

He shrugged. "I have a chain saw. I figured I'd skip the objections and get started while you were gone."

"I was going to call someone first thing in the morning. Anything I can't do myself, I can afford to pay for."

"There's nothing wrong with being a good neighbor." He cranked the saw again and made another cut.

She shut the door and stalked toward him, waving both arms. He made it through two more cuts before looking up at her.

He killed the saw and lowered it to his side. "If it'll make you feel any better, I'll take some of the pieces for firewood."

"And you'll let me pay you." Bryce wouldn't demand anything in return, but she hated being obligated to anyone. And that was how she'd feel if he kept doing things for her.

A muscle worked in his jaw. "I don't need your money, Andi."

She winced at the coldness in his tone. The differences in their families' income and social status had never mattered to her. It had to him. Maybe he still hadn't gotten over it.

"I know you don't. But I was planning to pay someone." She gave him a weak smile. "I'm trying to not take advantage of your generosity."

"It's not taking advantage when I insist."

"Then let me at least help. I'll haul and stack logs. We'll split the firewood."

As she moved to retrieve her groceries, a white Lexus turned into the drive.

Bryce stepped closer, the action protective. "Are you expecting someone?"

"No."

The car came to a stop behind the Accord. The driver's door swung open and a businessman climbed out. At least, that was what she assumed he was. He looked to be in his midfifties, dressed in typical business attire: dark suit, pale blue shirt and a striped tie. With a receding hairline and a paunch that spoke of too many hours behind a desk, the guy looked harmless enough. But she was glad to have Bryce next to her.

The visitor stopped a few feet from where she stood and removed a business card from a metal holder. "I'm Melvin Drysdale with Choice Property Development." He cast a sideways glance at Bryce. "If this isn't a good time, I can come back."

Andrea took the card. "You can talk freely in front of Bryce. He's my neighbor and keeps an eye on the place."

"Pleased to meet you, Bryce. I'm here to hopefully relieve you of your responsibilities." He turned his attention back to Andrea. "My group would like to buy your property. I'm sure we can arrive at a price you'll be more than happy with."

She drew her brows together. "It's not even on the market. How did you know—"

"The obituary was in the paper. I'm sorry for your loss."

"Thank you. I haven't made a decision yet." She pocketed his card. "I'll get in touch with you if I decide to sell."

He looked around. "This is a lot of land to keep up, and the house is pretty run-down. Your life is in Atlanta. Do you really want to deal with all this?"

Uneasiness sifted through her. "How do you know where I live?"

"You're listed on the property appraiser's website as half owner."

"With my address?" Since the tax bills went to her father, probably not.

Drysdale shrugged. "I did my homework."

She crossed her arms. "This place has been in my family for generations." And no one was going to push her into making a decision before she was ready. "If I decide to sell, I'll contact you. Right now, it's too soon. I just buried my parents yesterday."

"I know it's difficult." He walked to his car and opened the door. Instead of getting in, he looked at her over the Lexus's roof. "Keep in mind, it's often easier to pick up the pieces and move on if we don't have unfinished business hanging over us."

She clenched her fists, struggling to hold on to her cool professionalism. "Tell me, Mr. Drysdale, have you ever had to pick up the pieces and move on?" She didn't give him a chance to respond. "I'm guessing not. If and when I decide to sell, I'll let you know. And the timing will be my decision."

Drysdale bobbed his head. "Yes, of course. Again, I'm sorry for your loss. Take some time to get your bearings, then give me a call."

He got into the car, turned around and sped down the drive.

Once he pulled onto Ranger, Andrea released a sigh. "Did you get the same kind of vibes from him that I did?"

"What, the stubborn, sleazy, condescending ones?"

"Yeah, those."

"Totally." He gave her an encouraging pat on the back. "Don't let him pressure you into a decision you might later regret."

"I won't. I don't let people push me around." She gave him a wry smile. "Except my mother. Not many people had what it took to go up against her, not even my dad."

After putting away the groceries and changing into a sweatshirt and an old pair of jeans, she returned to the front yard, where more cut limbs had joined the others. "Have you checked the mail lately?"

"Not since the day before you first arrived. The regular mail lady knows not to put anything in the box, but sometimes a substitute will deliver the flyers and coupon papers."

She shrugged. She may as well check. There'd been four mail-delivery days since Bryce had last looked. She made her way down the drive, dried leaves crunching beneath her feet. Behind her, the saw started up, the pitch rising as Bryce pressed whirring metal blades to wood. Maybe she'd check the shed for some earmuffs. A pair of leather gloves, too.

When she reached the street, she waited for a car

to pass. The driver raised a hand in greeting. Probably someone who lived farther up Ranger. She didn't know him. After having been gone twelve years, there'd be a lot of people she didn't know.

She stepped in front of the box and swung the metal door downward. Lifeless eyes stared back at her. Dried blood was caked around one side of the mouth. The rest of the furry body disappeared into the shadow of the box.

A scream shot up her throat, and she stumbled backward, hand over her mouth. Bryce continued working, his back to her. Leaving the box open, she stalked up the driveway, her initial shock pushed aside by anger. What she saw had Matt written all over it.

She circled Bryce and held up a hand. As soon as his eyes met hers, he killed the saw.

"What's wrong?"

"You need to look in the mailbox."

He laid the saw on the ground, then covered the distance at a jog. When he reached the box, his jaw clenched. "A dead squirrel in your mailbox. I would take this as a threat."

"Or someone trying to really annoy me. And I'm pretty sure I know who."

Bryce reached in to remove the dead animal, and she cringed. He was wearing gloves, but still. She watched him turn the body over and inspect it.

"I'm guessing it was hit by a car, then put in the box. It also happened recently enough that it hasn't started to decay. I'll toss it into the woods."

"Or bury it."

Vultures usually disposed of wildlife struck by cars,

and that was okay. They were nature's cleanup crew. Death was part of life.

But this one bothered her—the thought that it might have been killed intentionally, just to take vengeance on her.

She pressed a hand to the metal door to close it, then leaned down to look inside. She had mail after all, pushed toward the back. She reached inside the box and pulled it out.

It wasn't mail. At least it hadn't gone through the post office. There was no envelope, no address or stamp. Just a piece of notebook paper folded in thirds, "Andrea" printed across the outside.

Bryce's eyes widened. "Don't handle it."

She dropped it back into the box. After placing the squirrel on the ground, he retrieved and unfolded the sheet.

Andrea moved to stand beside him, her gaze sliding over the words. A block of ice settled in her stomach, chilling her all the way to her core.

This was no simple prank. It was a threat, no matter how much she wanted to believe otherwise.

She scanned the words again, darkness pressing down on her with each one—

"Being where you don't belong can be deadly."

FIVE

Fire shot through Bryce's veins. This time Matt had crossed a line. "Come on."

Leaving the squirrel lying where he'd put it, he charged down the street with Andi right behind him. At the end of the Langman drive, Matt's old Charger sat near the house, front end jacked up, tools scattered around it. Matt was always tinkering. Everything he knew about mechanics he'd learned from his dad. But there was one big difference. Jimmy Langman had held a job at a garage in town for the past twenty years. Matt had never kept one more than two months.

Bryce climbed the porch steps and knocked loudly enough to be heard at the four-lane. While he waited, he looked around. Matt was nowhere to be seen, but several items belonging to either him or his dad littered the porch. A tattered jacket hung from the railing, and a pair of tennis shoes sat near the door. Gray with a neon green swish, they'd been classy at one point. Now they were worn and stained with grease.

When the door finally opened, Mr. Langman stood there scowling. "Stop all the racket already. What's the cotton-picking emergency?"

"Your son's been harassing Andi since she arrived, and it's going to stop now."

The old man's eyes shifted her direction and narrowed. "If she's going to threaten my boy for being on her property, she'd better stay off mine, or I'll trespass her."

"If that boy of yours keeps up the threats, he's going to jail. Andrea has inherited the property and has every right to enjoy it in peace."

Langman's bushy eyebrows lifted. "Inherited? Her old man's gone?" His nostrils flared. "Good riddance."

The final words were barely audible. But Andi's sharp intake of air said she'd heard them, too. No wonder Matt had such hatred for the Wheatons. He'd learned it from his father.

Matt stepped into the room and shuffled to the door. "What's wrong?"

Bryce locked gazes with his former friend. Matt knew exactly why they were there. The self-confident grin proved it. Bryce held up the paper and shook it. "The dead squirrel is pretty serious. But threats like this can land you in jail."

Matt shrugged, not even trying to read what was there. He didn't need to. He'd written it.

"I'm warning you. Stay away from her. And stay away from the Wheaton property."

"If you think it was me, prove it."

"I intend to."

He spun and stalked to where Andi waited at the bottom of the steps. He'd have taken her hand if he weren't still wearing the contaminated gloves. But he wasn't removing them until he had the note tucked into a plastic bag. Matt had probably worn gloves. But Bryce wasn't going to rule out the possibility of prints being left until the department did.

Andi headed down the drive next to him, fists clenched and eyes filled with determination. "This property has been in my family for four generations. If I decide to sell it, it'll be because I want to, not because some greedy property developer wants to get his hands on it or a nasty neighbor is trying to scare me away."

"Good for you."

He admired her spunk. And though he hoped she'd keep the property, he'd support her in whatever decision she made.

When she reached her driveway, she cast a glance at the squirrel lying at the base of the mailbox. Bryce bent to pick it up. If Andi wanted it buried, he'd get out the shovel and start digging.

As they walked toward the old house, Andi drew in a deep breath and released it in a sigh. "I'm usually a decisive person. I knew right away I was going to get rid of the place in Atlanta. My two-bedroom condo is plenty for me. Selling my parents' seven-thousand-square-foot house made total sense."

She continued around the side of the house. "The decision about this place is harder. Keeping it doesn't make much sense. I don't know that I'll even make it up here. But every time I think about letting it go, I feel sick."

"Why wouldn't you make it up here? You're only two hours away."

"My work schedule doesn't leave time for much else. Corporate America." She gave him a rueful smile. "But I enjoy what I do."

He frowned. "How many days a week do you work?"

"Usually six." She opened the door to the shed. "My team works Monday through Friday. Saturday is my time to catch up on whatever I didn't get done that week and organize things for the next. Sunday, I do chores at home."

He watched as she fished through the lawn tools for a shovel. She'd always had enough ambition for five people. She'd graduated high school at the top of her class, with the goal of obtaining a graduate degree from one of the Ivy League schools. According to Dennis, she'd succeeded.

But the Andi of twelve years ago knew how to have fun and didn't mind taking time out for drawing, stargazing and hanging with friends.

Did she really love working that much? Or was there something else behind her desire to keep such an insane schedule?

He took the shovel she handed him and moved toward the edge of the woods. "Sometimes it's good to slow down, take time out for things you enjoy."

"I do. I mean, I don't work *all* the time."

"When's the last time you did something just for fun?"

"Thanksgiving."

"Holidays don't count. Before that."

"Six weeks ago."

He stopped just inside the tree line. After laying the squirrel on the decaying bed of leaves, he drove the shovel into the hard ground. "What did you do six weeks ago?"

"Took my team out for dinner."

"That's work."

"No, it's not."

"Okay. Tell me why you took them out. If I were to ask one of them that question, what would they say?"

"To reward them. We'd completed a big campaign."

"That's an employee incentive. Definitely falls into the category of work."

She crossed her arms and frowned up at him. "We were talking about my deciding whether or not to sell the property. How did we end up here?"

"You said you didn't know if you'd even have time to come up here and use this place, or something to that effect."

"Okay, so I did." She pursed her lips. "There's nothing wrong with being ambitious."

"No, there's not. But when people have too much ambition, they're workaholics." He slanted her a glance. "Anyone ever accuse you of that?"

"More than once. But in the corporate world, that's encouraged, even rewarded." She heaved a sigh. "Maybe I *do* need to keep this place. It'll force me to take time off and at least make occasional trips up. Otherwise, it wouldn't be practical to spend the money for upkeep. And I'm all about practicality." She paused. "So there's my decision."

He stopped his digging to look at her. "Just like that?"

"Just like that. I think I knew all along I wouldn't be able to bring myself to sell it. And I don't have to. I can keep up my condo in Atlanta and still afford the maintenance on this place." She leaned back against a tree, a relaxed smile touching her lips. "With that decision, I feel like a weight has been lifted off me."

Yeah, him, too. But it was more than that. Her decision had left him with a sense of elation that he had a hard time explaining, even to himself. Laughter bubbled just below the surface, clamoring to get out. If he let everything he was feeling flow, Andi would think he'd lost his mind.

But Andi was one of his oldest friends. Friends were important to him. Tanner was a mile away, over on 294, with his fiancée, Paige, in the cabin at the back of Tanner's property. Colton and Mandy lived a short distance the other direction, on Hilltop. And when Andi came up, she'd be right next door. All his closest friends within a one-mile radius.

That was the only reason for his giddiness.

He looked down at the shallow hole he'd dug. "If you want this any deeper, you'll have to get me a pickax."

"That's good. He's getting a better burial than he would've if he hadn't ended up in my mailbox."

Bryce laid the squirrel in the hole and scooped dirt over it. After packing it down, he spread dried leaves with the edge of one boot.

Andi lifted her shoulders and then let them fall. "Now that the decision's made, I guess I need to call Melvin Drysdale."

He walked to the shed and returned the shovel to its place against the side wall. "Want me to get rid of him for you?"

"I can handle him."

He had no doubt about that. She didn't get where she was without being able to handle people.

He followed her inside, where she retrieved the card Drysdale had given her and slid her phone from her back pocket. Ten or fifteen seconds after she punched in the number, a smile climbed up her cheeks. "Voice mail. I get to take the coward's way out."

Her message was short and sweet. She thanked him for his interest but let him know she'd decided to keep the property.

"Another task knocked off my to-do list." She dropped the card in the trash. "In the last fifteen minutes, I've made the decision to keep the property and gotten rid of Drysdale. Now we're going to finish getting that tree out of my front yard. A productive afternoon, wouldn't you say?"

"Quite." He certainly had no complaints about how the day was shaping up. Any decisions that brought Andi back to Murphy on a semi-regular basis were good ones. And the longer she planned to stay on this trip, the better.

He also had her safety to think about. Even with a security system and Cooper standing guard, she wasn't totally safe at the old house. But better next door than two hours away.

Whatever trouble Dennis Wheaton had found, it probably didn't originate in Murphy. It likely followed him from Atlanta.

And if it followed Dennis from Atlanta, it could easily follow Andi back.

The tantalizing scent of chocolate chip cookies filled the kitchen. Andrea took the final tray from the oven and placed it on a rack to cool. One dozen was already sealed in a plastic container, with another dozen and a half on a plate covered with foil. She'd picked up ingredients when she'd been at Ingles, not intending to use them until she'd finished sorting through the house and putting everything away. But she'd accomplished enough in the yard this afternoon to justify goofing off.

Andrea returned the pot holders to the drawer and turned off the oven. She hadn't baked in years. She hadn't had the time. With a great bakery a few blocks from her condo, there'd been no need. But her purchases had never made her kitchen smell like this. If she was going to take up baking, she'd also have to get a gym membership. Her promise to indulge in only one cookie had fallen by the wayside. She'd polished off three before finally sealing up the container.

But she was giving away the rest. Now that she'd decided to keep the property, she'd be hiring a handyman to help with projects. The cookies would be a bonus.

She shrugged into her jacket, then picked up the foil-covered plate, which was still warm. That one was going to Bryce. He'd never let her dad pay him, and he wasn't letting her pay him, either. But no man turned down homemade chocolate chip cookies.

After taking a flashlight from the drawer, she opened the front door. The porch light spilled over the yard in a semicircular glow, holding back a wall of darkness. She locked the door behind her and pocketed the key. At seven in the evening, no one was likely to be prowling around, but it never hurt to be cautious.

After picking her way along the trail, she stepped into Bryce's yard and stopped, memories bombarding her. His porch light was on. A swing hung from the roof at one end. How many hours had they spent sitting there, talking and laughing, sharing kisses in the moonlight?

But those weren't the images that played through her mind. Only one was there, stuck on pause: Bryce with Carla sitting in his lap, arms entwined around one another—

She forged ahead, refusing to dwell on the past. It happened twelve years ago. They'd barely been adults. What she'd experienced six months ago had been so much worse. Bryce's betrayal shouldn't even still bother her.

But it did. Eighteen or thirty, age didn't matter. Betrayal stung regardless.

She shook off the thoughts and climbed his porch steps. Deep-throated barks answered her knock. Bryce was right. Cooper would be a good guard dog. She'd go ahead and bring him home when she left. She still wasn't thrilled with the arrangement. But it made Bryce feel better. And it was only temporary.

The door swung inward, and Bryce frowned down at her. "What are you doing here?"

"Uh, cookies?" She'd expected a little friendlier greeting.

"You shouldn't venture out alone after dark." The frown was still there. "If you do have to go outside for something, please call me."

"Okay, I will." He was overreacting. Someone was on a treasure hunt. No one had tried to hurt her. Well, they had, out on 60, but that was to keep her away from the house while they did their search. Now that was done.

His gaze dipped to what she held, and his expression softened. "Come in."

After taking the plate, he drew in a slow breath and peeked under the foil. "You made these?"

"Yep. Just now."

He picked up one and took a large bite. "Mmm, my favorite. You remembered." He closed the door behind her. "Thank you."

The smile he gave her did funny things to her insides. Yes, she remembered. Chocolate chip had always been his favorite. Not only had she made them for him on several occasions. They'd also made them together. A sudden sense of nostalgia struck her, along with an awareness of something lost, precious moments that could never be regained.

She cleared her throat and looked down at the dog, who appeared to be having a hard time containing himself. He kept shifting his weight from one side to the other, his tail wagging at a furious pace.

Bryce grinned. "Andi, meet Cooper."

"Hello, Cooper." Andrea held out a hand.

Bryce patted the dog's back. "Shake."

Cooper lifted a paw toward his master.

"Not me, silly. Shake Andi's hand."

He continued to paw Bryce's jean-clad leg.

"We're still working on some of the commands. But he's doing great, considering where he was when I got him. Six months ago, you'd have rather taken your chances with an ax murderer than share a house with him. I ended up replacing a great pair of hiking boots, along with some belts and a uniform, after he reallocated them for chew toys." He ruffled the fur behind the dog's neck. "This guy did more for getting me to pick up after myself than eighteen years of my mom's nagging."

She laughed, bending to pet the dog. When she straightened, she glanced around the room. The furniture had been changed to something more modern than what his grandparents had had, and the walls were now a toned-down mustard color instead of antique white.

But that wasn't what had snagged her gaze and held it. It was the five framed sketches hanging over the living room couch—each drawn by her. Two were portraits, one of her dad and one of Bryce. The others were scenes of activities they'd shared together—a visit to Hiwassee Dam, stargazing on her own back deck, Bryce leaning against the old well. Her dad must have given him the sketches sometime after she'd left and Bryce had had them matted and framed.

And kept them displayed. Had he simply appreciated the artwork? Or had he felt something for the artist all these years?

He grinned down at her. "There probably aren't many people who own a collection of early Andrea Wheaton originals."

She returned his smile. "No, you're the only one."

"Have you continued with your artistic endeavors?"

"Not unless you count choosing the color scheme and furnishings for my condo." That had been another argument. Her mom had insisted she use the family's interior designer, but Andrea had stood her ground. And she was glad she had. She couldn't be happier with the result. Every square inch of the place reflected her personal touch.

"That's a shame. I hope you pick it back up again."

She shrugged. "It's been so many years since I touched a charcoal pencil, I probably wouldn't remember what to do with it."

"You had incredible talent. It would all come back with a little practice." He extended a hand toward the couch. "Have a seat. I'll share my cookies with you."

"Those are for you. I already ate too many."

She took a seat and he sat next to her, the sketches now behind them. She'd also done a self-portrait and given it to Bryce on his seventeenth birthday. That one wasn't displayed. She didn't expect it to be. Carla wouldn't have appreciated having to look at a sketch of her new boyfriend's ex every time she came over. Any girlfriends Bryce had had since probably wouldn't have, either.

The only one she could put a name or face to was Carla. Although her dad had kept her up to date on some of the people in Murphy, he'd been fairly tight-lipped about Bryce.

"You said someone recently put you through the wringer." As soon as the words left her mouth, she wished she could draw them back. Sure, they'd agreed to renew a friendship. But his love life was none of her business. If he shared his, he'd expect her to relay her own pathetic story. Before she could take back her comment, he spoke.

"Her name was Pam. We met through mutual friends. She'd moved here from Franklin to escape an abusive boyfriend."

She shook her head. "That's something I'll never understand. Both guys who hit women and women who put up with it."

"Sometimes they think they can't do any better, or the abuser convinces them they deserve it. Pam grew up in a really dysfunctional home. I was amazed she had it together as much as she did. But she still had lots of stuff to overcome. I thought she was doing pretty well."

"So how did it end?"

"He finished his jail time and she went back to him."

"Oh, no." The woman had to have been crazy to walk away from a kind, gentle man like Bryce.

"You guys could have been sisters."

His tone was soft, but the words had the same effect as a bucket of cold water being poured over her. Was that why he'd gotten involved, because Pam had reminded him of her?

A heavy silence hung between them, until Cooper approached to put a big paw in her lap.

"So now you're ready for that greeting." She gave it a couple of shakes.

For the next two hours, the conversation stayed light. Finally, she rose to leave.

Bryce stood also. "Give me a second to get his bed, and I'll walk you home."

He disappeared down the hall, then emerged a short time later, carrying a large fur-covered object.

"You think he'll be all right in my living room?"

He clipped on the dog's leash and moved toward the door. "He should be fine."

She hoped so. If he was in her room, she'd wake up every time he shifted positions. Over the past six months, she'd grown too accustomed to sleeping alone.

The dog loped along the trail in front of them, stopping twice to lift his leg. At least he was getting that out of the way.

Once inside, she took the bed from Bryce and dropped it against one wall. It was the end of the living room closest to the hall. She could have her privacy without Cooper feeling too isolated.

Bryce rested one hand on the doorknob. "If you have any problems, call or text me."

"I'm sure we'll do fine." She had no experience with dogs, or animals of any kind. But how hard could it be?

She locked the door behind him, then got ready for bed, allowing the dog to follow. When she'd finished putting on her pj's, she clapped her hands and stepped into the hall. "Okay, Cooper, time for bed."

His ears lifted, but he stayed where he was. Maybe she was supposed to whistle. That was going to be a problem.

"Cooper, come." She waved a hand, motioning him toward her. He crossed the room and joined her in the hall. After some more coaxing, he stepped into his bed, turned two full circles and plopped down with a thump.

"Good dog." She petted him a few times and turned off the living room lights. It was early enough, so she could spend some time reading.

She still hadn't decided how long she'd stay. After next week, she'd be down to five weeks of vacation. If she wanted to take some long weekends, she'd better not burn through all of it. Maybe three weeks. By then she'd be ready to head back.

As she slid between the crisp sheets, a sense of heaviness settled over her like a cloak. Tension crept across her shoulders, and her insides tightened. What was wrong with her?

She picked up her phone and touched the Kindle app. Reading before bed had been a longtime habit. It was the surest way to shut down her brain so she could get some quality sleep.

The last page she'd read came up, midway through the newest book by one of her favorite women's fiction authors. She fluffed the pillows behind her and settled in.

After reading a few pages, she lowered the phone and rolled her shoulders, but the heaviness wouldn't leave. She recognized this feeling. It was the same thing she always felt when facing something she dreaded. Like a lunch date with her mother. Now it was the thought of going back to Atlanta.

Well, she was just going to have to deal with it. Sure, her ex was there. But she wasn't the first woman to have her self-esteem trampled by a cheating husband. And she certainly wouldn't be the last.

Soon she'd go back home and continue doing what she'd been doing for the past six months—avoiding routes that would take her anywhere near his office or the home they'd shared. She was even avoiding the hospital when she could.

And that was what she'd continue doing until thoughts of Phil with his new girlfriend didn't conjure up any more emotion than a trip to the mailbox. In the meantime, she'd occupy every spare moment with work.

The heaviness increased, pressing down on her until her shoulders ached. Now that she'd decided to keep the Murphy place, she didn't want to go back to Atlanta. At all.

She didn't even want to return to her job. The realization stunned her.

What was wrong with her? She loved her job. It defined her and gave her life meaning.

It also consumed her.

Bryce's words rang through her mind. *Sometimes it's good to slow down.*

She didn't know how to slow down. When she was younger, her mother wouldn't let her. When she got older, she wouldn't let herself.

If she didn't go back to her job, what would she do?

An image flashed through her mind, her pregnant friend, face glowing with love for her expanding fam-

ily. She wanted to sell her business and had insisted
Andrea would be the perfect fit.

No, out of the question. She'd be crazy to give up a
stable, high-paying job for the headaches of self-em-
ployment to earn a fraction of what she was currently
making. Totally impractical. And as she'd told Bryce,
she was all about practicality.

She pushed the thoughts aside and returned to reading until her eyes grew heavy. Finally, she placed her
phone on the nightstand and curled up on her side.

Her thoughts grew more random, that telltale sign
that sleep wasn't far away. She drifted on the sea of
nothingness, the tide drawing her further from consciousness. Until the click of toenails against the hardwood floor pulled her back.

She opened her eyes. Cooper stood in her doorway,
half in and half out, black body silhouetted against the
dim glow of the bathroom's night-light.

"Cooper, go lie down."

He emitted a soft whimper.

She tried the command again. It didn't work any
better than it had the first time. She heaved a sigh.
Bryce had warned her. Cooper was used to sleeping
in his room. In a strange house, away from his master,
she couldn't expect him to be content alone in the living room.

"Okay, Cooper. You win."

When she dropped his bed at the foot of hers, he immediately plopped down and curled up, head resting on
his front paws. She crawled back into bed and resumed
her favorite sleeping position.

Outside, the wind picked up, a faint, distant howl.

She soon found herself again hovering at the precipice, ready to slide into unconsciousness.

Another sound began, much closer than the wind. It was soft and low-pitched, followed by silence. Then again, repeating in a steady rhythm.

She opened her eyes. *Great.* A snoring dog.

Something scraped across the bedroom window, and tension spiked through her. She willed herself to relax. It was only a tree branch. The house was securely locked—this time with newly installed dead bolts.

And Cooper was sleeping at the foot of her bed. His presence brought more security than she'd expected, and she was glad to have him there. Snoring and all.

Whether from the break-ins, the dead squirrel in her mailbox, the threatening note, the run-in with Matt or the visit from Drysdale, she wasn't sure.

But a sense of uneasiness had wrapped around her.

And it wouldn't let go.

SIX

An old Beatles tune played in the living room, making the old house feel much less lonely. Andrea placed a stack of sweaters in the open box on her bed. There was no need to keep them. She'd outgrown them years ago, along with the other items in the box.

The music faded, and the first strains of "Here Comes the Sun" drifted into the room. As soon as Bryce left after picking up Cooper, she'd looked for some happy music to serenade her while she cleaned and sorted. She had plenty to choose from. Her dad grew up in the sixties and early seventies and had an enviable collection of CDs at the Murphy house. The Beach Boys, the Rolling Stones, Elvis and numerous others had a permanent place on the Wheaton shelf.

At least at this Wheaton residence. Pop music had never found its way into the Atlanta house. Her mother wouldn't have stood for it. Anything not high-brow enough to be performed by the London Philharmonic was beneath her.

Andrea folded down the flaps of the box and sang along. The lyrics weren't deep, but they were fun. She'd always liked that era of music because her dad had. She liked her mom's symphony music, too. But there'd been something special about blaring the Beatles through the house, her and her dad singing at the top of their lungs.

She toted the box into the living room and set it on top of another one near the door. She now had every room back in order except the master bedroom.

The "get rid of" stack was smaller than she'd anticipated, partly because there wasn't that much clutter. After her grandparents had passed away, her dad had donated their clothing and personal items to the Humane Society thrift store. And since this wasn't her parents' primary residence, the majority of their personal possessions weren't here.

If her mother were the one tackling clearing out the house, it would be much barer. Andrea hadn't been that unemotional. Too many of the items had sentimental value. Throughout her childhood, the Murphy house had been her retreat, the special place she and her father shared. They'd built so many memories.

She picked up a chunk of quartz displayed on the bookcase. She'd found it during one of their trips to the Hiwassee Dam. That was the time her father had tried to teach her how to skip rocks. His would skate across the smooth surface, bouncing three or four times. Hers would land in the lake with a splash. She never did get the hang of it.

She laid the rose-colored stone back on the shelf. Her mother would look at it as a meaningless hunk of rock, occupying space that should belong to an engraved Humidor vase, or some other collectible. She and her father saw it as yet another opportunity to say, "Remember when…"

She picked up a spiral-bound notebook she'd put on

the desk earlier and slid it under a roll of duct tape in one of the drawers. As she pushed it closed, a longing stirred, the desire to create. She tried to shake it off, but it only intensified.

When she'd cleaned up her bedroom, she'd come across one of her old sketch pads and a box of charcoal pencils. At the time, they'd meant nothing. Now they called to her.

She pulled the items down from the closet shelf and carried them into the living room. After positioning herself on the couch, feet propped up on the coffee table, she glanced around the room. Two old bottles sat on the rolltop desk. When she and Bryce had found them on the property as children, they'd thought they'd found buried treasure. In spite of the age of the bottles, most of their value was sentimental.

She put the pencil to the paper and began to sketch with short, quick strokes. Silhouettes appeared, and the objects took shape, growing more three-dimensional as she layered in the shading.

A sharp rap sounded on the door. Her hand jerked, and a short, dark diagonal line cut into the drawing. Two other knocks followed the first. She thrust the pad aside and grabbed her phone from the coffee table. Eight o'clock. Bryce wouldn't be bringing Cooper over for another hour.

She took a deep breath and tried to slow her racing pulse. Intruders didn't knock. And it couldn't be a ploy to see if anyone was home. With the rental car sitting in the driveway and all the lights on inside, the house obviously wasn't vacant.

She crossed the room and peered around the edge of the drapes covering the front window. A man stood on her porch, turned partially away from her. It wasn't Bryce. Standing in profile, he looked an awful lot like... No, couldn't be.

She moved to the side to shout through the closed door. "Who is it?"

"Melvin Drysdale."

She'd been right. What did it take to get rid of the man? A restraining order? She shot off a text message to Bryce.

Drysdale here.

Then she leaned forward to shout through the door. "Didn't you get my message? I've decided not to sell."

"I got your message, but I think you'll want to re-consider."

"The property isn't for sale."

"Everything's for sale at the right price." He paused. "Will you please come outside so we don't have to shout through the door? Or open the window? You know I'm harmless."

Yeah, he looked harmless enough. But this was a conversation she didn't need to have.

He continued before she could respond. "I've got an offer in my hand. All you have to do is sign on the dotted line."

She hadn't had an appraisal done, but the figure he rattled off was easily 50 percent more than the market value.

"This home belonged to my family. You can't put a dollar amount on that."

"What would your father want? Would he want you saddled with a deteriorating property, more trouble than it's worth, or would he want you to take the money and enjoy yourself?"

Heat built in her chest. How dare he claim to know what her dad might have wanted? Before she could respond, another raised male voice reached her from somewhere outside.

"He'd want her to follow her heart, which means keeping the place she loves so much."

Andrea swung open the door in time to see Bryce climb the three steps onto her porch. A leash was wrapped around his right hand, the other end attached to Cooper's collar. He'd positioned himself between the dog and Drysdale, which was a good thing. Cooper stood at attention, eyes fixed on Drysdale, a low growl rumbling in his throat.

Bryce gave the man a stiff smile. "I'm sure there are other comparable properties for sale in the Murphy area. I'd suggest you go talk to a Realtor and see what's available, because this one isn't."

A chilly gust blew through the open door. Dried leaves danced across the yard, the rustle growing and then fading. A similar gust had probably allowed Bryce to approach without the other man hearing him.

Drysdale shifted his gaze between the dog and the pistol holstered at Bryce's hip and backed down the steps. His eyes met hers. "Hang on to my card, because you'll change your mind. You'll find this place just isn't worth it."

Bryce cocked a brow, his expression cool. "Is that a threat?"

"Just stating facts." Drysdale spun on one heel and stalked toward the Lexus waiting in the drive.

Andrea stepped back to allow Bryce and his dog to

enter. "That man's got a lot of nerve." She closed the door behind them. "I'm glad you got my text."

"No more missed texts. I've got a notification on there now that you can hear at the other end of the house." He unclipped the leash from Cooper's neck, then drew his brows together. "Didn't Drysdale get your message?"

"He got it. He just figured he'd try to sway me to change my mind."

"Why?" He gave Cooper a hand motion, and the dog settled at his feet. "The property's pretty. It's got acreage with a small creek running across the back." The same creek ran through his own property. "But that's not hard to find up here. So why is he so dead set on buying this one when it's not for sale?"

"I don't know."

"Maybe he's working with the men who broke into your house. They're determined to find something before you do. Now they believe Dennis buried it. The best way to guarantee that you don't find it would be to convince you to sell the property."

She frowned. "That's kind of extreme. It would have to be something really valuable."

"Or really incriminating. Maybe they have more to lose if their secret gets out than the cost of this property."

When she moved to the couch, the dog followed, plopping down at her feet.

Bryce took a seat next to her and picked up the sketch pad she'd left on the coffee table. "Did you do this today?"

"I was working on it when Drysdale showed up."

A smile of approval climbed up his cheeks. "Good.

I'm glad to see you drawing again. You have too much talent to let it go to waste." He laid the pad back on the table. "Drysdale's out of Atlanta, right?"

"Marietta, which is a suburb of Atlanta."

He nodded slowly. "I'm going to run his name and see if anything shows up. Also, a friend I went to the academy with works for the Atlanta PD. I'll ask him to check to see if Drysdale is the subject of any investigations."

"I'd appreciate that. Something about the guy doesn't sit right with me."

"Me, neither. In fact, if you'll give me the names of your dad's business partners, I'll have him check those, too."

She nodded. "I'll write them down for you."

When Bryce walked out the door an hour later, he left with a handwritten list of names and no dog.

She knelt to cup Cooper's face in her hands. "I didn't think I'd say this, but I'm glad you're here."

Drysdale had made her uneasy from the first time she'd met him. Cooper's reaction had been even stronger. That deep growl hadn't stopped until Drysdale had gotten halfway to his car. If Bryce hadn't kept a firm grip on the leash, the dog might have taken a bite out of the man.

She rose, dread curling through her.

Animals often sensed the evil in people.

There was a reason Cooper didn't like Drysdale.

Bryce walked with Cooper along the trail leading to Andi's house. He held the leash but didn't have it connected to the dog's collar. It wasn't necessary. The dog wouldn't wander. If he did, one sharp command would bring him back.

He emerged from the trees right behind Cooper. It was early afternoon, but he'd have to leave for his shift in thirty minutes, and he wanted to check on Andi.

She'd gotten back yesterday after a trip to Atlanta to sort through her dad's home office. According to Andi, when he'd gotten licensed for financial planning and gone into business with his two partners, he'd kept some of his CPA clients and handled their books from home. Over the two-day period, she'd notified all of them about her father's death and returned their records.

Her parents' personal paperwork, she'd brought with her in boxes. Eventually she'd have to go back to her job and condo. The odds of her moving to Murphy permanently were almost nil.

He stepped onto the porch and rapped on the door. There was a bell, but it had stopped working years ago. Dennis had done whatever work was necessary to keep the old house from deteriorating. A nonfunctioning doorbell didn't fall into the must-be-done category.

The door swung open, and Andi invited him inside. "Is it that time already?"

"Almost. How's the paperwork coming?"

"Pretty good." She bent to scratch Cooper's neck. She was apparently getting used to him. Maybe she was even starting to like him. She hadn't complained about having him there, anyway. Other than the snoring.

Of course, he'd spent only two nights with her so far. Five days had passed since Sunday's squirrel incident, but for three of them, she'd been in Atlanta. And he'd worried about her the entire time she'd been gone.

Now she was back, at least for a couple of weeks.

During the hours he was at work, he was trusting her safety to Cooper, along with the alarm system Tri-State had installed yesterday. Now both doors and all the windows had sensors. He'd have preferred a motion detector in the living and dining area, but if Cooper decided to roam during the night, he'd set it off.

Andi moved into the dining room, where a chair was pulled away from the table. A manila file folder lay at that place, with several more stacked to the side. An open box sat on the floor, about one-half full of files.

"I'm fortunate my dad was an accountant. He really had his affairs in order. Since he added my name to everything, nothing will even need to go through probate. Usually kids have it much harder than this."

She sat down and picked up the single file folder and slid it into the box. "I found their life insurance policies. Let's just say I won't have anything to worry about for a long time. Of course, my dad's lawyer is working on locating all the assets."

He nodded. When everything was said and done, Andi was going to be a very wealthy lady. She'd always been well-to-do, but the money had belonged to her parents. Now it was all hers. Which put her even more out of his league.

She pulled the next folder off the stack. "Oh, wow."

He looked over her shoulder at what she held. It was labeled "Mercedes C300 Coupe."

"This was the car they died in." She ran a hand over the folder, then opened it. The file contained maintenance records.

She picked up the top receipt. It was from the Mercedes-Benz dealership in Atlanta. From where he stood, he couldn't read what had been done.

For several moments, Andi read silently. When she swiveled her head to look up at him, her jaw had gone lax.

"What is it?"

"Work the dealership did." She looked down at the receipt. "R and R brake pads, turn rotors, adjust calipers. This is dated November 2. Three weeks before the accident, my parents had the brakes redone."

She stood and started to pace. "My mom was driving. She always went a good five or ten under the speed limit. The road wasn't just familiar. She'd been on it so many times, she could just about drive it in her sleep. And tiredness didn't play into it, because she only made it about two miles from my aunt and uncle's place. Now I know there's no way the brakes failed."

She stopped her pacing to stand in front of him. "So how did she drive off the side of a mountain?"

"I don't know." Bryce's chest clenched. Was it possible someone tampered with the car? The brakes likely didn't fail...unless someone cut the lines. Or maybe Dennis and Margaret had a push from behind, the same as Andi had.

If someone killed Dennis to get his hands on something, he wouldn't hesitate to take out Andi for the same reason. If the motive was revenge, would the killer feel Andi deserved to die for Dennis's sins?

Andi closed the folder. "I've already contacted the investigators and asked them to look at the brakes." She frowned. "I don't know if they'll be able to tell anything, though. I saw pictures. The car didn't catch fire, but it was completely mangled."

"They have ways of finding out."

"My mom may have gotten distracted, even swerved

to miss a deer. But in light of everything that's happened, I don't think that's the case."

He didn't, either, which made his concerns for Andi's safety even greater.

Cooper rose from his spot in the corner of the room and walked to the back door.

"You need to go out, buddy?"

The dog's tail wagged. Bryce picked up the leash and hooked it to his collar. Without it, the dog would still be sniffing underbrush and tree trunks fifteen minutes later. Something about the leash said business.

Bryce walked out the door behind Cooper, who headed for the nearest tree. When finished, the dog stood at attention, sniffing the air.

"What is it? Do you smell something?"

Bryce scanned the woods, straining to hear any sounds of movement over the rustle of the breeze through the trees. Was Matt snooping around again?

After listening for another minute, Bryce gave a tug on the leash. "Come on, boy. Let's go in." It was probably just an animal.

Bryce opened the back door and followed the dog inside, casting a final glance at the woods. There was movement in the distance, a flash of color. Cooper had been right. Someone was out there.

"I'll be back."

Andi looked at him, brows raised. He'd answer her questions later. He closed the door behind him, then bounded down the deck's stairs, through the small backyard and into the woods.

After reaching the area where he'd seen someone, he stopped and listened. Nothing. He scanned the woods, turning in a slow circle. Three quarters of the way around, his gaze locked onto a figure some distance away, running toward the Langman property. In fact, he'd probably reached it by now and was no longer in Andi's woods.

But that didn't matter. He had been. And he'd been warned.

Bryce charged after him, but he had too much of a head start. Matt would probably be inside the house by the time Bryce emerged from the woods. But that wasn't going to stop Bryce from confronting him.

He headed for the Langman porch. The same as before, Matt's old man answered the door. "What are you accusing my boy of this time?"

"Let me talk to him."

"He ain't here. Went to jail last night. Arrested for drunk and disorderly conduct."

"Did you bail him out?" He usually did. That was part of Matt's problem. His daddy never let him face the consequences of his actions.

"Nope. Gonna let him rot in there for a couple of days first. Boy needs to learn a lesson."

A couple of days wasn't going to provide the lesson Matt needed. But Langman wouldn't receive that truth from him. The old man didn't show the hatred toward him that he did toward the Wheatons, but ever since Bryce broke off his friendship with Matt, Langman had treated him with cold disdain.

Bryce turned to go, but Langman's voice stopped him. "So, what did he do?"

"Nothing."

He descended the porch steps, and the door closed behind him.

Matt had done nothing. He wasn't even there.

Or Langman was lying, covering for him.

Checking out his story would be easy enough. He'd just look at last night's arrest records. Or put Matt's name into an inmate search.

He sincerely hoped it wouldn't be there. Then he'd know for sure Langman was lying and it was only Matt prowling Andi's woods.

Matt held a lot of animosity toward her. If he never saw her again, he'd be happy. But Bryce didn't believe for a moment that he wanted her dead.

Maybe the guys who ransacked her house were connected with Matt. Or maybe they were working on their own.

It didn't matter.

Something told Bryce they played for keeps.

SEVEN

Andrea dragged a twelve-foot ladder from the shed. The thing weighed a ton. Rather than a stepladder, it was an old, straight wooden one and had lain against the wall as long as she could remember. It had probably belonged to her grandfather. Maybe even her great-grandfather.

Now that she'd decided to keep the place, all the projects her dad had let go over the years screamed at her. She could afford to hire contractors to whip everything into shape. In fact, she'd already gotten recommendations from Bryce for a plumber to change out the toilet that let water continually trickle into the bowl and an electrician to figure out why the breaker tripped every time she plugged something into the bathroom outlet.

But tackling some of the jobs herself gave her something to do. Slowing down didn't mean she had to sit idle.

Leaving the shed door open, she gripped a rung and dragged the ladder across the backyard. She'd left Bryce out front, trimming limbs that hung too low over the driveway. He was probably working on cleanup now. She hadn't heard the whine of the chain saw for a while.

Instead, music filled the air. She'd brought the CD player out to the deck and plugged it into an exterior outlet. This time it wasn't the Beatles' greatest hits. She'd inserted an Elvis Christmas CD.

The world wasn't going to cancel Christmas just because her life had fallen apart. She might as well quit fighting it. Maybe she'd even get a tree, do a little decorating.

If you can't beat 'em, join 'em.

One of the few idioms that had never come out of her mother's mouth. Andrea hadn't been allowed to swim downstream with the masses. Her mother had always pushed her to be better and work harder than everyone else. And she had.

Not that it had done her any good. No matter how hard she'd tried, she'd never quite met her mother's expectations.

She stopped next to the deck and dropped the ladder parallel to the house. Now that the chain saw had fallen silent, the music helped drown out the hum of male voices next door. Apparently Mr. Langman had left Matt in jail less than twenty-four hours before breaking down yesterday afternoon and bailing him out.

Now Matt was hanging out with his friends, probably drinking and puffing on something other than tobacco. Every so often, raucous laughter rose above the other sounds. They had a fire going in the fire pit, too. She'd been catching whiffs of smoke each time the wind shifted.

After moving to the other end of the ladder, she gripped the sides and lifted, struggling against the weight as she worked it toward an upright position. The sky was gray, and the early December air held a bite, but with the exertion of her activities, she'd stopped feeling it some time ago.

"What do you think you're doing?"

She started, almost dropping the ladder. When she looked over one shoulder, Bryce was hurrying toward her. She'd asked him the same question when she'd caught him cutting up her tree last Sunday.

"Cleaning out gutters." She tilted her head upward to where leaves overflowed the metal sides and trees had sprouted in the trough.

"You don't need to be working off the top of a ladder."

She ignored his admonition and continued what she'd been doing. She needed to either get the thing fully upright or drop it. Since she'd gotten this far, she was determined to finish.

Leaves crunched as Bryce stomped toward her. His arms circled her, hands gripping the sides of the ladder, and the weight got suddenly lighter. He didn't release it until he had it securely positioned.

"Those gutters are almost ten feet off the ground. I'll take care of them."

His voice was low, filled with determination. When she turned to face him, he stared her down with his stern gaze.

But that wasn't what unsettled her. It was how he stood so close, exuding competence and masculinity. His North Carolina Tar Heels jacket was zipped in the front, and day-old stubble covered his jaw. A couple of wood chips had gotten trapped in his windblown hair, and her fingers tingled with the urge to reach up and remove them. Twelve years and one cheating spouse later, how could that electricity still be there?

She stepped to the side to put a little distance between them, suddenly aware of her own disheveled appearance. She'd found a faded pair of blue jeans with grass stains on the knees and donned one of her dad's insulated flannel shirts, rolling the sleeves to a point just above her wrists. Her hair had been in a neat ponytail when she'd started, but after two hours of yard work, most of the sides had escaped the scrunchie and blew into her face with each breeze. But she wasn't out to win any beauty contests, or even impress any men.

She planted her hands on her hips. "You got away with cutting up the tree because you started it when I wasn't here. I'm not going to attempt a toilet replacement, but I think I'm talented enough to handle cleaning out gutters."

"It has nothing to do with talent or ability. You could get hurt."

"I can get hurt driving to the grocery store."

She stalked to the shed and rummaged through the items on one of the shelves until she found what she was looking for. There was probably something more suited for cleaning out gutters than a hand spade, but it was better than using her fingers, with or without the gloves she wore. She'd found them on another shelf, not sliding her hands into them until she'd thoroughly checked them for spiders.

When she emerged from the shed, Bryce was standing by the door, expression stormy. He followed her across the yard. "I'm happy to help with anything you need done. And if you insist on paying someone, I know several people who would jump at the chance to earn some extra money."

"I'm going to hire people for some projects. Just

not everything." She climbed the ladder, spade handle stuffed into her back pocket. The rungs creaked with every step. She hesitated, adding *fiberglass stepladder* and *metal extension ladder* to her mental shopping list.

She shook off the uneasiness. The ladder wasn't rotten. The sides and rungs looked strong and solid. It was the nature of the material. Rocking chairs, old houses— wooden things creaked.

Once satisfied with her position, she scooped out a spade full of decaying leaves and let them fall to the ground.

"Why are you insisting on doing this?"

She looked down at him. "Can't you see? I'm enjoying myself."

"Cleaning gutters." The doubt in his tone was reflected on his face.

"Yes."

Bryce had accused her of being a workaholic. Maybe she was. But that wasn't what this was about.

She loved the Murphy house because of what it had meant to her father. Giving it the attention it deserved made her feel close to him. The projects she'd tackled so far had been almost cathartic.

Especially the ones outside. She'd almost forgotten how much she used to love nature.

When she looked at Bryce again, he shrugged. "Suit yourself."

He walked to the shed and emerged with a rake. When he disappeared around the side of the house, she resumed her work. It was something they'd agreed on. She'd tackle outside projects only if he was home. Once he left for work, she'd remain locked in the house with Cooper, alarm set.

Hanging on to the aluminum gutter, she stretched to the right and flipped a final scoop of leaves over the edge. That was as far as she could safely reach.

Once on the ground, she wrestled the ladder over, an inch or two at a time. When she'd finally gotten it positioned about three feet from where she'd started, she climbed it again, the creaks vibrating through the bottoms of her tennis shoes. She pulled the tool from her back pocket and stepped on the final rung.

It emitted the same unnerving creak. The crack of splitting wood registered a half second later and the step gave way.

A scream ripped a path up her throat. She released the spade and made a frantic grab for the side of the ladder, other hand still clutching the gutter.

The top of the ladder slid sideways, and she went with it, legs swinging in an attempt to find purchase. The gutter ripped through her gloved fingers as she fell, and she released the ladder, ready to try to break her fall.

Her right foot hit the ground first and turned inward with a snap. Pain shot through her ankle and up her leg, and she landed with a thud on her right hip. A second later, the ladder struck her shoulder, then fell across her left leg.

"Andi!" Panic laced Bryce's tone.

She looked across the yard to see him running toward her, expression a mix of concern and horror. He pulled the ladder off her leg and dropped to his knees next to her.

She shifted position and groaned. Her ankle and hip hurt. So did her shoulder and left calf where the ladder had struck her. Her right wrist, too. She'd apparently fallen on it when her ankle gave way.

Bryce put gentle hands on her shoulders. "Don't try to get up. I'm calling 911." He pulled his phone from his pocket.

She held up a hand. "Let me assess my injuries first. An ambulance might be a little overkill."

When she moved her foot, her ankle screamed in protest. Ice was definitely in order. She at least had a bad sprain, maybe even a break. She'd know more when she stood and put weight on it.

Her wrist was the same—a bad sprain. But she was sure nothing was broken. Some time in a brace, and she'd be good as new. The hip, shoulder and leg were probably just bruises.

"I think I'm okay." She lifted her hands, ready to allow Bryce to help her to her feet. Self-sufficiency wasn't going to benefit her at the moment.

After he'd helped her up, she gingerly tested the right ankle. She could put some weight on it as long as she kept the joint straight.

She limped to the deck, leaning on Bryce's arm, then sat on the steps. Movement in her peripheral vision drew her attention to the left.

Three figures watched from the tree line, Matt in the center. A guy she didn't recognize stood on Matt's left; Bradley Gunter was on his right. Bradley had always gotten into as much trouble as Matt. She'd never been sure who was the instigator. Maybe they both were.

When she glanced up at Bryce, she knew he'd seen them, too. He charged over to where the ladder lay on the ground.

She drew her brows together. "What are you doing?"

Instead of responding, he picked up one end. Two rungs were broken. She'd apparently taken out the second joint as she fell.

He turned the ladder, adjusting the angle. When he looked up, his face was red and a vein throbbed in his temple.

But the anger wasn't directed at her. His gaze was fixed on Matt and his friends.

"Bryce?" What had he seen?

Ignoring her, he stalked past her toward the woods that separated the Langman and Wheaton properties. Both Bradley and Matt's other partner in crime spun and disappeared into the trees, kicking up dead leaves as they ran. Maybe they were smarter than she'd given them credit for.

Matt wasn't. Though his stance projected wariness, he was just cocky enough to stand his ground.

Bryce didn't stop until he stood toe to toe with Matt. When Bryce spoke, his words were too low to carry to the deck. He grabbed Matt by the shirt collar and yanked him forward. Andrea gasped.

"Bryce." She rose from the deck and took a step. Pain shot through her ankle. She needed a crutch or walking stick if she didn't want to risk further damage to the joint.

What had set Bryce off? Whatever it was, it wasn't worth getting into a physical altercation. She had no doubt who would come out on top. But that wasn't the point.

Matt struggled to break free of Bryce's grasp. "Let go of me."

Bryce ignored the plea. Andrea clutched the rail and watched him drag Matt across the yard. Matt's eyes were wide, every bit of cockiness gone. At six foot two, Bryce was a good four inches taller and probably out-weighed Matt by fifty pounds. And Bryce was ticked.

Matt struggled some more, dragging his feet. "This is police brutality! I'm going to report you."

"Do you see a uniform? A badge? No, you don't. That means I'm not acting as law enforcement. Right now, I'm nothing but a concerned neighbor."

He gave him a hard shove, and Matt fell to his knees in front of the ladder.

"Andi could have been seriously hurt, maybe even killed."

Matt twisted his head around to look up at Bryce but didn't try to rise. "What are you talking about?"

"The ladder. You see these two broken rungs? Andi was standing on one of them when it gave way."

Andrea held up a hand. Bryce was overreacting, and he was going to get himself in trouble. "It's okay. This is what I get for using a ladder that was probably man-ufactured during the Civil War." She should have lis-tened to him when he tried to stop her.

"Your fall was no accident. This ladder might be old, but there's not a bit of rotten wood on it." His gaze locked with hers, and something there sent a block of ice straight to her gut. "There are hacksaw cuts halfway through the top five rungs, right where they go into the side rails. He intended for this to happen, if not to you, to anyone who might help you out around this place."

The air whooshed out of Andrea's lungs, leaving her hollow inside. That could have been Bryce. Or any of the people he'd referred to who would jump at the chance to earn some extra money.

Matt rose and backed away, arms raised and eyes as

wide as they'd been when Bryce dragged him across the yard. "Wait a minute. We heard her scream and came to see what was going on. You can't pin that one on me."

"That one?"

"Okay, I admit it. I put the dead squirrel in her box. I wrote the note, too. But I didn't do this. I swear. I ain't never tried to hurt nobody."

Bryce moved toward him. "If you don't want to be charged with attempted murder, I'd suggest you stay as far away from Andi and her property as humanly possible. If you're smart, you'll even avoid the whole right-hand side of your own."

Matt gave a slight dip of his head, then moved toward home at a good clip. After letting Bryce intimidate him, he wasn't demeaning himself further by running away. But he wasn't hanging around, either.

"I'm done for the day." Andrea started up the deck steps. "I need to ice my ankle, then wrap it."

The next moment, Bryce was beside her, sweeping her off her feet. She wrapped both arms around his neck and rested her head against his shoulder.

Her ankle was throbbing. But it was more than that. Over the past several months, her life had self-destructed. First her marriage. Then her parents. Now someone was trying to kill her.

And Bryce was there, offering her encouragement and support. They were friends. And friends went to bat for each other. But the fury he'd shown toward Matt and his fierce protectiveness toward her spoke of something deeper.

She tightened her hold, drawing from his warmth and strength. Right now, she needed him. She was hurting, both inside and out. The care he offered, whether as a friend or something more, she'd take.

Once inside, he gently laid her on the couch. "Are you sure you don't need a doctor? I'll drive you to Murphy Medical."

"I'm positive." If she changed her mind, she'd let him take her. She still had the Accord, and would for a while longer. She'd gotten word yesterday—they were totaling her Escalade. There was too much damage to the frame.

Her mom's car still sat in the garage of their Atlanta home. It was one of those two-seater BMWs, classy and sporty at the same time. Andrea planned to sell it. She was more of an SUV kind of girl.

She pushed herself to an upright position. "Spending a couple hours in the emergency room doesn't sound like fun. If I'm not going to get anything accomplished, I'd rather do something I enjoy."

"Then let me get you some ice."

He disappeared into the kitchen and returned a couple of minutes later with a zippered plastic bag filled with ice and wrapped in a dish towel. After propping her foot up on a pillow he'd put on the coffee table, he tucked the pack around it. "How's that?"

"Cold."

"It's supposed to be." He sat next to her. "So what did you have in mind for something fun?"

"I was thinking about watching a movie." She'd brought back a TV with a built-in DVD player from her parents' house, determined to prove to Bryce that she was slowing down.

"Can Cooper and I join you? He loves movies. Especially ones with dogs. I rented *Hotel for Dogs*, and he was mesmerized."

"I haven't seen it." Actually, if a movie had been released anytime in the past ten years, she probably hadn't seen it.

"If you want to watch it, I haven't returned it yet."

"You don't want to see it twice."

"I don't mind. Cooper will be thrilled."

She smiled. "We'd better keep Cooper happy if we expect him to continue his guard-dog duties. Otherwise he might go on strike."

"You have a point. I'll go get the movie. And the dog. But first we need to file a police report."

"I was thinking the same thing."

While he called dispatch, she chewed her lower lip. She was going to have to get a hasp and padlock for the shed. Originally a one-room cabin, her great-grandparents had lived there until the house was built sometime later. The oldest building on the property, it hadn't locked securely in years. Her dad had never worried about it. No one was going to steal a bunch of old tools.

Actually, no one had messed with the riding mower, either. It had occupied its same spot in the corner forever, until it finally gave up a few years ago. According to her dad, Bryce had been keeping up the small portion of the property that wasn't wooded ever since.

Bryce finished the call and pocketed his phone. "Do you believe Matt?"

Her stomach tightened. That same question had circled through her mind for the past several minutes. "I never thought I'd say this, but I do. When you said what you'd found, he was as surprised as I was. I don't think he's a good enough actor to fake that kind of shock."

"I was thinking the same thing." He put his arm

around her and pulled her against him. "I don't want to let you out of my sight."

She closed her eyes, resisting the urge to lean into him. She shouldn't let him hold her this close. It was muddling her thinking.

Because right now, all she wanted was for him to hold her and never let her go. She needed to get a grip. If she didn't get her head back on straight, she was going to do something stupid.

She snuggled more tightly against him.

There'd be time for rational thinking later.

Tomorrow.

Bryce closed the door on a silent, empty house and jogged down the porch steps. Cooper was still at Andi's, already walked and fed. Bryce had taken care of that early this morning.

After law enforcement left last night, he'd come home for the dog and a handful of movies. He'd also brought over a frozen lasagna. It wasn't a home-cooked meal, but at least she hadn't had to make it herself.

They'd ended up watching two movies. At Andi's insistence, the second one had been an action-adventure flick. She'd said it was the least she could do after he'd sat through two viewings of *Hotel for Dogs*. He was pretty sure she'd enjoyed the testosterone-charged show as much as he had.

Actually, he'd enjoyed both. He'd sat on the couch next to her, his arm around her, Cooper at their feet. Maybe that wasn't how "just friends" did movies. But having Andi snuggled against his side had seemed so natural. Maybe it was because of the many times they'd done just that. Not there. They'd never had a TV at the house growing up. But he and Andi had watched their fair share of movies cuddled together at the old Henn Theater downtown. All these years later, it still felt right.

He stepped onto her porch and rapped on the door. This morning he was taking her to church, but not to either of the two she'd suggested. Colton and Tanner had invited him to theirs numerous times, and he'd always offered excuses. Now that he'd decided to go, he'd be in trouble with his friends if he went somewhere else. They'd all occupy an entire row at MountainView Community Church.

Andi opened the door and waited for him to enter. She had her weight shifted to one foot, a crutch under each arm.

He frowned. "Are you sure you're up for this?"

"Positive. I'm pretty good at maneuvering on these things." To prove her point, she made her way into the dining area and back again. She still hadn't gone to the doctor. Fortunately, Colton's wife, Mandy, had the crutches tucked away in a closet, souvenirs from an ACL tear she'd suffered as a high school cheerleader.

A few minutes later, a horn beeped. When they walked out the door, Tanner was sitting behind the wheel of his Silverado, and his fiancée, Paige, was climbing out the passenger side.

She held up a hand in greeting. "Us girls will sit in the back. You guys take the front. A lot more leg room."

Bryce approached them and made introductions. Other than the brief meeting the night they'd caught Matt prowling in the woods, Andi didn't know Tanner. And she hadn't yet met Paige.

After helping Andi into the truck, he took a seat up

front. Soon the women were engaged in conversation behind him. They seemed to hit it off well, which was good. Andi liking his friends was important to him. If she was going to be spending time at the old house, he planned to include her in their get-togethers.

When they arrived at MountainView, they met Colton and Mandy just inside the door. There were more introductions, and by the time they took their seats near the front, the service was beginning. After a welcome and opening prayer, the worship band struck their first notes and song lyrics appeared on a screen over the drummer's head.

Several of the songs were modernized versions of familiar Christmas carols, and Bryce sang along softly. Andi stood next to him, smiling as she belted out the words. She'd always had a pretty voice. He didn't.

When the song service ended, the pastor took the podium. His message had a Christmas theme. The second week in December, Bryce had expected as much. He knew the Christmas story. Attending church at least once during the season had been a tradition in his family.

The pastor began his message talking about Jesus being Emmanuel—God with us. That wasn't a new concept for Bryce, either. He cast a sideways glance at Andi. She was leaning forward, wearing a gentle half smile. Since she was newly divorced and having just lost her parents, the thought of not being alone would probably resonate with her.

The next scripture named Jesus as Savior. As the preacher expanded on the point, Bryce frowned. It wasn't the first time he'd heard Jesus referred to as Savior. But now something about the thought disturbed him. Jesus being sent as a Savior implied that mankind needed saving.

When he pulled his attention back to the pastor, the man was reading from First Timothy, a statement made by the Apostle Paul—"Jesus Christ came into the world to save sinners, of whom I am chief."

What? The man wrote over half of the New Testament, and he thought he was the worst sinner who ever lived?

When they stepped out into the sunshine some time later, Andi smiled up at him. "I'm glad we came." Her features held a serenity that he hadn't noticed before. He hoped she'd found peace inside those walls.

He'd found the opposite.

As he walked toward Tanner's truck, one statement circled through his mind, spoken by the pastor near the end of his message—"Without Christmas, there's no Easter, and without Easter, there's no salvation."

He'd always considered himself a pretty good person, at least since Dennis Wheaton pulled him onto the right path. He figured when he got to the gate, Peter would consult the book, see all his good deeds and let him in.

But maybe he had it wrong. What if he wasn't good enough? If the Apostle Paul needed saving, what did that say about him?

He climbed into Tanner's truck and fastened the seat belt. Now that church was over, they were all heading over to Colton and Mandy's house, where a large Crock-Pot full of roast, potatoes and carrots waited. An afternoon spent with his closest friends, talking and laughing, was just what he needed.

Since Andi arrived back in Murphy, hardly a moment had gone by that he hadn't worried over her safety.

This afternoon he'd lay it aside. With her tucked away in Colton's house, surrounded by people, he could finally let down his guard.

As far as the uneasiness he'd left church with, he would set that aside, too. He'd have plenty of opportunity to delve into it more deeply later. Judging from Andi's reaction to the service today, she'd likely be making church attendance a regular part of her life.

And as long as she was in Murphy, whatever was a regular part of Andi's life would also be a regular part of his.

EIGHT

Bryce sat at the computer, nursing a cup of coffee and checking out world events. He had cable and often listened to the news if he was home for it, but keeping himself updated this way was more efficient. He could scan headlines and click on only the things that interested him.

His phone lit up next to the laptop, and he cringed. As soon as Andi was out of danger, he was going back to his old notification. What he had on there now sounded like Alvin and the Chipmunks trying to wake the dead.

It was serving its purpose, though. He hadn't missed a text since he set up the new alert.

He picked up the phone, and his pulse kicked up several notches. It was from Andi. You up?

He released a pent-up breath. Not a someone's-trying-to-kill-me text. He responded. For a while.

Have you had breakfast?

Hmm, if she wanted to cook for him, he certainly wouldn't complain. No.

On my way with Cooper.

Oh, no, not alone. He jumped up from the table and grabbed the jacket hanging on a hook beside the door. He shrugged into it as he descended the porch steps. A fine layer of frost covered the ground, and a chilly wind cut right through him.

Leaves crunched under his feet as he made his way toward the trail, the cold seeping through his socks. Maybe he should have slipped into some shoes, too. No, he'd deal with frozen feet before he'd let Andi walk over alone.

Up ahead, a door shut. He emerged from the woods in time to see Andi descend the steps, a foil-covered plate in one hand and a walking stick in the other.

She'd made a lot of progress with her ankle over the past four days. She still kept it wrapped and used a stick when on uneven ground, but the limp was almost gone. She'd said her wrist was doing fine, too, as long as she didn't bend it too far. The bruise on her leg had turned an angry blue-black. She'd lifted her pant leg and showed it to him, claiming she had a matching one on her shoulder and an even larger one on her hip.

As she made her way toward him, Cooper trotted along in front of her. Bryce knew the instant the dog saw him. Cooper bounded toward him, ears bouncing. Seconds later, large paws slammed into his chest.

"No, boy. Down." He lowered the dog to the ground, laughing. "We're still working on some things."

"He's excited to see you. He'll be glad when he's not stuck babysitting me anymore."

He took the plate she held and followed Cooper back down the trail. "Actually, he does the same thing when we're headed over here. I'm almost afraid he's going to choose you over me."

"I don't think you have anything to worry about." She paused. "Why are you barefoot? It's thirty degrees out here."

"I'm not barefoot. I'm wearing socks."

"Which are probably frozen to the bottoms of your feet."

He frowned. "You might be right. I didn't take time to get my shoes. I don't like you stepping out the door alone."

"That's why I texted you. But I figured you'd wait at your front door for me. I'm easily in shouting range of you."

Yeah, but shouting range wasn't good enough. He wanted to keep her in visual range, too.

He swung open the door, then tilted his head toward the plate. A mouthwatering aroma was seeping around the foil. "What's in here?"

"It's called a giant pancake." She stood her walking stick by the door and followed him inside. "Super easy. You mix up the ingredients, then bake it in a cast-iron skillet. Slather melted butter over it when it's finished, sprinkle with sugar, and voilà, breakfast."

He placed the plate on the dining room table, and she sank into a chair.

"When my dad and I would come up here, mornings always included giant pancakes." She gave him a wistful smile. "We never had them at home. I think it was just something special for the two of us here."

He took two glasses from the cabinet. "I assume giant pancakes go good with orange juice."

She grinned. "Giant pancakes go good with everything."

After setting the table, he plopped a can of dog food into a bowl and put it on the floor. If Cooper didn't eat first, he'd stare at them with soulful eyes throughout their entire meal.

"One more thing. Dry socks. I can no longer feel my toes."

When he walked back into the room, Andi removed the foil from the plate to reveal eight pie-shaped pieces, already cut.

"You won't let me pay you for the work you're doing, but I figured you wouldn't turn down breakfast."

"No payment necessary. Your dad was more like a father to me than my own. I've always been happy to help out." He flashed her a teasing smile. "But I never turn down food."

He took a seat, then pulled two pieces of pancake onto his plate. "I got a call from my buddy in Atlanta during my shift last night."

"Anything interesting?"

"John Lassiter has a thing for driving fast. He averages a speeding ticket every quarter. He's a few points away from losing his license. Mark Barrand is in a lawsuit with the IRS. There's apparently some dispute over back taxes."

"And Melvin Drysdale?"

"He's been married several times. His last wife disappeared. He was a person of interest, but they never could prove his involvement. They still haven't found her."

"He probably hid her body under the floorboards so he doesn't have to share his wealth with her."

That scenario wouldn't surprise him. He stabbed his next bite. She'd asked him to check out her dad's partners and Drysdale. He'd done more. "I had him run your dad's name, too."

Her fork stopped halfway to her mouth, and her eyes met his.

"Nothing. He's completely clean."

Her shoulders dropped as she released a breath she'd apparently been holding.

"I hope you don't mind that I had him checked out."

"Under the circumstances, that was the smart thing to do." She heaved a sigh. "You know, this was my dad's favorite time of the year. My mom always had professional decorators come in and deck out the Atlanta house for Christmas. I think she was competing for the most spectacular house on the block."

She gave him another wistful smile. "We had so much fun doing it ourselves here—going to town, picking out the tree, loading it on a blanket on top of my dad's car. If we had ever damaged the paint, my mom would've killed us both."

He returned her smile. He'd been part of those preparations more than once. He and Andi had always spent the actual holiday with their respective families, but they'd made some great memories during those three or four weekends leading up to Christmas.

She fixed her eyes on the picture hanging on the wall opposite from where she sat. It was her own sketch, a scene from inside the Wheaton living room next door. A decorated Douglas fir stood in the corner, next to the fireplace. A fire burned inside, and stockings lined the mantel, names written in cursive. One said "Andi," one said "Dad" and one said "Bryce." A dog was curled up on the hearth. It wasn't part of the original scene. Andi had added it in memory of the black Lab Bryce had lost then.

When Andi met his gaze, her eyes sparkled with anticipation. "I want to get a tree and decorate the house for Christmas, the same as Dad and I used to do. I've just got to figure out how to get it here. Throwing it on top of the rental car is probably not a good idea."

"We can use the Sorento. I'll even take you today. We have plenty of time before I have to head in to work."

She finished her juice, then stood to take their empty dishes to the sink. "I've got some things I'm working on at the house. Can you pick me up in two hours?"

"Sure. Cooper and I will walk you home. With shoes, this time."

He slipped his feet into the tennis shoes he'd left in front of his recliner last night. When he opened the door, Cooper stood at attention, waiting for the command.

"Come on, you can go."

The dog darted outside and down the porch steps. Andi retrieved her walking stick and followed, and Bryce brought up the rear.

Cooper headed straight for the trail. He'd traveled the route enough that he knew the way. The dog had almost reached the corner of the house when he suddenly stopped. His ears lifted, and muscles rippled beneath his black coat.

Bryce rushed forward, tension spiking through him. "Cooper, stay."

Before he could grab the dog's collar, Cooper bolted away, charging into the backyard, toward the woods. Bryce gave a second and third command. Cooper ignored those, too, his barks echoing as he ran.

Andi held up a hand. "I'll make it the rest of the way. Go find your dog."

"Lock yourself inside. I've got to get my weapon." No way was he charging into the woods unarmed.

As soon as Andi had locked the door, he sprinted back to his house. When he emerged, Cooper was still barking. As near as he could tell, the dog had stopped somewhere near the back of Andi's property. Did he have Matt cornered?

Or someone else?

Bryce crept deeper into the woods, the weight of the pistol reassuring. Maybe he should call for backup.

And risk bringing units out for nothing more serious than an animal or a snooping neighbor. No, he needed to check it out.

As he skidded down the steep incline toward the creek, the barking grew louder. Ahead, black stood out against the browns and greens of nature.

When Bryce reached him, Cooper was at the base of a pine tree, looking up. Bryce shook his head. Just what he'd suspected. The dog had cornered a raccoon.

He pulled the leash from his pocket and clipped it to Cooper's collar. "Come on, goofball. Leave it alone."

With a tug on the leash, Bryce turned to head back up. To the right, a shallow cavern had been gouged from the side of the steep slope. That was the place where gold had been mined on the property.

The deepest part had long since been filled in. According to Dennis, it had happened when Andi's great-grandfather brought operations to a halt after a freak accident claimed one man's life. As kids, he and Andi would climb down the jagged slope and pretend they were old-time gold prospectors. He hadn't been there in years.

But someone had.

He clambered down to the bottom of the grade. The area that Andi's great-grandfather had filled so long ago was now dug out, with shovel and pickax marks left behind. A five-gallon bucket was tucked into the back of the hollowed-out area, two sluice pans dropped inside. Had Dennis known about the recent activity there? Probably not.

Bryce looked around him, searching for a hint as to where someone had entered and exited the property. The creek was only about fifteen feet away. During the spring thaw, it would grow to a width of two or three feet. Now it was little more than a trickle.

He scanned the opposite slope. He'd never met the owners of the property to their rear. But they likely weren't the ones tampering with the old mine. He'd already caught Matt on the property once.

Bryce marched through the woods, still holding Cooper's leash. When he stepped into the Langman backyard, Matt and the same two friends he'd been with Saturday were sitting around the fire pit. Smoke rose between them. But what wafted to him on the light breeze smelled sweeter than burning pine logs.

He stopped to stand between Matt and Bradley, who passed the rolled cigarette he'd been holding to the third guy. Cooper stood watching, curious but not aggressive in the slightest.

Bryce leveled his gaze on the stranger, who looked to be in his early twenties. "You new to Murphy?"

"Yeah. Moved here three weeks ago."

"Where to?"

"Up on Panther Top." He tilted his head toward where Ranger Road ended farther up the mountain.

"You live with your parents?"

He lifted his chin. "Just till I get my own place."

"Where'd you move from?"

"Tampa."

Bryce nodded. This wasn't the first time he'd seen it—parents take the kids out of the city and move them to a quaint mountain town with almost no crime. Then they hook up with the Matts of the community.

"I'm Bryce Caldwell. Live two doors down."

"Danny Carlson."

"Nice to meet you, Danny. Tractor Supply's looking for help. So are several other businesses around town. Getting a job will be good for you. Help keep you out of trouble."

Matt took the cigarette from his new friend. After hauling in a long drag, he held it for several moments, then blew it out slowly. "If you came over here to harass me and my friends, you can go ahead and leave."

Bryce shrugged. "Just getting acquainted."

He looked at the other two. If there was still gold on Andi's property, it was probably better to keep that fact quiet. Of course, knowing Matt, he'd probably already blabbed it.

Bryce leveled his gaze on him. "I'm curious about something. What'd you find in the old mine next door?"

"I don't know what you're taking about."

"I can tell you've been digging."

"Wasn't me."

"Come on, no one else knows it's back there."

Matt took one last drag, removed the end from the clip and tossed it into the fire. "So what if it *was* me?

After what Old Man Wheaton did to my great-grand-father, I'm entitled to some of the Wheaton fortune."

It wasn't an admission, but it was the closest he was going to get. "I was just wondering if there was anything left or if they got it all out way back when."

Matt shifted his gaze to the fire. "Nah, nothing there. It's a dead mine."

"That's too bad."

Bryce lifted a hand in farewell and headed back into the woods. When he reached Andi's deck, she opened the door before he could knock. She'd apparently been watching for them.

"You got him." She heaved a sigh of relief and sank into a chair at the table. "I was afraid he was going to keep on going. There are hundreds of acres of woods out here." She paused. "Did you find anybody?"

"Yes and no. Cooper had run almost to the creek. You remember the old gold mine?"

Her eyes sparked with interest. "Yeah?"

"Matt has dug out a lot of what your great-grandfa-ther filled in. He's been coming onto your property and panning for gold for who knows how long."

"He admitted it?"

"In so many words."

She lifted a brow. "Has he found anything?"

"He said no. But I'm pretty good at knowing when people are lying."

She nodded slowly, brain working behind her blue eyes. "No wonder he doesn't want me here. But it's stupid for him to try to run me off. If someone else owned the property, Matt wouldn't be any more welcome here than he is now."

"Maybe he isn't trying to scare you into selling.

Maybe he just wants you to stay in Atlanta, the same as your father's been doing."

"Then the place would be vacant and he could come here whenever he wanted without getting caught."

Bryce sat opposite her, and she rested her chin in her hand.

"I wonder if that's what my dad hid, a large gold nugget."

"How would anyone know?"

"Maybe someone overheard him inquiring about its value."

He picked up a pen from the table and tapped it against the oak surface. "So let's say there's a rich vein of gold there. Your great-grandfather dynamited the opening of the mine, figuring no amount of gold was worth a man's life. For decades, it sat there untouched."

"Until Matt."

He nodded. "Your dad caught Matt snooping around and went to investigate. When he discovered Matt had reopened the mine, he figured he'd have some fun himself."

"My dad loved the outdoors. And he enjoyed trying new things. I could totally see him doing something like that." She pursed her lips. "But why wouldn't he have told me?"

"How much time did you spend alone with him in recent months?"

"Not as much as I should have." Her gaze dipped to her hands, which were clasped on the table.

He covered them with one of his. "You were both busy. My point is, he probably wouldn't have said anything in front of your mom, knowing how she felt about the property. And maybe at first he didn't realize just how much gold he was sitting on."

She pulled her hands free, straightening her shoulders. "And once he did, that's when he called you to set up a time to talk." She sat back in the chair, a smile climbing up her cheeks. "I knew it had to be something like this. I couldn't believe my dad would ever get involved in something illegal."

The grief and tension that had hung over her for the past two weeks had lifted, and the enthusiasm she projected was contagious. But clearing Dennis of wrongdoing didn't remove the danger.

"We still haven't ruled out foul play in your parents' accident. Or figured out how Drysdale plays into all this."

She pursed her lips. "Maybe he learned about the gold from Matt. I could see Matt bragging about some huge gold nugget he supposedly panned from my great-grandfather's abandoned mine."

"Does Drysdale seem like the type of person who'd run in the same circles as Matt?"

"He wouldn't have to. He could have been in hearing range when Matt was talking about it. Or maybe not Drysdale himself. Maybe somebody who knew somebody who knew Drysdale. You know, six degrees of separation."

He nodded. It was possible. Maybe Dennis Wheaton had been sitting on a small fortune and Drysdale had somehow gotten wind of it.

If that was the case, had Drysdale tried to convince Dennis to sell, then had him killed when he refused? The plan would have been almost foolproof. The only heir lived in Atlanta and hadn't stepped foot on the property in over a decade.

But Andi hadn't followed the plan.

And now she was the only thing standing between Drysdale and the property he was so determined to get.

It was a position that could prove to be deadly.

Andrea rose from the table and snagged her purse. "Let's go get that Christmas tree."

Bryce stood, too. "From the Rotary Club?"

"Yeah. Then we can hit Walmart. I'd like to use the same decorations, for old times' sake. But I'd rather start with new lights."

Bryce opened the door for her, then reached around to twist the lock. "Remember those old light strands where if one bulb burned out, half the strand went dark?"

She groaned. "How could I forget? I was always the one that had to dig through the branches and find the dead bulb without destroying the decorations."

After locking the dead bolt with the key, she grabbed her walking stick and let Bryce help her down the steps. Walking around the house wasn't bad. Maneuvering steps and trekking across unlevel ground was still a challenge.

"Mind if he goes with us?" Bryce tilted his head toward Cooper. "He loves car rides."

"What dog doesn't?"

As she climbed into the Sorento's passenger seat, she stifled a smile. Christmas tree shopping with Bryce. It wasn't what she'd envisioned when she first arrived in Murphy two weeks ago. But a lot had happened over the past two weeks that she hadn't envisioned.

Certainly not the unexpected sense of peace she'd found here. Or even that she and Bryce would be well on their way to forming an amicable friendship. It would never go any further than that, which was fine. That wasn't what she wanted. But she was glad to have her old friend back.

When they pulled into the lot fifteen minutes later, Cooper stood in the back seat. Bryce stepped out of the truck and held up a hand. "Sit."

The dog complied, and Andrea closed the passenger door. "I'll make this quick. I know you've got work this afternoon."

"We've got plenty of time. I'll even be able to help you set up the tree and start decorating."

That was going to bring back some memories. She and her dad would always drive up the morning after Thanksgiving and buy a tree. Then they'd spend Friday afternoon and evening decorating. Most years, Bryce had been there, too, adding his own touches. The year they were both thirteen, they'd sat side by side on the couch, stringing popcorn. For every piece they strung, they ate two. It took them an hour to get a two-foot section completed.

They pulled from the lot a short time later with a Christmas tree tied to the roof. The Walmart stop didn't just yield lights. She also threw in a couple of Christmas CDs. One could listen to Elvis only so many times.

Bryce turned onto the four-lane, headed for home. "Are you going to decorate your condo, too?"

"No need. Christmas is less than two weeks away. I'll be here at least that long." She sighed. "Then my break will be over."

"You don't sound pleased."

"I love my job. The pay's good. I work with great people. But my stomach ties itself in knots every time I think about going back."

"Then don't."

"I can't just quit."

"People do it all the time."

She gave a wry laugh. "Not responsible, practical people."

"Sometimes you have to go out on a limb, take the plunge."

"I've never quit a job without having another, even better one lined up."

He cast her a sideways glance. "I bet you wouldn't starve before you found something else."

"That's beside the point. I could never bring myself to give up a good-paying job without something to step into. I'm too practical."

But maybe she did have something to step into. Maybe that chance run-in at Ingles wasn't coincidental after all.

Her pulse picked up speed, and her stomach fluttered with the same sense of anticipation she always got at the prospect of a new challenge.

A fresh start. A new life. It wasn't practical. But it was exactly what she needed.

She removed her phone from her purse.

"Who are you calling?"

"Angie Stanger. I ran into her at Ingles the other day. She's selling her store and decorating business, and I'm going to buy it."

He cocked a brow. "When you said you usually don't have a problem making decisions, you weren't kidding."

She smiled. "When I know what I want, I act immediately."

And this was what she wanted. It made absolutely no sense, but it felt 100 percent right.

Every job she'd ever had, her mother's connections had gotten her foot in the door. And her mother had never let her forget it. It didn't matter that she'd worked harder and longer than anybody else. According to her mother, she wasn't responsible for any of her own success.

Andrea pressed the Google icon and tapped the microphone. "Designs by Angie." The business name displayed, and she touched the screen. In a short time, she'd be saying "Designs by Andi." Or maybe she'd choose a different name altogether.

Excitement warred with trepidation. She'd never run her own business before. Hopefully the MBA would help. But no matter how much book knowledge she had, some lessons she'd have to learn by trial and error.

One thing was sure: this venture was completely her own. Whether she failed or succeeded, she'd have no one to blame or credit except herself.

Angie answered the call, her tone cheery and professional at the same time. Soon the professionalism fell away and she released a happy squeal.

Andrea smiled, Angie's excitement fueling her own. In career decisions, there were more things to consider than pay level and benefits. Sometimes the least tangible aspects were the most important—things like job satisfaction and doing what one loved. Having control of the job rather than the other way around.

Andrea finished the call and smiled over at Bryce.

"I'm going next Monday to check out the store, look at the books and so on."

Five more days. She'd have scheduled it earlier if Angie wasn't overwhelmed with a huge decorating job in Chattanooga. If the meeting went like she expected it to, she'd be giving two-week notice to her employer as soon as she got home. Maybe even from Angie's parking lot.

Meanwhile, she'd use the next five days of downtime to work on the house. If the store and decorating business were a step down from her current management position, the old Murphy house was a leap away from the elegance of her condo. But it didn't matter. She'd always loved the old house, even in its semi-run-down condition.

Bryce pulled up next to the Accord. "Cooper can wait here a few minutes while we haul the tree in."

"Good plan." They'd get the tree inside, then bring the dog in on the leash. When Bryce was gone, she never let Cooper run free. She hadn't felt confident enough in her ability to control him. After this morning's wild chase, she probably never would.

She helped Bryce wrestle the tree off the roof, then wrapped her arms around the top while he grabbed the trunk.

"You sure you can carry that with your bad ankle?"

She cast a glance over one shoulder. "I'm fine as long as you don't make me walk backward."

Soon the tree was lying on the floor in front of the fireplace, and Cooper had curled up against the opposite wall. The two bags of lights waited on the couch.

While Bryce went to the shed to look for a hacksaw,

Andrea retrieved the tree stand and boxes of decorations from the middle bedroom closet.

Tedious chores occupied the next fifteen minutes—rearranging furniture to make room in front of the window, trimming the trunk and getting the tree secured in the stand.

"Now the lights." She held up a hand. "Wait, I almost forgot." She walked to the master bedroom, still favoring her right ankle, and returned with the CD player. She'd carried it back there earlier when she'd worked on the bedroom. Soon the first strains of "Sleigh Ride" filled the room.

Bryce lifted a brow. "We're not going to listen to one of the new ones?"

"We can't do the tree without Elvis. It's tradition."

She handed him a box of lights, then set to work removing a second strand from its package. The CD was almost finished by the time they placed the last strand.

Bryce stepped back. "I can't believe we actually got six hundred lights on a six-and-a-half-foot tree. If you open the drapes, you could light up your whole front yard."

She gave him a playful punch. "Maybe it *is* a little extreme."

But she and her dad had always gone overkill on the lights. The ornaments, too. Her dad had said the overabundance of decorations made the tree look cheery. If there was any Christmas she'd need cheery, this was it.

Bryce glanced at the clock. "Unless I'm going to work dressed like this, I'd better head for home."

"Thanks for all your help. Now that the lights are strung, the rest of it is all fun stuff."

"I still hate to bail on you."

She shrugged. "I'm used to decorating alone. Phil never helped."

"Your ex?"

"Yeah." The first few years she'd decorated a nine-foot-tall artificial tree alone. The last few she hadn't even bothered. When Phil had been in medical school, his hours had been long. In residency, they'd been even longer.

"What happened?" He paused. "If you'd rather not say, I understand."

She crossed her arms. She really *would* rather not say. Telling the story involved admitting she hadn't been able to hold on to her husband. As if she was somehow deficient. But Bryce had told her about Pam. That was what friends did, shared their hurts.

She drew in a stabilizing breath. "He's a neurosurgeon. I worked my tail off putting him through medical school, then supported us while he did his residency. I knew someday it would be worth it. He'd have a great-paying job, and we'd reap the rewards of all that sacrifice."

"And?"

"Nine months ago, he joined a successful neurosurgery group. Six months ago, I came home from work early to find him with our next-door neighbor."

"Oh, man. That stinks. I'm sorry."

"Thanks. I'm getting over it." Or maybe she wasn't. Otherwise, she wouldn't still feel like throwing up every time she thought about it.

He moved toward the door. "Is it okay if I stop by after my shift? It'll probably be a little late."

"Sure. I might be in my flannel pj's."

"The acrobatic cats."

"You noticed."

She closed the door behind him and threw the dead bolt. As she removed decorations from the first box, the CD ended and the house fell silent.

She took a second one from its case, another Elvis Christmas album, and swapped it with the first. Moments later, music swelled. But the house still felt empty. She willed back some of the holiday spirit she'd felt with Bryce at her side and pulled garland from a box.

That one holiday, they'd proudly displayed the stubby popcorn garland front and center. It hadn't made it to a second Christmas. The braided ribbon garland had survived the years. So had the pom-pom-and-soda-straw garland. Half the fun of trimming the tree had been making new decorations to add to the eclectic collection they pulled out of the closet every year.

Once she had the garlands arranged, she started on the ornaments. She was trying. Really hard. She was decorating, and she'd do some baking—iced sugar cookies in the shapes of bells, trees, candy canes and snowmen. Maybe she'd even attend MountainView's Christmas Eve service.

MountainView was a little larger than the church she'd attended with Bryce and her father, but not by much. This past Sunday, sitting a few rows from the front with Bryce next to her, had brought back memories. Except this time it was different. She had a mission. She'd gone searching for something. She couldn't say she'd fully found it, but she was on her way. The future services she planned to attend would help. So would the Bible that currently lay open on her bedside stand.

She pulled another ornament from the box and folded

back the tissue. A jolt hit her, shooting all the way to her toes.

It was a wallet-size family photo in an oval frame that she'd decorated with ribbon and paint and glitter. She'd been about ten.

She inserted a hook into the loop and hung it from one of the branches. Though she'd known it, the reality hit her full force. While Phil was bringing his new girlfriend to his family's Christmas gathering, she'd be spending her first holiday without her parents.

She sank onto the couch, despair settling over her.

A sense of loneliness that even Elvis's rich voice couldn't dispel.

NINE

Bryce walked through the woods, the flashlight beam illuminating the trail in front of him. He'd parked the cruiser in his driveway, then headed right over.

It would be fun to see what Andi had done with the place and reminisce over decorations he hadn't seen in more than twelve years. Although Dennis had continued to come without Andi, he no longer bothered to decorate. The decorating was likely for the kids' benefit rather than his own.

Bryce stepped from the woods and moved toward the house. Andi had forgotten to turn on the porch light for him, but a glow seeped around the edge of the drapes hanging at the front window. Knowing how many lights were on the tree, he wasn't surprised.

He knocked and immediately called, "It's me."

A few seconds later, the door swung open. Cooper pushed past Andi to give him a nudge and a tail wag. After Bryce greeted his dog, Andi stepped back to allow him entry. True to her word, she was dressed in the cat pajamas.

"Sorry. I'm going for comfort." She grinned. "Comfort and maybe a little bit of rebellion."

He lifted a brow. "How's that?"

"You know my mom. She was all about appearances. From the time I was old enough to realize I was a girl, she made sure my hair was styled and I was dressed to meet the president. Of the country club, at least, if not the United States." She closed and locked the door behind him. "By age fifteen, that included makeup. If she could see me now, I think she'd figure out a way to come back, just to give me one more of her infamous lectures."

Bryce shook his head. No wonder Andi had enjoyed escaping to Murphy.

"No need to apologize. You look cute." Actually, she looked better than cute. This casual, playful version of Andi was much more appealing than the uptight, professional one. This was the Andi he'd fallen in love with so many years ago. He cleared his throat, reminding himself they were just friends.

"The tree looks great." He moved close enough to study the ornaments and lifted a hand to touch one.

That was the year Dennis had made little boxes out of poster board and let Andi and him turn them into miniature Christmas presents. Bryce had wrapped them in her grandmother's leftover quilting fabric and passed each one to Andi to decorate with ribbon, berries, spray-painted pine needles and tiny bows. If his guy friends ever learned of the activities he'd done over here, they'd have grounds for blackmail.

She walked farther into the room and sank onto the couch. "There's nothing like sitting in front of a fire in the wintertime in a pair of flannel pj's."

He followed her gaze. Behind the fireplace screen, flames danced atop neatly stacked logs. She'd helped

Dennis build a fire so many times, he wasn't surprised she could do it on her own.

When he moved to stand in front of the fireplace, Cooper plopped down at his feet. Heat rose, warming his hands, still cold from the walk over. Three stockings hung across the mantel, the left one in memory of the man who had been a father to both of them.

His chest clenched. Dennis Wheaton's death was going to leave a hole in more than just Andi's life.

He crossed the room to where she sat. "Knowing you'd pulled all this out, I was afraid I'd get here to find you sad."

"Believe me, I had a brief period of feeling sorry for myself, even had a good cry. But I never wallow in self-pity for long."

Yes, Andi had developed an amazing inner strength. He'd sensed it almost from the moment she arrived.

He sank onto the couch next to her, letting his arm rest behind her back. He had to agree with her remark about sitting in front of a fire in the wintertime.

A warmth that had nothing to do with burning logs filled his chest. The scene brought a sense of contentment that he hadn't felt in a long time. The tree, branches heavy with fond memories. The woman he loved, even if only in friendship, sitting next to him. His dog—the dog they were now sharing—lying on the hearth, against a backdrop of dancing flames.

This exact scene had hung on his dining room wall for the past five years. The impact was like a boulder crashing into him, and he was left with an odd sense of having been caught in a time warp. Andi's long-ago sketch had materialized right in front of him. Cooper was even curled up on the hearth, standing in for old Sport.

He closed his eyes, once again seventeen, sitting next to the woman he was sure he'd spend the rest of his life with. He curled his hands into fists, trying to capture and hang on to that moment in time, when the future was bright with promise and he hadn't yet made the biggest mistake of his life.

"I really messed up."

She didn't ask what he meant. Her thoughts were probably following the same track his were. "Don't worry about it. We've all made our share of bad decisions. When you broke up with me, I sort of understood." She turned to look at him. "I knew exactly what I wanted. I was even ready to defy my mother by not choosing the son of one of her society friends."

"Yeah, your mom wouldn't have been thrilled." His throat tightened with that same sense of inferiority he'd felt as the kid from the wrong side of the tracks falling in love with the rich girl.

"But we would have had my dad's blessing." She gave him a sad smile. "Anyway, even though you were the only boyfriend I'd ever had, I knew what I wanted. But I understand that you didn't."

"You'd seen the world. I'd barely been outside North Carolina. Your lifestyle seemed so worldly. I thought the only way I'd know you were the one was if I experienced life, dated some other girls."

"I actually understood all that, even at eighteen." She shifted her gaze to stare into the fire. "What I didn't understand…"

He waited for her to finish her thought. When she

didn't, he finished it for her. "…was how I could move on so quickly."

"Yeah."

But he hadn't moved on. It had only appeared that way. "As soon as I walked back home from your house, I started having second thoughts, wondering if I'd made the right decision. I kept thinking, what if I came to realize you *were* the one and you'd already found someone else."

He heaved a sigh and continued. "An hour or two later, Carla showed up."

She'd lived catty-corner across Ranger for years. They'd played together as children and sometimes hung out as teens. Other than her comments about how crazy he was to tie himself to a long-distance relationship when there were all kinds of girls in Murphy, she hadn't made any moves on him. Or he'd been too dense to see them.

"We were sitting on the porch swing, talking. I told her I'd broken up with you so we could date other people but was afraid I'd made a mistake. She was determined to show me I hadn't."

Andi crossed her arms in front of her, pulling them tightly over her torso. "You looked like you were enjoying the lesson."

"Of course I was." He wasn't going to lie to her. "I was an eighteen-year-old guy. But when I looked up and saw you standing there at the edge of the woods, eyes filled with pain, I knew I'd just sealed shut the door to any possible reconciliation in the future. And I wanted to rip out my own heart."

He'd shoved Carla off his lap and hurried after Andi. Before he could catch her, she'd locked herself in her house and refused to come out. Thirty minutes later, she and Dennis were pulling out of the driveway, heading to Atlanta.

"I never got a chance to talk to you after that. I just want you to know what you meant to me and how sorry I am that I hurt you. Over the years, I've kicked myself more times than I can count."

Her hands fell to her lap, and she looked up at him, searching his eyes. Was she looking for sincerity? If he was projecting one-fourth of what he felt, she'd know without a doubt.

He reached up to touch her cheek. "I never had any more to do with her after that. I couldn't look at her without thinking of what I'd done to you."

When he let his finger trail along her jaw, she closed her eyes. They'd agreed to be just friends. That was all she'd wanted.

And it was all he'd wanted, too. After everything Pam had put him through, he didn't have the energy to fight his way past Andi's barriers.

But he didn't feel any of those barriers now. And he wanted nothing more than to kiss her.

When she opened her eyes, they were filled with uncertainty. But there was something else. A cautious hope.

He leaned closer, and her eyes drifted shut again. His lips brushed hers, the briefest touch before she turned away.

She crossed her arms again. "I'm sorry. I'm not ready for this. I don't know that I ever will be."

He sighed. Her walls had gone right back up. Thinking they'd ever have more than friendship had been nothing but a pipe dream. The scars ran too deep.

"That's all right. I'm totally fine with just being friends." He'd temporarily lost his head. It wouldn't happen again.

A log shifted, sending sparks spiraling upward into the chimney. Cooper looked behind him, then settled back down.

"I made some eggnog." Andi pushed herself to her feet and headed toward the kitchen. On her way past the CD player, she hit Play.

A half minute later, the refrigerator door opened and closed and glasses clanked against a backdrop of "Winter Wonderland."

"I also made macaroons."

She returned carrying a tray that held a platter of cookies, their glasses of eggnog and two small plates. As she bent to lay it on the coffee table, "Winter Wonderland" died mid-phrase, and the lights clicked off, leaving only the glow of the fire.

Bryce reached for Andi, tension spiking through him. "Stay here."

He pulled his flashlight from his pocket and clicked it on. There were no storms in the area. He'd stepped from his car under a clear sky, an almost half-moon casting its soft glow over the landscape. No reason for the power to go out.

But seemingly unexplainable power outages happened occasionally. Sometimes someone hit a power pole on the four-lane, or a transformer burned up, or a limb came down across a line.

"What happened?" Andi's voice was paper-thin, with an underlying quiver.

"I'm going to look out the side and see if there's light in my direction."

Leaving her sitting in the living room, cookies and eggnog untouched, he darted down the hall to the master bedroom. When he swept aside the curtains, his uneasiness ratcheted up several notches. A soft glow shone through the trees—his own porch light. His power was on.

So what happened to Andi's?

Out front, glass shattered, followed by an almost simultaneous scream. A long string of fast, ferocious barks punctuated the wail of the alarm. He dropped the curtains into place and ran from the room, panic pounding at his heels.

At the end of the hall, Andi yanked a blanket from the back of the couch, her frame silhouetted against the flames still dancing in the fireplace. But a glow seemed to come from somewhere else, too.

He ran into the room. Cooper was nowhere to be seen. Flames engulfed the love seat that separated the living room from the dining area. Andi swung the blanket down hard, and the fire spread over the front of the small couch to lick at the living room rug.

He grabbed the blanket from her. "Start a pan filling with water, then call 911. The alarm system might not do it." Although the battery backup was supplying power to the alarm, he wasn't counting on the phone lines not being cut.

As water ran in the kitchen, he beat the sofa over and over. When the blanket caught fire, he dropped it and stomped on it, along with the rug, which also had flames working their way across it.

"No dial tone." Andi's words were laced with panic. A fair share transferred to him. Someone hadn't just cut her power. He'd also broken off contact with the outside world.

She ran around him to snatch her cell phone from the coffee table. They'd knocked both glasses of eggnog over. The cream-colored liquid spread across the table and dripped to the floor.

Andi straightened. "One bar." After frantically punching the screen, she pressed it to her ear.

When Bryce had the last of the fire beat out, Andi lowered the phone. "Not enough service to get through."

"We need to go to my house."

"I'm not leaving my place unattended."

"And I'm not leaving you here alone. After we make that call, we'll come back and keep watch until they arrive."

He hollered for the dog, who slunk into the room from the direction of the kitchen. Before leading Andi out the door, he hooked on Cooper's leash and drew his weapon. Outside, faraway sirens wailed. As he crossed his yard and climbed his porch steps, they grew closer.

Bryce locked the three of them inside and pulled out his phone. Maybe the emergency vehicles were for them, maybe not. He wouldn't leave it to chance. He dialed 911 and soon had the confirmation he wanted. The alarm company had picked up an interruption. Not getting an answer on Andi's cell number, they'd dispatched the police.

Bryce pocketed his phone and stared at Andi, preparing himself for a battle. The cat pajamas made her look relaxed and playful. But he wasn't deceived. She was going to be as adamant as she'd be wearing a power suit. "You're not going to be able to stay at your place."

"I know. I've got to get the window fixed, clean up the damage from the fire."

"You're not going to be able to stay after that, either."

She flung up her hands. "Why keep the house if I can't use it?" Her volume was several decibels louder than normal.

He raised his voice to match hers. "And what good is the house if you're dead?"

She drew in a breath, the action seeming to calm her. "If these creeps wanted me dead, they'd have already succeeded."

She sank onto his couch. "Somebody doesn't want me here, and he's trying to scare me off. Maybe it's Matt. Maybe it's Drysdale. Maybe it's someone else entirely." She crossed her arms. "Whoever it is, it's not going to work."

He heaved a sigh and sat next to her. "Andi, come on. This isn't the time for stubbornness."

She stood and started to pace. When she spoke, her voice was low and controlled.

"All my life, my mother has tried to dictate everything I've done, from what I wore to the jobs I held to who I married. I'm through." She pointed toward the property next door. "That's my home. It's been in my family for four generations. No one's going to take it from me, and no one's going to make me leave. Eventually, they'll see that and give up."

"Or eliminate the obstacle."

"No one is going to try to kill me over it."

"What about your parents?"

She stopped her pacing. A shadow crossed her features and worry settled in her eyes.

Then determination pushed it aside. "Monday, I'm

meeting with Angie to discuss the terms for buying her business. I'm not going to back out. I'm here to stay."

Bryce shook his head, anger rolling in his gut. He was faced with an impossible situation.

A very determined woman.

A possible killer.

And neither of them willing to step away.

Andrea's gaze circled the dimly lit room, and she sought out a clock. It sat on the nightstand next to her bed, one of those older-style ones with hands. Almost 9:10 a.m.

Wait, that wasn't her clock. Where was she? And why was she still sleeping at 9:00 a.m.?

She pushed herself upright, and the events of the prior night slammed into her with the force of a tidal wave. Someone had tried to burn her house down. If Bryce hadn't been there, they might have succeeded.

She swung her feet over the side of the bed. The scent of smoke wafted upward. She needed to wash her pajamas. They reeked. But since it was the only pair she'd brought, she'd worn them, smoke and all.

Bryce had offered to loan her a T-shirt and some sweatpants, but she'd turned him down. Sleeping in his clothes felt too…intimate.

More memories rushed forward, and she stifled a groan. He'd tried to kiss her. And she'd almost let him. What had she been thinking?

She hadn't been. She'd let all the emotion that went with Christmas muddle her brain.

Throughout the afternoon, she'd pulled one memory after another from the dusty old boxes. No wonder she'd been a puddle of mush by the time he'd arrived.

Then he'd piled that apology on top of her already volatile emotions. It had been so heartfelt, it had just about done her in.

Until last night, she'd never given him the opportunity to explain. She'd run inside the house and told her father that she wanted to leave. *Now.* It wasn't until they were on Spur 60, headed toward home, that she'd opened up and spilled the whole painful story. Her dad had listened, offering sympathy but no advice. Another way he'd been the polar opposite of her mother.

In the next weeks, Bryce had tried. But she'd ignored his calls and deleted his texts without reading them.

His apology last night had touched her. But it didn't change anything. They already had a meaningful friendship. As far as anything deeper, it wasn't just a twelve-year-old wrong that was keeping her from falling in love.

Phil had never apologized. No sorry-I-hurt-you-but-I-don't-love-you-anymore sentiment. He'd said she was overreacting, that a lot of successful men slept with other women.

Maybe so. But she wasn't willing to share. As long as she remained single, she didn't have to worry about it.

She gathered some clean clothes from the bag she'd brought over a few hours ago. A hot shower would be pure bliss. Hopefully Bryce wouldn't mind her tying up his hall bath for a while.

When she opened the bedroom door, the scent of coffee lured her toward the kitchen. The shower could wait. She padded barefoot down the hall.

Bryce smiled at her over the top of his computer screen. He sat at the table, nursing his own cup of coffee. "Good morning, Sleeping Beauty."

She wrinkled her nose. She was so *not* Sleeping Beauty. "What are you up to?"

"Checking out the headlines."

She opened a cabinet door, then closed it and moved to a second one.

"Left of the sink."

"Thanks." She took down a mug painted with a whitewater rafting scene and filled it. After adding some half-and-half from the carton in the fridge, she joined him at the table. "Did I make the news?"

"Not this news. I'm sure there'll be a story about the fire in next week's *Cherokee Scout*." He closed the laptop. "What's on your agenda for today?"

"Laundry, for starters. It was time anyway, but I've got to wash these pajamas before I wear them again."

"You won't be allowed back in your house until the investigation is finished."

"Wonderful."

"They may let you get some more things out of the unaffected rooms. But you'll need to wash your clothes here."

She took a sip of coffee, the heat warming her from the inside out. After calling 911 last night, they'd gone back over to her house to wait. Bryce had immediately figured out what had happened to her power. The shed door was open, the padlock snapped with bolt cutters. Inside, the fuse for the house had been pulled. The instant he pushed it back in, the lights came on. The phone wasn't as easy. Someone had cut the wires in the box mounted on the side of the house.

With the lights on, they'd been able to check out the damage. Charred remains of something lay in front of the love seat. Based on how quickly the fire had spread,

Bryce suspected someone had soaked an object with gasoline and thrown it through the broken window.

The love seat itself was burnt beyond repair. So was the rug. She'd strip and refinish the hardwood floor. It needed to be done anyway. But there'd probably forever be a large area darker than the rest of the floor, a permanent reminder of how blessed she was not to have lost her home.

As far as who had set the fire, the list of suspects was short—Matt Langman and Melvin Drysdale. Would Matt go to that extent to try to scare her off? If he burned the house down, he could come onto her property anytime he wanted. There'd be no one there to stop him.

But that scenario seemed off. Leaving threatening notes, putting dead squirrels in mailboxes—that was Matt's style. Trying to burn down houses, especially with people in them, didn't fit. According to her dad, all Matt's crimes had been petty.

That left Drysdale as the more likely suspect. She drew her brows together.

Bryce studied her. "You look like the wheels are turning."

"Yeah. The last time Drysdale came by to try to push me into selling, he told me to hang on to his card because I'm going to find that this place isn't worth it. I thought he was talking about all the work. Now I think it was a warning."

"The investigators will be checking him out."

She nodded. She'd thrown his card away but had retrieved his number from the call log on her phone.

She finished her coffee, then washed her cup and put it back in the cabinet. If she was going to crash at Bryce's for a few days, she could at least be a neat houseguest. She snagged the clothes she'd laid on her dresser earlier and crossed the hall to the bathroom.

Thirty minutes later, she emerged, wet hair wrapped in a towel and all traces of smoke removed. When she reached the kitchen, Bryce was standing at the stove, stirring scrambled eggs. The toaster had been pulled away from the wall, and waves of heat rose from the two slots. A knife lay propped up on the edge of a butter dish. A plate already held two finished slices.

He looked over at her. "Feel better now?"

"You have no idea."

The toast popped up. "If you want to butter those last two, we're almost ready to eat."

She helped him get everything to the table, then sat in the chair adjacent to his. "Watching you with your laptop earlier got me thinking. I need to get mine and connect it to your Wi-Fi, or I need to borrow yours."

"I'm finished. Help yourself." He pushed it in her direction. "What do you want to look up?"

"Melvin Drysdale."

"My buddy already did."

"He was focusing on investigations, criminal history, stuff like that."

She slid her plate over and pulled the computer next to it. She could work and eat at the same time. She'd done it for years.

"So, what are *you* going to focus on?"

"Everything else."

She brought up the internet and typed Drysdale's name into a search engine. The first two results were obituaries. "Since he likely hasn't faked his death, we'll assume these aren't him."

Bryce slid his chair up next to her and pointed at the screen. "Melvin Drysdale, president and CEO of Choice Property Development."

"That matches what was on the card he gave me."

She spooned a couple of forkfuls of eggs into her mouth. Bryce was already a third of the way through his.

She scrolled a little farther. "Priscilla Drysdale, Wife of Real Estate Mogul Melvin Drysdale, Disappears."

She clicked the link and scanned the article. The information was the same as what Bryce's friend had relayed, but didn't include the fact Drysdale was a suspect.

There were links to several more articles about projects he'd been involved in, but nothing that jumped out as being important.

She opened a new window and filled in the search bar.

"North Carolina Division of Corporations database?"

"Just seeing if he has his hands in anything other than Choice Property Development." She would check Georgia, too. But since he was dead set on acquiring her North Carolina property, she figured she'd start there first.

She clicked the link, and the search screen for the Secretary of State appeared. She searched by company officials, then tried again by registered agents. Both produced no results.

"Now Georgia." She took another bite of eggs. They were rapidly moving toward the cool side. As often as she worked while eating, she was used to cold food, too.

When she'd brought up Georgia's search window,

she typed "Melvin Drysdale" into the "Officer Name" field. The results showed six businesses.

Bryce leaned closer. "If those are all the same Melvin Drysdale, he's a pretty busy guy."

"Or *has been* a busy guy." She pointed to the last column. "Half of them show a status of dissolved. Only three are currently active."

One was Choice Property Development, which was no surprise. Drysdale was listed as the CEO. The other officers' names didn't ring a bell.

"Let's check out these businesses." She clicked the back arrow. "Terra Minerals Limited." Her pulse kicked up speed as she clicked the link. "Sounds like a mining company. Drysdale is the chief financial officer."

"What kind of company is it?" Bryce's tone held some of her own excitement.

"That's not given here. Just says 'Domestic Profit Corporation.' I'm sure they have a website."

Fifteen seconds later, she'd navigated to the page. "Bingo. They're a mining operation. No wonder Drysdale is so determined to get his hands on my property."

Had Matt found gold and blabbed it to the wrong people? Knowing him, he'd embellished the story. A lot.

She looked at Bryce, mind spinning. "Drysdale may have tried to buy the property from my dad. Then when my dad refused, Drysdale had both of my parents killed, figuring with my life in Atlanta, I'd be happy to unload the property."

"You might be getting ahead of yourself. Are you sure Terra Minerals actually mines gold?"

She clicked on "About Us" and scanned the company information. Disappointment doused the excitement she'd felt moments earlier. "They mine kaolin."

"What's kaolin?"

"China clay. It's used in making china and other tableware, but its biggest use is in the paper industry."

He looked at her with raised brows. "How do you know this stuff?"

"I did a research paper on mining my freshman year of high school. Earth science."

"And you remember."

She shrugged. "They mine a lot of it in Georgia." She pulled her lower lip between her teeth. "But mining kaolin is nothing like mining gold. It's not likely that one company would do both."

"Unless Drysdale is involved in two different companies."

She clicked the back arrow. "Nope. The other one is Executive Group Financial Services, definitely not a gold mine." She shook her head. "Property development, mining and financial services. Drysdale's got his hands in a little bit of everything."

She followed the link to check out the last company. "He's the vice president on this one." She shifted her gaze to the name above Drysdale's and gasped. "John Lassiter. One of my dad's business partners."

"Could be a different John Lassiter."

"And a different Mark Barrand as CFO?"

Bryce nodded. "Okay, that's too much coincidence."

When she read the last name, a dark heaviness descended on her, wrapping her in dread. "My dad is listed as the secretary. Why wouldn't he have told me he was a principal in another endeavor?" She looked at Bryce, silently pleading for an explanation that didn't put a stain on her father's integrity. He didn't offer any.

She shifted her gaze back to the computer screen.

"When Drysdale first showed up, he said he saw the obituary, and that's how he knew the property might be for sale. But he and my dad were in business together, along with my dad's two partners. Why didn't he mention that?"

The same reason her father hadn't. Nausea churned in her stomach, and she put a hand over her mouth. The breakfast she'd managed to consume between clicks was threatening to make a reappearance.

"When was the company formed?"

She lowered her hand. "Two years ago."

"About a year before the big money started coming in." Bryce's voice sounded tight, pinched. He obviously didn't want to believe it any more than she did.

So everything wasn't about gold.

Or maybe it was. If her father mentioned the presence of gold on his property to one of his business partners and that person mentioned it to Drysdale, Drysdale might have decided to have it checked out. Maybe he learned the Wheatons were sitting on a small fortune, one he was determined to have for himself.

As improbable as her theory sounded, that was the explanation she'd cling to. Because the alternative was unthinkable. Her sweet, honest father would never have been involved in anything shady.

There had to be a legitimate reason for the financial success he'd seen within months of forming the new company.

And a logical reason why he'd chosen to keep those details from her.

TEN

The dryer buzzed, and Andrea strode into the laundry room off the side of the kitchen. It felt good to be home. She'd been there the past three days.

Last Friday she'd learned that investigators had finished collecting evidence, and she was free to return to the house. It helped that the damage had been confined to such a small area.

The fire was still under investigation. Bryce knew the investigators. Actually, he seemed to know everybody. Although he'd gotten them to promise to notify her of anything they found, she wasn't expecting any earth-shattering news. What happened was pretty clearcut. Someone had broken a window and thrown a flaming object inside. What she really wanted to know was who. No lab tests were likely to reveal that.

She opened the dryer door and removed her bedspread. She'd finished her clothes on Saturday, her smoky pajamas two days before that. Those, Bryce had thrown in with his own smoky clothes. Today she was tackling the bedding. Since she and Bryce had beat out the fire before smoke could fill the house, it probably wasn't necessary. But it made her feel better.

Things were almost back to normal. The phone company had replaced severed wires, and Bryce had padlocked the box. She'd also called the same handyman who'd replaced the window after the first break-in. She'd be using him on some future projects, too. Especially ones that involved ladders.

She headed down the hall with the still warm bedspread. She'd received another call on Friday, too—regarding her parents' accident. The investigation had been inconclusive. The underside of the car had simply been too mangled, brake lines ripped loose along with everything else. If there'd been any brake fluid left on the ground where they'd parked at the lodge, several hard rains had destroyed the evidence before any questions had been raised.

She'd just finished putting the bedspread on her bed when a knock sounded on the front door. That would be Bryce, with Cooper.

When she opened the door, the dog almost knocked her down bounding inside. He made two circles around the living room, then stood, looking up at her, body quivering with excitement.

She dropped to one knee and cupped his face. "What's this all about? You just saw me this morning."

"I think he got spoiled having both of us for a couple of days." Bryce's smile died. "You already know how I feel about you coming back home."

Yeah, she did. He'd made it clear. She'd also made her thoughts on the matter clear. "If I'm going to let these creeps run me off, I might as well sell the property to Drysdale."

Before he could offer any further argument, her cell phone rang, and she swiped it from the coffee table.

Tension crept across her shoulders. She didn't recognize the number.

After she gave a tentative "Hello," the caller identified himself as Gilbert Ormand, the fire investigator. They weren't finished, but he was calling to give her what they had so far.

She glanced at Bryce. It helped to know people who knew people.

As Ormand talked, she paced. Bryce stood leaning against the doorjamb, watching her, arms crossed.

"We didn't get any viable prints from around the window. And with the hardness of the ground and the fact that it's covered in leaves this time of year, there weren't any footprints left behind."

Andrea sighed. Two pieces of evidence that could point to who was trying to scare her off.

Mr. Ormand continued. "There was an almost empty gas can against the side of the house, a short distance from where the fire was started. Several prints were lifted from that and came back belonging to Matthew Langman."

Andrea stopped pacing, her jaw lax. "He's my neighbor. He's threatened me several times."

"Yeah, that's what Bryce said. Police talked to Matthew and his father. The younger Langman claimed his gas can had gone missing the day before. Langman Senior gave his son an alibi, said he'd sat in the living room all evening, playing with the Xbox."

So Matt had an alibi. His father. Which, in Andrea's opinion, wasn't an alibi at all. Ormand went on to say that Drysdale had an alibi, too. His was more convincing. But that might only mean he had someone else doing his dirty work.

"The arsonist tied a bunch of rags around a rock, so it would throw well, then soaked everything in gasoline and lit it."

Andrea nodded. That was no surprise. Seeing the charred blob lying there, she'd assumed as much.

When she ended the call, Bryce looked at her with raised brows. "Well?"

"They found a gas can. Guess whose prints were all over it."

"Matt's."

"Of course, Matt claims someone stole it, and his old man has given him an alibi."

"Why am I not surprised?"

She took a seat on the couch. "If Matt *is* the one behind all this, he's not working alone. There are at least two others."

Bryce sat next to her. "The two who broke into your house."

"Right. And Drysdale. I have no idea what his involvement is, but as badly as he wants my property, I'm sure he's connected somehow."

"We already know he was involved with your father."

"That, too." She drew in a deep breath. "Ormand said he has an alibi during the time of the fire. He'd taken a girlfriend out to dinner in Atlanta and dropped her off at home at nine thirty, which doesn't give him enough time to have made the trip to Murphy. She corroborated his story. So did the restaurant."

"He could still have someone working for him, like the two guys who broke into your house."

"My thoughts exactly." She crossed her arms. "Matt probably knows a lot more than he's letting on. Eventually he's going to mess up."

"Like leaving the gas sitting where he used it?"

"Yeah. That's a major careless mistake. He probably soaked everything, then laid the can down. By the time he broke the window, set the ball of rags on fire and tossed it into my house, his focus was on getting out of there, and he forgot to pick up the gas can." She gave Bryce a wry smile. "I think all the drugs he's taken have killed a few too many brain cells."

She pushed herself to her feet. "I'd better get ready for my appointment with Angie. I'd hate to go looking like this."

"There's nothing wrong with the way you look."

The warmth in his tone sent goose bumps cascading over her. When she met his gaze, the same heat was reflected in his eyes. She crossed the room, ignoring the effect his obvious appreciation had on her.

"I'm in sweats and no makeup. I've spent the morning cleaning house and doing laundry." But that made no difference to him. He'd always thought she looked good and had never hesitated to say so. It touched a chord with her now even more than it had then.

She tamped down the longing and grinned at him over one shoulder. "Remind me not to rely on you for fashion advice."

He laughed. "I'm a guy. That's usually not one of our strong points."

He headed toward the door and she followed, ready to lock it behind him.

"By the time you come home tonight, you'll be living next door to the proud new owner of Designs by Angie. Or maybe I should say Designs by Andi. At least the negotiations will be underway."

His face lit with a smile of his own. "I'm proud of you."

"Why?" Being director of marketing for a Fortune 500 company, dozens of people under her, was a lot more impressive than taking over a tiny one-woman operation in Murphy, North Carolina.

"You're stepping out of your comfort zone, embarking on a new life. It takes a lot of guts to do that."

Her heart swelled with the approval in his eyes. He seemed to instinctively know what a woman needed. What *she* needed. Too bad he wasn't willing to expend the energy required to develop a relationship. And too bad she wasn't willing to let down her guard enough to try again.

After he left, she strode toward her room to get ready. Fortunately, her ankle was pretty well healed. A week earlier, and she'd have been limping into the store with a walking stick.

When she returned to the living room, Cooper had jumped up on the couch and was stretched out across two-thirds of its length.

She planted her hands on her hips. "Does your daddy let you up on the furniture? I don't think so." She pointed at the floor. "Down."

The dog obeyed but looked at her with sad eyes. Bryce had assured her he wouldn't destroy the house while she was gone. Since Bryce would be leaving for work before she returned, he'd had to bring the dog over before she left.

"All right. I'll go get your bed." Bryce had bought a second one to keep at his house so the original could stay at hers. After plopping it down in front of the hearth and checking the water bowl, she headed out the door.

Tomorrow she was going car shopping. Maybe she'd even go this afternoon. There was a GM dealership in Murphy.

She'd pretty much decided to get another Escalade, maybe in a different color. Her old one was gray, a hue Cadillac had named Bronze Dune Metallic. Now she wanted something bolder, something that reflected her new sense of adventure. Red. Metallic red, if that was an option.

She slid into the rental car, tossing her purse into the passenger seat. After pulling onto Ranger, she gave it a little gas, allowing the car to gradually gain speed as she wound downward toward the four-lane.

Halfway there, she tapped the brake going into a curve. Something didn't feel right. The pedal was squishy. A second later, it hit the floor.

Her heart leaped into her throat. She pumped the brake several times. Now there was no resistance at all. When she yanked on the emergency brake, nothing happened.

Panic pounded through her as she continued to gain speed, tombstones on both sides of her a blur. The road made a sharp curve left, the steep slope to the right deep enough to roll the car if she didn't make it.

She slid around the final curve, tires squealing. As she shot onto the four-lane, she swiveled her head to the left. The huge grill of a semitruck bore down on her. The horn blared, blending with her own scream. She barely cleared the truck's path as it skidded past behind her.

She flew across the break in the median and became temporarily airborne as she cleared the slightly raised eastbound lanes. Any speed she'd lost crossing the four-lane, she quickly regained on Little Ranger Road's downhill slope. Another sharp curve was just ahead of her, to the right this time.

She was going too fast to make it. Her tires lost traction and she skidded across the oncoming lane.

A chain-link fence stood ahead of her, trees looming just behind it. A half second later, her whole world exploded in white.

Then everything went black.

Bryce walked up his driveway, flipping through the envelopes he'd just retrieved from the mailbox. Mostly junk. He'd toss those into the trash, unopened, as soon as he got inside. The rest...

The wail of a distant siren pulled his thoughts from the mail. Uneasiness trickled through him. Sirens in Murphy weren't a common occurrence, especially this far from town.

He rolled his shoulders in a slow circle, trying to dispel some of the tension. Andi would have left fifteen or twenty minutes ago. She was probably in town already, pulling up to the store.

The wail grew louder. Another one joined the first, rising and falling in a different pattern. Bryce knit his brows. There was more than one emergency vehicle.

He pulled his phone from his pocket. He'd check to make sure Andi was all right. Then he'd be able to get on with his afternoon, which in another hour would involve heading to work.

After bringing her up on his contact list, he touched the screen and put the phone to his ear. It rang once. Twice.

The sirens reached their loudest, faded slightly, then

fell silent. His stomach tightened. That was close, like just past where Ranger met the four-lane.

Andi's phone rang a third time. Then a fourth. When her message came on, he disconnected the call and closed the distance to his Sorento at a jog. The sirens likely had nothing to do with Andi. Maybe she was still driving and would call him back when she stopped. Or maybe she'd arrived at the store early and was already in her meeting.

But it wouldn't be that difficult to put his mind at ease.

After cranking the SUV, he backed to the right and jammed the vehicle into Drive, kicking up gravel as he shot toward the road.

When he reached the four-lane, he almost crumpled in relief. Lights flashed on the opposite side, a hundred feet or so ahead on Little Ranger Road. Andi would have pulled into the median and made a left to head toward town. She'd have had no reason to continue straight.

He waited for a vehicle to pass, then crossed the highway. The Ranger Community Center was just ahead, a good place to turn around. He pressed the brake, ready to make his left into the center, but then changed his mind. The emergency vehicles weren't far beyond it. The victims could be people he knew.

As he approached, he slowed to a crawl. A Cherokee County Sheriff unit was stopped along one side of the road, an ambulance on the other. He drove slowly between.

When he looked left, his heart stuttered. Just past the ambulance, the chain-link fence that ran along that side of the road was mangled, a section of it missing. Down the slope beyond, the rear end of a car was barely visible. Dark blue, like Andi's.

He whipped the Sorento off the road in front of the sheriff vehicle. *God, please don't let it be Andi.*

No, it couldn't be Andi. She knew which way town was.

He jumped from the car and ran across the road. Definitely a Honda Accord. It had sailed through the fence, sideswiped several trees, then come to an abrupt stop against two others. He skidded down the gentle slope to where emergency personnel were working to extract the driver. He wouldn't disturb them or get in their way. He just needed to know whether it was Andi inside.

When he circled around to the front of the car and looked through the windshield, he had to grab the hood to stay on his feet.

It *was* Andi. Her head was tipped to the side, her eyes closed. Blood trailed from a gash on the side of her face, soaking into her blouse.

A paramedic standing at the open driver's door carefully lifted her head and held it steady while another one fastened a brace around her neck. Bryce stood with his heart in his throat, watching them work to stabilize her.

Another figure moved down the slope toward him. Sam Williamson, dressed in Cherokee County garb. He'd started with the department about a year ago, working patrol.

Sam tilted his head toward the car. "You know her?"

"She's…my neighbor." His neighbor, and so much more.

"Any idea what happened? To have struck this hard, this close to the four-lane, she had to have come off Ranger Road flying."

He shook his head. "She was headed to town. She should have turned at the highway."

Instead, she'd gone straight through without stopping.

Because she didn't have any brakes.

Realization slammed into him. Someone cut her brake lines. Whoever was after her didn't just want her gone from Murphy.

He wanted her dead. The same as her parents.

Her mom had missed a curve and driven off the side of a mountain. Andi told him the investigation was inconclusive. But he didn't need investigative results to know what had happened. Mrs. Wheaton had missed a curve because someone had tampered with the Mercedes's brakes.

He grasped Sam's forearm. "Make sure they check her brakes. And she needs around-the-clock protection at the hospital."

Sam lifted his brows. "That's some pretty serious stuff."

"Believe me, some serious things have been happening. We can't let her out of our sight."

He wasn't going to let her out of his. He had three weeks of vacation banked. If he had to use every bit of it protecting Andi, he'd do it.

This was just what he'd feared. Dennis wouldn't sell the Murphy property, so someone had removed him as an obstacle. That same person was now going after Andi. With no one else to inherit, the estate would likely be liquidated and the property would go to the highest bidder.

Bryce placed the call to the department. He'd do an official vacation request later, but this would cover him for today. Finally, the paramedics had Andi removed from the car and stretched out on a spine board, ready to load her into the ambulance. She was still unconscious.

"You're taking her to Murphy Medical?" He knew both paramedics. He'd gone all the way through school with one and worked some accidents with the other.

"Yeah, for now. We've got her stabilized. If necessary, she'll be transferred to a trauma unit."

After shooting off a quick text to both Tanner and Colton, he headed for the hospital. When he arrived, the only information he was able to get was that the doctor was sending her to X-ray.

He took a seat in the waiting room and checked his phone. Tanner and Colton had both texted him back. Tanner still had another couple of hours to finish his shift but was going to try to cut out early. Colton was on his way. A district attorney, he apparently wasn't in court this afternoon.

Within minutes, the automatic glass door opened, and Colton walked into the emergency waiting room. "What happened?"

"She was going to town. Missed the curve on Little Ranger."

Colton's brows knitted as he took a seat. "Little Ranger? What was she doing over there?"

"My thoughts exactly. I haven't talked to her, but I think I know what happened. She got to the bottom of Ranger and had no brakes. In light of everything that's happened, I believe someone tampered with them."

Colton frowned. "She shouldn't be staying there alone."

Bryce released a frustrated breath. "Try telling her that. She's developed a stubborn streak a mile wide."

His leg began to bounce, heel tapping against the floor. "She has an alarm system. I've secured the house as best as I can. I've even got Cooper sleeping with her to alert her if anyone tries to come in. But I'm still about to go out of my mind worrying about her."

Colton's eyes widened and understanding filtered in. "That's her, isn't it?"

"What do you mean?"

"The one you told us about. You've never gotten over her."

Bryce heaved a sigh. There was no use trying to evade the question.

"Yeah, that's her." And now that she was lying injured on a gurney somewhere in the hospital, he realized how much she still meant to him.

By the time the doctor came out to talk with him, Bryce's nerves were coiled so tightly he almost sprang from the chair.

"She's awake, but disoriented, which is understandable. We've run X-rays and a CT scan. We don't have the results yet, but you can go back and see her now."

He followed the doctor, leaving Colton sitting in the waiting room. When the doctor slid the curtain back on its track, Bryce stepped around him into the small area.

His knees went weak as shock collided with relief. A figure was lying on the small bed, sheet tucked around her, head held immobile by a cervical collar. Small cuts and abrasions marked her face and arms, and a decent-sized bruise seemed to be forming on one cheek. The spine board they'd used at the scene was still beneath her.

His heart twisted. She looked so small and frail, encased in plastic and linen. He drew closer.

She was awake, staring at the ceiling. The collar didn't offer her any other option. Her eyes shifted to meet his and the edges of her mouth lifted in the start of a smile. It was small, barely noticeable. But it melted his heart.

He loved this woman. He could no longer deny it. He'd told himself that he'd be content with nothing more than friendship.

But somewhere between that conversation in her living room and today's accident, everything had changed.

No matter how much he'd tried to fight it, he'd fallen in love with her all over again.

Or maybe he hadn't. Through the long years apart, as she'd married and had her life and he'd gotten on with his, maybe he'd never stopped loving her.

Maybe deep down, in some sectioned-off corner of his heart, too painful to explore, he'd loved her all along.

ELEVEN

Bryce pulled away from Murphy Medical Center, Andi next to him.

She crossed her arms and leaned back in the seat. "I can't believe they kept me for three days."

"The doctor was concerned about your memory loss." When she'd first woken up, the events surrounding the accident were a complete blank. She remembered cautioning Cooper to be good and walking out the door. The next thing she was aware of was waking up in the ambulance on the way to the hospital.

"By the next morning, I was completely back to normal. Mentally, anyway. I feel like I've been run over by a truck."

"No trucks. But you did do battle with several trees."

She shifted position and winced. "I think they won." She paused. "I need to go back to the house."

"Andi, we talked about this." She'd agreed to stay with her aunt and uncle in Asheville, two hours away. He'd packed her clothing into her two suitcases and currently had them in his back seat, along with her laptop. Meanwhile, Cherokee County deputies would watch her place, hoping to catch whoever was behind the attacks.

Yesterday, they'd gotten some preliminary results of the investigation. The cable to the emergency brake had been cut. The other lines hadn't, as he'd initially suspected. Instead, someone had loosened both bleeder screws on the driver's side. After she'd slowed two or three times, there wouldn't have been enough brake fluid left to stop the car.

Investigators hadn't found the tool used to cut the emergency brake cable, but a bleeder wrench lay a short distance from the gravel drive, partially concealed by dried leaves. They'd lifted prints but didn't have the results back yet.

Andi held up a hand. "Don't worry. I haven't changed my plans. I just need to get some stuff."

"It's not safe."

"When I come back, the house may not even still be standing. There are pictures and things there that I can't replace, memories of my father."

He heaved a sigh. "Fifteen minutes max. And we'll wait for backup." He pulled over to make the call, then headed toward Ranger.

When he turned off the four-lane, instead of traveling up the road, he pulled into Ranger United Methodist Church's parking lot. On a Thursday afternoon, it was empty. After circling the lot, he stopped to wait at the entrance. The church sat high on the hill to his left, its cemetery sprawling beside and in front of him.

His cell phone rang, and he pulled it from his pocket. The call was from the detective in charge of her case.

Bryce's pulse kicked up. "Any new developments?"

"We got an ID on the prints we lifted from the wrench. Matt Langman."

"Have you talked to him?"

"Yeah. Same as before. He checked his tools and said his wrench is missing."

"Has he been arrested?"

"We kept him for questioning, then released him. Since he leaves everything outside, easily accessible to anyone, the evidence wasn't strong enough to hold him."

Bryce nodded. Either Matt's threats were getting much more serious, or someone was setting him up. He was inclined to believe the latter. The gas can and wrench left behind were too convenient.

He disconnected the call and filled Andi in on the details. He'd just finished when a cruiser turned onto Ranger. He followed it to the Wheaton house. While one deputy kept watch outside, the other waited in the living room.

After boxing up some photo albums and mementos Andi and Dennis had collected, they pulled ornaments from the tree, leaving it essentially bare. They all had sentimental value, since they were handmade. Finally, everything Andi wanted to keep was boxed up. They loaded the items into his truck and thanked the deputies.

In two hours, they'd be in Asheville. Though Andi had initially wanted to go back to her condo in Atlanta, he'd talked her out of it. That would be the first place her attackers would check.

He followed the cruiser up the drive. At the end of Ranger, it pulled into the median, ready to complete a left turn.

Bryce waited for two vehicles to pass. By the time he was ready to pull out, the cruiser was moving down the highway, headed toward town.

He lifted his foot from the brake. Before he could step on the gas, Andi gasped.

He swiveled his head to look at her. "What?"

"I've figured it out. My dad's note. Turn around."

After a glance in his rearview mirror, he backed into a drive on their right. But he wasn't leaving the safety of the vehicle until he knew what she had in mind.

Excitement radiated from her. "I've felt all along that Dad left the note for a reason. It was a message to me. He wanted to tell me something that wouldn't be obvious to anyone else."

Yeah, it wasn't obvious to him, either. He drew to a stop in her driveway. "Go ahead."

"My dad talked about burying secrets deep. I've wondered all along if he meant it figuratively or literally. Now I know. He physically buried something."

Bryce frowned. "If it was buried deep, like the note said, I don't know of anywhere on your ten acres that that could have been accomplished easily. I think I proved that burying the squirrel."

Andi turned in the seat to face him more fully. "I don't think he had to dig the hole. I think it was already dug."

"What do you mean?" His jaw went lax. "The well."

What was it Andi had told him? Dennis had said that instead of collecting wishes, the well collected burdens.

She reached for the door handle, but he held up a hand.

"Wait."

Her shoulders dropped. "No one's here. Your friend already checked everything out."

She was right. Gary had circled the house the entire time they'd been inside and had seen no one.

"We'll be back on the road in no time." Her eyes

were pleading. "I just have to know before we head to Asheville. You can even stand guard with your gun."

She climbed from the truck, and he got out the other side. "Wait."

But she was already headed around the side of the house at a jog. He followed her into the woods, weapon drawn and eyes peeled for any signs of movement.

It was dusk. They had maybe another twenty minutes of daylight left. If Andi was right, they'd have what they wanted in five.

When they reached the well, Andi pulled the bucket up, hand over hand on the rope. As she worked, he continued to cast glances around them.

Finally, she grasped the bucket's handle and looked inside. Her face fell. "It's empty. I thought for sure this was it, that we'd find the answer here."

She set the bucket on the edge of the well. It leaned at an angle, as if the bottom wasn't flat. When she turned it over, something was affixed there with pieces of duct tape, crisscrossed over one another.

Bryce's pulse kicked into overdrive. Dennis had probably died for whatever was taped to the bottom of that bucket. And whoever killed Dennis wouldn't hesitate to take out him and Andi, as well.

He scanned the woods again and froze. Had he just seen movement near the back of the property?

He tightened his grip on the pistol. "We need to go. Now."

"Not without this." Andi pried one end loose and, with a jerk, peeled the whole thing back. The rip of glue letting go seemed to echo in the silence.

Then there was another sound, much closer than where he'd seen movement earlier.

This one turned his blood to ice.

It was the telltale click of a hammer being pulled back on a revolver.

Another click followed and a third.

Icy fingers danced down Andrea's spine. She'd never been around guns. But she'd watched enough detective shows to know what she'd just heard. Even if she hadn't, Bryce's expression would have given it away. Every bit of color had drained from his face.

"There's three of us and two of you." The words came from beyond them, deeper in the woods. The voice belonged to Drysdale.

She stood frozen, too afraid to move. Bryce had wanted to wait for backup. She'd been in too much of a hurry.

Dear God, what have I done?

Drysdale spoke again. "Drop the gun and kick it away from you."

After several moments' hesitation, Bryce did as he'd been told.

"Now hands in the air."

Andrea raised her arms, still holding the package, and watched Drysdale approach. Two men flanked him. One was huge. They all held pistols. Though only Drysdale had spoken, she was pretty sure the others were the two who'd ransacked her place.

"Now head toward the house. If either of you try anything, we'll shoot you both."

"Here, take it." Andrea shook what was in her hand—a small padded envelope, folded in half, duct tape stuck to one side. "You can have the gold. Take anything you're able to pull out of the mine. I don't want it."

Drysdale snatched the package from her hand with a condescending snort. "Do you really think this is all over a few gold nuggets?"

Dread trickled over her. When she'd learned about the gold, she'd clung to that theory with every bit of determination she had. It hadn't been the most practical explanation. But it had been better than considering the alternative, that her father had gotten involved in something illegal and finally decided to clear his conscience.

"Now move. We're going in the front door."

Drysdale's command sliced across her thoughts. She obeyed, Bryce walking next to her.

"I need my keys. They're in Bryce's truck, in my purse." So was her phone. Maybe she'd have an opportunity to slip it into her pocket and eventually get off a quick 911 call.

Drysdale marched them around the side of the house and into the driveway. She'd left her purse on the front floorboard. After opening the passenger door, she leaned in and unzipped it, but before she could slip her hand inside, Drysdale's voice stopped her.

"Wait. Bring it out here where we can see you."

Her heart fell. So much for trying to retrieve her phone. She straightened and pulled her keys from the front pouch.

"Now toss your purse back into the vehicle."

She did as Drysdale commanded, then let the armed men direct her toward her front door. Maybe she could enter the alarm code incorrectly and pass it off as nervousness.

As soon as she opened the front door, the alarm

sounded its entry tone, waiting for the code. Her hand shook as she lifted it to the panel.

Drysdale spoke close to her ear. "Think about what you're doing, because if the alarm goes off, we'll shoot you both right here."

She punched in the four numbers and the alarm fell silent. When she cast a glance at Bryce, his eyes were alert and tension radiated from him. The two of them were outnumbered and unarmed. But if any opportunity for escape presented itself, Bryce would be all over it.

"Python, find something to bind the cop."

Drysdale's words sent panic spiraling through her. With Bryce tied up, their chances of escape would plummet.

The larger man looked around him. "What?"

"Rope, tape, anything."

There was no rope inside, but the desk drawer held duct tape. If the men were the same ones who'd ransacked her house, they'd know that.

After a moment's hesitation, the man called Python walked to the desk, then opened and closed drawers until he found the right one. Drysdale made a motion with his pistol.

"Tape his hands behind him."

After laying his weapon on the bookcase, he grabbed one of Bryce's wrists. When Bryce resisted, he gave that arm a twist. Bryce winced but didn't make a sound. At a well-muscled six foot two, Bryce wasn't a small guy. But Python was huge. He'd probably gotten the nickname because of the size of his arms.

Two seconds later, Andrea was trapped against the smaller man's chest, his arm around her throat and the cold barrel of the pistol pressed against her temple.

Words hissed against her ear. "If you don't wanna see your girlfriend's brains blown all ova this room, you betta do what you're told." It was the New Englander with the attitude.

Bryce put his hands behind his back and allowed the man to tape his wrists together. But the determination in his eyes was unmistakable.

The New Englander lowered the gun but didn't release her. She watched, helpless, while Python shoved Bryce backward onto the couch and taped his ankles.

What were they going to do, shoot them? No, if that was their plan, they'd have done it outside and left their bodies in the woods. They had something else in mind.

Bryce didn't deserve any of it. She should never have let him get involved. She looked at Drysdale. "What do you want? The property? I'll sell it to you. In fact, I'll give it to you. Just let Bryce go. He has nothing to do with this."

"I don't want the property."

"You've hounded me to sell it to you. Let Bryce go, and I'll sign it over to you, no strings attached."

"I don't need the property anymore. I'm guessing everything I want is in this little package."

"Then take it and leave." Bryce's tone was cold and commanding. "You're already under investigation for the murder of Dennis and Margaret Wheaton. You might get away with it, But if you follow through with whatever you have planned here, there'll be nowhere you can run that they won't find you."

Ignoring Bryce, Drysdale nodded toward Python. "Shut him up."

Python balled up one meaty fist and drew it back.

Andrea released a shriek, which was cut abruptly short as the other man clamped his hand over her mouth.

"No, the tape, you idiot." Drysdale's tone was sharp. "I want him conscious."

As Python tore off a six-inch strip of duct tape and pressed it over Bryce's mouth, Drysdale removed a folding knife from his pocket and sliced open the envelope. Inside was a zippered plastic bag. He pulled out the contents, and Andrea held her breath. Whatever her father had hidden, he'd wrapped it in several paper towels. Drysdale unfolded them, dropping each to the floor, then held up a thumb drive. "Where is your computer?"

"In Bryce's truck." She cast a sideways glance at the man still holding her. "He and I can go get it."

Maybe she'd have another shot at getting her phone.

"You stay here." The command came from Drysdale. "Slater, go get it."

So that was the New Englander's name. It could be a nickname, like Python, but it wouldn't hurt to remember it.

Slater released her and moved toward the door. As he turned to throw the dead bolt, her gaze slid to his shoes. They were tennis shoes, worn and dirty. She'd seen them before. Had he been wearing them while he'd ransacked her room as she hid under the bed?

She couldn't remember. She'd been too terrified to notice details.

He disappeared out the front door, then came back a minute later with her laptop. Drysdale pushed aside a water glass she'd left sitting on the coffee table and opened her laptop. After taking a seat on the other end of the couch from Bryce, he booted up the computer and inserted the thumb drive.

She'd give almost anything to learn what was on that drive, but she couldn't see the screen from where she stood. Python and Slater were positioned on either side of her, their weapons tucked into the waistbands of their jeans. But judging from their alert stances, neither had let down his guard.

Her father had probably uncovered some things that could send Drysdale and his partners to prison and had saved the evidence, intending to show it to Bryce.

Was his hesitation in going straight to the Atlanta police because he was struggling over having to turn in his partners?

Or was the struggle over turning himself in?

For several minutes, Drysdale leaned forward, scanning whatever was there. Finally, he looked up, nodding. "Just what we suspected. Lassiter was right. When he found Dennis at the office late on a Saturday night, he knew he was up to something. He was acting too weird." He closed the cover, and his gaze met Andrea's. "The man has good instincts. He followed your dad, figured out he was headed up here."

Andrea pursed her lips. So why didn't Lassiter just follow her dad all the way to Murphy and get what he wanted? Because men like Drysdale and Lassiter never did their own dirty work. They always had others do it for them.

Drysdale continued. "Lassiter said we needed to have his office and cell phones bugged. It paid off."

The pieces of the puzzle started to click into place. One of her dad's partners had listened in on his conversation with Bryce. Then they'd had to come up with a way to silence him before that meeting could take place.

Drysdale nodded to Python. "Restrain her, too."

As the man jerked her hands behind her back, Drysdale shook his head. "I would never have expected that out of Dennis. What kind of man double-crosses his partners?"

Andrea stared down at Drysdale, eyes narrowed. "You should have known better than to bring in someone like my dad. As smart as he was, he was bound to figure out what you were up to, and he was too honest and upright to keep quiet."

Drysdale's face reddened, and he sprang to his feet. She'd obviously hit a nerve.

"If you think dear daddy was so honest and upright, you need to be enlightened." He circled the coffee table, grabbed her by the hair and forced her to her knees.

Bryce slid forward on the couch and struggled to his feet. Python shoved him back down, then stepped up beside Drysdale.

"Come on, boss, we need to do what we came for and get out of here."

Do what we came for?

"No. I want her to know what kind of man her father really was." He turned the laptop around and opened the cover. A long list of files filled the screen, many titled "Geological Report," each followed by an address.

Had someone done a geological report on her family's property and found the probability of a rich gold vein? But Drysdale had said it wasn't about the gold.

Bending at the waist, he clicked on a file titled "Investors." A spreadsheet appeared, line after line of names, dates and amounts.

She looked at the entries more closely. With each name, there were dates with funds taken in, and much larger amounts paid out three months later. Drysdale scrolled down, where increasingly more investors were listed.

It didn't take Andrea long to assign meaning to what she was looking at. Drysdale and his partners were involved in a Ponzi scheme. Maybe her father had been, too. The realization was like a kick to the gut.

If he'd been involved, there was one consolation. He'd gathered the evidence, brought it here and contacted Bryce. Law enforcement. Maybe he *had* allowed himself to get caught up in the scheme. But he'd made the decision to turn everything over to the authorities.

Drysdale closed the folder with a smirk. "So your father wasn't so pious after all."

Maybe he wasn't. But he'd done the right thing in the end.

Drysdale nodded at Python. "Finish restraining her."

Python shoved her sideways, and her head hit the floor with a thud. While large hands wrapped tape around her ankles, Drysdale trained his weapon on Bryce. Slater kept his pointed at her.

When he finished, he tore off a final six-inch piece. He was planning to gag her, too. This was her final opportunity to scream for help.

But it wouldn't do any good. All her neighbors were too far away to hear. Except for possibly Matt and his father. And she couldn't expect help from either of them.

Besides, screaming would be a sure way for her to end up with a bullet in her head. Bryce, too.

Drysdale's gaze shifted to Bryce. "Tie them together, back-to-back. I don't want any chance of them escaping."

A cautious sense of relief filtered through her. If Drysdale was concerned about them escaping, he apparently didn't have plans to kill them. He just needed to secure them well enough that they couldn't call for help until he and his thugs were long gone. In fact, they probably had a private jet ready to take them to Grand Cayman or somewhere. Trying to scare her into selling the property didn't work, so maybe this was the backup plan.

Python pressed the short piece of tape over her mouth and brought her to a seated position. After jerking Bryce to his feet, he dragged him around the coffee table and shoved him to the floor behind her.

Once they were positioned back-to-back, Python circled their upper bodies three or four times with the tape.

Escape wouldn't be easy. Maybe some time would pass before they figured a way out of their predicament. If nothing else, eventually someone would check on them. Her aunt and uncle were expecting her tonight. If she didn't show up, they'd try to contact her. When that failed, they'd call the police.

"Slater, go get the gas."

Drysdale's words jarred her from her thoughts. *Gas?*

Dread wrapped around her, dark and thick and heavy. It bore down on her, pressing the air from her lungs. Her mind scrambled for an explanation, any explanation, all the while avoiding the obvious one.

When he returned a few minutes later, holding a gas can in one gloved hand, all denial fled.

Drysdale and his men planned to burn the house down with them inside.

Panic pounded up her spine and settled in her chest, sending her heart into a frenzied rhythm. At her back, Bryce twisted in a futile attempt to escape.

Slater started at the back door and sloshed gas along the wall, following the perimeter of the room.

It splashed onto his jeans and shoes, and as he turned the corner and headed into the living room, he left wet footprints on the hardwood floor. After moving across the front and finishing the fourth wall, he splashed what was left in the can onto the couch.

Drysdale stood, staring down at her, shaking his head. "It wasn't supposed to come to this. I'm not a believer in the daughter paying for the sins of the father. But you brought it on yourself. Nothing happened until you refused to sell me the property. Almost nothing."

He glared at Python. "His instructions were to get up here and find the evidence. When he learned you were headed back up, he took it on himself to run you off the road. Had to drive his truck home and come back in Slater's vehicle, then thought I should have to pay for the damages."

Python crossed his massive arms. "How was I supposed to look for evidence if she was staying at the house? Running her off the road bought us time."

Andrea watched him, her final question now answered. He only thought it had bought them time. He hadn't counted on her getting off that slope and making it to the Murphy house less than two hours later.

Drysdale ignored the argument, his attention still on Andrea. "All you needed to do was sell. A few No Trespassing signs, and our secret would have been safe until we could locate what your father had taken, no matter how long it took."

He walked with Python to the back door. Slater followed, shoes still leaving wet tracks.

Shoes that looked familiar and she wasn't sure why. *Matt's shoes.*

That was where she'd seen them, sitting on Matt's

front porch. The men were going to set the house on fire and leave Matt's gas-soaked shoes somewhere nearby.

That was why Drysdale hadn't shot them. He wanted to make sure none of the evidence led to him.

And all of it pointed to her antagonistic next-door neighbor.

The three men walked through the dining area and slipped out the back door. A minute later, Python stepped back inside and dropped a flaming stick on the floor.

The fire spread rapidly, following the path along the wall and licking at the curtains. Soon the entire double room would be engulfed in flames, with her and Bryce in the center.

God, please save us. Her biggest takeaway from the church services she'd attended the past two Sundays was that God was with her, not just at Christmas but all the time.

Please send someone.

He could do it. She had no doubt. She'd never questioned the greatness of God. She'd just believed in a distant God who didn't involve himself in the lives of people.

But the past two Sundays, she'd been introduced to a God who was much closer, a God who cared about every detail of her life—*God with us.*

She still believed in the greatness of God.

But if He chose not to answer, she only hoped that the smoke would take them out before the flames.

As flames traveled around the perimeter of the room, Bryce struggled against the tape holding him. Behind him, Andi screamed against hers, her cries little more than a muffled whimper. He'd never have let the man restrain him if the other hadn't been holding a pistol to her head. *God, help me get us out of here.*

He glanced frantically around him, pulse pounding in his ears. Tied as they were, they'd never get on their feet. Even if they could manage it and somehow hop to either door, they wouldn't be able to escape before the flames consumed them.

Their only hope was getting loose. Duct tape tore easily once the edge was ripped. He had a folding knife in his front pocket but no way to reach it.

His gaze settled on the coffee table. If he could tip the glass over and smash it with his boot, maybe they could use a piece of it to cut the tape. With the table at his right side, he'd have to turn ninety degrees to do what he had in mind. He rocked back and forth, pulling Andi with him, rotating a little with each movement. Andi likely had no idea what he planned to do, but she worked with him anyway.

A high-pitched whine sounded over the crackle of flames. His heart leaped. Sirens. Was help on its way?

No, that was impossible. The flames wouldn't be visible from outside for another couple of minutes. Then they'd spread fast. By the time someone called and emergency personnel arrived, it would be too late to save them. It was up to him.

He lifted his legs and tipped over the glass. When he brought his heels down hard, it shattered. Two curved sections, almost two square inches, lay among the smaller pieces.

Flames climbed up the back of the recliner, and smoke billowed above their heads. Bryce scooped the glass off the table and onto the floor. Now that Andi had figured out what he was doing, positioning them so he could reach it went much faster.

He picked up one of the larger pieces and slid it between her fingers. She immediately tightened her grip, holding it firm. He rubbed the edge of the tape against the glass.

Fire danced across the front of the room, moving up the gas-doused tree with a roar. He attacked the tape with renewed vigor. The piece of glass twisted, and pain went through his wrist, razor-sharp. Moisture trickled into his palm. Andi had lost her grip. She may have gotten cut, too.

Clasping his hands, he jerked his wrists outward. At the rip of tape, he heaved a relieved sigh. After a second tug, his hands were free. It took only a minute to slice through the tape that wrapped his ankles and bound the two of them together.

He removed it from their mouths, then worked on freeing her hands and ankles. Blood coated his palm and dripped from the ends of his fingers, making the glass slippery. His wrist was bleeding pretty badly. He'd deal with it once he'd gotten them both to safety.

A coughing spasm overtook him, and he pressed his jacket to his mouth. The whole perimeter of the room was engulfed in flames, the couch and curtains now on fire. They couldn't get to either door.

A wave of dizziness swept over him. Still on his hands and knees, he swayed sideways. The whole room was spinning. He blinked several times, trying to make it stop.

He had to get out. And he had to save Andi. He didn't know about her, but he wasn't ready to meet God. Two weeks ago, he would have thought he'd be welcomed through the pearly gates. Now he knew better.

"Come on." Andi took one of his hands and started to stand.

"Stay low. The smoke…"

The sirens seemed to be closer, somewhere out on the four-lane. Or maybe the squeal was inside his head.

Andi crawled toward the hall. "Follow me."

He forced his limbs to cooperate. Andi was ahead of him, casting repeated glances over her shoulder. He was moving through a tunnel, the walls closing in on him.

When they reached the master bedroom, she slammed the door behind him. Good thinking. It would buy them some time. He opened his mouth to say so but couldn't seem to formulate the words.

She threw open the front window. "Come on. We'll climb out through here."

He grasped the footboard and pulled himself onto the bed. She'd told him to do something, but he could no longer remember what.

She spun to face him. "Bryce?"

A second later, she'd closed the gap between them. When she looked at her hands, she gasped. "You're bleeding. You got cut when the glass slipped." She checked his wrist. "Lay down, and keep pressure on it. I need to find something I can use for a tourniquet."

She pushed him back onto the bed. Something slid from his pocket. She'd taken his phone. She stalked into the bathroom with it pressed to her ear. Her words drifted to him. "We need an ambulance and a fire truck." She rattled off the address.

The sirens grew closer. That had to be what he was hearing. His ears were ringing, but this was much louder, more piercing. Someone must have called before Andi did. Or the vehicles were responding to a different location.

Andi stepped into view, holding what used to be a washcloth. It was now cut into strips. She also held… a toothbrush?

She tied one of the strips loosely around his forearm and slid the toothbrush underneath. As she turned it, the makeshift tourniquet tightened. The bleeding gradually stopped. Once satisfied, she tied another strip to secure everything in place.

There was a crash at the other end of the house. Maybe the roof had caved in. No, someone was there. There were shouts, raised men's voices.

Andi hurried to the open window and screamed for help. When Bryce pushed himself upright, the room spun and darkness moved in on the edges of his vision. Two figures appeared at the window.

"We need help." Andi's voice held panic. "Bryce has lost a lot of blood. I don't think he can make it out on his own."

Someone climbed through the window and dropped to the floor.

Matt?

No way was Matt risking his life to rescue them. Loss of blood was making him delirious.

But his rescuer *was* Matt. Andi looped one of his arms over her shoulders and Matt positioned himself under Bryce's other arm. Outside, the sirens reached ear-piercing level, then fell abruptly silent.

Andi and Matt brought him to his feet, and the darkness encroached further. As they lifted him into the window opening, strong hands outside gripped him around the torso and pulled him through. His rescuer tried to place him on his feet, but his knees buckled and his eyes drifted shut.

Someone dropped to the ground beside him and nestled a shoulder under his arm. That would be Matt. Was Andi still inside? He needed to help her.

But his legs wouldn't work. Matt and his other rescuer dragged him away from the house and laid him on the ground. Bryce forced his eyes open and looked up into the face of Jimmy Langman. Red and blue lights flashed around him.

"Andi…"

Soft hands wrapped around one of his. "I'm here."

She was safe, and so was he. Neither of them were going to meet God tonight. But the thought had shaken him. At the earliest opportunity, he was going to find out what it took to be ready and make sure he was.

Soon Andi's driveway held both an ambulance and a fire truck, in addition to the two sheriff cruisers that had arrived.

As the paramedics worked on him, bits and pieces of conversation drifted to him from nearby, questions from Andi that he couldn't make out, responses from Matt that made no sense—

"…the hospital…the old mine…buried…wearing my shoes…called the cops…fire… Bryce's truck…"

His eyes fell closed.

The words faded.

And everything went silent.

TWELVE

Andrea gave two raps on the doorjamb, then entered Bryce's hospital room.

He smiled from his bed, where he'd raised the back and propped a pillow behind him. "Hello, stranger."

"Hey." She returned his smile, her heart swelling. She loved him. After they'd both come so close to losing their lives, she could no longer deny it. Had last night's events had the same impact on him? If so, would he be willing to give a relationship a shot?

Would she?

His gaze slid over her. "Since you're dressed in street clothes rather than a hospital gown, I'm guessing they didn't keep you."

"They treated me for smoke inhalation, then released me this morning. I just finished all the discharge paperwork. Paige is picking me up when I'm ready to leave, but I figured I'd come up here and bug you first."

She'd gotten a hold of Tanner through the Murphy Police Department, and he'd given her Paige's number. She now had it programmed in her phone. She'd met her less than two weeks ago, but they'd instantly connected. Paige had lived through her own traumas.

Bryce nodded. "If you hold out a while longer, I might be able to join you. The doctor's releasing me today. I'll have to see him in ten days to have the stitches removed."

He held up one arm, with its thickly wrapped wrist. "He said as much blood as I lost, I was blessed to be alive. We nicked an artery." He grinned, shaking his head. "I can't believe you stopped the bleeding with a washcloth and toothbrush."

"Necessity is the mother of invention."

He took her hand with his good one and squeezed it. "I owe you my life."

"I owe you mine. If you hadn't broken the glass and cut the tape, we'd have died in the living room."

"And as unlikely as it seems, we might both owe our lives to Matt and his father."

"I prayed that God would send help, and He did, in the most unexpected way." She frowned. "But both of them made it clear they weren't doing it for us."

His brows drew together. "Then why?"

"Matt knew I was in the hospital, and you were spending all your time with me. He figured he'd take the opportunity to snoop around the old mine. While he was there, three men approached. He said he barely got himself hidden before they started poking around, talking about something being buried there, and once the Wheaton kid was out of the picture, they'd dig up the whole area if they had to."

"So why did he call the cops?"

"He didn't like them horning in on what he was doing. But what really did it was seeing the one guy wearing his shoes. He knew they were going to do something bad and make it look like he did it, the same as they'd done with the gas can and wrench. So he ran home and called the cops, not realizing we'd come back."

Bryce nodded. "So Matt didn't suddenly develop a Good Samaritan gene."

"'Fraid not. Anyway, a short time later, he slipped back over to see what was happening and saw Drysdale and his guys jogging away from the house. He started to follow them, hoping he'd be able to lead the police to them, then got scared and doubled back. That's when he realized the house was on fire and called 911 again."

"No wonder they got there so fast."

"Yeah. They were responding to Matt's calls, not mine. Matt didn't go around front until the police were almost there. That's when he saw your truck and realized we were inside. He ran home to get his dad. They kicked in the door, and I screamed for help. The rest you know."

Bryce pursed his lips. "Maybe they *were* watching out for their own interests, but we still owe them a huge debt of gratitude."

"I tried." She'd thought this could be the start of reconciliation between their families. But she wasn't holding out hope. There was as much animosity between them as there'd ever been. "They both said to keep my thanks. Langman said if we had died, Matt would have taken the blame and never seen the light of day, and that was the only reason they did what they did."

Bryce shrugged. "Maybe someday. You never know what the future has in store."

She nodded. The words were truer than he probably realized. She'd have never guessed when she showed up in Murphy last month, that in so short a time, she and Bryce would go from uneasy acquaintances to...

To what?

Bryce had dispelled the tension between them by laying it all out—he wasn't interested in anything deeper than friendship. At the time it had been a relief. That was when she'd been sure she'd wanted the same thing. And falling in love hadn't even been a dim possibility.

Should she do what he did, have a heart-to-heart talk and let him know exactly how she felt?

No. She'd already experienced the ultimate rejection once this year. If Bryce told her he didn't have those kinds of feelings for her, she'd want to go to bed and stay there.

Besides, if Bryce *was* interested in renewing a romantic relationship, she wasn't even sure she could go through with it. Maybe she would come to realize her walls were too thick, her heart too tattered to love again.

She pulled her hand from his grasp to slide a chair up to his bed. "Paige said as soon as you get out, we're all getting together at Tanner's for a party. She's calling it a celebration of life and justice."

Bryce lifted a brow. "Since we'll be celebrating justice, is it safe to assume Drysdale and his goons have been caught?"

"Yep. And police are going to be investigating everything Drysdale was involved in." She frowned, dread wrapping around her like a cloak. "I know it's not likely, but I keep hoping they'll uncover evidence that totally absolves my father."

His eyes filled with sadness. "That's sometimes hard to prove, piecing everything together after the fact. If they don't come to that conclusion, it doesn't mean your dad *was* involved, just that they can't eliminate the possibility."

"Thank you." She gave him a weak smile. She appreciated his words. But he wasn't just trying to make her feel better. He was probably trying to convince himself, too. Finding out her dad was innocent would be as important to him as it was to her.

A man wearing a white jacket entered the room. A stethoscope dangled from his neck, and he held a clipboard. "Are you ready to get out of here?"

"More than you can imagine."

While the doctor gave Bryce instructions on the care of his wound, she stood back and waited.

Today was Friday. Next week, she'd be moving ahead with the purchase of Angie's business. Though she'd missed her appointment at the store, Angie had visited her in the hospital after her car wreck, and they'd had numerous phone conversations. Soon she wouldn't just be a Murphy resident. She'd be a Murphy business owner.

And she'd be living right next door to Bryce. So close, but never more than friends. Maybe quitting her job and moving to Murphy on a permanent basis had been a mistake.

She crossed her arms and leaned back against the wall. She'd made the choice abruptly, without thinking it through. Maybe it was time to give it a little more thought, before she proceeded down a track that couldn't be reversed. One she regretted.

Backing out of her purchase of Angie's business after giving her word would be a stinky thing to do. But it wasn't too late. Nothing had been signed, no money exchanged.

And she hadn't shut the door on her Atlanta job. She'd given notice but promised to be available remotely as long as needed. As dismayed as the company had been to lose her, they'd probably be pleased to bring her back on. If they hadn't already filled it, they'd likely even hire her for her old job.

Staying in Murphy or going back to Atlanta. Both choices had pros and cons.

Could she pray for wisdom? Was *God with us* just for comfort and protection? Or could it also apply to guidance?

She hoped so.

Because she was in serious need of some.

Bryce sat in Tanner's living room, surrounded by some of his favorite people. He'd been released from the hospital this afternoon. As promised, his friends had planned a celebration—a dinner of taco salad, complete with cake.

Colton and Mandy had brought meat and tortilla chips. Tanner had provided sour cream, salsa and cheese, and Paige had cut up lettuce and tomato. The four of them had gone in together on a cake from the Ingles bakery.

Since Bryce's friends had insisted that the party was in his and Andi's honor, they wouldn't let the two of them bring anything. Now he was sitting on the couch next to Andi, pleasantly full and sweet tooth satisfied.

Tanner stood to gather the empty cake plates and grinned at Bryce. "Since there are no more crazies stalking Andi, you're not going to know what to do with yourself."

Bryce smiled, too, a sense of lightness filling his chest. He'd caught them up on everything that had happened over the past few days. "Number one will be taking the obnoxious notification off my cell phone. I've been listening to Alvin and the Chipmunks on steroids for the past two weeks rather than risk missing another text from Andi."

"I'd be doing the same thing." Colton cast a loving glance at Mandy next to him. He'd been alternating between hugging eighteen-month-old Liam and bouncing him on one knee since they'd finished eating.

Mandy smiled and patted his leg.

A pang shot through Bryce. Seeing the happiness his friends had found shone a spotlight on his own loneliness.

Colton stood, holding his son against his chest. "We've had fun, but it's past this little guy's bedtime."

Andi pushed herself to her feet. "I think I'll head out, too. It's been a long day."

Bryce agreed. By the time they'd left the hospital, it had been early afternoon. Andi had asked Paige to drop her off so she could pick up another rental car and get checked into a motel. Then Paige had left him at the Wheaton place to get his Sorento. Fortunately, it was undamaged.

After hugs from the women and pats on the back from the men, Colton and his family loaded into their Highlander and Andi climbed into her vehicle, this time an Explorer. The two SUVs rolled up the drive, and Bryce made his way to his own.

Tanner followed him, but Paige disappeared inside. She lived in the cabin at the back of Tanner's property and wouldn't be joining Tanner in the house until after their wedding next April.

Tanner stopped next to his SUV. "Are you going to let her get away twice?"

Bryce looked at him, but his friend's attention was

on the Explorer, now making its turn onto 294. "What's that supposed to mean?"

"You know what I mean. You've kicked yourself the past twelve years for letting her get away the first time. Now you're getting a second chance. She's clearly in love with you. And you're going to blow it again."

He frowned at his friend rather than giving him the shove he wanted to. "Have you been talking to Colton?"

Tanner shrugged.

Yeah, just what he thought. His friends were conspiring against him.

Tanner gave him a nudge. "What are you afraid of?"

"Nothing." He'd given the answer on reflex. He'd answered too quickly, because what he'd said wasn't even true.

He *was* afraid. Afraid of rejection. Afraid she'd agree to pursue a relationship with him, then back off. Afraid now that he'd fallen head over heels in love with her, she'd go back to her ex-husband.

Tanner stared him down. "I don't believe you."

"Believe what you want." He opened the door to the Sorento and slid into the driver's seat. Before he could close the door, Tanner stepped into the opening.

He heaved a sigh. Colton and Tanner were the only two men on the planet who could push him like that.

"What do you want?"

Tanner leaned against the open door and rested a hand on the roof. "I want you to be happy, bro. So tell me why you're getting ready to make the biggest mistake of your life a second time."

He crossed his arms. "Okay, let's say she agrees to date me. What do you think will happen if her ex realizes what he lost and wants her back?"

"From the little I know of Andi, I'd guess she'd tell him to take a hike."

Bryce banged his head against the headrest a couple of times. "I'm a cop. Her ex is a neurosurgeon. You think there's any way I can compete with that?"

Tanner gave him a *get real* look. "The creep cheated on her."

"And Pam's ex beat her up. Repeatedly. That didn't stop her from dumping me and going back to him."

"I think Andi's got it together better than Pam did."

She did. But she was also practical. She'd been in love with the guy once or she wouldn't have married him. Sure, when she'd caught him with his girlfriend, she'd been hurt. But she'd also been hurt all those years ago when she'd stepped out of her woods and caught *him* with Carla.

They were two entirely different situations. But it didn't matter. If given the opportunity, restoring her marriage would be the more practical choice.

Tanner looked ready to shake him. "You're not competing with anyone. You're the one she loves."

Bryce gave him a doubt-infused glance. "She told you that."

"Not directly. But Paige commented on it. She had it figured out the first time she met her. And it's as obvious on you as it is on Andi."

He sighed. "It doesn't matter. She's been burned. She's got walls around her heart a mile thick. I don't have what it takes to break them down."

"Then maybe you need to figure out what it does take and work on getting it." He stepped back. "Think about it, bro."

Tanner shut the Sorento's door and raised a hand in farewell.

As Bryce headed up the drive to begin his short trip home, conflicting emotions tumbled through him. Tanner made it sound so easy. Of course, he'd found the girl of his dreams and was still flying high. Tanner and Paige were perfect together.

And so were he and Andi. They always had been. He'd seen it way back when they were teenagers. Then he'd lost sight of the fact.

He made a left at the four-lane and headed toward Ranger. Tanner was right. He *did* love her. And if he let her go again, he was going to regret it for the rest of his life. Whatever effort he had to expend, Andi was worth it.

Tanner had said he needed to figure it out. He had to somehow break down the walls she'd built around her heart.

Could they roll back time and return to the way they were?

No, they couldn't. They were different people. They couldn't have what they had before, a love that was pure and innocent. Maybe even a bit naive.

But that didn't mean they couldn't have something just as satisfying. Even more so. Something deeper. More meaningful because of everything they'd gone through to get there.

But first, Andi would have to be willing to take a chance on him. The only way he was going to get past her defenses was to convince her that he really did love her the way he'd said he did all those years ago. With a love as big as the sky. Always and forever.

Whatever he did, it would have to be something special. Mere words wouldn't do it. Neither would gifts.

A plan began to form. By the time he pulled into his driveway, it was taking shape. He wouldn't be able to pull it off alone. He'd need help.

A partner in crime.

And he knew just the person.

THIRTEEN

Andrea stood back, watching people enter the large room, gazes filled with appreciation. With its wooden floors, brick walls and open-beam ceiling, the Hackney Warehouse was rich with character and a popular venue for weddings and other events. This one was an engagement party, the first job Andrea had done without Angie's assistance.

She'd moved ahead with purchasing the business and, in the three weeks since Christmas, had accompanied Angie on four decorating jobs. She couldn't say God had spoken to her. But He'd given her peace about the decision. Wasn't that sort of the same thing?

She'd also gained peace about something else. She wasn't sure whether to credit God with it, but she was thanking Him anyway. The investigation was progressing well. Drysdale and his cronies had tried hard to implicate her father, but they hadn't been able to totally cover their tracks. Her father's assets were still frozen, pending the final results of the investigation, but what had been uncovered so far was encouraging.

Her father's partners had had quite a thing going. Drysdale had been acquiring bogus geological reports showing rich mineral deposits, and Lassiter and Barrand had been presenting the information to investors. They'd brought her father in a year and a half earlier. Judging from the changes she'd noticed in him, he'd discovered something was off about nine months before he died. With so much evidence pointing to him, that might have been why he'd wanted to get some direction from Bryce first.

A woman approached, wearing a rust-colored sweater dress with a wide black belt and fur-topped black boots. "Everything's absolutely perfect. Everyone's gushing about the decorations." Blond curls bounced as she gestured.

Andrea gave her an appreciative smile. Shelby Peters was her client. She radiated excitement, and Andrea had to tamp down some unexpected jealousy. If she was going to envy all her brides-to-be, she'd gotten into the wrong line of work.

She cast a glance around the room to take in the decorations that everyone was "gushing" about. Tulle-covered strands of lights wound around the columns, and swags of tulle and lights hung from the ceiling. Long rows of tables were draped in white linen, with centerpieces of tulle, flowers, greenery and candles every few feet.

A DJ had set up in the corner and was already providing music for the attendees. Soon one hundred and fifty guests would sit down to a full catered dinner. Shelby and the groom-to-be had obviously spared no expense.

She brought her attention back to her client. "So where is the handsome guy?" All her dealings had been with Shelby, and she had yet to meet the groom.

"He should be here shortly."

When Bryce walked into the room, Andrea's pulse picked up speed and her stomach rolled over. Dressed to a tee in a suit and tie, he looked better than good. She needed to stop reacting to him, no matter what he was wearing.

Since the fire, she'd been living in town, so with the exception of church and a couple of gatherings with Bryce's friends, she hadn't seen much of him.

She should have known she'd be likely to run into him tonight. He knew everybody. If Shelby or her fiancé had been Murphy residents for any length of time, he'd be a friend of at least one of them.

He walked toward her, his warm smile making her weak in the knees. She silently scolded herself. Even if he *was* interested in a romantic relationship, it would never work. If she couldn't hold on to him back then, what made her think she could hold on to him now? Or that she had what it took to keep any man's love? She hadn't been able to make her relationship with Phil last. Even with a marriage license.

When Bryce reached her, he was still smiling. It was more disarming up close.

"You outdid yourself. Everything looks great."

"Thank you." She was pleased with the effect. And she'd thoroughly enjoyed the process. Any doubts she'd had about whether she'd made the right decision had dissipated with her first job. The creativity that she'd been so sure was too deeply buried to resurrect had come charging to the surface like a geyser.

Bryce looked around the room. "Isn't Paige here? She'd said she was working with you."

"She went to the ladies' room."

The employee that usually helped with decorating jobs had gotten sick, but Paige was able to clear her schedule and step in last minute. Shelby had insisted that they both stay and enjoy the festivities. That wasn't typical. Usually, she'd clear out before the first guests arrived and come back when the event was over to tear down.

"So, are you a friend of the bride or the groom?"

"I know them both really well."

More guests arrived, and Andrea recognized several familiar faces. Tanner was on the guest list, as were Colton and Mandy. They'd apparently left Liam with a babysitter.

Soon the DJ stopped the music to tell everyone to take a seat. When Paige and Tanner sat on one side of her, and Mandy and Colton sat on the other, she tamped down disappointment. Bryce had taken a seat at the opposite end of another row rather than sitting with her. And why not? She wasn't the only friend he had.

The DJ cleared the guests to go through the buffet line, one long table at a time. Soon everyone had their food, and the hum of conversation rose against a background of love songs.

She'd just finished eating when the DJ stopped the music and called Bryce up. He hurried forward and grabbed the microphone.

"Is everyone having a good time?" Applause rose around her. "How's the food?" More applause, even louder.

What was Bryce doing up there? Was he the best man, ready to toast the groom-to-be? Had the man even arrived? If he had, Shelby hadn't introduced him.

"I want to start by asking a very special lady to join me up here."

Andrea nodded. That would be Shelby. They were apparently close.

"Andi Wheaton."

Her stomach rolled over and dropped several inches. She swiveled her head between Paige and Mandy. "Me?"

They both smiled. "Yes, you."

When she sat in stupefied silence, Paige gave her a little push. "Go."

Andrea rose from her chair and made her way to the front corner of the room. What was he doing?

She released a breath. He was going to recognize her for the decorations. Next he'd recognize the caterers.

When she reached him, he turned her to face the crowd and looped an arm over her shoulders, his other hand still holding the mic. "This is Andi Wheaton. Her business is Designs by Andi, formerly Designs by Angie. She's responsible for the decorations tonight."

The room filled with applause and whistles. Heat crept up her neck and into her cheeks. But Bryce was giving her free publicity. She'd take it.

When the applause died down, he dropped his arm from her shoulders and took her hand. "I first met Andi when we were about six and she and her dad came to visit. By age twelve, I started to realize girls were pretty cool and Andi was especially intriguing."

Some chuckles went around the room. Her cheeks were now on fire. What was Bryce doing? This wasn't about them. It was Shelby's party.

But Bryce continued. "By age fourteen, I was hope-lessly in love. At least as in love as one can be at that age." Some more chuckles. "At age fifteen, I realized she was in love with me, too, and we shared our first kiss."

Andrea closed her eyes. *Oh, God, please open a hole in the floor and let me disappear.* She was so going to kill Bryce when this was over.

She opened her eyes and sought out Shelby, who was sitting in the front row, next to a young man Andi was sure had to be her fiancé. He'd apparently slipped in after they'd gotten up to fill their plates.

If Shelby had a problem with Bryce horning in on her special night, she didn't show it. In fact, she wore a radiant smile.

Bryce continued, his tone somber. "When I turned eighteen, I lost her."

The room fell totally silent, so quiet there wasn't even a cough or rustle of clothing. Andrea clenched her teeth. She needed to put a stop to this before Bryce embarrassed her, or himself, any further.

"This is Shelby's party." She hissed the words, hoping they'd reach his ears but not the microphone. "Anything you have to say to me can wait."

Bryce ignored her. "Shelby, can you please come up here?"

If she couldn't stop him, maybe Shelby could. Maybe she'd throw him out. Maybe she'd throw them both out.

But she didn't look like someone ready to expel guests from her party. When she stepped up beside them, she was smiling even more broadly. Bryce's smile matched his friend's.

"Andi, meet my cousin, Shelby. My *married* cousin." He lifted her left hand, where both an engagement and wedding band circled her ring finger.

"But—" She looked from Shelby's hand to her face,

then back to Bryce, feeling like the only one not in on some practical joke. "If Shelby's already married, why are we here?"

Shelby gave her an apologetic smile. But there was too much joy behind it for the apology to look sincere. "Sorry. I'm afraid I got you here under false pretenses." After a playful wave, she walked back to her seat.

Andrea might have followed, but her brain was too stalled out for her to do more than stand dumbstruck. Bryce turned her toward him and took both of her hands in his. Instead of speaking to her, he angled his face to the crowd.

"I'm going to do something now that is more than ten years past due."

He dropped to one knee, still holding her hands. Now his eyes were on her and no one else. Her mind spun. Actually, everything else inside seemed to be spinning, too.

"Andrea Wheaton, I love you with all my heart. Will you do me the honor of marrying me?"

Her jaw sagged. "You're proposing here?"

He released one of her hands to sweep his arm wide, indicating all those looking on, the caterers standing against the wall behind the long buffet table, the decorations.

"This engagement party is yours. If you'll say yes."

The pieces tried to fall into place, but she was still having a hard time wrapping her mind around everything. Bryce had planned all this. The whole thing had been his idea. Not only had he spent a fortune on the elaborate party, he was risking humiliation in front of all his friends if she said no. He had to be seriously in love with her.

But what if it didn't last? What if someone better came along? Going through that kind of rejection again would destroy her.

He squeezed her hands, doubt creeping across his features. She'd waited too long. But how could she make a decision like that spur of the moment? Would she ever be ready to let down her guard?

He continued to stare up at her, emotion swimming in his golden-brown eyes. Had his gaze ever held that much love? Had Phil's? She didn't think so.

"You love me?" Her words were the merest whisper.

"More than you can imagine."

"Always and forever?"

"Always and forever."

She looked around the room. Bryce had proved his love for her in a dramatic way. How could she still question his commitment?

She couldn't.

She gave his hands a tug, a silent command to rise. When he was on his feet, she pulled her hands from his grasp. Uncertainty flashed in his eyes for only a moment, turning to relief, then pure joy, when she slid her arms around his neck. His encircled her waist.

"Yes." She turned her head toward the crowd and spoke more loudly. "Yes."

Once again, applause rang out, but this time it didn't die down for some time.

The first strains of "Always and Forever" filled the room, and the overhead lights went out, leaving only the strands of tiny white lights that she'd used in her decorating.

As Luther Vandross crooned the words in his smooth,

rich voice, Bryce began swaying to the music, and she fell into step with him.

He bent at the waist, mouth close to her ear. "Do you love me?"

"Yes."

"I want to hear you say it."

"I love you. I've been falling back in love with you bit by bit ever since I returned to Murphy. I think it started when I walked into your house and saw that you had my sketches proudly displayed. By the time you helped me set up the tree, and we were sitting side by side on the couch, a fire in the fireplace, I was hopeless."

"But you didn't let me kiss you."

"Because I was scared. I was scared of everything I was feeling for you and scared of being hurt."

He leaned close, his face inches from hers. "I don't want you to ever be afraid again."

No, she wouldn't. How could any doubts take up residence in her mind when he looked at her like that, as if she were the only thing in his life that he truly cherished?

He leaned closer still. He was going to kiss her, but this time she was ready.

His lips met hers. The awkwardness she should have felt knowing they had one hundred and fifty sets of eyes on them lasted all of three seconds. The DJ standing a few feet away, the party guests, the rows of tables—everything around her faded. It was just the two of them, her and this man she'd loved and then lost and then found again.

Warmth flowed through her, the sense of having come home. This was where she belonged. Right here in Murphy. In Bryce's arms.

When he pulled away, she almost protested. Her eyes met his, and the same adoration she'd seen earlier was shining from his face.

"You know when *I* started to love *you* again?"

"When?"

"I don't think I ever stopped."

He twirled her around and drew her closer. Her heart soared with the music.

Bryce loved her, and she loved him.

Always and forever.

With a love as big as the sky.

* * * * *

Mary Alford was inspired to become a writer after reading romantic suspense greats Victoria Holt and Phyllis A. Whitney. Soon, creating characters and throwing them into dangerous situations that tested their faith came naturally for Mary. In 2012 Mary entered the speed-dating contest hosted by Love Inspired Suspense and later received "the call." Writing for Love Inspired Suspense has been a dream come true for Mary.

Books by Mary Alford

Love Inspired Suspense

Forgotten Past
Rocky Mountain Pursuit
Deadly Memories
Framed for Murder
Standoff at Midnight Mountain
Grave Peril
Amish Country Kidnapping
Amish Country Murder

Visit the Author Profile page
at Harlequin.com for more titles.

GRAVE PERIL

Mary Alford

Before the mountains were brought forth,
or ever thou hadst formed the earth and the world,
even from everlasting to everlasting, thou art God.
—*Psalms* 90:2

To anyone facing an insurmountable mountain in their life. Know that God is with you through each step of the way.

ONE

The rain that had followed Jamie Hendricks from Louisville came down harder as she reached the Appalachians. The mountains had a way of attracting dramatic weather. Today was no different. Dark gray storm clouds gathered atop Darlan Mountain, obscuring it from view and spreading spindly fingers of fog throughout the valley below.

Still, even in the growing darkness, the beauty of the mountains drew Jamie in, filling her with memories that were mostly good…until she thought about that horrible day.

In spite of everything she'd done to deny it, this was home.

Yet nothing about this trip was the heartwarming homecoming she'd longed for throughout the years.

I know who killed Charles Dalton…

Her uncle's chilling words were her constant companion. She wouldn't be here now if it hadn't been for Uncle Paxton's call.

As soon as Jamie reached the sign for Darlan, Kentucky, at the city limits, she grabbed her cell phone. Once more, she tried to reach her uncle, like she had periodically since leaving Louisville. The lack of service surrounding the mountains did little to reassure her, and her uneasiness grew. Their last conversation dominated her thoughts, as did the fear she'd heard in his voice.

"Where are you, Uncle Paxton?" Frustrated, Jamie tossed the cell phone on the seat beside her.

As she drove down Main Street, the ugliness of the last year she'd spent here was everywhere around her. From Givens Grocery, where she'd first heard the whispers about her father's guilt from patrons of the store, to the cold stares she'd received from her classmates at Darlan High School at the end of the road. Her father had been convicted of killing Charles Dalton even before a jury of his peers passed judgment.

Losing her mother to cancer at five had been difficult, but watching her father being hauled away to prison for something he didn't do was devastating. An only child, Jamie and her father had become inseparable after her mother's death. Back then, she couldn't imagine her life without him in it.

It took everything inside Jamie not to turn the car around, ignore Uncle Paxton's concerns and head back to Louisville, where she'd tried to keep the past buried for so long.

Help me, Lord. I have to stay strong for my uncle.

Even though she was exhausted beyond belief, Jamie didn't make a single stop in town. Paxton needed her. She headed toward the county road that would lead up the mountainside to her family home, where he was waiting for her.

A part of her prayed Uncle Paxton had finally found the evidence needed to clear her father's name, while another part knew that, no matter what, the damage was written in stone. Her father's conviction had destroyed so many lives, Noah's included. And it had been the death knell for her future with Gavin.

As she headed up Darlan Mountain, the rain seemed determined to play its part in the story of her return, just as it had the day long ago when she'd left town, thinking it would be for good. Back then, it had been as if the skies themselves were weeping right along with Jamie.

Jamie switched the wipers to high as the downpour made it difficult to see. Fog descending from the mountaintop took away the rest of her visibility. It was as if she were driving blindfolded.

Growing up, there had been half a dozen families living up on the mountain. With the decline of coal mining in the county in recent times, that number had shrunk to only two.

Forced to slow the car's speed to a snail's crawl, Jamie passed the last house up the mountain before her family's home.

Don't look, her heart urged, yet Jamie couldn't help it. The Dalton home was dark save for a single light that appeared to be coming from the kitchen. Gavin was home, his reasons for returning to Darlan far worse than hers. He'd come back to bury his Grandmother Ava.

When Uncle Paxton first told Jamie about Ava's passing, she'd wanted to come home for the funeral, yet her last conversation with Gavin stood in the way. Ten years might have passed, but she hadn't been able to get those ugly parting words out of her head. She'd pleaded her father's innocence. Gavin hadn't believed her. Her seventeen-year-old heart had broken into a thousand pieces. In that same heart, Jamie had believed Gavin would not welcome her presence at Ava's funeral.

Edging around the side of the mountain, past the Dalton place, Jamie focused her entire attention on the limited view before her. Gavin was her past. She was here for her uncle.

Jamie barely cleared the curve when a set of head-lights suddenly appeared in her rearview mirror, taking her by surprise and temporarily blinding her. Up until now, she hadn't seen a single soul since she'd reached Darlan.

The lights continued to grow bigger as she squinted. The driver appeared to be speeding up, in spite of the road conditions. What was he thinking, going so fast around such a dangerous corner?

Beyond the Dalton place, her family home was the only other house up on the mountain, and yet the vehicle continued to come on strong.

By now, the driver should have seen her and slowed down.

I know who killed Charles Dalton... Her last phone conversation with Uncle Paxton inserted itself into her thoughts, unwelcome.

In the driver's-side mirror, she was able to make out what appeared to be a monstrous SUV mirroring her every move. It wasn't Uncle Paxton's vehicle. He drove a truck.

Someone was following her.

Jamie reached for her cell phone again. But the service was nonexistent, and she wasn't sure who she would try to call. Paxton wasn't picking up, and the text message he'd sent soon after their final conversation warned her not to trust anyone from the sheriff's department.

Fear slithered into the pit of her stomach. She was on her own.

The vehicle quickly closed the space between them to within a few feet of her car, and the lights turned on bright. The driver was deliberately trying to intimidate her.

Jamie struggled to shut down the panic. If she wanted to survive, she'd have to figure a way out of this.

Uncle Paxton's worried declaration continued to niggle at her thoughts: *I'm in real trouble, Jamie. I know who killed Charles Dalton, and because of it they're coming after me!*

What had her uncle uncovered that had sent him into such a panic, and how was it connected to the person tailing her now?

Jamie moved as close to the edge of the road as safely possible, hoping she'd misunderstood the driver's intent and the vehicle would try to pass. It continued right on her bumper. She increased her speed. The SUV did the same. This was no misunderstanding.

If what Uncle Paxton said were true, his life could be in danger.

Red Plume Lane was just up ahead. If she could make it there, she could turn around and head back down the mountain. Hopefully get away before the driver tried something lethal. She didn't dare take Red Plume, as it dead-ended not too far past the intersection.

Jamie's hands tightened on the wheel. She spotted the road up on her left.

Please, Lord, help me...

It was now or never. With all her strength, Jamie whipped the steering wheel to her left and spun the car around, sliding on the wet road and almost losing control.

Somehow, she managed to keep the car from slipping off the road. Once it was straightened out, Jamie floored the gas and peered in her rearview mirror. She caught a glimpse of the vehicle turning around. The SUV was coming after her still. The other vehicle's powerful engine raced closer. There was only one option left. If she could reach Gavin's house, she knew—no matter what their past might be—he would help her.

Jamie watched in horror as the SUV lurched forward, its headlights growing huge before it rammed into the back of her car, throwing her forward.

She clutched the wheel tightly to keep the car from veering off the road. Her heart flew into her throat. The driver was deliberately trying to run her off the road.

Even with the gas pedal on the floor, her car was no match for the powerful SUV. Before her brain had time to process what to do next, the vehicle smashed into her again, this time harder than before. Her head slammed against the steering wheel. For a second, Jamie thought she would black out.

Her car swerved to the left and spun around. She fought to keep it on the road, but her efforts were futile as the car plunged nose first into the rain-filled ditch and the world around her blurred.

While Jamie held on to consciousness by a thread, she was vaguely aware of the SUV rolling to a stop beside her. The driver's door opened and she saw a man in khaki pants heading her way.

With her heart pouring adrenaline through her body, Jamie squeezed her eyes closed. If she pretended to be unconscious, maybe he wouldn't hurt her.

The man stopped next to her and opened the door. He leaned down. She could feel him studying her and was terrified he'd finish what he started and kill her right then and there.

"She's out cold. Check the back. Maybe she has some of it with her." He hit the trunk button and Jamie could hear it opening.

"There's nothing here," a second man said, then closed the trunk with a slam. "Doesn't look like he was ever with her. He's still out there somewhere. We'd better find him and the stuff before *he* arrives."

The man hovering over her still hadn't moved. Was he debating whether or not to kill her?

"Let her be. We don't need the hassle of covering up another murder. She didn't see anything, and we need to get out of here. There's a house down the mountain. They could have heard the noise."

After what felt like a lifetime, the man near her finally spoke. "Yeah, well, I hope you're right about that because I know her."

It took everything inside of Jamie not to react to those terrifying words. She thought she recognized the man's voice. He pretty much confirmed it.

While she kept as still as her heart would allow, the man finally moved away. With her eyes shut tight, she heard the SUV turn around and head up the mountain. They were going to her house!

We don't need the hassle of covering up another murder. They'd killed someone else. Her thoughts went to Gavin's father. Were these the men responsible for killing Charles? If so, then they were going after Uncle Paxton now.

Even with the noise of the engine fading in the distance, Jamie was terrified to move. It was the thought of what would happen when those two came back and decided to finish the job that finally forced her into action. She had to get out of there. Had to find Paxton.

Slowly, she opened her eyes. Her head ached. The world around her spun and her stomach threatened to heave. Squeezing her eyes closed, she waited until everything stopped spinning.

Smoke billowed from the wasted engine of her car. She was stranded out here on this secluded stretch of road, and she had no idea when her attackers might return.

As she struggled to free herself from the seatbelt, she felt blood oozing from a gash on her forehead. Her body ached from the jarring impact of the vehicle slamming into her.

Once she'd freed herself, Jamie grabbed her cell phone and scrambled out of the car. She fought to keep from passing out as she waded through the almost knee-deep water in the ditch up to the road.

The isolation of the area was far worse than she remembered. Her home was still a good mile up. With the vehicle out of commission, there was only one option left. She'd have to walk out.

The no-service indicator on her phone did little to ease her mind. Without knowing what those men would do to her when they came back down the mountain, she couldn't risk keeping to the road. She had to stay out of sight.

While she thought about her best route to stay hidden, another set of headlights rounded the bend in the road some distance down from her. Someone else was coming!

Jamie's heart slammed against her chest. She searched the surrounding darkness for somewhere to hide. The mountainside was covered in trees. She raced across the road and into the woods there.

The vehicle continued to advance at a much slower pace than the one following her. As she watched, a beat-up truck came to a stop behind her car. She couldn't see who was driving, and until she knew who it was, she wasn't about to come out of hiding.

It took a second for Jamie to regain her bearings. As a child, she'd played in these woods and knew them all by heart. As much as the idea of going to Gavin for help didn't appeal to her, there was no doubt that she needed it. Those men had been looking for Paxton and something else. He'd told her he'd be waiting for her at the house. If those men found him there, she couldn't imagine what they'd do to him.

Gavin Dalton pulled up as close behind the wrecked car as he could get, his headlights on bright. It sat nose first in a ditch, filled with water up to the floorboards. Smoke plumed from its engine. The driver's door stood open. It didn't look as if anyone was inside. Where had the driver gone?

Today of all days, this was the last thing he needed. He'd heard the noise that sounded like vehicles colliding up the mountain, and his conscience wouldn't let him not go to render aid.

Barring the day he'd buried his father, today had been the worst day of his life. He'd had to say goodbye to his beloved Grandmother Ava. Even after seeing her in the casket, he still couldn't believe his rock was gone. She'd practically raised him. He'd never really known his mother, since she'd died when he was still a baby, right up here on this same mountain. Her car had run off the road one winter's day. It had been just Gavin, his dad and Ava for as long as he could remember.

When he got the call that Ava had passed, it had floored him. Ava had suffered a massive heart attack while sitting out back on her favorite bench, no doubt watching the sunset over Darlan Mountain, as she had for going on seventy years.

Gavin had been doing the same thing minutes earlier when he'd heard the crash.

As a CIA agent, he'd seen a lot of bad things. His instincts just naturally veered toward trouble. Turned out, this time he was right.

While he continued to stare at the wreckage before him, he noticed something that didn't jibe with the car ending up in the ditch of its own accord. The back bumper was crumpled in several spots. It appeared someone had deliberately forced it off the road. He scanned the area. His concern for the missing driver doubled.

Always lend a hand, Gavin. Mountain folk look out for one another. He could almost hear his grandmother reminding him of this. Ava had lived that creed throughout her life. *She* never once failed to lend a hand when someone was in need.

Even though he'd been gone for ten years, he understood why Ava had loved this place so much. It was in her blood. His, too. This was one of the reasons it was so hard to think about selling her home. Still, now that she was gone, he couldn't imagine living there, and his job as a member of the CIA specialized antiterrorist unit known as the Scorpions took him out of the country for months at a time.

Excuses…all of them. The real reason he didn't want to hold on to the house was that he saw his father everywhere around the place. The brutal way Charles Dalton's life had been taken from him would forever mar Gavin's memories of life on the mountain. Shot to death by his best friend and business partner.

And so he'd come to a difficult decision. He planned to get in touch with the local real estate agent the next day. Put the house on the market and see what happened.

Now, as he took in the extent of damage to the car, he realized there was a good chance that whoever was driving the vehicle had been injured.

With that disturbing thought still ringing in his head, Gavin grabbed his flashlight and got out, clicking the light on. Tucking his service weapon behind his back, he waded into the water and slowly eased to the open door.

As he approached, the empty driver's seat confirmed that no one was inside. He shone the flashlight into the back seat. There was a suitcase and what looked like a laptop bag. In the passenger's seat, a purse. The sight increased his unease. Why would the driver leave her identification behind?

Gavin pulled out the wallet tucked inside the purse. The name on the driver's license froze him in place and sent his heart back in time. Jamie Hendricks. The car in question belonged to his high school sweetheart. The woman he'd once loved with all his heart.

He glanced frantically around. Where was she?

Jamie wouldn't have simply walked off for help without taking her purse or locking the car up with her belongings inside. He flashed the light around, yet there was no sign she might have been thrown from the car.

What if Jamie been taken against her will by the driver of the second vehicle? His gut clenched at the thought.

He remembered his grandmother telling him about how much the crime rate had increased over the past ten years in Darlan due to the flood of drugs rolling through the community.

Gavin whispered a prayer for a safe outcome, then went into action.

"Jamie!" he yelled as loud as he could, hoping she could hear him if she was still close by. His voice echoed down into the valley below. "Jamie, it's Gavin Dalton!"

Across the road, something rustled in the bushes. It could be a wild animal. Hogs were everywhere around these hollers. He homed the flashlight in on the direction of the noise and saw movement.

With his heart wrenching like crazy, he yelled, "Put your hands in the air and show yourself before I shoot! Now!"

He kept the flashlight focused on the parting bushes as someone—a woman—emerged. She squinted as the light hit her eyes. One hand went up to shield them.

It had been ten years since he'd last seen her, but he'd thought about her—and what might have been—just about every day of his life.

Seeing her now felt almost surreal. He couldn't believe Jamie was back in Darlan and that someone had run her into the ditch.

She ran across the road and into his arms. He could feel her shivering in reaction to what had just taken place, as well as to the chill of the night air.

Time melted away as he held her tighter. She still felt the same in his arms as she had all those years ago. They'd been so close once. He'd planned to ask her to marry him the summer before they were both scheduled to leave for university.

And then *that* day happened. His world had changed forever when her father killed his. Their life together and the future he'd once envisioned for them had splintered into a million pieces. A chasm stood between them that was impossible to breach. For the first time in their lives, they'd stood on opposite sides of something.

Gavin pulled himself together and moved a little away so that he could get a good look at her. Even terrified, she was still the prettiest girl he'd ever known. Her normally sparkling green eyes reflected the horror of what she'd gone through tonight.

She had a bloody gash on her forehead. Clumps of her golden-brown hair were matted into it.

Jamie drew in a breath and took a step back, as if realizing what she'd done. Gavin let her go. The lethal past was firmly in place between them once again.

"I was scared they were coming back again. Gavin, someone ran me off the road." Her voice shook. He didn't doubt for a second how terrifying the experience had been.

"You're hurt." His immediate attention went to her injury. He examined the gash gently with his fingertips and couldn't keep the anger from his tone. Someone had tried to harm her, and he had no idea why.

She drew in a shaky breath and pulled away from his touch. "No, I'm fine. It just scared me."

"Jamie, you're not. That looks like it needs stiches."

He indicated the wound, but she shook her head, trying to play the injury down.

"I'll be fine. It looks worse than it is."

While he doubted it, he knew it was pointless to argue. Jamie could be stubborn when she wanted to.

"I heard the crash from my place. What happened?"

She was shaking so much that it appeared to be a struggle to get words to come out. "I'm not sure. I was driving home when an SUV came out of nowhere. I thought it was just some kids playing around until they forced me off the road."

He didn't want to believe she'd been deliberately targeted in such a frightening way. "Are you sure it was on purpose? The road is wet. It's hard to see with the rain and the fog."

She waved his theory away. "I'm positive. Gavin, they were inches from my bumper the whole time. When I tried to turn around and get to your place, they rammed my car twice. The last time I lost control, and that's when I was run off the road by two men."

He frowned at her answer. It was not the one he'd wanted to hear. "Did you get a good look at the vehicle?"

She shook her head. "Not really. It happened so fast. I know it was an SUV and that it was big. And I think it was black or maybe dark brown."

It wasn't much to go on. "After you crashed in the ditch, did the SUV keep going?" He hadn't heard the vehicle drive past his house.

She hesitated, sending a bunch of alarm signals up for him. "Yes. They're heading up to my house."

He stared at her, trying to understand the meaning.

"Why would they be heading to your house…?" Then it finally clicked. "Where's Paxton?"

"He's supposed to meet me there. Gavin, we have to help him. I'm afraid they'll hurt him."

His thoughts reeled. Why had someone tried to hurt her or Paxton? "What's Paxton gotten himself involved in this time?" Gavin couldn't keep the hard edge from his tone.

"I wish I knew." She didn't look at him, leaving him with the impression she wasn't telling the whole story. Jamie didn't trust him. That hurt to consider.

His mouth tightened in revulsion as he thought about how bad the outcome of the wreck could have been.

"What aren't you telling me, Jamie? There's no way what happened to you here doesn't involve one of Paxton's harebrained theories in some way."

She finally faced him, her defiance clear. "I told you I don't know anything, so will you help me or not?"

Before he could answer, the noise of another vehicle coming up the mountain interrupted their conversation.

Jamie turned frightened eyes to him. "What if it's connected to the other vehicle? We have to get out of here now."

She was right. Standing on the side of the road like this, they were exposed, sitting targets. Together, they hurried back to his truck. Before they had the chance to get inside, red and blue lights flashed behind them.

Relief swept through Gavin. "It's okay. It's the sheriff."

Yet, instead of relaxing, Jamie appeared more panicked. She shook her head. "No, Gavin, we have to get out of here now. Uncle Paxton warned me not to trust anyone at the sheriff's office."

Hearing her uncle's claims, Gavin's distrust grew. Paxton had been on a mission to prove his brother hadn't killed Charles ever since the man had been convicted of the crime. When Noah died of miner's lung two years into his life sentence, Paxton's efforts had gone into overdrive. He'd even enlisted his good friend, Gavin's grandmother, Ava Dalton, in the hunt for evidence.

Before Gavin had time to ask why Paxton didn't trust the sheriff's office, the patrol vehicle chirped its siren once then pulled alongside the truck.

Gavin grabbed her hand and squeezed it. "Let me handle this."

The passenger window came down. A shockwave rolled through Gavin upon identifying the man sitting inside the white police SUV. Andy Lawson was the last person Gavin would have expected to be elected sheriff of Darlan County, in spite of the fact that his father had once held the position.

He and Andy had gone through their entire school years together. Andy was a borderline juvenile delinquent whose father had had to bail him out of trouble throughout most of his high school years. Gavin couldn't imagine how this man had become sheriff, except on his father's merits.

Andy seemed about as shocked to see Gavin. "Gavin Dalton? I heard you were back in town. Sorry to hear about your grandmother. She was a great gal."

"Thanks, man." Gavin somehow got the words out. He knew good and well Andy and his grandmother had never gotten along. Ava had been very vocal about Andy's lack of discipline and had spoken to his father about it on numerous occasions.

At one time, the Lawsons lived on the mountain before moving to town. Their property backed onto to Ava's. When Gavin was younger, Ava had run cattle on that part of the place. Through the years, several head had gone missing. Ava was convinced Andy had had something to do with it. Gavin and his dad were inclined to agree, but without hard proof tying Andy to the missing cattle, there had been no way to prove it.

Andy looked past Gavin and spotted Jamie. "I didn't see you there, Jamie. I had no idea you were back in town, too. Is this your car? Looks like you had a doozy of a wreck. Are you hurt?"

Gavin could feel Jamie's unease growing. She managed to shake her head. "No, I'm fine."

"What happened here?" Andy asked, still without even looking at the car. Immediately, his lack of interest in the car's obvious damage garnered Gavin's concern. As far as he could tell, the man hadn't given it more than a cursory glance. As a sheriff, it was an odd way to investigate an accident. Unless he already knew about what happened and was checking to see if Jamie was still alive?

"It was my fault, I'm afraid." Gavin jumped in with a made-up explanation to get Andy's attention off Jamie. "I accidently hit Jamie. I was taking a ride up the mountain when I came to the bend. I guess I was going a little too fast for the road conditions, and I tagged her."

"Have you talked to Paxton lately?" Andy's immediate change of subject surprised them both.

Jamie edged closer to Gavin. "No…why?"

"No reason," Andy answered a little too quickly. "I just had a few more questions for him since he was the one who found Ava after she died." He frowned.

"Why are you back in Darlan, anyway? Did you come for the funeral?"

Jamie quickly grasped at the excuse he'd provided. "Yes, that's right."

Gavin wasn't surprised that Andy hadn't been at his grandmother's funeral, considering their past relationship, but neither Jamie nor Paxton had attended, either. Not that he could blame Jamie after the way things ended between them. Still, Paxton had been a good friend of Ava's. Unless he hadn't been able to attend because he'd gotten himself into trouble.

Andy accepted her answer without questioning it. "Well, if you see him, tell him I'd like to have a word. You need me to call a tow truck to get you out of the ditch?"

Something was definitely off with Andy's way of handling the whole situation, and Gavin was anxious to get rid of him. "No, that's okay. I'll give Marty a call and have him pull it out for Jamie."

After another suspicious look, Andy nodded. "Alright, then. If you two don't need me, I'm heading home. My shift just ended a little while ago. I was at the end of the road by the intersection when I heard the ruckus up here and decided to come check it out. Glad I did. You need a ride to your house, Jamie? I'd be happy to give you a lift. That way I can check in with Paxton. Get the answers I need and then be on my way."

"You can't," Jamie said in a rush, then amended her answer when Andy appeared more suspicious. "What I mean is, he's not home. He went to Jamesville for a few days to gather supplies for the mine."

"You don't say… That was kind of sudden, wasn't

it?" Andy scowled at her answer. He'd come just short of calling her a liar.

Gavin stepped in. "I can give Jamie a ride. You're on your way home, and since Paxton's not there, anyway, it would be a wasted trip." He'd seen that Andy knew Jamie wasn't telling him the truth. Would he push to go to her house? If so, Gavin wasn't about to let Jamie head up there alone with Andy.

"Suit yourself," Andy mumbled, finally ending the silent standoff. "Have Paxton call me when you talk to him, you hear?"

Jamie nodded.

Andy put the vehicle in gear and gave them a two-finger salute before making a U-turn in the middle of the road to head back down the mountain.

Once he was gone, Jamie let out a huge sigh. "I don't trust him for a minute. He was definitely fishing for something." She looked as pale as a sheet.

Gavin had a dozen different questions running though his mind. "Why does Andy need to talk to Paxton so urgently? I spoke to the coroner. Ava had a heart attack, and that caused her death. Even though Paxton found her, what questions could he possibly still have?" He watched Jamie closely. "Did Paxton tell you anything else about my grandmother's death?"

She appeared frazzled by the events of the evening. "No, only that Ava had died and he was the one who found her."

None of it added up in Gavin's mind. Why was the sheriff so concerned with finding Paxton?

His gaze narrowed. As far as he knew, Jamie hadn't been home once since she'd left, with the exception of attending her father's funeral.

"What else did Paxton say to get you to come back here? It had to be big." There was no disguising the bitterness in his tone. He couldn't help it. Her sudden exit from his life had been eating at him for years.

The way things had ended between them after the trial, well, it had been devastating for him as well as her. Gavin knew he was mostly to blame for it. He'd been grieving for his father while Jamie kept insisting that Noah was innocent. He hadn't been able to handle it any longer and lost his temper. Told her he didn't believe her. That he'd never believe her. It had been the end of them. He'd always regretted saying that to her. Even though it was the truth, it added yet another wedge between them that made it impossible to overcome. He'd hoped that once things settled, he and Jamie could work things out. That hadn't happened.

The tears in her eyes as she'd looked at him still haunted him. That had been the last time he saw her, standing in front of her family home, begging him to believe her.

Jamie left town without so much as a word, and his future happiness crumbled around him.

He'd moved away shortly afterward, to attend university, and then later joined the CIA. They'd both left Darlan behind, and now the only family member tying him here was gone.

Like Jamie's Uncle Paxton, his grandmother had never believed Noah Hendricks murdered her son. She'd gone along with every single one of Paxton's crazy ideas to clear Noah's name, much to Gavin's dismay. It was about the only thing he and his grandmother had ever argued about. In Gavin's mind, there had been no other explanation. Noah had shot his father when he found out Charles was thinking of selling the mine he owned to a large corporation.

Jamie didn't look at him when she answered. "He said he had finally found proof that would exonerate my father of killing Charles. I know what you're thinking, but this time there was something in his voice." She intercepted his disbelieving look. "I can feel it, Gavin. This time I believe he really knows who killed your father."

Gavin ran his hand across the back of his neck. "Jamie, we both know who killed my dad. Just because Paxton and you can't accept it doesn't mean it isn't true."

She squared her shoulders and took him on, arguing her case. "Your grandmother didn't believe Noah was capable of killing Charles. Your own grandmother."

He'd heard enough. "Jamie, a jury of Noah's peers convicted him of the crime, remember?" When tears filled her eyes, he regretted his outburst. "Look, I'm sorry it happened. I loved your dad. He was like family...until, well, you know. And I'm sorry he had to pass away in prison like that. I can't imagine how that was for him and for you. But it's time both Paxton and you let go of this vendetta and got on with your lives. Before what Noah did that day poisons what's left of them."

TWO

No matter what the jury had said, Jamie would never believe the kind and gentle man she remembered her father being would ever be capable of harming his good friend Charles.

She choked back old memories from childhood. Her father used to read her stories from the Bible each night before she went to sleep. Even when her mother was still alive, the bedtime Bible reading was *their* time together. Her father was a Godly man. Noah never once missed a church service, and was a deacon for most of his adult life. Noah Hendricks went out of his way to help anyone in need.

So it didn't matter what the jury declared or what Gavin chose to believe; Noah and Charles had been much closer than friends. They'd been like brothers. And Noah would never hurt his brother.

Yet it was pointless to have this ugly conversation with Gavin again. They'd gone over it a dozen times in the past. She'd pled her father's cause with all her heart, and Gavin hadn't believed her.

The anger simmering in his eyes told her nothing had changed. But Gavin had. He'd left here a sweet young boy who'd stolen her heart. The man standing before her now had a hard edge about him.

He was still as handsome as ever, with straight blond hair that touched the collar of his shirt. A good six inches taller than she was, Gavin had been a star athlete in high school. He still looked as if he could run a football.

Jamie forced her straying thoughts back to the moment. "Uncle Paxton could be in real trouble by now."

Gavin blew out a frustrated-sounding sigh. "Come on. Let's get you inside the truck where it's warm." He reached for her arm, but she shook him off. "Jamie, I'm not letting you walk into what could prove to be a dangerous situation. I'll take you to my house where you can warm up, and then I'll go and check on Paxton." He headed for the driver's side of the truck, but she didn't budge. Gavin turned back. "Jamie…"

There was no way she was going anywhere but to look for Paxton. "I'm going home. Paxton needs me. If you won't take me there, then I'll walk."

He stared at her as if she'd lost her mind. "Jamie, it's a good mile up the mountain still."

She lifted her chin. "Will you take me home, or do I walk?" Staring up at the man she'd once thought she would spend the rest of her life with, she realized how young and naive she'd been back then. So foolish. Or maybe it was just a matter of their circumstances simply being too much for them to overcome.

Gavin's blond hair was soaked through, as was the Stetson that looked like the same one he'd owned ten years ago. There were lines that hadn't been there on the younger Gavin's face, but the velvet-brown eyes were still the same, and when he looked at her, she could almost picture the old Gavin. Her Gavin. The carefree one who always caused her heart to do a little somersault.

"Okay, I'll take you," he bit out, clearly not happy with the turn of events. "I'll go get your things from the car and then I'll take you home." He'd always called her stubborn when she was standing up for something she believed in. Especially when it was something they disagreed on.

It was that same stubbornness that had seen her through to becoming a criminal defense attorney and pursuing her passion of working to help those wrongfully convicted…like Noah. Her father was right there with her through each new case she took on.

Gavin waited until she had gotten into the truck before slamming the door a little harder than necessary.

She watched him tramp down the damp road then wade into the ditch to get her things. He'd changed a lot since she'd been gone. Grown up. Matured.

He grabbed her purse from the front seat and then took out her bag and laptop and headed back to the truck.

Opening the rear door, he placed her things inside, took off his hat, then got behind the wheel.

"I'll call Marty Roberts when we get service. He can tow your car out of the ditch and get it home for you tomorrow. Maybe he can recommend a good repair shop in town."

"Thanks," she said and managed a smile. She could almost hear the remorse in his voice. Did he regret his earlier outburst?

She wondered if Gavin had kept in touch with Marty or any of his high school friends after he left town.

Somehow, she doubted it. Like her, Gavin had cut ties, keeping his contact limited to only Ava.

Their gazes locked. After a moment he smiled, and her breath stuck in her throat. She'd forgotten how much she loved that smile.

"What's on your mind?" he asked when she continued to stare at him, mesmerized. Her heart drummed like crazy. Memories, both good and bad, gathered in her mind. The way things had ended with Gavin stunted her ability to form any lasting relationships. Jamie had thrown herself into her work, each new case taking a little bit more of her soul. The injustice she'd seen was heartbreaking.

One case, in particular, still haunted her. It was the first one she'd ever worked, an elderly man accused of killing his wife. The man had already served thirty years in prison when she found him. Jamie and her team worked hard to get him exonerated and gain his freedom. He'd died a few days later.

Jamie looked away and cleared her throat. "Nothing. I was just thinking about Ava. I'm sorry, Gavin. She was a sweet woman, and I loved her a bunch. She'll be missed."

Through the years, Jamie had kept in touch with Ava, who had been like a grandmother to her, as well. The only subject that she refused to discuss with the elderly woman was her grandson. It had taken a couple of phone calls before Ava finally relented on that topic. Still, she always insisted that Gavin loved Jamie, that she just needed to give him time to recover from the loss of his father.

But there had been one thing that Ava didn't know.

Jamie hadn't had the courage to tell her about her last conversation with Gavin.

"Thanks," Gavin managed by way of an answer and returned his focus to the road ahead.

Jamie recalled how Ava had practically raised him, with Charles and Noah spending so much time at the coal mine trying to make it a success. She couldn't even imagine how hard Ava's death had been for him.

Because of the details of her grandson's life that Ava had dropped into their numerous conversations, Jamie knew Gavin had joined the CIA. He was fighting terror. Ava was so proud of her grandson.

"How long are you staying in Darlan?" she asked when he didn't make an effort to say anything more.

He glanced her way again, some of the hardness leaving his face. "Not long. I'm just settling Ava's affairs. I'll be putting her house up for sale, and then I'm heading back to Colorado." His voice was rough with emotion. She could see how hard this decision had been for him.

It tore at Jamie's heart to think of someone else living in Ava's home, but mostly because if Gavin was selling the place, it meant he was leaving town for good this time. That hurt like crazy. Part of her had always hoped there would be a second chance for them in the future, even though her life was in Louisville and his was in Colorado. She wanted to cry for the younger Jamie, whose heart had been torn beyond repair.

Somehow, she'd let go of the pain. She had no right to blame him for moving on. After all, she'd done the same. Jamie hadn't been back to Darlan since her father's funeral. The only time she saw Paxton was when he came to visit her in Louisville.

Besides, Gavin was her past. Her future was the law. She'd devoted herself to righting the wrongs of the justice system because she couldn't bear for another innocent person to die in prison like her father had.

When she couldn't think of a single thing to say to fill the silence, she turned her focus to her last conversation with her uncle. There had been something in Uncle Paxton's voice. She'd never heard him sound so afraid before.

He'd told her he knew who killed Charles, and yet when she'd questioned him about it, he'd refused to talk over the phone. Instead, he'd begged her to come home. Said he needed her. Had he been afraid of someone listening in on his conversations? Someone from the sheriff's office, maybe?

Gavin rounded the final bend and her house appeared off to the right of the dead end. Not a single light was on in the place. Uncle Paxton had promised to be here, yet his truck was nowhere in sight. Neither was the SUV that had run her into the ditch. Where had those men gone? There was no other way down the mountain except the road they'd come up or cross-country.

The rainy night kept the moon and the stars from providing light. The isolation of the area sent a chill speeding down her spine.

Gavin stopped the truck in front of the house and stared up at its darkness.

"I thought you said Paxton was meeting you here. Where's his truck? And where is the vehicle that ran you off the road? I don't like it, Jamie. Something's wrong." Gavin scanned the surrounding countryside. "The men in the SUV must have gone cross-country."

Was Paxton with them, or had he managed to escape?

Gavin put the truck in Reverse.

"What are you doing? We can't leave," she said in a panic when he backed out of the drive. "We have to find him."

He pointed to the opposite side of the road. "We need to get this truck out of sight. After what happened to you and our run-in with Andy Lawson, I don't like being out in the open like this."

Gavin slowly pulled the truck into the woods so it was out of sight and yet they still faced the house.

Once he'd parked, he stared up at the house with the same worry written on his face that she knew was on hers.

"Give me a second to check things out, then I'll come get you when I know it's clear." When she didn't respond, he looked over at her. "Jamie?"

Jamie couldn't answer because something alarming had caught her attention. A light in the woods close by. "What is that?" She pointed to it. Was it Paxton roaming the woods, hurt, or was it something far more deadly? Maybe it was the men who'd run her off the road, searching for Paxton.

She could see the uneasy set of Gavin's jaw. "Stay here while I go check it out," he said in a clipped tone. "Make sure you lock the door, and don't open it for anything or anybody. I'll be right back." Gavin got out of the truck. It was then that she noticed the gun he'd tucked inside the waist of his jeans.

He started to shut the door and suddenly the seriousness of the situation hit home and Jamie was afraid for him. She grabbed his arm. He stopped. Looked into her eyes. Her chest grew tight. She couldn't say what she really wanted to. Couldn't bring the past up again.

"Be careful." She breathed a little unsteadily. Their eyes held for a moment longer. She'd have given anything to know what he was thinking right then.

He slowly nodded and closed the door, waiting for her to lock it before he hurried away.

Jamie stared up at the house that had been her home for so long. Where was Uncle Paxton? And why was the sheriff so determined to speak with him?

Her thoughts churned with all the unanswered questions. The man in the SUV knew her. She'd recognized his voice. But trying to make sense out of something that was beyond her understanding without talking to Paxton was useless.

The darkness of the house was alarming. A disturbing thought came to her. What if Uncle Paxton was hurt inside? Maybe he'd hidden his truck somewhere and hiked in, worried that someone might be watching the place. If the men had gone inside and found him... She didn't want to think about what might have happened.

Ignoring Gavin's warning to stay in the truck, Jamie opened the door and got out.

She hadn't set foot inside her childhood home since her father's funeral. The dark windows and lack of light coming from inside sent chills down her spine and did little to ease her fears.

Jamie kept replaying her last conversation with her uncle. Paxton had been frantic. After ten years of searching for evidence to clear Noah of murder, Paxton believed he'd located it. Why now, after so long?

She'd lost track of the numerous theories her uncle had come up with through the years. But this time felt different. What happened on the road back there seemed to back up the feeling.

Jamie continued to stare up at her old home as the rain soaked through her jacket and into her bones. Up here in the Appalachian Mountains, night came quickly and thoroughly. There was no light to keep the darkness at bay, making it hard to see your hand in front of you.

Her foot had just cleared the first step when Jamie noticed something she hadn't before. The front door stood ajar. Unease scurried down her spine. She could still hear the fear in her uncle's voice when he'd called to beg her to come home.

"Uncle Paxton, are you in there?" Jamie called out. The only answer was the familiar noises of the mountains. Locusts chirped. Somewhere close by an owl hooted. She could no longer hear Gavin moving through the woods. How long had he been gone? Was he in trouble?

The usually breathtaking night sky was obscured by clouds. The dampness of the mountains sent chill bumps up her arms.

She grabbed her cell phone. This time, the phone picked up enough service for her to make the call. She dialed her uncle's number. Inside the house, Paxton's phone rang and then went to voicemail. Paxton never went anywhere without his phone.

Jamie's feet felt glued in place. Something was wrong.

She needed God's strength to push her legs into motion. Her uncle could be hurt.

With her prayer for courage chilling the night air, her heart thundered as each creaky step took her up to the gaping door.

Drawing in a deep breath, Jamie pushed the door the rest of the way open. She swallowed back fear and stepped inside. The house was pitch black, but what she could make out scared the daylights out of her. The room was in complete disarray. Furniture was turned over. All the drawers on her father's old antique desk stood open. Some had been pulled out completely.

Someone had ransacked the house. They'd been looking for something.

Jamie tried the light switch. Nothing happened. The power was off. Was it just a coincidence—or something more?

"Uncle Paxton, where are you?" she yelled one more time, knowing it was pointless. Her uncle wasn't here. Whether by his own will or someone else's, he was gone.

She spotted his phone lying on the floor and picked it up. The last call he'd made was to her, hours earlier.

Apprehension filled the pit of her stomach, and she looked nervously around the place. She'd been foolish to come here alone, going against Gavin's warning. Now she was on her own, and someone had obviously been here recently.

Jamie headed for the door, the hair on her arms standing at attention, the need to run overwhelming. She'd barely gotten halfway across the living room when someone grabbed her from behind, restraining her in a vice grip. Jamie screamed and clawed at the man's arm, but it was pointless. She was no match for his strength. He clamped a hand over her mouth to silence her.

Behind her, what sounded like a scuffle took place, then another man grabbed Paxton's phone, which she still clutched in her hand. "I've got *his* phone. Let's get him out of here now," she heard the man say. It was the same voice from earlier!

The man restraining her shoved her away hard. She stumbled forward. Before she could regain her footing, something smashed against her temple.

Jamie dropped to the floor, disoriented. The last thought she had before she lost consciousness was that she was here alone, and something bad had happened to her uncle.

In the distance, Gavin picked up the noise of what sounded like a four-wheeler's engine firing. The light he'd been following for a quarter of a mile disappeared, returning the mountain to its previous darkness.

Did it belong to someone out hunting, or was it connected to what had happened to Jamie earlier? He didn't believe in coincidences this big. Whoever was out here was up to no good.

Gavin headed for the last place he'd seen the light. The house behind him was still dark. Jamie had expected Paxton to be waiting for her there. Part of Gavin prayed that this would turn out to be just another one of Paxton's ridiculous theories.

Out of the corner of his eye, he caught movement. Gavin whirled in that direction, his flashlight in one hand, his weapon in the other. "Don't move or I'll shoot!"

A man he didn't recognize froze where he stood. Gavin kept the light aimed in his eyes as he moved closer. The man squinted against the brightness, but did as asked and stood motionless.

"What are you doing up here?" Gavin asked without lowering his weapon.

The man hesitated, no doubt trying to come up with a believable answer.

"Nothing. I was just doing some squirrel hunting. This type of weather is perfect for it. Can you lower the light and the weapon, buddy? I'd hate to get shot for no reason."

Gavin didn't buy his story for a second, and he sure wasn't prepared to lower his gun until he knew what the man was up to.

"Oh, yeah? Well, you're on private property. Did you get permission from the owner to be out here?" Gavin knew the answer already.

The man appeared sheepish. "No, sir, I didn't. But I figured the owner wouldn't mind if I rustled up a little food for the table."

Gavin noticed that the man didn't have a shotgun with him, but he caught sight of a bulge beneath his jacket. "What do you know about what happened down the road tonight?"

The man grew visibly ill at ease at the mention of the wreck. He edged closer to Gavin.

"That's far enough," Gavin warned.

The man stopped dead in his tracks. "I don't know what you're talking about. Look, I'm sorry to be hunting on your property and all. It won't happen again." He turned to leave through the woods behind him, but Gavin put a stop to it.

"Not so fast." In the distance, a single gunshot reverberated through the night. The man stopped dead. Gavin flashed his light in the direction of the shot. Nothing moved.

"Who else is out here with you?" Gavin demanded. When the man made no move to answer, Gavin edged closer with his gun aimed at the man's chest. "You need to come with me. Now."

The man took a step closer. "Alright, don't shoot. I'll come with you. But for the record, whoever fired that shot isn't connected to me."

Gavin pointed the gun in front of him. "Get moving."

The man made to move past Gavin, then grabbed a log from the ground and whirled around, slamming it hard against Gavin's side. Pain raced from the contact point down the side of his body. As he was stunned by the attack, the man had the advantage and kicked Gavin on his injured side. Gavin dropped to the ground, his breath leaving his body in a whoosh.

Through the pain, Gavin could just see the man running away as fast as he could. Before he reached the woods, two other people emerged from the direction of the shot, and the three disappeared from sight.

Gavin dragged himself to his knees. Holding his injured side, he drew in air and waited for the world to settle before he slowly staggered to his feet.

There was no doubt in his mind that the man had been lying. He'd been up to no good, and so had his partners.

With his legs threatening to give out underneath him, Gavin took off in the direction the men had gone. He'd traveled a short distance when he realized that he was heading back to the road he and Jamie had just come up, only a little way from her house.

Once he reached the edge of the woods, he spotted the road and started down it. Another vehicle was parked behind tree coverage and out of sight from the road. A dark SUV, like the one Jamie described earlier.

Before Gavin could reach the vehicle, the driver fired

the engine, splitting the quiet of the night. They were getting away. He ran toward the vehicle. The driver apparently spotted him and shoved the SUV into Drive and the car went screaming down the mountainside.

Gavin stopped in the middle of the road and stared after it. Who were these men, and why were they coming after Paxton?

He headed back in the direction he'd come. *He said he had finally found proof that would exonerate my father...*

What had Paxton uncovered that would make him believe he could clear Noah's name after all these years?

A chilling thought occurred to him. What had the man who'd fired the shot been shooting at? Had they been inside Paxton's house? Fear raced through his body. He'd left Jamie sitting outside alone.

Gavin started running as fast as he could through the woods toward Paxton's house, ignoring the pain in his side. Whoever had forced Jamie off the road would have knowledge of her relationship with Paxton. They'd known where she was going tonight. Had they been waiting for her at the house to finish the job?

When he reached the clearing beside the house he noticed there were still no lights on inside. He rounded the corner and spotted the truck. Nothing moved so he hurried over. Jamie was nowhere in sight. There was little doubt in his mind that she'd gone looking for her uncle inside the house.

Gavin rushed up the steps. The door stood open. Inside, nothing but darkness greeted him. As his eyes adjusted, something moved close to the sofa. He drew his weapon, then he heard a moan and realized it was Jamie lying on the floor. She was hurt.

He dropped down to his knees beside her, his heart in his throat. "Jamie, are you okay?"

Please, God...

Slowly, she opened her eyes and stared up at him with terror on her face. She tried to sit up, but he stopped her.

"Don't try to move. We don't know how serious that wound is. Coupled with what happened earlier, you could be hurt. I'm calling for help." He reached for his cell phone to dial 911, but she stopped him.

"No... Gavin, you can't." She struggled to a sitting position. Her fingers probed a spot on the left side of her head. "Gavin, they have Uncle Paxton."

He stared at her, trying to comprehend what she meant. "What do you mean, they have Paxton?"

"Someone came up behind me and grabbed me. They took Uncle Paxton's phone, and I think they took him hostage, as well. Before I knew what was happening, they hit me with something." She shivered when she spotted the fireplace poker lying nearby. "They came here looking for Paxton. I'm positive they found him."

There was no doubt in his mind that whoever had come after Paxton was connected to the men he'd run into. The man with the light had probably been stationed out back as a lookout.

He shared his misgivings. "He was probably part of the group I came across in the woods out back. I'm sure they're the same ones who ran you off the road earlier. They were driving a large SUV..."

He stopped when he remembered the gunshot. *They came here looking for Paxton. I'm positive they found him.*

His gaze held hers. "Jamie, I heard them shooting at something."

Her hand flew to cover her mouth. "Oh, please no. Gavin, Uncle Paxton could be hurt. We have to go after them."

He blew out an exasperated sigh. "We don't know where they were headed. We need help. These guys are obviously dangerous."

She shook her head before he even finished the thought. "No. For all we know, they're acting on Andy Lawson's orders. I told you Paxton warned me that, no matter what happened, I shouldn't reach out to the sheriff. There had to be a reason for the warning. After everything that happened here tonight, I believe him."

Gavin's gaze narrowed. "Is there more to the story than what you've told me?"

Immediately, he watched as she put up a wall between them before answering, confirming the belief that she wasn't telling him everything.

"Someone tried to run me off the road earlier and now Uncle Paxton is missing, and they've obviously searched the house. I'd say that's enough proof Paxton stumbled onto something."

Gavin peered around the darkness. She was right. The place had been tossed. Those men had to be looking for something in particular. His guess was they hadn't found it, and so they'd taken Paxton because they believed he knew where it was.

He couldn't imagine what Paxton had gotten himself involved in.

"Why would your uncle ask you to meet him here?" he asked in amazement. "Paxton had to know this would be the first place those men would look for him. Why put your life in jeopardy?"

For this, Jamie had no answer. "I don't know. He

must have had his reasons, though. Gavin, I'm worried about him."

Gavin couldn't ease her fears any because he had the same bad feeling in his gut. Chaos surrounding them. It looked like a bomb had gone off. "Are you sure you don't have some idea what Paxton might be involved in?"

She started to say something, but seemed to think better of it. "I don't. I told you everything I know."

Their eyes held. He knew her well. Gavin could see there was more to the story than what she'd told him. She didn't trust him. There was a time when they'd been close. Shared everything. That had ended the day her father killed his.

Jamie slowly got to her feet. She was less than steady, and he grabbed her waist.

"I'm okay." She shook off his help.

"Wait here. Let me take a look around," he told her in an annoyed tone. He was annoyed with her for not trusting him. He was the same Gavin she'd once claimed to love. More than anything, he was angry at the way things had turned out between them and their two families.

He searched the rest of the rooms on one side of the house. When he came back to the living room, she was nowhere in sight.

Fear shot through him. "Jamie!"

She stuck her head out of her dad's old bedroom. "I think Uncle Paxton's in real trouble. You have to see this."

"I told you to stay put." He sounded ticked off because he was. She never did listen to reason. Some things hadn't changed one bit.

He followed her into the room.

"We have to find out who took him before it's too late. Paxton's hurt." She used her phone as a flashlight. The light bounced off a six-by-eight-inch spot on the carpet. It looked like dried blood. The second he saw it, all his anger toward Jamie evaporated.

She was right. Whatever Paxton had become involved in had landed him in some serious trouble, and Gavin wasn't sure they would be able to find him before it was too late.

THREE

She drew in a frightened breath and racked her brain, trying to recall where she'd recognized that one man's voice from. Yet no matter how hard she tried, the recollection remained elusive.

"We have to find out where they took him before it's too late. If these are the same men who killed your father, they won't hesitate to do the same to Uncle Paxton once they have whatever it is they're looking for." With Paxton's warning not to go to the local authorities, they were on their own and she had no idea where to start.

Was it possible that the sheriff's office was somehow responsible for Charles's death and had covered it up? If that were true, and with Paxton shooting off his mouth around town for years about Noah's innocence, they'd have to find a way to silence him if he'd accidently stumbled onto the truth.

Gavin examined the destroyed house. "I have no idea what's going on, but it's obvious Paxton has gotten himself into some real trouble. When I went into the woods following the light, the man I ran into said he was hunting, but he was lying. When I heard the shot and tried to take him in, he attacked me. Then he and two of his partners got away."

For the first time, Jamie noticed that he was holding his side. "You're hurt." She hurried over and touched his hand, but he grabbed hers and pulled it away.

"I'm okay." His tone held anger.

She stared into his eyes, hurt by his reaction. "What's going on here?"

He blew out a breath. "I wish I knew. Are you sure there's nothing more you and Paxton talked about in the past? Anything that might shed light on how to find him? It doesn't matter how small it may seem."

She wondered how much to tell him about recognizing the man's voice, and what the two had said when they believed she was unconscious. Gavin had expressed doubts before. Did she dare trust him with what she'd overheard? Or would he think she was as paranoid as Paxton? She couldn't face his rejection again.

"Only what I've already told you. Uncle Paxton believed he'd found the evidence that would clear my father's name. He couldn't talk about it on the phone, but told me no matter what happened, I shouldn't talk to the sheriff's office. He begged me to come home. I could hear the fear in his voice." She suppressed a shudder. Paxton wasn't afraid of much. This had gotten her attention right away.

She lifted her shoulders in a shrug. "You know the rest."

Jamie could see that what she said didn't make a lot of sense to a trained law enforcement agent.

"And you're positive they took him?" When she couldn't hide her hurt that he didn't believe her, he added, "Paxton would obviously have expected someone to show up here at some point. Especially if he believed the sheriff's office was involved. Maybe he got wind of what was happening and slipped away before they arrived. Those men could have been trying to trick you into thinking they had your uncle. Maybe see if you would lead them to Paxton."

Jamie didn't believe it. "There was a scuffle. They *had someone*, Gavin. Even if it wasn't Uncle Paxton, they took someone against their will. And Uncle Paxton was here recently. He left his phone behind. I know my uncle. He never goes anywhere without his phone. The man who took it from me said, 'I've got his phone. Let's get *him* out of here.'"

She could see that he still wasn't fully convinced. "Let's not jump to any conclusions just yet. Paxton's smart. He might have heard the accident happening down the mountain and gotten out of here before those men arrived. You know how sound travels up here. If he left in a hurry, he might leave his phone behind."

While that made sense on the surface, Jamie couldn't let go of what the man had said.

Jamie squared her shoulders, ready to argue what she believed was true. "They took him, Gavin. What are we going to do to get him back?"

They faced each other in a silent standoff. She'd find her uncle with or without his help.

Before he could form an answer, a noise outside drew their attention away from the conversation. It sounded like multiple cars heading up the mountainside.

Gavin hurried outdoors with Jamie glued to his side.

"They're coming this way!"

He listened for a second. "You're right. I'd say they're about at my house right now. Go back inside. I'll be right there." He headed for Ava's old truck and got out the shotgun and shells she kept there, while Jamie didn't move.

"Hurry, Jamie. We need to get out of sight before they arrive," he said once he'd reached her side again. She turned on her heel and ran inside, heading for the window.

Gavin slammed the door shut behind them, then locked it.

She could see three sets of headlights flashing through the wooded area near the road. They were almost to the house.

"Do you still remember how to use one of these?" Gavin asked and handed her the shotgun.

"I think so." At one time, she and Gavin had hunted game in the area together. She was an excellent shot. Although it had been years since she'd shot a gun, she was confident she could handle the situation.

The first vehicle rolled to a stop out front, its lights on bright. She and Gavin quickly ducked away from the window. Seconds later, two more cars came to a halt.

"I can't tell how many men there are out there, but I'm guessing it's a bunch." Gavin turned his head and stared at her.

"What do you think they want?" The panic growing inside her made it hard to breathe normally.

He shook his head. "Whatever Paxton started obviously didn't sit well with these guys."

There's nothing here... The men who had run her off the road had been looking for something more than just Paxton.

"This is the sheriff's department. You, inside the house, come outside with your hands up." She recognized the voice right away. It was the man who ran her off the road.

The name of the deputy played through her memory. Now she knew why that voice had sounded so familiar earlier. She'd grown up with Dan Miller.

He'd been right. They did know each other.

"We're outmanned," Gavin said. "If we stay, we'll be in custody and we'll be of no help to Paxton if that happens."

"Last chance. We know you're in there." A brief silence followed and then the men opened fire. Jamie and Gavin hit the floor at the same time as bullets riddled windows and walls.

"Wait here," Gavin said once the shots had ended. He crept low to the ground and went to her dad's old bedroom. More shots took out the window and sent glass flying. After the noise of broken glass faded, an eerie silence reigned.

"I don't see anyone back behind the house," Gavin said after he returned. "We have to get out of here before we're trapped inside. Just the two of us won't be able to hold them off for long."

What he said was true, but they wouldn't get far on foot. The people outside would eventually storm the house and see it was empty. They'd come looking for Gavin and Jamie.

Gavin crept to the window once more. "They're just sitting there. Almost as if they're waiting for something or someone." He came back to where she was.

"They don't want to bring Uncle Paxton in, they want to kill him," Jamie said.

"I'm not sure they're after Paxton at all," Gavin said. "I think they know *we're* in here."

She stared wide-eyed at him. Was Gavin right?

"Sorry, I know this is hard. Let's get going. Stay as low as possible. We don't know what they have planned for sure, but they could be sending men around behind the house at any moment. At any rate, we don't have much time."

He went to the back door and cracked it, then whispered, "I don't see anyone yet. We have to be as quiet as possible, which is going to be hard, seeing as there's no moon or stars visible through the clouds."

Gavin tucked his weapon behind his back and slung the shotgun over his shoulder before easing out the door. He took her hand. They'd taken only a couple of steps when a board squeaked beneath their feet. Gavin froze. Seconds ticked by, yet the men out front didn't seem to have heard it. They continued to talk amongst themselves.

Gavin pointed to an area straight behind the house where someone had cleared a large part of the property back there.

"We can't afford to go back for the truck," he whispered. "If we head out that direction, we can circle through the woods behind the house until we reach the road again. Once we get to Ava's place, my car is there. We'll have a means to escape. But if Andy is involved in this, then he knows we're together and were heading up here. You have to wonder if these men do as well."

Easing carefully off the porch, together they headed toward the cleared area as fast as they could. It was early autumn in the mountains, yet already the leaves had begun falling, making each step precarious.

Once they reached the top of the hill behind the

house, they stopped. Jamie looked behind them. She could still hear the men talking.

"Charge the house." Dan Miller gave the order. Unease balled in her stomach. Uncle Paxton had been right in warning her against contacting the sheriff's office.

"Hurry, Jamie. It won't take them long to realize no one's in the house." Gavin started running and she followed. They couldn't afford to get caught now. Paxton was in real danger. Whatever her uncle had uncovered, these men wanted him dead because of it.

Once they topped another hill, there was no time to rest. They headed down the other side at breakneck speed.

Jamie hadn't been back here in years, but she could see that Paxton had made an effort to clear the entire space out recently. The dirt appeared freshly turned. He'd told her previously that he wanted to start farming the space behind the house. That explained the clearing out, but Paxton wasn't one to stick with a plan for long. Maybe this time was different.

With the recent clearing, the countryside was littered with felled trees that made the going slow. Jamie stopped for a second to gather her breath. From behind them, she could hear the men's voices carrying.

"There's no one inside," one of the men said.

Her gaze shot to Gavin. "They can't have gotten far. Find them," Dan Miller ordered. He was clearly the one calling the shots. Where was Andy Lawson in all this? Was he trying to keep his hands clean?

Gavin grabbed her hand. "We need to hurry."

As they rushed deeper into the woods, Jamie spotted what she at first thought was a fallen log. She stopped.

Gavin reached her side. "What is it?" he asked, glancing behind them.

"There." She pointed to the object, which wasn't anything as innocent as a log. A body lay face down. Someone was dead in the woods.

"Oh, no... Gavin." Her deepest fear was that it was Paxton. She couldn't look. Jamie didn't want to see her beloved uncle lying dead on the cold, wet ground.

Gavin knew exactly what she was thinking because he thought the same.

Jamie had turned away. She couldn't watch. "Please tell me it's not him," she whispered, almost as if in prayer.

Slowly, Gavin eased the body over. Momentary relief rushed over him. "It's not Paxton," he assured her, but he knew the man lying dead there. And so did Jamie.

She turned. Her hand clapped over her mouth in surprise. "I can't believe it. That's Terry Williams. What happened to him?" she asked in shock.

Terry and Paxton had been good friends for as long as Gavin could remember. Was Terry dead because of something Paxton uncovered? The man had a single gunshot wound in his forehead, assuring Gavin this was no accident. The wound was fresh. There was no doubt this had been the shot he'd heard earlier.

"He's been shot," he told her quietly. "Terry has to be the person those two took from your house."

Tears were in her eyes. "I still can't believe it. Why would someone want to harm Terry? He's just a kind, gentle soul who's never hurt anyone."

Gavin could think of only one explanation. "This

thing is quickly escalating. We have to get off this mountain before we end up like Terry."

"We can't leave him like this." Jamie's voice broke as she looked at the man lying on the ground.

Gavin got to his feet and helped her up. Behind them, he could hear the noise of men making their way through the woods.

"They're coming up pretty fast." Gavin did his best to cover the body with leaves. "That's all we can do for now." He looked into her eyes. "I promise we'll come back for him. We'll give him a proper burial once this is all over."

She slowly nodded. "Which way do we go from here? I'm all turned around."

Gavin tried to regain his bearings. He pointed to the right. If his internal compass was correct, that should take them to his family home.

Several flashlights scanned the area behind them. They were all out of time. "Run, Jamie," he told her.

"There. Up ahead. I see them!" one of the men pursuing them yelled.

"Duck!" Gavin barely got the words out before shots were fired. Bullets flew past them. Jamie dove for the nearest tree, with Gavin close behind her.

They couldn't stand still and wait for the men to capture them. Gavin pointed up ahead. If they could stay behind tree coverage and out of sight as much as possible, they might stand a chance of reaching the house.

He tossed her the shotgun. "Go ahead of me. I'll cover you." She hesitated, not wanting to leave him behind. "It's okay. Hurry, Jamie."

With one final look his way, Jamie turned and

headed for the next tree while Gavin opened fire, forcing one of the men to retreat.

When there was a lull in the firefight, Gavin dashed after Jamie. The men must have seen the movement because they started shooting again.

Gavin flattened against another tree and edged out just enough to fire.

The air was thick with gun smoke. When a tenuous silence reclaimed the area, Gavin ran as fast as he could. He'd almost reached Jamie when more rounds exploded around him. One hit its mark.

Gavin yelled out in pain as the bullet seared into his left side. He almost lost his footing; his hand touched the ground as he stumbled several times, but managed to keep from falling. It was imperative that he stay mobile and keep moving. Once he was stable, he held on to his wounded side as blood seeped through his clothes.

Jamie had turned at the sound of his scream.

"Don't stop!" he yelled and waved her off when she started for him. They had to keep going.

It felt as if they'd been running for hours. Ignoring the pain and the faintness, Gavin hit the road just a little behind Jamie. The world around him spun and his stomach heaved as he came close to passing out. They were almost to Jamie's downed car. Just a little bit farther to Ava's place. He just had to hang on.

Jamie hurried to his side.

"We need to get out of sight before they catch up." He pointed to the wooded area on the opposite side of the road. In his condition, it might as well be on the other side of the moon. He wasn't sure he could make it another foot.

Blood soaked his hand, and his vision blurred. It

was a struggle to keep from losing consciousness. He blinked hard and forced back the nausea.

Jamie grabbed him around the waist and together they left the woods. Crossing the road meant they were out in the open and exposed.

His breathing became more labored. They reached the opposite side of the road and Gavin was thankful for the cover of trees. He needed to rest.

"No, we can't stop. We have to keep moving. It's not much farther to Ava's," Jamie told him, yet putting one foot in front of the other was a near-impossible task. He leaned heavily against her, losing track of time. How long had they been out here?

"There it is," Jamie exclaimed and he forced himself to focus.

The light he'd left on in the kitchen came into view. He almost lost hope. From where he stood it seemed miles away, and he wasn't sure he had the strength to make it to the light.

Behind them, he could hear their pursuers. They'd reached the road.

"Go ahead of me. Get to the house. Call the state police." His words slurred. He couldn't hang on much longer.

Jamie ignored what he said. She kept her arm around his waist and helped him along as best she could. He winced in pain, his strength slowly ebbing away. They had to reach the house. It was their only chance. If he passed out now, it was all over.

With each step jarring through his injured body, they made it to the edge of Ava's property.

"We're almost there, Gavin. Hang on a little bit longer. Please, just hang on." He barely registered the desperation in Jamie's voice.

He thought he managed a weak nod, but wasn't sure if it was real or a hallucination. The house came into view. Almost there. The steps leading up to the porch loomed in front of him like an insurmountable fortress forcing him to stop long enough to catch his breath.

"Come on, Gavin. We can't stop now. We're almost there. Just one step at a time."

Perspiration beaded his forehead. He pulled himself up onto the first step and pain shot through his side. He squeezed his eyes closed, fighting back bile.

The next step was just as difficult, as were the rest. Once they reached the porch, he struggled and somehow managed to take out the key, yet he couldn't hold it steady enough to open the door.

"Here, let me." Jamie took the key from his unresisting hand and slipped it into the lock.

The world around him became fuzzy. Gavin collapsed against Jamie, his full weight almost bringing her to her knees. He had no idea how she managed to keep them both upright.

"Hang on, Gavin," Jamie said, sounding out of breath. She pushed the door open. His grandmother's living room flashed before his eyes. It was the same view he had every single time he entered the familiar room. He was coming home.

He mumbled something unintelligible.

"What did you say?" Jamie asked, clearly not understanding. He had no idea, either. The sight in front of him brought tears to his eyes. He loved this old house. Had loved the woman who owned it more than anything. He couldn't imagine not calling this place home ever again.

"Home." The word was barely distinguishable. It would never be home again. Not without Ava.

"Yes, we're home." Jamie obviously hadn't understood what he meant, and he was too weak to try to explain it.

She put both arms around his waist and all but dragged him over to the sofa, stopping long enough to catch her breath. She was a slender thing. He couldn't imagine how difficult it was for her to haul his six-foot-plus frame from the door to the sofa.

Gavin groaned as pain shot up his side when Jamie managed to lower his wounded body.

Each breath he took hurt like crazy. His shirt was wet with his own blood.

He closed his eyes and tried to gather enough breath into his body. When he opened them again, he saw Jamie hurrying back over to the door. The darkness outside disappeared when she slammed it closed and relocked it, sliding the custom-made locking system his grandmother had installed back into place.

Ava. He'd buried his grandmother today. Gavin couldn't get the image of her lying in that coffin out of his head. Tears gathered in his eyes again. He slumped down onto the sofa, his world turned sideways. He was barely aware of Jamie saying his name before his eyes drifted shut and everything, including her, vanished completely.

FOUR

"Gavin!" Jamie screamed and ran to his side. He'd slumped down against the sofa seat, his eyes closed. "Gavin." He still didn't respond.

Jamie jerked his jacket open and recoiled at the muddy red spot covering his shirt where blood had soaked through. Gavin was in real trouble, and she had no idea how to help him.

"Stay with me, Gavin." She shook him gently. His eyes barely opened. He mumbled something she didn't catch before his eyes dropped shut again.

"Gavin, wake up. I need you. Please, wake up." She shook him harder. It took several tries before he finally roused.

Confused, he stared up at her for the longest time, as if he didn't know what was going on. Her fear must have registered through the disorientation. He reached up and touched her cheek gently. "Don't worry, Jamie. It's going to be okay." His words were still slurred and he winced. The simple effort of speaking was difficult.

Gavin drew in several shallow breaths then tried to sit up. He clutched his side, pain etched on his face before he slumped back against the sofa.

"Gavin, you've been shot. What do I do? How can I help you?" Her voice shook. His pain scared the daylights out of her. The thought of losing him like this was terrifying.

"Check the security system. The monitor is on the desk. We need to see if they followed us here," he forced out.

Jamie hurried to Ava's old desk and clicked on the monitor. Five different angles of the property came into view. What she saw there was terrifying. Armed men dressed in sheriff's uniforms were easing toward the house.

"They're here, Gavin." As she watched, three of the men cleared the front porch. Miller was one of them.

"We know you're in there. Come out with your hands up," Miller ordered.

Jamie turned toward Gavin who held his finger up to his lips.

"Break the door down," Miller told one of his men.

The man slammed his shoulder against the door, but it didn't budge. They didn't know the advanced security measures Ava had put into place. Steel reinforced doors, with state-of-the-art locking systems on all windows and doors. The place was a virtual fortress. When Ava had first told her about the security upgrade, Jamie couldn't imagine what the woman was expecting to happen. Now, she was grateful that Ava had taken such extreme precautions.

After several more tries without avail, Miller's phone rang and he answered it, speaking briefly to someone. "He needs us back there. Let's go. They're not going anywhere. Not in his condition."

Jamie watched the men leave the way they came, her hands shaking.

She went back to Gavin. "We have to get you out of here before they come back. You need to be checked out at the hospital." He was fading fast.

"We can't. They'll be checking all the hospitals. You're going to have to dress the wound yourself," he murmured.

Wide-eyed, she stared down at him. "I might hurt you."

He grabbed her hand, forcing her to be still. "There's no one else who can help me. It has to be you. You can do this."

Dread wrapped its slithery arms around her. Gavin was right. She was all he had, and she would do everything in her power to take care of him.

"You're right. I can," she murmured without really feeling confident that she could.

As she stared into his eyes, unwelcome feelings resurfaced. She'd spent years trying to deny it, but that didn't change the truth. She still cared for Gavin and couldn't bear it if something bad happened to him.

"Thank you." He managed a smile, and tears filled her eyes. She didn't want to lose him.

Hugging him close, she was careful not to hurt him more. When she would have pulled away, he cupped her face. "Thank you, Jamie."

Theirs had been a love story that had ended with two broken hearts. Now they were facing a life-and-death situation in which the outcome was unpredictable. There were no guarantees they'd survive to find Paxton, whether dead or alive.

He let her go and drew in several labored breaths while Jamie prayed for strength.

"You need something to sanitize the wound and some dry bandages." His voice was barely audible, the injury draining his strength.

"Okay. I'll get them."

He smiled at her attempt at bravery. "That's my girl. You have to be quick, though. We don't know how much time we have."

She got to her feet, went to the master bathroom, and she grabbed alcohol and a towel to help with the bleeding. The medicine chest contained only a box of Band-Aids. She'd need something much bigger to wrap the wound up securely. In the hallway linen closet, she found fresh sheets. Ava always kept them available in case someone dropped by for a visit and decided to stay.

Jamie ripped one of the sheets into strips that would serve as bandages. Once she had everything she needed, she went back to Gavin. His eyes were closed again and he was so still.

Dropping the supplies, she hurried to his side, kneeling next to the sofa. "Gavin!"

He slowly opened his eyes, saw all the worry on her face and did his best to reassure her. "I'm okay, I was just resting. Are you ready?"

She wasn't anywhere close, but Gavin needed her to be strong, and she'd do anything for him.

"Yes, I'm ready."

Sitting down next to him, she slowly unbuttoned his shirt. The wound was a bloody mess. The effort of pulling his shirt free left him drained of energy. She couldn't imagine how difficult it was going to be dressing the wound.

Jamie didn't realize he was watching her, no doubt seeing all her fears, until he spoke. "I'll be okay. I'm tough," he assured her.

She gently wiped the area around the wound clear of blood, then cleaned it with the alcohol. He cringed as the medicine hit the wound and stung. One hand gripped the side of the sofa.

Once she'd finished cleaning the spot, Gavin slumped back against the sofa, exhausted.

"We're almost done," she said gently, then folded some of the bandages and placed them over the wound.

"You'll need to apply pressure until the bleeding stops." Gavin forced the words out through clenched teeth.

Blood still oozed from the wound. Jamie placed her hands over the bandage and pressed hard. Gavin squeezed his eyes shut and bit his bottom lip.

"I'm sorry," she whispered, hating that she was the one to cause him pain. "I know it hurts."

It felt as if it took forever before the bleeding finally subsided. After removing the bloodied bandage, she put a clean one in its place, then took several strips of cloth and eased them around his waist until the wound was secured.

When Gavin lay back against the sofa, Jamie hurried to the kitchen and brought a glass of water over. She sat back down. "Here, take a sip."

She held his head up so that he could drink. He managed a single swallow then collapsed again.

"I'm not sure what to do next," she said. With Gavin so weak, they couldn't leave the house. They wouldn't get very far. If Miller and his men showed up again, would they find a way inside?

He didn't answer, and she shook him once more. Gavin didn't respond. Fear gripped her and Jamie grabbed his wrist, feeling for a pulse. It was there, weak but steady.

Jamie leaned back against the sofa. What if Gavin didn't wake up? What if the men showed up again? When her fear threatened to take control, she hit her knees and prayed.

"We need Your help. Please make him better."

Still kneeling close to Gavin's side, she watched him closely. Although he still hadn't moved and he was so pale, he seemed to be resting more comfortably, which was probably the best thing for him right now. Would they be able to stay hidden long enough for him to recover his strength?

Jamie got to her feet and killed the lights, then went over to the window. Nothing could be seen through the darkness. Feeling helpless, she let the curtain drop and went back to check on Gavin. He was sleeping peacefully. She took one of Ava's quilts from the closet and placed it over him for warmth.

Laying the shotgun on the coffee table, she took the Glock that Gavin had tucked close to him and shoved it into her jacket pocket.

It had been years since she'd been to Ava's home. Probably the last time had been when she was a teenager. While most things still looked the same, there were some significant differences.

She'd noticed the first when she'd locked the door. The locking system was like nothing she'd ever seen before. Even though Ava had told her she was putting in the security measures, Jamie still couldn't reconcile it with the strong but sweet woman she'd known for so many years. What was Ava expecting to happen to her that she needed such sophisticated protection?

In several of their conversations after Jamie first left the area, Ava had told her about how heroin had the county of Darlan in a stranglehold. Had Ava been afraid of someone breaking into her home and stealing from her to support their habit?

Jamie couldn't help but wonder if what was happening to her and Gavin was in some way related to the drug problem in Darlan. Was that what Uncle Paxton was trying to warn her about? If so, then how did the heroin connect to the sheriff's office or to a ten-year-old murder? There had to be a connection.

An uneasy thought made her shiver. Ava Dalton had made it clear to anyone who would listen throughout the years that she didn't believe Noah had killed her son. Was her death really due to a heart attack, like the coroner claimed, or because someone wanted to silence her, as well?

While she tried to make sense of the impossible, the monitor on Ava's desk suddenly flashed on, giving views of every part of the property. Someone was here. Jamie hurried over to the screen and studied it. What had triggered the sensors? Then she saw it. Several of the same armed men from earlier were making their way through the woods behind the house.

Horrified, she watched as the men methodically marched across the yard. Once they reached the house, they stopped and then unexpectedly left the property.

They were looking for something in particular. Why hadn't they returned to the house? Were they standing back, waiting for her and Gavin to emerge so that they could arrest them...or worse?

Jamie went back over to where Gavin still rested peacefully. As much as she wanted to wake him up and tell him what had just happened, she knew rest was the best medicine for him now.

With nothing else to do but wait, Jamie went into the kitchen. She needed something to do. Without turning on any lights, she made coffee. When she'd woken that morning, the only thing on her mind had been defending her client, who was down to his last appeal. And then Uncle Paxton had called, and her life in Louisville had taken second place to her only living relative. She'd managed to get Adam Sullivan's upcoming trial extended for another week. She prayed it would be long enough to save her uncle.

Now, exhausted beyond belief, Jamie was afraid to let her guard down for a second. She'd watch over Gavin until he was stronger. No matter what, she wouldn't let him down.

With coffee in hand, she went over to the monitor. Nothing stirred outside. Had the men truly moved on in their search, or were they still out there somewhere, waiting for them to come out into the open before they'd attack?

Gavin's eyes felt glued shut. It was a struggle to force them open. Where was he? It took a moment before he remembered what had happened. Jamie being run off the road. The race through the woods that resulted in his being shot. The desperate trek to his grandmother's house. He was home. The room was dark. Where was Jamie? The only light was coming from somewhere behind him.

It took all his strength to make it to a sitting position. Breathing was a struggle.

Someone hurried his way. Jamie! She was safe. He could see the concern on her face. Had something happened?

"Don't try to move. You're still very weak." The gentleness in her tone matched her eyes.

"How long have I been out?" he managed in a barely audible voice. His side hurt like crazy, and he felt as weak as a kitten.

"Several hours. You lost a lot of blood, Gavin."

He knew she was worried about him, but there was an edge to her voice that had him concerned. "Something else happened while I was out." It wasn't a question.

She sat next to him. "Yes. Not too long after you passed out, your grandmother's security system went crazy. Several of the same armed men from earlier made their way through the woods behind the house. They searched the yard as if they were looking for something, yet once they reached the house, they stopped and then unexpectedly left the property. It was…strange."

Gavin shook his head. "I have no idea what they could be looking for."

"Me either, but I don't think we can afford to stay here much longer."

She was right. Miller would want to take both him and Jamie in for questioning. He'd try to find a way to silence them. Gavin couldn't let that happen. Paxton had stumbled onto something big that definitely involved the sheriff's office, and he and Jamie were outnumbered. Miller and his men would keep coming after them. Using their badges, they'd be unstoppable.

"How often do you and your uncle talk?" he asked, the question taking her by surprise.

"Maybe once a week, sometimes more, depending on our schedules. Why do you ask?"

Because I'm desperate. Because I'm afraid I can't keep us safe, was on the tip of his tongue, but he couldn't voice his fears aloud. Jamie was counting on him.

"I'm just thinking Paxton might have said something in passing that didn't make sense at the time, but in the light of what's happened tonight, might be helpful in finding him."

Gavin could see her replaying their previous conversation over in her head. "Paxton told me he was closing down the coal mine for a while to do some repairs. At the time, I didn't think anything of it, but the last time I spoke to him, he told me that the mine was still closed." She stopped to look at him. "He was barely making a living as it was. There was no way he could afford to have the mine closed for so long. I'm wondering if maybe he was doing more than mining down there."

Since Gavin's father's murder and Noah's incarceration, prior to passing away, the mine that the two friends had worked together for years had been sitting mostly untouched. With Charles's death, controlling interest had gone to Ava. She'd let Paxton mine it as he saw fit. Ava had told Gavin occasionally that while Paxton and his friend Terry Williams worked the mine, they'd never found the mother lode that Noah and Charles believed existed beneath the mountain.

"Ava mentioned on several occasions how the use of the drug heroin had gotten really bad in Darlan. I remember her talking about it when I first left Darlan ten years ago. Do you think this has something to do with drug trafficking?"

He managed a nod. "Possibly. You think Paxton could be hiding whatever Miller and his men are looking for at the mine?" Gavin asked, then considered the possibility. It made sense in a way. That would explain why he wasn't mining. "Does anyone besides you know about the repairs?"

She shook her head. "Not as far as I know."

Even if Paxton hadn't discussed the repairs with anyone, the mine would be the first place Miller would look after he checked Paxton's house. There were no guarantees they'd find him there alive. Still, they had to try, because right now, they had no idea why the sheriff's office was willing to kill the older man.

"We need to get to the Darlan Mountain Mine as soon as possible." He grabbed the sofa arm and tried to stand. His knees threatened to buckle, and the world swam before his eyes. Gavin sank back down. He'd never felt so weak before. How on earth was he going to protect them, should something happen?

"You need to rest," Jamie insisted. "You were shot. You've suffered a tremendous blow to your system."

He closed his eyes until the world settled down. "There's no time. We need to get out of here while we still can. Miller and his men could return at any moment."

"At least let me change your bandage, and then I'll make you something to eat. It'll give you energy."

As much as he wanted to get to the mine as fast as possible, Jamie was right. He needed something to boost his strength.

He watched as she skillfully removed the bandage

and treated the wound before wrapping it again. While the spot was still red and swollen, at least the bleeding had stopped.

Jamie gathered the used bandages and got to her feet. Before she could walk away, he clasped her hand, holding her there. She looked down at him with uncertainty written on her face.

"Thank you," he murmured with an attempt at a smile, while wanting to say so much more. He still cared for her, and he couldn't think of anyone he'd rather have on his side.

She returned his smile. "I didn't do anything you wouldn't have done for me."

"Maybe, but still, thank you."

She squeezed his hand and then stepped back. "You're welcome." He watched as she hurried away, and he tried to get his chaotic heartbeat under control. Feelings still existed between them, but he'd made so many mistakes with Jamie. Now they were facing a life-and-death situation, and he was injured. Could he keep them safe?

Gavin slowly struggled to his feet and followed her to the kitchen. She caught him coming her way and hurried to his side.

"You need to lie back down."

He shook his head. "I need to get back on my feet as soon as possible. Moving around will help."

Resigned, she shrugged and handed him some coffee. He accepted it gratefully and took a sip. He'd forgotten how refreshing a simple cup of coffee could be.

"There doesn't appear to be much in your grandmother's fridge besides eggs and bacon."

To Gavin it sounded like a feast. "Sounds good to

me." Slowly, he lowered himself down to one of the stools in front of the bar. Trying to hide his exhaustion from her was impossible, yet there was nothing that could be done about it. Although being shot had taken its toll, the fast-paced life he led as a spy was catching up with him, as well. He'd been burning the candle at both ends for years. He'd been in Kandahar when he'd learned about his grandmother's passing. He'd caught the first flight home to Darlan.

Even though he'd been home for almost a week, Gavin had barely spent any time at Ava's house. Too many bittersweet memories were stored up here. All the Christmases he and his father would go out to the woods and cut down a tree for his grandmother. Ava always wanted the biggest tree they could find. The Easter egg hunts as a child. He could picture Ava in just about every square inch of the homestead. Even after witnessing his grandmother's body being lowered into the ground, Gavin still couldn't imagine death conquering her.

Jamie set a plate of bacon and eggs in front of him, then touched his hand. "I miss her, too. I still can't believe she's gone."

Gavin swallowed emotions that he wasn't ready to deal with just yet. "Yeah, I can still see her standing where you are, making all those amazing meals she used to put together as if it were nothing at all. Especially during the holidays."

Jamie smiled, reminiscing. "I remember that one Christmas when we all got together over here. That was a great day."

He remembered the time she mentioned, too. He and Jamie hadn't yet started dating, but he'd known he was crazy about her, even back then. Every time he'd looked at her, his young heart had gone crazy.

"Your grandmother told me you went to work for the CIA. She was proud of you."

There was much more that she wasn't saying, but he wasn't surprised that she and Ava had talked. His grandmother was always dropping hints about their conversations whenever she spoke to Gavin. Ava had always adored Jamie.

He nodded. "After my father's death, I stopped believing in anything good. I joined the CIA and then later...got married." He slid her a look. She was clearly surprised. "I became driven by my career for a long time, and because of it, my marriage collapsed around me. Emily deserved better than what I could give her."

Gavin watched as Jamie processed what he'd said. Was it just wishful thinking on his part, or did she actually seem unhappy about what he'd told her?

"I had no idea you were married. Ava never mentioned it." She swallowed visibly. "I'm sorry it didn't work out, but I understand about failed relationships. I haven't been able to keep anything together long enough to even be called a relationship."

He smiled at her admission. "I knew I had to do something to redeem myself. When I was offered a job with the Scorpion team, I finally found my purpose. I love the men and women on the team, and it was through my comrades that I came to know God. He changed my life. Gave me a purpose. Now, I can't imagine my life without God in it."

Jamie returned his smile. "I'm happy for you. I know the importance of faith in my own life. It's proven itself so many times in the past."

She took her plate over to the bar and sat next to him. "Why do you think they took his phone?" she asked, her forehead knitted together into a frown.

Gavin put down his fork. "They were probably trying to find out who he spoke to recently. Maybe track his movements." He stopped and shrugged.

Without Paxton, all their questions would remain unanswered.

"I just hope he's okay," she said, and he could hear the concern in her voice.

He swiveled to face her. "Paxton's a tough old guy. He'll be okay." He tried to reassure her while hoping he hadn't lied, because he had a bad feeling. Something was terribly wrong in Darlan.

Gavin finished his meal and struggled to his feet, intent on washing off his plate.

"Here, let me do that." Jamie took both plates over to the sink and rinsed them off while Gavin eased around the great room, hoping to regain some of his strength.

"I have some pain medicine in my bag, along with some antibiotics. I'll just go get it."

She watched him leave with a worried look on her face. She was probably wondering how they were going to make it out of this thing alive in the condition he was in.

Once he found the medicine, he took the correct dosage and went back to where Jamie had finished clearing away their breakfast. Outside, it was just getting light.

Jamie glanced out at the breaking dawn. "Why would they kill Terry? He's the sweetest guy. He'd never hurt anyone."

Growing up, Terry Williams had been part of Gavin's life every bit as much as Paxton had. Terry and Paxton had been friends for as long as Gavin could remember. Terry grew up a miner and proud of it, but he was also one of the nicest men Gavin had ever known. He remembered how, after his father's death, Terry had stopped by pretty much every day to check on him and Ava.

He shook her head. He didn't want to tell her, but the only explanation was that Terry had been killed because of his relationship to Paxton. Someone thought Terry knew something important.

Gavin slowly went over to the monitor and checked the cameras outside. "I don't see anyone. We should probably take this opportunity and get out of here while we still can. I'm going to gather some things we might need along the way."

He went back to the room he'd used as a child and grabbed his backpack, filling it with supplies—extra bandages and medicine, a flashlight and a lighter. His backup weapon and ammo for the Glock and the shotgun, along with a knife and rope. Useful things to have when entering a mine.

Doing the simplest of things was difficult. He had to stop periodically to regain his strength. If they had to fight their way out of a situation, he wasn't so sure he would survive it.

"We'll have to take my rental car," Gavin told her when he came back to the living room.

With his grandmother's old truck still in the woods near Jamie's home, they'd have no choice. But the path to the mine was a rough one, especially coming up the back way like they'd be doing. They wouldn't be able to make it the full way up by car.

Jamie didn't seem nearly as confident about what

they would be forced to do. "Gavin, you've lost a lot of blood. I don't think you're up to the challenge of walking the rest of the way to the mine."

He could see she was worried about him. She came over to where he stood and gently touched his arm. "Let me check out the mine on my own."

Gavin understood her fears, but there was no way he was going to let her go down there alone.

He shook his head. "It's too dangerous. We don't know what we'll find once we're in the mine." And he couldn't stand the thought of anything happening to her.

"Gavin…" She bit back whatever else she'd been about to say before giving in. "Fine."

"As soon as it gets light, we'll head out. Hopefully, those guys will have moved on."

As the world outside grew light, he prayed for the strength to keep them safe. Because right now, he wasn't nearly as convinced they'd walk out of this thing alive.

FIVE

Just making it out to the car drained Gavin's energy at an alarming rate. Jamie took the backpack from him and put it in the back seat, then hit the garage door opener and the door slowly slid open.

"You'll have to drive. I don't trust myself behind the wheel." His voice was little more than a whisper. Jamie was frightened for him. If they were attacked, could she protect him?

Once she'd helped him get his six-foot-plus frame inside the compact's passenger seat, Jamie rounded the back of the car and glanced around the filmy light of a new day. So far, there didn't appear to be anyone around. Where had Miller and his men gone?

Jamie got behind the wheel and backed out of the garage. Gavin tucked his Glock beneath his seat. The shotgun was hidden behind the back seat.

"Ready?" she asked. The tiniest of nods did little to clear away her concerns. She eased down the long drive pitted with potholes. Ava and her husband, Henry, had built the house close to the edge of their property when they were first married. Ava had told her that the spot where the house sat was the first place she and her husband had kissed. It was a sweet story that had stuck with Jamie through the years. Tough as nails, Ava had also had a gentle side that very few people other than family and close friends ever got to see. It was what had made her so special. Jamie fought back tears at the memory.

As much as she didn't want to give in to her fears, Jamie couldn't help but worry about her uncle's safety. She believed if Paxton had been able to reach out to her, he would have by now. The Darlan Mountain Mine was the only logical place where Uncle Paxton would go to hide out. It was his second home—though anyone who knew him would realize this. Would they be too late?

Jamie stopped when she reached the road, her hands sweaty on the wheel. Once she was positive no one was coming, she pulled onto the mountain road and headed back toward her family home. Her thoughts returned to the frightening events of the previous night right here on the mountain. Dan Miller, the man whose voice she'd recognized from the past, someone sworn to serve and protect, had tried to run her off the road.

Their car barely made it out of the drive before a deputy sheriff's SUV appeared behind them, seemingly from nowhere, flashing its lights. With the previous night's encounter still fresh in her mind, Jamie stared at the rearview mirror in horror. "That looks like the same sheriff's deputy who came to my house last night. He's the one who ran me off the road."

Gavin sat up straighter in his seat and squinted behind them. "We need to pull over. We don't want to give him any reason to arrest us. Find a wide spot and stop. Maybe we can find out what he knows."

It was the last thing she wanted to do, but Gavin was right. If they ran, they'd look guilty.

Jamie eased as far off the road as the narrow shoulder would allow. There was no doubt in her mind that Miller had ordered Terry's murder. If he was capable of doing such a senseless thing, he wouldn't hesitate to silence them if he saw them as a threat.

Gavin covered her hand on the wheel. "Try to relax. We don't want to tip him off that something is wrong."

She stared into his eyes, saw the strength she'd always been able to lean on in the past, and slowly nodded.

Miller got out of the SUV and made his way over to the car. With a quick prayer for their safety running through her head, Jamie lowered the window.

The deputy's gaze went from Jamie to Gavin, recognizing them both.

"I'm surprised to see the two of you together again. What are you up to so early this morning?" The suspicion in Miller's voice made it clear he was on alert.

Jamie did her best to sound confident. "I ran into Gavin, and we started reminiscing about when we were younger, growing up here on the mountain. I guess we lost track of time. I'm just heading up to my house now."

She found it strange that Miller didn't ask about her car. Did he suspect she knew it was him who'd run her off the road?

"Have you seen Paxton lately?" he asked with an edge to his tone.

It took everything inside of her not to look away. "No, I haven't. Why do you need him?"

"Because we found Terry Williams's body in the woods behind your place last night. We believe Paxton may have murdered his friend."

The allegation struck her like a blow. Miller was

trying to frame Paxton for Terry's murder. "That can't be true. Uncle Paxton would never hurt Terry. They've been friends since they were kids."

Miller wasn't moved by her defense of her uncle. "That may be, but it doesn't change the fact that Terry was found on your property. And people do strange things when their livelihood is threatened."

Fear froze her expression. "What are you talking about?"

Miller smiled smugly. "I'm thinking Terry was going to turn Paxton in for trafficking heroin. Paxton had to get rid of him quickly before that happened. And now Paxton has disappeared, which certainly makes him appear guilty. We know this because we went to your house last night and he wasn't there. Someone else was, though."

Miller's unwavering gaze held hers. Jamie ignored the reference to them being at the house. "Uncle Paxton didn't do what you're accusing him of. He's in Jamesville."

Miller clearly didn't believe her, but for the moment he had nothing to hold them on. "You can be sure I'll check on that. You'd better hope he's there. In the meantime, if you talk to him, tell him to turn himself in. We wouldn't want anything bad to…happen to him if he tried to flee."

Her eyes widened at the threat.

With a final tap on the side of the car, Miller made his way back to his vehicle.

Jamie put the window up with trembling fingers. "What do we do now?" She turned to Gavin.

He peered in the side mirror. "We can't go to the

mine, that's for sure. Not with him watching us. Let's head up to your place for now. See if he follows."

Jamie eased the car back onto the road and headed up the mountain. A quick check in the rearview mirror confirmed her worst fear. "He's still coming. Miller's not letting us out of his sight. I can't believe they're trying to frame Uncle Paxton for Terry's death when they're the ones who killed him." She shook her head. "We can't let that happen."

Gavin continued watching as the deputy kept his distance, making it clear he was following them. "We'll do everything we can to keep Paxton safe. But first, we have to find him before they do."

Jamie did her best to keep her speed steady. She couldn't believe what had happened since she'd been home. Less than twenty-four hours ago, her biggest concern had been freeing a wrongfully accused man. Now she and Gavin were trying to stay out of jail long enough themselves to find her uncle, before Miller and his goons took care of whatever problem he posed.

As Jamie rolled to a stop in front of her place, Gavin surveyed the house and surrounding mountainside. The sheriff's department didn't have deputies stationed around. They weren't expecting Paxton to return. Why? He noticed Miller stop a little way down, concealed by a group of trees. "We still have our tail. Let's hope he gets bored after a while and leaves us alone, because if he doesn't, there's no way we can go to the mine. We'd be leading him straight to Paxton, assuming he's hiding there."

Jamie was staring at the spot where he'd left his truck. "Gavin, your truck's gone."

He craned his neck behind them. Miller and his men had

moved Ava's truck "I have no idea what's going on here, but I sure don't like it. Let's get inside and out of sight."

He grabbed the backpack filled with supplies and got out of the car, followed by Jamie, and hurried up the steps to the house. The front door was blocked by crime-scene tape.

"What should we do?" She glanced up at him, her eyes filled with worry.

"We go inside. This is your home, and Miller didn't try to stop us when we told him what we were doing." Gavin ripped the tape away from the door and opened it. Jamie hesitated a second, then went inside with a final look at the deputy.

In the light of day, the damage done there was even more alarming than what he'd seen the night before. The destruction left from the hail of bullets was shocking. Shattered glass was everywhere. Broken knickknacks littered the floor of the great room. Furniture was riddled with bullets. Gavin recalled the bloodstains in the bedroom. Someone was injured here. Gavin was positive Terry had been shot where they'd found his body. So whose blood was this? The only explanation was that it had to be Paxton's. The bloodstain didn't appear big enough to be fatal. Maybe he'd been injured by Miller and his men and managed to escape. That would explain why they were still looking for Paxton.

Jamie peeked out the window. "He's not leaving. We can't risk going to the mine and leading him to Paxton."

Gavin joined her by the window. "We won't be able to drive there. We'll have to go on foot. For the time being, we'll stay here. See if he leaves. If not, then we'll have to go back to Ava's and head out after dark."

He looked into her eyes and saw the fear she couldn't

hide. Everything inside of him wanted to protect her, but he had to know what they were facing, and Jamie was still holding something back. "I need you to tell me what you haven't yet. Paxton's life might depend on it. You said Miller ran you off the road last night. Are you sure?"

She stared at him for the longest time, evidently surprised, then blew out a sigh, her voice little more than a whisper. "I'm positive. I recognized his voice." She turned to face him fully. It was time to tell him everything. She could trust Gavin. He'd risked his life for her. "He was with someone. They were looking for something in particular. They searched the trunk. The other man said, 'We'd better find him and the stuff before they arrive.'" She shivered, recalling the conversation. "But what was the most frightening was what the other man said next. He said, 'We don't need the hassle of covering up another murder.'" She looked into Gavin's eyes and said, "I think they were talking about your father's murder."

Startled, he couldn't let himself believe what she was saying. Sure the man's words were disturbing, but he wasn't ready to make that leap just yet. "We don't know that. It could mean anything." The hurt on her face was hard to take. She would never give up on proving her father's innocence.

"What do you think they were looking for?" he asked gently, needing to steer the conversation back to safer ground.

She blew out a sigh. "I have no idea, but whatever it is, they're willing to kill for it."

As he looked around the place in the light of day, he saw things that he hadn't earlier. The rooms had been ransacked, but the house looked as if it hadn't been lived in for quite some time.

"Was Paxton still living here?" Gavin asked.

She obviously found the question odd. "As far as I know, yes. Why?" She looked around and saw what he had.

Jamie tried the lights once more. "The electricity was off last night as well. I thought maybe those men had turned it off." She went over to the desk and rummaged around. "There are several months' worth of electricity bills here. The power has been shut off."

"Paxton obviously hasn't been living here in a while. But if he's not staying here, then where?" Their gazes locked.

"The mine. That's the only explanation. The only place where he'd feel safe," Jamie insisted.

She began roaming the small living space where she'd grown up. He wondered if being with him again had brought up any unresolved feelings for her. It certainly had for him.

He'd practically grown up in this house, as well. Even before he and Jamie started dating, the two families had spent a great deal of time together. He remembered Sunday meals here with Noah praying over the food. Noah was like a second father to him, which made what he did that much harder to accept.

Gavin swallowed regret and searched for something to say to fill the awkward silence. He left his spot by the window and sat down on the dusty sofa, the injury drawing down his strength.

"Ava told me you'd become a criminal defense attorney." Jamie shot him a surprised look, and he smiled. "We talked a lot about you," he said in answer to her unasked question. "She was proud of the work you did. She said you were trying to help those who couldn't help themselves…like your father." The last part was difficult to say.

Jamie looked away. He couldn't tell what she was thinking.

There was something he needed to say. "I never told you how sorry I was to hear about Noah's passing, but I was. In spite of everything that happened, he was still like family, and I hated thinking about him in that place. Hated that he passed away there."

Jamie cleared her throat. "Thank you," she murmured, her voice unsteady. "I had no idea when I chose this career path how many cases there were of people being wrongfully incarcerated. It's heartbreaking." She told him about an elderly man by the name of Adam Sullivan whose case was similar to her father's. As she spoke, he could see tears glistening in her eyes. Her passion for her work was obvious.

He slowly got to his feet and went over to where she stood. He took her hand and held it. "I'm sorry," he managed and wished he could erase the ugly past for them both.

After a moment, she nodded and squeezed his hand, then moved away, wiping tears from her face. "It's okay. I love the type of work I do, but it can be emotionally exhausting."

Jamie went back to the window and looked out. "He's still there." She turned back to him. "I don't think he's leaving."

"There's no need to hang around here any longer. Let's head back to Ava's. I just hope we can make it until nightfall without Miller trying something."

He could see the thought was terrifying, and he tried to reassure her.

"Why don't you grab some personal things? If Miller stops us and asks why we were here, you can tell him you came to pick up a few things before heading back to Louisville."

While Jamie looked around the place, Gavin watched Miller's vehicle. If the deputy stopped them, and Gavin was certain that would happen, he would search the car looking for anything that might give him the location where Paxton was hiding. His backup weapon and extra ammo for the Glock and the shotgun, along with a knife and rope might give away too much.

Gavin quickly found a safe place to store them. They could stop back by the house to retrieve the items before heading to the mine.

He moved the bookcase enough so that he could stuff the things behind it and prayed Miller wouldn't grow suspicious and search the house again. He shoved the medicines and extra bandages in his jacket pocket.

"What are you doing?" Jamie asked when she spotted him kneeling near the bookcase. She held a collection of trinkets in her hand.

He straightened awkwardly. His injury made everything more difficult. "It wouldn't do for Miller to find those things in the backpack, and I'm pretty sure he saw it in the back seat. I can't leave it here. He'll wonder where it is." He held the now empty bag open, and she placed the few items inside.

"There's nothing we can do for Paxton right now. Let's get out of here."

With one final look around, Jamie opened the door

and stepped out into the foggy morning. Gavin followed her out to the car.

"He'll stop us. Once we're on the road again, he'll stop us and search the car and the bag. Try to appear as calm as you can."

Jamie got behind the wheel once more and started the car, glancing his way. He couldn't begin to hide the toll his injury had taken on his body. He was barely hanging on.

"Gavin, are you okay?" The worry in her voice confirmed how bad he must look.

He managed a nod and tried to sit up straighter. "I'll be fine. I just need to get back to the house and rest for a while. It's going to be tough making it to the mine on foot." He touched her hand. "You should try to rest, as well."

She put the car in gear and eased past the deputy's parked patrol vehicle. They'd barely cleared the bumper when the deputy fired the engine and red and blue lights strobed behind them.

"You were right. He's going to stop us." Jamie breathed the words out fearfully.

Gavin watched Miller turn the vehicle around and come after them. "Relax. If he sees you're nervous, he'll suspect we're up to something."

Jamie stopped the car and drew in a shaky breath. Behind them, Miller got out of his patrol car and headed their way. Gavin prayed for strength for himself and for Jamie not to fall apart. He had a feeling that Miller was just looking for a reason to take them in.

SIX

Deputy Miller advanced with his weapon drawn. Horrified, Jamie whirled to Gavin. "He's got his gun out." She couldn't hide the terror in her voice.

Gavin clasped her hand and held it. "It's going to be okay."

She wasn't nearly as sure.

"Get out of the car with your hands up," Miller ordered when he reached the back of the car.

Jamie couldn't stop shaking. "What should we do?"

Gavin turned in his seat. "We do as he asks. Get out slowly with your hands in the air. The last thing we need is another gunshot wound to deal with."

The damage the bullet had done to Gavin's body was starting to show. He could barely get out of the car on his own. She was worried Miller would notice something off in his behavior and look closer. Would he arrest them? Or worse?

Jamie stepped out of the car and put her hands in the air. Gavin slowly did the same, his face pale, pain etched there.

"What's this about, deputy?" Gavin asked, somehow managing to keep his voice strong.

Miller motioned the gun at Jamie. "Get over there next to her."

As she watched, Gavin plastered a blank expression on his face and obliged.

"What were you two doing back there?" Miller kept the weapon trained on Gavin.

"I went to pick up a few things from my house," Jamie said. "The last time I checked that wasn't illegal. I told you where my uncle is."

Miller didn't answer. "Pop the trunk and get over there." He motioned them to the opposite side of the road.

"Dan, I'm a CIA agent. We have the right to know why you've stopped us," Gavin told him.

Miller immediately grew wary. "You joined the CIA?" He didn't seem convinced, but he changed his demeanor a little.

"That's right, and I know you're violating our civil rights by not telling us why you pulled us over…again. We told you everything we know about Paxton. Unless you have evidence that ties us to some crime, you need to proceed very carefully."

Miller actually appeared afraid. "She's related to Paxton. We believe he's guilty of murder at the very least. That gives me the right to search this vehicle if I think it's been involved in a crime."

"Only this isn't Jamie's vehicle. It's my rental car." Jamie could tell that Gavin was fading quickly.

"He's right. I'm a criminal defense attorney in Louisville. Without Gavin's permission you can't search the vehicle."

She stepped closer to Miller, hoping to keep his attention off Gavin. "And you have no proof that Uncle

Paxton is guilty of anything. Even if he was, I'm certainly not responsible for his actions."

"If you aren't guilty, you won't mind me searching the car," Miller challenged. "Unless you have something to hide?"

Now was not the time to argue their civil rights. She needed to get Gavin out of here as fast as possible.

"Fine, search the car and then let us be on our way." She hoped she sounded more confident than she felt inside.

Miller popped the trunk himself, then looked around, reminding her of the way he and his partner had searched her vehicle the day before. He'd been looking for something in particular. Was that the reason he'd insisted on searching the car now?

Once Miller was satisfied there was nothing incriminating inside, he opened the driver's side back door and spotted the backpack.

"What's in here?" He shot them a questionable look, then took the bag out and unzipped it, dumping the contents onto the ground. One of the little figurines her mother used to collect broke into a dozen pieces on the pavement.

Tears filled Jamie's eyes. That was one of the few possessions that she still had of her mother's.

Miller tossed the bag on the ground beside it and headed back to his vehicle with one final warning. "You'd better be telling the truth about where Paxton is, because if I find out different, you're both in big trouble, CIA agent or not. And make sure you get that wrecked car out of the ditch as soon as possible. If we have to tow it, it'll cost you."

He got back into his vehicle and slammed the door

hard. As he drove past them, he crushed the remaining pieces of the memento into dust.

Jamie hurried over to the items that were left and dropped to her knees, clutching her mother's precious collectibles against her chest.

Gavin came over, awkwardly crouching beside her. He gently put the rest of the figurines into the bag and zipped it closed. "I'm sorry about that," he murmured earnestly. "He had no right to do that."

She brushed aside tears and got to her feet, holding out her hand to him.

He took it with a grateful smile, using her strength to pull himself to his feet. He stumbled into her. Jamie put her arms around his waist to steady him, then struggled to get him back to the car.

He all but fell into the seat, and her fear for his well-being increased. Jamie quickly closed the door and grabbed the bag. Putting it on the back seat, she got behind the wheel.

Gavin leaned against the headrest with his eyes closed.

"Gavin!" She shook him, and he slowly opened his eyes.

"I'm okay." He slurred his words, indicating it was far from the truth. "We need to get out of sight as soon as possible. I don't trust Miller not to change his mind and come after us again. He can make us both disappear if he wants to."

Jamie put the car in Drive and headed down the mountain, going as fast as she dared. Once she pulled onto Ava's property, she slowed the car's speed. Every single bump in the road had Gavin cringing in pain.

"I'm sorry," she murmured, hating that she'd hurt

him. She pulled the car into the garage and out of sight, hit the button to close the door and killed the engine.

Next to her, Gavin didn't move a muscle. Every time she saw him like this, she was terrified. Would he pay with his life for Miller's crimes? "Gavin, we're here."

He slowly turned his head and looked into her eyes.

"I'm going to need you to help me. I don't think I can manage it on my own."

Jamie stuffed down her fear and got out. Once she'd unlocked the home's side door, she went around to Gavin's door and opened it.

"Easy does it." She slid her arm around his waist. He flinched as he draped his arm over her shoulders and shifted sideways so that he could put his feet on the ground.

It took all of Jamie's strength to lift his tall frame out of the car. Gavin leaned heavily against her, and she struggled not to collapse beneath his weight.

They slowly moved inside the house, and she helped him over to the sofa.

"Rest now," she said once he was lying down. "Where are the pain pills?" she asked and he patted his jacket pocket.

Jamie dug them out and poured a couple of pills into her palm, then got a glass of water from the kitchen. She braced the back of his neck so that he could swallow the medicine. The exertion of simply driving to her house had been too much. How would they ever make it all the way up Darlan Mountain to the mine?

"Gavin, what can I do to help you?" she asked, because she was out of ideas.

He dragged in a breath and closed his eyes. "Rest is the only thing that will help me. We'll wait until night-

fall. They'll be watching the place, have no doubt—
Miller might not be around, but I'm guessing one of
his men is. There's no way we can give them the slip
in broad daylight. I don't think I could make it even if
we could. If we stand any chance at getting to the mine
alive, we have to wait."

Someone was shaking his arm. Frustrated, he tried
to bat the hand away. "Gavin, you have to wake up.
The sheriff is here." He recognized the panic in Jamie's
voice right away. His eyes flew open and he stared into
Jamie's frightened face.

"Is he alone?" he asked and forced his injured body
up to a sitting position.

"Yes, it's just Andy."

Gavin rubbed a hand over his sleep-weary eyes. "We
have to let him in. He knows I'm here, at the very least.
If I don't answer, he'll suspect something is up."

He stumbled to his feet with effort, unable to keep
from wincing. Jamie hurried over to help steady him.
Gavin closed his eyes and waited for the nausea to go
away.

"I'm okay," he said once he felt a little steadier. She
let him go. Gavin slowly went over to the door. Before
he unlocked it, he did a quick sweep over the room,
looking for any red flags. The monitor!

"Cover the screen up with a blanket," he whispered,
and Jamie rushed over, grabbed the blanket from the
sofa and tossed it over the monitor.

Gavin opened the door, startling Andy, who appeared ready to leave.

"I was beginning to think you weren't home, after
all." Andy took a step forward.

"Sorry, Jamie and I were out back talking and I almost didn't hear you knock. Come inside." Gavin stepped away to let Lawson in.

Andy spotted Jamie and took off his Stetson politely. "Good to see you again, Jamie. I wondered where you'd gone. I stopped by your place before I came here." Andy didn't mention the carnage there and Jamie somehow managed to keep her reaction to herself.

"After what happened there last night and with there being no electricity, well…" She left the rest unsaid.

Her comment seemed to come as a surprise to Andy. "What happened there last night?" he asked with concern.

Why hadn't Miller updated the sheriff about what they'd done?

"Your deputy and some of your men fired on us. They shot up the place, as I'm sure you're aware," Gavin told him.

Lawson turned pale. It was a moment before he could speak. "I'm sure they had reason after what happened to Terry. Terrible thing."

But Miller and his goons hadn't known about Terry until after they'd shot up the house. Gavin kept that bit of information to himself.

"Poor Terry. He was such a good man," Lawson continued. "That's actually why I'm here. You understand that I need to ask you some questions, Jamie, seeing as Terry's body was found on your property and all."

Jamie's brow knitted together in confusion. "We already told Deputy Miller that we didn't know anything about what happened to Terry."

This bit of news came as an obvious surprise to Lawson. "You did? When did you speak with Dan?"

Gavin frowned. Something was definitely off about Lawson's lack of knowledge.

"Earlier today," Gavin supplied. "He stopped us on the way back from Jamie's house. She needed to pick up a few things there. Sheriff, we don't have any idea what happened to Terry, and neither of us have seen Paxton since we got here. As Jamie told you before, he's not in town."

Lawson scanned the room. "Everything okay here?" he asked and indicated a single blood-stained bandage that had fallen off the coffee table almost out of sight. He'd missed it when he looked around the room.

Gavin's gaze locked with Jamie's. He was aware of her drawing in a shaky breath.

"Everything's fine. That must have been something Ava left out before..." He stopped short. Couldn't say the word. He still couldn't believe she was gone.

Lawson accepted his answer, but Gavin was left with the impression that he didn't really believe him.

Gavin needed to do something to take Lawson's scrutiny off the house. "Do you have a time of death for Terry?"

Lawson turned his attention back to Gavin. "The ME says sometime between six and ten last evening."

"That's a pretty wide gap. Anyone could have gone up there and killed him." Gavin knew the time of death was closer to six—around the time he'd spotted the man in the woods.

"That's true enough," Andy said and nodded. "As I recall, you and Jamie were heading up there around that time."

Jamie shifted nervously, garnering Lawson's attention again.

"We did go up there yesterday, but the power was off. Gavin offered to let me stay here."

Lawson didn't look away. "That so?"

"Yes, that's so. We left after just a few minutes. It was too dark to see anything."

There was no doubt Lawson didn't believe her. "Why didn't you get the items while you were there last night?"

Jamie let go of a breath. "Like I said, it was dark by then. There was no way I could see anything inside the house. I decided to wait until daylight. We were heading back from the house this morning when your deputy stopped us and searched us at gunpoint, which was totally unwarranted. We had done nothing wrong and were more than cooperative."

Lawson clearly had no idea what his deputy had been up to. "I'm sure he had his reasons for the search. This is a murder investigation, after all."

"What caliber of weapon was used to kill Terry?" Gavin asked, because he didn't like the direction the interrogation was going. He was positive Terry was killed with a shotgun.

The sheriff wasn't as forthcoming with this detail. "Sorry, but I can't divulge that information. This is an active investigation, and you two were in the area at the estimated time of death. You'll understand that, until I can clear you both, I can't give out details of the case."

Gavin couldn't tell if the sheriff was trying to cover up something or if he was really serious.

"I've been trying to get in touch with Paxton since yesterday. He's not answering his phone. I did some checking around Jamesville, over where the miners buy their supplies. No one remembers seeing him in the last few days. You have any idea where he really is, Jamie?" Lawson asked in a low tone that bordered on threatening.

Jamie hid her uneasiness badly. "I have no idea. He told me he was going there for supplies. Maybe he changed his mind and went somewhere else."

Lawson didn't believe it. "That's pretty strange for him to be away from the mine for so long, don't you think?"

Jamie stood up straighter and squared her shoulders. "Not really. Uncle Paxton told me that he was thinking of taking a few days off to visit some friends soon. Maybe he decided to do that instead."

Lawson finally nodded. "That makes sense. Still, if you hear from Paxton, I need to speak with him as soon as possible. Tell him to call me directly. And if you two come up with anything relevant to the investigation, I'd ask that you do the same." He donned his hat and headed for the door.

With a puzzled look Jamie's way, Gavin followed him. "Thanks for stopping by, sheriff. If we hear anything, we'll let you know."

"Where's the truck?" Lawson asked out of the blue.

At first Gavin wasn't sure what he was talking about. "'Scuse me?"

Lawson pointed to the driveway. "Ava's truck. I didn't see it parked outside."

Gavin struggled to come up with a believable answer. "Oh...it's out back. I was cutting down some dead trees on the place."

The excuse was about as thin as the ice on William's Pond in wintertime, but it was all he could come up with.

"Speaking of, I noticed Jamie's car still up on the side of the road. I figured you hadn't had time to call your friend to tow it with everything going on. I gave him a call. He's going to pick it up sometime tomorrow."

Gavin was surprised by Lawson's kindness. "Thank you," he managed.

"No problem. It's best not to leave cars unattended for too long. You wouldn't want someone to come along and vandalize it."

He still didn't buy the sheriff's motives. "No, we would not."

Lawson looked him in the eye. "I meant what I said earlier. Let *me* know if you have anything useful."

Gavin closed the door with an uneasy feeling in the pit of his stomach. Why had Lawson been so insistent that they reach out to him and him alone? What was he up to?

SEVEN

"What was that about?" Jamie asked the second she was certain Lawson had gone.

Gavin slowly made his way back to the sofa and sank down. "It sounds as if he had no idea what Miller is up to, which is kind of strange."

She could see the effort of dealing with the sheriff had drained Gavin's energy. "You should lie down for a while and rest." She didn't want to say it aloud, but she had no idea if Gavin would be ready to make the hike up to Darlan Mountain.

Gavin shook his head. "I'm fine. I'm just trying to make sense of all of this."

She sat down next to him and took his hand. "I know you are, but it's hard. Nothing adds up. Do you think Miller is acting without Andy's permission? Andy certainly seemed in the dark about his actions."

Gavin turned so that he could look into her eyes, and her heart went crazy at the emotions she saw there. "He has a lot of other deputies working with him. How can Lawson not know?"

"Some sort of power play, you think?" she asked, and he shook his head and then leaned back against the sofa and closed his eyes. She knew no matter what was going on, he needed to rest. Otherwise, they'd never figure it out.

Jamie focused on their joined hands. "We're both tired and running on empty. Why don't you rest while I make us something to eat?"

His eyes opened and he smiled over at her. "That would be nice." When she started to get to her feet, he held her there. "I'm sorry this is happening to you, Jamie. You don't deserve any of it."

Jamie's heart went out to him. He was fighting so hard for her. She returned his smile. "You don't deserve what's happening, either. I know how hard it was for you losing your father and now Ava. I'm just so sorry, Gavin. But I'm thankful for your help. I can't imagine trying to do this alone."

His smile disappeared. He looked so serious. "You and I were friends for a long time before…well, before what happened. I'd do anything for you. Always will."

The lump in her throat made it hard to force words out. "I feel the same way about you. Maybe after this is all over, we can find our way back to being friends again." She really wanted that to happen.

Something darkened his expression. He reached up and touched her cheek gently, and her eyes closed, her heart racing in response to his touch. Was she only fooling herself, thinking they could simply be friends again?

With her emotions raw and close to the surface, she stumbled to her feet and he let her go. Without another word, she left him alone.

Jamie opened the refrigerator and stared at the meager contents without seeing them. It hurt to think about what might have been. She'd been so in love with him back then. Her world had revolved around the time they spent together. Friday night football games. Saturday night at the local drive-in in town, where all the kids went to hang out. Sunday afternoon cruising around town in Ava's old pickup truck. They'd spent every possible moment together, and yet it hadn't been enough. She'd gone to bed each night anticipating the next time she'd see him.

And then that day had happened and everything crumbled at her feet. She'd watched her father be taken away in handcuffs. Her seventeen-year-old heart couldn't take it all in. Visiting Noah at the jail with her uncle, Jamie had never seen her father look so desolate. The tears in his eyes haunted her to this day.

The trial that followed had been nothing but a sham. Her father's attorney kept insisting that he should take a plea, but Noah refused. He was innocent, and innocent people didn't go to jail.

The day the verdict came in had shattered that belief. Her father was going away for the rest of his life. There hadn't even been time to hold him one more time before he'd been escorted off to Eddyville, to the maximum security prison there.

She and Paxton had visited every chance they got. Uncle Paxton had vowed he'd find out the truth and get his brother free. It hadn't happened. Noah had died in a prison infirmary of miner's lung, and Jamie hadn't been able to get to him before he drew his final breath.

The funeral had been one of the most devastating days of her life. Jamie had thought she would never stop crying. She still remembered Ava's kindness that day, even though her father was considered a murderer by the town he once loved. Ava had organized a luncheon at the church, and she and Paxton had been treated with kindness. Jamie would forever be grateful for Ava Dalton's friendship. Now Ava was gone and someone was trying to silence Paxton for something he knew. Jamie was terrified that she and Gavin wouldn't be able to unravel the truth before it was too late and she and Paxton became the final victims of a nightmare that started ten years earlier.

Something startled Gavin awake. He looked around the darkened room. There had been movement. He'd sensed it.

Gavin struggled to a sitting position. The light from the monitor captured his attention right away. Jamie stood close by. He got to his feet and went over.

"What is it?" he asked, making her jump.

She pointed to the screen that showed the road in front of the house. "Miller came back about a half hour earlier. He was alone, until now."

There were two additional patrol vehicles out there. The reality of it sent his thoughts churning. They needed to get out.

"They're getting ready to storm the house. Jamie, whether or not they have any proof, they're going to arrest us. We have to leave now."

"There's a shortcut I remember from childhood. It should get us to my house faster. We can gather the supplies and head to the mine."

Gavin nodded. "Good. Let's get going. On foot, it's not going to be easy." He stumbled a little as he headed for the back of the place. When she didn't follow, he turned, seeing all her doubts.

"Are you sure you're up to this?" she asked.

He wasn't, but they were all out of choices. "I'll be fine." He tucked his weapon behind his back, and she grabbed the shotgun.

"I have more ammo at your place, but we need to take

extra just in case Miller has people stationed at your house. I think Ava keeps some extra shotgun shells in the hall closet. I'll grab some bullets for the Glock I have in my bag along with the binoculars."

He found his backpack, shoved the medicine inside along with extra bandages, and then headed for his room when she stopped him. "I'll get them. You just take it easy."

Gavin couldn't imagine how bad he must look. He sat down at the desk and continued to watch the monitor. The men were getting out of their vehicles. They didn't have much time.

"Jamie, we've got to get out of here now," he called out, and she came running into the room. He pointed to the screen. "They're coming this way. We'll never get away in time. Not with this." He pointed to his wound.

Her troubled gaze held his.

There was only one place he could think of for them to hide out in a pinch. "Ava has that old root cellar on the place. I think I can find it in the dark. Hopefully, they won't think to check there."

He turned off the monitors and slung the backpack she'd loaded with ammo over his shoulder. "We can't afford to use a flashlight," he told her. "Stay close to me."

She followed him out the back door, and they listened carefully. "I don't hear anything." He was worried. "I don't like it."

Jamie took his hand, and together they stepped off Ava's beloved back porch and headed out. Even though the yard was well maintained, they were still walking in the dark. The clouds hid most of the stars. The moon hadn't come up yet.

"It's just over there. Getting the door open will be a pain, though," he whispered.

Once they reached the cellar a little way from the house, Gavin grabbed the door handle and pulled. It took everything inside of him to keep from screaming in pain.

"Let me help." Jamie took hold of the door with him. Together they managed to lift it. He prayed the deputies hadn't heard the noise they made, but sound carried through the hollers.

They stopped and listened. "I don't hear anything, do you?" she whispered.

"No, but let's get out of sight as quickly as possible." Gavin went inside and held out his hand to Jamie.

"Be careful, it's been years since I've been down here. I don't know what kind of shape the stairs are in."

Once she was inside, he piled as much brush as he could in front of the door and then shut it as quietly as possible. Holding hands, they slowly made their way down the steps. When he reached the bottom one, he dug out the flashlight from his backpack and shone it around. Cobwebs clung to everything in sight. The place was covered in several inches of dust. He remembered his grandmother telling him that, with her advancing years, she hadn't canned anything in a long time. The cellar had sat unused for a while.

As he flashed the light around, he quickly noticed that the condition of the place was far worse than he thought. One of the walls appeared close to collapsing. Gavin pushed aside the image of the cellar entombing them inside its dusty walls.

"We can't afford to keep the light on. With the walls in such bad shape, the flashlight's beam will show through." He turned off the light and she moved closer, shivering. He would give anything to be able to reassure her it was going to be okay, but nothing could be further from the truth. He wasn't sure how much Miller knew of the property, but most of the older houses around these parts had root cellars.

He held her tight. Being close like this reminded him of all those times in the past when he and Jamie would slip off to a quiet place to be alone. He'd hold her, as he was right now, and they'd sneak kisses. He'd been crazy about her. Back then, he'd thought he would spend the rest of his life right here in Darlan with her at his side.

He'd been wrong. Neither one of them could have foreseen the tragic outcome that would drive them apart.

Outside, the noise of footsteps could be heard, rousing him from memories of the past. The men were almost right on top of them now. Jamie clutched him tighter.

"Any sign of them?" Miller asked. He sounded as if he was just outside the door.

"No, and there's been no movement at the house. Maybe they didn't come back to the house like you thought. They could have headed out of town." A voice he didn't recognize responded.

While the conversation continued, it sounded as if they were moving away from the cellar.

"How long do you think we should wait here before we leave?" Jamie whispered.

Gavin had no idea. Miller was law enforcement. He could be standing close by, waiting for them to slip up. "A little longer. If we leave before they've cleared the area, we might be walking straight into an ambush."

EIGHT

It felt as if they'd been huddled in the rotting old root cellar for hours, and Jamie wasn't sure what the worse danger was: the men searching for them outside or the man standing a breath away.

Holding him close, she could feel Gavin's steady pulse against her ear. But her heart was breaking all over again for what might have been.

If it weren't for the danger they now faced, it might have been ten years earlier. Before Gavin's final words imprinted themselves in her head.

He moved slightly. They faced each other. Did he feel the same way?

"Jamie…" He whispered her name, his voice rough with emotion. Her breath hung in her throat at the possibilities hidden there. She couldn't go back to the hurt.

She stepped back. His hands fell away. Would there ever be a time when they could be together without the past clouding their feelings?

"How long do you think we've been here?" she asked, needing to bring things back down to a less emotional level.

He dragged in a breath. "I'm not sure. Maybe an hour." She could hear the pain in his tone. She couldn't imagine how difficult the trek through the woods had been for him.

"How are you holding up?"

"Hanging in there, I guess." He didn't sound good.

"I think I saw a chair in the corner. You should sit down for a bit."

He didn't argue. "I think that's a good idea." Gavin felt his way over to the area where the chair was and eased his weight down. Jamie heard it squeak.

He leaned back, exhausted by the effort.

Lord, he needs Your strength. Please help him, Jamie silently prayed.

Outside, a sound captured her attention. "I hear voices again," she whispered and knelt next to him.

She reached for his hand, and he held it as a flashlight's beam bounced off the holes in the walls.

"We didn't check the cellar. They could be hiding in there." A voice she didn't recognize moved closer.

"They're not in there. But just to be sure…" Miller stopped. Before Jamie knew what the man intended, shots split the quiet of the night and whistled past them. Jamie grabbed hold of Gavin. They both hit the ground. Gavin tucked her in close, his body sheltering hers in a heroic measure that was just like Gavin.

Another round of shots kicked up dirt inches from where they lay. Then silence followed.

"Come on, let's get out of here. If they were in there, they're dead now. I don't want to have to explain this to the sheriff."

Leaves crunched beneath their feet as they walked away. After what felt like an eternity, Gavin slowly eased to his feet, holding his injured side. He dropped down to the chair. Immediately, Jamie was at his side, worried.

."Are you okay? You didn't get hit again?" Fear gripped her heart. He couldn't take much more.

Gavin barely managed an answer. "No, but I'm not okay. I think I reopened the wound."

She took the flashlight from him and shone it on his side. He was right. Blood seeped from the wound to stain his shirt.

"I put some extra bandages in the backpack," he forced out.

Jamie unzipped the bag and then helped him slide off his jacket before she unbuttoned his shirt.

"It's not too bad." It was a lie to reassure him. Nothing could be further from the truth. The wound appeared red and inflamed. She tossed the bloodied bandage away, then packed the wound with strips of cloth and rewrapped it.

Then she knew he needed to hear the truth. "You need medical help. If this gets infected…" She didn't finish.

"I'll be okay for the moment." She wanted to believe him, but in her mind, she couldn't imagine how he was going to make it to her house, much less the mine. "Gavin, you're barely able to stand by yourself."

He framed her face and looked into her eyes, silencing her. "I'll be okay. We have to keep moving. It's our only option. Right now, they believe we've left town. That won't last for long."

His answer wasn't the one she needed, but they were all out of choices.

Jamie helped him to his feet, then grabbed the backpack and slung it over her shoulder. With the shotgun in one hand and the flashlight in the other, Gavin leaned heavily against her as they stumbled up the stairs.

"Kill the flashlight. Let me go out first," Gavin said

in a near whisper. Jamie moved out of the way and let him ease the door open.

He stepped out into the dark night while Jamie's heart hammered in her ears. She couldn't hear a sound. Had Miller and his men headed back to their vehicles?

Please, God.

Gavin held out his hand. "I believe they've left," he said softly. "Let's get going. Which way to the shortcut?"

In the darkness, it was hard to find. "It's been years since I came out here. I believe it's this way." She pointed to the right, where nothing could be seen but blackness. At night, the hollers could be deadly. One wrong move and you could fall into one of the half-dozen abandoned mine shafts to your death. Or stumble off the side of the mountain.

She and Gavin started walking in the direction she'd indicated. Jamie hoped her memory proved true and they weren't running in circles.

With Gavin struggling to put one foot in front of another, Jamie tried to get her fuzzy brain to make sense of what they'd been through so far. Was this really all related to drugs? How did Sheriff Lawson fit into all of this?

"Where exactly will this way put us out at?" Gavin asked. He stopped and dragged in several labored breaths. Jamie's fear for him increased.

Somehow, she shoved aside her troubled thoughts. "Back off to the side of the house. I hope they aren't still watching it."

"Let's hope not," he managed. Guilt tore at her heart. She'd put Gavin's life in danger by turning to him for help.

"What do you think they did with Ava's truck?" she asked.

"Probably hauled it off somewhere and searched it

for whatever they were looking for at your house. They probably dumped it in one of numerous old mine shafts once they didn't find what they were looking for, to get rid of any evidence that would tie it to us. They'll do the same to you and me if they find us."

Those ominous words hung between them in the chilly night. "This has to be related to the drug problem in Darlan somehow," Gavin said, and Jamie suppressed a chill. "Still, why do they think Paxton would know anything about that?"

Jamie drew in a breath and voiced her beliefs. "Uncle Paxton told me he'd found proof that my father didn't kill yours. What if he's right and your father's death had something to do with drugs?"

Seconds ticked by before Gavin answered. "I think we should stick with what we know," he said quietly and he had no idea how much those words hurt to hear.

Jamie struggled to hold on to her composure. She didn't care what evidence they tried to falsify to prove their case against her uncle, there was no way she'd ever believe Paxton was involved in such a destructive thing.

"I can see the house." Jamie pointed up ahead, and Gavin followed her. "We're almost there." Her eyes skimmed his face, no doubt seeing the exhaustion he couldn't hide. "Do you think you can make it?" she asked gently.

He managed a nod, conserving his energy. Truth be told, he'd never been so happy to see anything than he was to see her old house. The hours in the woods had depleted what little strength he had left. It was a struggle to put one foot in front of the other.

Once they drew closer, Gavin glanced around, trying to pick up any abnormal movement. While he didn't see anything unusual, he couldn't help but feel they might be walking into an ambush. He took out his night-vision binoculars and zoomed in on the house. "I don't see anyone around the place. Let's hope it's empty."

They slowly eased down the rise and toward the back of the house.

Gavin stepped up on the porch and froze. Someone had left the back door standing slightly ajar. It hadn't been that way earlier.

"They've been here since our last visit." He pointed to the open door. "Miller must have searched the place again. Maybe he thought we left something incriminating behind."

He drew his weapon, eased the door farther open and went inside. He was almost halfway across the living room when he heard it. *Click, click, click.*

"Run, Jamie!" he yelled as he turned and ran as fast as he could, all but dragging her along with him.

They'd barely made it out the door when the house exploded. Both he and Jamie flew some twenty feet through the air.

For a moment, he lost consciousness. The heat from the fire brought him to. He stared up at the blaze. Where was Jamie?

Gavin struggled to his feet. The world around him swayed. It was as if everything had gone mute. While his hearing had taken the brunt of the explosion, he could feel blood trickling from several facial wounds.

Once the world stopped spinning, his only thought was for Jamie. Ignoring the pain in his side, he searched frantically for her. She'd landed a little way behind him. He could see her crumpled body lying still. Gavin covered the space between them as quickly as his broken body would allow, fear following him every step of the way.

"Jamie." He called out her name as he reached her side, then knelt next to her. He felt for a pulse. After he'd assured himself it was there, he touched her arms and legs. Nothing appeared broken. She had several cuts, as well, and she was bleeding.

He shook her. "Jamie, wake up."

She slowly opened her eyes. When she saw him, she grabbed him around the waist and held him tight, shaken.

"What happened?" She barely got the words out.

"The house was set to explode when someone entered it. No doubt all entrances were wired. They were probably expecting Paxton to return."

She pulled away and stared at the blazing inferno behind him. "I can't believe it. We almost died. Gavin. What are these men after?"

He shook his head. "I wish I knew. Right now, we've got to get out of here. They'll see the explosion and come looking to see if Paxton is dead."

As if in response to his words, the sound of a vehicle could be heard making its way up the mountain toward the blaze.

"Do you think you can walk?" he asked.

She nodded. "Yes, I think so."

He wasn't nearly so sure, but they didn't have a choice. He managed to get to his feet and held out his hand. She took it and slowly stood. For a second, she leaned against him and his arms tightened around her. He wondered if she was hurt worse than he'd originally thought.

"I'm okay," she said and pulled away, the moment gone.

Behind them, the noise of a vehicle coming to a stop could be heard.

"Stay here. I'll be right back," Gavin told her, and then keeping within the coverage of the trees, he crept closer. Gavin counted at least four armed men. He slowly eased back to where Jamie was hidden. If this was Miller and his men, and they spotted them, with both of them still shaken from the explosion, Gavin wasn't so sure they would survive another run-in.

NINE

Jamie watched the men staring at the fire. She and Gavin had moved a little deeper into the woods. From where they stood, she could see the front of the house quite clearly. The men weren't there to put it out. Through the blaze, she couldn't make out who they were, but they didn't seem a bit surprised by the explosion. They were talking amongst themselves as if nothing had happened.

A cell phone rang. "No one's here," one of the men said. "We're not sure if he's inside. The fire's still burning pretty bad." The man listened for a bit. "Alright. We'll see you in a few." He ended the call. "He's on his way up here now."

Several of the men didn't appear pleased by the news. They grumbled amongst themselves, then went back to watching the fire, talking and occasionally laughing.

While Jamie and Gavin watched, another vehicle pulled up. This time Jamie recognized the deputy's SUV.

"That's Miller," she whispered.

Dan Miller got out of the vehicle and went over to the men. Jamie tried to focus on what he was saying. "I'm going down the mountain to make sure no one sees the fire and decides to come and investigate. We still don't know who set it off?"

"No, there's been no activity around. Whoever was in there is probably dead," the man who had been on the phone answered.

"Did you search around the place?" Miller demanded, clearly not satisfied with the way things had gone.

The silence that followed angered him more.

"Well, do it," Miller all but yelled at the man. "Paxton's smart and he knows we're after him."

"You heard him. Get to it." The other man took out his anger on the men with him.

"We've got to get out of here now." Gavin grabbed her hand, and they started running as fast as they could.

"Hold on. I see someone over there!" one of the men yelled. "There's two of them."

"That's Jamie and Gavin. We can't let them get out of here alive."

Her heart thundered with each step. There were five of them. Even with the weapons she and Gavin had, they couldn't hold them off long.

Gavin looked behind them. The men had cleared what was once the side of the house and were coming toward them full force. "We need a diversion."

She remembered they were close to a boarded-up mine. "There's that old abandoned mine that collapsed years ago. It's not too far from here. If we can get some space between us and those men, we can hide there."

Gavin's silence told her the idea was not a welcome one, but they were all out of options.

"Gavin, it's our only chance."

"Do you remember the location well enough to find it in the dark?"

She hadn't been there in years, but she had a general recollection of where it was.

"Yes, I can find it."

He let her hand go and she stopped, turning to face him. "What are you doing? They'll be here soon."

She saw him smile sadly. "I'm going to do an old-fashioned shoot-out. See if I can buy you some time."

Jamie shook her head. "You can't stand them off alone. You're outnumbered."

"I'll be fine. I'm right behind you. Just keep moving."

"No, Gavin." She didn't want to leave him behind. She couldn't bear the thought of something happening to him.

"Go, Jamie." With one final look into his eyes, she turned and started running as fast as she could.

"Over there!" one of the men yelled and started firing in Jamie's direction. She barely made it behind a tree before bullets rushed past her.

When there was silence again, she started running and didn't look back.

Behind her, more shots fired, followed by another weapon engaging. Gavin.

Someone yelped in pain. It took everything inside of her not to turn around and go back to make sure he was okay. She knew she couldn't do that. Gavin was a trained CIA agent. Better equipped to handle the situation than she was, even wounded.

Jamie reached the area where the abandoned mine had collapsed. It had once been one of the oldest working mines in Darlan County. In the dark, and trying to recall the location from memory, it took longer than she'd expected, but she finally found the boarded-up hole in the side of the mountain. Nothing about it was inviting.

The mine had been sealed off for a long time, since she was a child. When it had collapsed, it had trapped six miners below. The rescue team hadn't made it to the site of the disaster in time to save any of them.

Jamie yanked away enough boards to get inside. Shoving aside her fear of spiders and creepy-crawly things, she squeezed through the opening and did her best to replace the boards in case the men happened her way.

What if the area where she stood was unstable? It had been years since anyone had been in here. If it collapsed, she'd be buried alive. With difficulty, she shoved the fear aside. She was trying to save her uncle's life. She had to be strong.

The gunfire had stopped. Where was Gavin? She couldn't let herself consider that he might have been captured, or worse.

As Jamie stared into the blackness surrounding her, she heard something alarming nearby—what sounded like footsteps coming her way at a fast pace.

She clasped her hand over her mouth as the steps halted next to the mine. Someone shoved one of the boards free. Jamie inched away from the entrance as a flashlight's beam illuminated the area where she had just been.

"I don't see anyone. The place is unstable. They wouldn't hide there. Let's keep going."

After a moment, the footsteps faded into the distance. Jamie let go of the breath she'd held on to.

Just as she'd begun to relax, another set of footsteps came to a stop next to the mine entrance.

"Jamie, are you in there?" Gavin whispered so quietly that she almost didn't hear him. Relief overtook her fear.

"Yes, I'm in here." She thanked God for keeping him safe.

He shoved the rest of the boards free and held out

his hand to her. She ignored it, going straight into his arms and holding him tight. Happy to be out of the musty mine.

"Which way were they heading?" he asked when she finally let him go.

She pointed up ahead. "Toward the Darlan Mountain Mine. Gavin, what if Uncle Paxton's in there somewhere hurt?"

With Gavin close by, they started walking toward the mine at a fast pace while Jamie tried to control her fears.

She didn't want to think what would happen to her uncle if those men stumbled on him in the belly of the mine.

"We need to reach the mine before they do." Gavin couldn't believe what had just taken place. In the firefight, he'd managed to hit one of the men. Soon after, he'd heard a vehicle leaving. He assumed it was Miller going down the mountain to make sure no one else happened their way. Miller was a coward who didn't care if his men got injured trying to protect whatever illegal activity he and the rest of his team were up to.

To stand a chance of saving Paxton, they'd have to reach the mine before the men.

He and Jamie had been walking for a little while when he heard a noise behind them that sounded like more vehicles coming up the mountain and he turned. Two patrol vehicles, with their lights flashing, rolled up on the scene of the fire. No one got out. Was Andy Lawson in one of them? Gavin had no idea how Andy fit into the picture. He hadn't been part of the previous attack at the house, and he hadn't been lying in wait outside Ava's home. Was he the person calling the shots?

"You think they'll call the fire department to put the

fire out, or will they let it burn to the ground?" Jamie asked with emotion weighing in her voice. This was her family home. She'd lived there most of her life.

Gavin tugged her into his arms. "They were hoping they killed the person they were after, namely Paxton, but now they know it was us inside the house. They won't let up. They'll let the fire burn itself out, and then they'll cover the whole thing up, somehow."

"They have to be stopped. We can't let them get away with this." He could tell she was close to losing it.

He turned her in his arms so that he could look into her eyes. "They won't. I promise you, I'm not going to let them get away with what they've done."

She held him close and nodded against his chest. He'd do everything in his power to figure out what was happening here.

"One thing is for sure. If they set the explosives to catch Paxton, then he's still alive and out there some- where. And the sooner we get to him, the better." He just hoped they located Paxton before the men look- ing for him.

"You're right. We have to find him before they do."

The cloudy night made the going more difficult the higher up the mountain they went. Still, Gavin didn't dare risk using the flashlight to light their way. It would be a glaring beacon to those men.

"What I can't understand is why Paxton hasn't been living at the house. How long have Miller and his men been chasing him?" Gavin wondered aloud.

"I can't believe I had no idea what was happening to him. Every time I spoke with him, he never let on that anything was wrong. I just assumed he was stay- ing at the house still." She sighed softly. "I noticed he'd cleared a lot of space behind the place. He told me a while back that he wanted to do some farming back there. It doesn't make sense."

She was right. Why had Paxton cleared the area only to let the power be shut off? "You can't think of anything he might have said in passing that might help us clear up what's really happening here?"

He had to believe that Paxton would have mentioned something about the situation to his niece, if only by accident.

She thought about it for a second. "When he called this last time, he mentioned that he didn't trust any police, especially the sheriff's office here, and hadn't for a while. When I asked him why, he never could tell me anything in particular. Or maybe he was afraid to say it over the phone." She looked up at him. "I'm sorry. I should have pressed him for answers. I just thought... well, I thought he was being Uncle Paxton." She stopped for a second. "He loved my father so much, and he was determined not to let him take the blame for killing yours."

Gavin didn't want to have this discussion again. He admired her loyalty to her father, but he couldn't share her faith in Noah's innocence.

One of Gavin's previous conversations with Ava ran through his head. She'd defended Noah fervently as well, refusing to believe him guilty. Ava, Noah and Paxton had always been close, along with his father.

When he couldn't think of anything to say, they continued walking again.

"What do you think Miller and his men are really up to by escalating the violence?" Jamie asked when the silence between them grew.

There was only one answer that made sense in Gavin's mind. "They're trying to cover up something.

Probably something they're involved in that Paxton found out."

Jamie shook her head. "Like what?"

"I'm not sure. Ava seemed particularly worried about the influx of drugs into the area causing an increase in crime. She blamed the sheriff's office for not doing more to curtail the drugs."

"I remember her telling me the same thing," Jamie said, making him curious as to how often she'd spoken to his grandmother.

"She always was crazy about you. I'm glad you two stayed in touch."

Jamie smiled at him. "We didn't talk as often as we should have. That was my fault. There were certain things that we just couldn't move beyond and it was hard…" She stopped, but he understood.

"Still, thank you for keeping in touch with her. I admit, there were times when it was hard for me to talk to her as well. Too many bad memories, I guess."

He didn't say as much, but calling Ava had been difficult because every time he spoke to her it reminded him of the woman he'd lost.

It was the main reason he'd left Darlan behind in the first place. Everywhere he looked, he'd seen the past. His father. Jamie. What might have been. Yet the guilt was still there, even after he left and Ava had needed him. Oh, she would never have said as much, but she'd wanted her only family member close. Instead, he'd been running from a troubled past he couldn't escape, and it had tainted his entire existence.

He couldn't imagine where his life might have gone if he hadn't joined the Scorpions. After his marriage ended, he'd been in a bad place. Several times, he'd called Ava, wishing he could pour out his darkest thoughts to her, but he hadn't been able to say a word. He hadn't even told his grandmother that he'd gotten married in the first place. How was he going to tell her he'd made a mess of it? Through his brothers and sisters in the Scorpion unit, he'd found God and his life had been changed.

Still, he regretted the way things ended between himself and Emily. She was sweet and kind and she reminded him of Jamie. He'd been drawn to her because of the bad place he'd been in since his father's murder. They'd met while he was back in the states in between missions. He'd been searching for something positive and latched onto her light. They'd eloped after knowing each other less than a month and it wasn't long before the marriage started to fracture.

Emily wanted to meet his grandmother, but Gavin always had one excuse or another not to. Mostly, he believed he knew Ava would tell him he'd acted irrationally. She'd have been right. He had been floundering and grabbed on to Emily hoping she could save him.

His drive to succeed became another way of dealing with his grief. And if he was being truthful, Gavin had realized his marriage was a mistake as well. He'd thrown himself into his work more because of it, leaving Emily alone for long periods of time. Soon, it became too much for her to bear and she filed for divorce. He'd failed her.

Gavin would give anything to be able to go back in time and rewrite the past. Apologize to Emily. Be there for his grandmother. Believe Jamie. But he couldn't, and he had to live with the results of his decisions for the rest of his life.

TEN

They reached the rise above the Darlan Mountain Mine. Down below, the trailer that had served as an office for as long as Jamie could remember appeared dark. Nothing stirred.

Jamie started down toward it, but Gavin stopped her. "Hang on a second. We need to make sure it's clear." He unzipped his backpack and took out the binoculars once more, then scanned the building and the surrounding area. "I see them." He knelt down low and Jamie followed.

"Where are they?" she asked.

He pointed to the edge of the woods close by. "Over there. They're heading for the trailer." He handed her the binoculars. Three men advanced on the trailer. While two waited outside, the third went in. In a matter of seconds, the man returned to his friends.

Jamie listened carefully as their voices carried from the valley below. "No one's been here since the last time we searched the place," one of the men said, then murmured something Jamie couldn't catch.

"We'd better check the mine. They might be hiding in there," another man said.

The third man, who had been talking on his phone, went back over to where his buddies were. "Hold up a second. He wants us back at the house. Something's come up."

One of the men wasn't happy with the new orders. "They could be in there. We can take care of the problem once and for all."

"And I told you he wants us back at the house now. Something's going on," phone man barked, not liking that his orders were questioned.

The second reluctantly turned away. "Alright, but if they get away because we missed them inside, it's on him."

The three slowly eased back into the woods and out of sight.

Jamie let out a breath, then looked at Gavin. "What do you think that was about?"

The worried expression on his face didn't ease Jamie's mind any. "I have no idea, but I sure hope they haven't found Paxton."

If she and Gavin were wrong and Paxton wasn't in the mine, then it might cost her uncle his life.

"My gut tells me he's in the mine somewhere. This might be our only chance to check it out without them watching it," Gavin told her. "First, let's take a look inside the trailer."

As they drew near, Jamie could see broken glass everywhere. The place had been broken into by Miller's men. With her weapon at the ready, Jamie prepared herself to enter, with no idea what they'd find inside.

"Wait, Jamie." Gavin stopped her before she could go inside. She turned to him. "Let me check it out first." He was afraid of what they'd find inside.

As they stood facing each other, inches apart, Gavin unexpectedly touched her face. The tenderness in his eyes sent her heartbeat racing.

"I'll be right back." He dropped his hand and turned away, and she gathered in a much-needed breath.

Within seconds of entering the trailer, Gavin came back out. "You need to see this."

Jamie followed him. She stopped just inside the door and stared in disbelief at what she saw there. The file cabinet was open and files had been scattered all around. Paxton's desk was turned over.

"Oh, no." She clasped her hand over her mouth at what she saw on Paxton's office chair—what looked like more bloodstains in several spots. Coupled with what they'd found at her house, Jamie was almost certain something terrible had happened to Uncle Paxton.

Gavin spotted the blood, too, and came to her side. "We don't know that it's Paxton's."

She managed a nod. "What were they searching for in here?"

He looked around at the chaos and shook his head. "I don't know."

She scanned the interior of the trailer. Half of the file folders were empty of paperwork.

"What was in the files?" Gavin asked, evidently noticing the same thing.

Jamie shook her head. "In the past, it was just purchase orders for supplies and such and employee information, but as far as I know, the mine hasn't been working in months. Besides Terry, there are no other employees."

"Why would they care about a few purchase orders or employee records?" Gavin asked.

She shook her head. "What happened to make them leave like that before they searched the mine?" Had they found Uncle Paxton?

Gavin pulled her closer. "It could be anything. The sooner we get inside the mine, the sooner we have answers."

While he was right, she dreaded going down in there again. The last time stood out in her mind. She'd come here after they'd found her father standing next to Charles's lifeless body. She'd stared at the bloodstained ground and couldn't believe what was happening.

"Are you okay?" Gavin asked. The concern in his eyes told her he'd read her thoughts.

She managed a nod and he let her go. Jamie watched him kneel down and pick up several of the files lying on the floor.

"This one's marked revenue." He grabbed another one. "Purchase orders." Several papers were in the file. "There's certainly nothing of any importance here. Why take the files…unless…"

"They were looking for something else. Maybe they thought they'd find a clue as to where whatever they're missing might be found. Maybe that's why they took some of the file contents," Jamie reasoned.

"I don't think Paxton would take the chance of leaving anything important here, where he knew they could gain access easily enough." Gavin said, unconvinced.

Jamie lifted her shoulders. "You're right, it sounds silly. Knowing Uncle Paxton the way I do, I can't see it, either."

Gavin got to his feet and tossed the file folders down on the floor once more. "We're not going to get any answers here. Let's get to the mine."

They left the trailer, and Gavin flipped on his flash-light. "Hopefully, those men are far enough away that they won't see the light. We're going to need it down there."

She sensed his reluctance to enter the mine, and she certainly understood. He'd come to the mine and seen his father lying dead. Going back down there would bring back the ugly memories of that day.

As they headed to the gaping black void that was the entrance, Jamie couldn't help but feel as if the truth behind the decade-old murder that had been hidden for so long was about to rise, finally, to the surface. One way or another.

Gavin hadn't been inside the mine since they'd found his father. After what happened to Charles, he'd sworn never to go down there again. Yet here he was. He had to put aside the devastating memories of that day, and help Jamie find Paxton.

Still, it was hard to push aside all that he'd lost. He stopped at the entrance, stuck in place. Unable to put one foot in front of the other.

Jamie turned back to him. "I know it's hard," she said gently.

He managed a smile. "It is. I haven't been here since…that day."

She took his hand. "Me, either. You can do this, Gavin. I know you can."

The fear in her eyes urged him on. She needed him. He'd do it for Jamie.

He squeezed her hand and then aimed the flashlight through the entrance. Drawing in deep breaths, together they went inside to purge old memories once and for all.

The temperature dropped by degrees the farther down they went. The place was just as dark and dank as he remembered.

Right away, it became clear it hadn't been a working coal mine in quite some time. The road used to access the mine was showing signs of lack of use. There were more pot holes than road left, which seemed to indicate the mine hadn't been in use much longer than what Paxton had indicated to Jamie. So, what had her uncle been doing down here, if not mining, and why did Terry have to lose his life?

The ceiling was so low that they had to bend over to walk. They reached the spot where the single mine shaft divided into two separate tunnels.

"Which way?" Gavin asked. The one to the right was where they'd found his father. He didn't want to go that way.

Gavin couldn't hide his unease from her. "There's nothing much going on to the left. That's just where the supplies are stored, if I remember correctly."

He drew in a breath. "Okay, right it is."

Gavin flashed the light down the tunnel. The narrow entrance did little to reassure him.

They started walking, their steps echoing off the walls. Maintaining a bent-over position was hard on the back. Gavin could feel the stress on his injured side, too. As hard as he tried, he couldn't shake the bad feeling growing in the pit of his stomach. What if they were walking into a trap? He didn't understand why the men had suddenly backed away from hunting them. They knew he and Jamie were still out here. The mine was the only logical place for them to go. So why let them get away?

They reached another fork. A similarly narrow shaft veered off to the right and looked as if it was ready to collapse. He didn't like the looks of it.

Jamie shook her head. "This part of the tunnel wasn't there the last time I was here."

"You're right, but I feel we have to check it out." He flashed the light down the passageway. It seemed to go on for a long way.

As they made their way farther into the bowels of the mountain, the shaft suddenly ended. Gavin examined the wall closely, then tapped it with the flashlight. "It's fake," he exclaimed in disbelief.

Jamie came up beside him. "Why would my uncle build a fake wall?" Their eyes met as they both realized. Something valuable was hidden behind it.

"Let's find out." Gavin slammed the end of the flashlight against the wall, and pieces easily crumbled away. In no time, he'd made a hole large enough to crawl through.

Behind it, they found something alarming.

"Oh, no." Jamie stared in shock. "Gavin, is that..."

"Yes, heroin, and lots of it." Gavin couldn't believe what he was seeing. Had Ava been right all along and everything that had happened to them so far, his father's death, even, came down to a bunch of drugs? If so, how did Paxton fit into what they'd uncovered?

Jamie went over to the stacks of drugs. "But why is it here?" she wondered aloud.

Gavin didn't want to voice the obvious, but she must have seen the look on his face.

"No way. No matter how bad it looks, Uncle Paxton's not involved in these drugs."

He wanted to believe her, but someone had obviously

brought the drugs in and gone to great lengths to keep them hidden. Paxton was the obvious choice.

Gavin didn't voice his thought aloud. "Whatever is really going on here, we need help now, because this thing has gotten way out of hand." He knew getting anyone from law enforcement involved wasn't something she wanted to do, but in his opinion, they were all out of choices.

Before she could answer, a noise echoed through the mine.

"What was that?" Jamie asked.

Gavin turned. He could hear voices coming from behind them. "Miller's men. They're coming after us. We have to hurry."

He grabbed her hand, and still in a doubled-over position, they made their way back to the main tunnel. Once they were back on track, they raced down the narrow passage and deeper into the mine.

"I see them up ahead." Miller! He and his men were closing in.

"The drugs are here as well," one of Miller's men yelled.

"Leave the heroin where it is for now. Hurry up. They're getting away," Miller ordered.

Shots rang out behind them, bouncing off the walls and dislodging rocks.

Was Miller crazy or just that desperate? One false shot and the whole place could come down. "Hurry, Jamie. This place is unsteady. It could collapse at any moment." As they continued running down the narrow passage, Gavin pulled Jamie in front of him. "Keep going," he told her when she turned back to him, confused. He wasn't going to let one of those stray bullets strike her. He'd die first.

They moved as fast as they could. Up ahead, the passage suddenly split into two separate directions.

"Which way?" Jamie said in a tense whisper.

Gavin had no idea. "Just pick one." Before they could choose a passage, the world around them rumbled and shook.

"Get down!" Gavin grabbed Jamie and ducked as low as he could as huge chunks of rock splintered from the crumbling walls inches from them. The mine was caving in around them. Close by, the ceiling rained to the floor beneath the compromised walls, and immediately the world was plunged into darkness as dust and debris became so thick that he could taste it.

The flashlight fell from his hand. Gavin could feel the grit from the blanket of dust covering both him and Jamie, instantly filling his lungs. He coughed violently and wiped tears from his eyes. Jamie buried her face against his chest. It felt as if the world would never be steady again. And then an eerie silence replaced the noise.

Gavin tried to collect his thoughts. They were trapped inside the mine with their outside air supply cut off and surrounded by dense black. And Miller and his men now had access to the drugs. They didn't need Gavin and Jamie any longer. They'd let them die down here, and no one would ever be the wiser.

Jamie coughed and tried to clear her lungs of the dust while Gavin searched around for the flashlight and found it. He tried the switch. Nothing. The flashlight had broken in the collapse.

Near the place where the tunnel had caved in, Gavin heard footsteps. Someone was coming close.

"Let's get out of here," Miller said. "There's no way they're getting out alive. Come on, we need to move the drugs to a safe place."

Footsteps faded. Miller and his men had entombed them down here. Would it prove to be their final resting place?

ELEVEN

The pitch blackness surrounding them was terrifying. The air was clogged with coal dust. Jamie fought back fear. She didn't want to die here without knowing what had happened to her uncle. With no idea where the two shafts would lead, they had to keep moving. Keep fighting. "Gavin, we can't let them win. We can't die down here."

In the darkness, he gently framed her face. He was so close, and she needed him so much. "I'm not going to let that happen. We are not going to die down here. We'll locate Paxton and find out what's really going on with the drugs," he assured her with so much confidence that she almost believed him.

Gavin got to his feet and pulled her up beside him. For a moment, she clung to his strength.

"I'm right here. I'll always be right here," he said and held her close.

"I'm so glad you are. I can't imagine going through this without you."

His lips brushed across her forehead. "I'm glad I'm here, too." He took out his phone and flipped on the flashlight app, illuminating the rubble surrounding them.

Jamie looked around at the destruction. "If we'd been

standing closer to the collapsed side, we might both be dead."

"Don't think about that now," Gavin told her. Even covered in dust, he'd never looked more handsome.

She managed a smile for his sake. "We both look like we've survived a war."

He chuckled at her description. "Yeah, but we're alive, and that's all that matters. Let's keep moving. We need to find another way out of here and fast." She knew he didn't want to say it, but their air supply would only last so long.

"I'm not sure which path to take."

Gavin shone the light both ways. "I don't think these passages were here the last time we were in the mine. Your uncle added them for a reason. Maybe he was expecting something like this to happen, and he wanted to be prepared for it."

Jamie prayed that in the process of digging out the extra passages, Uncle Paxton had found another way out of the mine.

"Let's go right," Jamie said and he nodded. It was as good a choice as any. While they came prepared to go into the mine, their resources would sustain them for only so long.

They headed down the passage with no idea where the path would lead them. What if they ran into another dead end? They'd be trapped inside their own tomb.

Her mind kept going back to the heroin they'd found and what Miller had said about it. "Do you think the sheriff's department is involved in smuggling drugs?" Until recently, the thought would have been unimaginable.

"It's looking more like they are. What I don't understand is why."

Was it just her imagination, or was it getting harder to breathe? "I can't help but believe, we're missing something important that will tie everything together."

Gavin shook his head, helpless. "I've been racking my brain trying to come up with something that would shed some light on the situation. There has to be more going on here than Miller and his men smuggling drugs. Something bigger…" He stopped, his gaze latching onto hers. "I remember something my grandmother told me shortly after my father died. She mentioned that a corporation had started buying up lots of the old mines across Kentucky. They approached my dad about buying the Darlan Mountain Mine. My dad had refused their offer flat out. Ava said Dad mentioned that he felt threatened by the man who came to see him." Gavin shook his head, frustrated. "I'm not sure what that has to do with anything, though."

She thought about what he'd said. "Maybe nothing, but it's certainly curious and the same thing happened to Uncle Paxton not too long ago. He said some people offered to buy the mine from Ava. She still had controlling rights, but she'd turned over the management of the mine to Paxton. When he told Ava about the offer, she refused to sell out right." Jamie stopped walking and faced him. "Did Ava tell Sheriff Lawson about the threat at the time? It certainly would indicate someone else might have had a reason to harm your father."

Gavin shook his head. "She tried. But the sheriff wouldn't listen. He felt he had enough evidence to convict Noah for killing Charles. The case was closed."

Jamie couldn't believe she'd never heard the story from Ava. "As far as I know, she never mentioned the previous offer to Uncle Paxton. Still, it's strange. Do you think it was the same person who offered to buy the mine before?" She hesitated. "Gavin, maybe the people trying to buy the mine are the ones who really killed your father."

The disbelief in his eyes hurt like crazy. He still believed Noah was capable of killing his father. Nothing had changed.

"As much as I want to believe you, Noah was convicted of the murder and there was never any evidence to prove someone else was involved," he said quietly. His answer was not what she wanted to hear and she struggled to keep it together. "I'm sorry, but I'm not ready to go there yet."

What little hope she held on to evaporated. Would he ever believe her? She lifted her chin. "You may not be, but there's no doubt in my mind my father didn't kill yours." Yet arguing this point again wasn't getting them anywhere and they were running out of time.

Jamie drew in a steadying breath, then let the resentment go. "There's plenty of abandoned mines around. Why not use them instead of calling attention to themselves by trying to buy out the Darlan Mountain Mine?" She shook her head. "And how do these people fit in the heroin trade, if at all? What does any of this have to do with the sheriff's office?" she said in a frustrated tone.

"For one, most of the abandoned mines around have collapsed. They'd have to dig them out to store anything there. Still, it would make more sense than buying an active mine and shutting it down. Something's off here, I just don't know what." He shrugged helplessly. "Maybe I'm being naïve, but I can't help but believe that Andy Lawson isn't involved in this thing."

Jamie couldn't share his belief. "How can he not be? He's the sheriff. Those are his men."

Gavin stood his ground. "I know, but I remember

Andy from school. He was a punk and he got himself into a lot of trouble growing up, but I don't think he's capable of murder."

While she didn't share his opinion of Andy's innocence, Gavin was a trained officer. He'd faced this kind of thing more times than she had. "You think Dan Miller is the mastermind behind it all?" Jamie knew the man somewhat from the past. He was intelligent, but she didn't believe he would have come up with the plan to smuggle drugs through the county on his own.

"It's possible, I guess. Miller is certainly cunning enough, but I think this is beyond his scope. There's a bigger player involved here."

Jamie couldn't imagine who that might be. Right now, however, she was just terrified they would run out of air before they could get out of the mine alive.

Gavin tried the phone. "There's no service. I'm not surprised. We're pretty far under the mountain, but we're heading north."

"That means we're heading in the direction of the wilderness. Gavin, there are miles and miles of woods out there. If we make it out of here alive, we'll have to hike out."

Remaining positive was a hard thing to do under their circumstances. If they found a way out, trying to navigate their way through the wilderness surrounding the mine could prove its own challenge, not to mention the unpredictable weather. It was just the two of them with limited resources and no one looking for them. They were in big trouble.

With every breath they took sucking up what precious little air remained in the mine, Gavin's faith was faltering, but he wasn't about to give in to the doubts. He had to keep fighting.

Being with Jamie again made him realize that he'd never stopped caring for her. The argument she'd made concerning the people trying to buy the mine being connected to his father's death made sense, but why hadn't any of this come out before now if it were true? Still, whatever the truth proved to be, whether his father's murder was at the hands of Noah or someone else, together they'd figure it out, then maybe they could finally break the shackles of the past.

Yet as hard as he tried, he couldn't understand how the heroin and the sheriff's department might be connected to the big business trying to buy his family's mine. Without more to go on, it was useless to speculate. Survival was the only thing that mattered now, and he needed something to take his mind off their impossible situation. He found himself wondering about Jamie's life back in Louisville.

She had grown into a strong woman in spite of what she'd had to overcome. She'd weathered the storms thrown at her, and she was still standing.

"Tell me about your life now. Are you happy?" he asked, because he wanted her to be.

She didn't look at him. He sensed it wasn't a subject she liked to talk about. Especially with him.

"I suppose. As happy as anyone can be with the past we have. I love my job. Helping others who are wrongfully accused get their freedom back feels like I'm helping my dad a little." She shrugged.

He stopped and reached for her hand. "I'm sorry you had to go through that."

She turned to face him, swallowing hard. She looked into his eyes and his heart broke. The pain he saw there assured him how difficult her father's conviction and death had been for her to deal with. He should have been there for her.

Gavin drew her close, wishing for a second chance with her. Their eyes held and he brushed a strand of hair from her face. Even covered in dust, her hair powdered white, she was beautiful, and her beauty stirred him inside.

"Regardless of what happened between my father and yours, you needed me and I let you down." He tipped her chin. Saw tears in her eyes. Hated himself for his part in her pain. He leaned close. Her eyes closed, and his lips claimed hers. The tiniest of sobs escaped before she kissed him back with all the pent-up emotions from their past. The danger they faced, the death that was closing in all around them, just faded away. It was the two of them again and it felt like she belonged in his arms.

Jamie pushed free suddenly, and he let her go. She turned away. The past and its heartache was still standing between them. Would it always be?

More than anything, Gavin wished he could believe what she said about Noah's innocence. Yet the conviction wouldn't let him.

"We should keep going. There has to be another way out. We just have to find it."

Gavin let the past go and glanced around, spotting something he hadn't seen before. A small light off to the right. As much as he wanted to believe it was a way out, he knew it wasn't. It would still be dark out. Still, it was something they needed to investigate.

"Look over there." He pointed to the light. "What is that?"

He and Jamie went closer. "It's a door." He tried to open it. "It's not budging." Their gazes locked.

"Uncle Paxton," Jamie said. "He must be in there."

"Can you hand me your shotgun?" he asked, and she gave it to him. He slammed the butt of the weapon hard against the door. It took several tries before it flew open and they faced a room filled with light.

"Let's go see what's inside," he told her and went through the door first. What he saw was shocking. There were several file cabinets set up, much like those in the trailer.

He went over to the first one and pulled out a file, letting out a low whistle at what he saw there. "Paxton clearly hasn't been mining for a while, but he has been gathering massive amounts of evidence." Jamie looked over his shoulder. "There are dozens of files with surveillance photos in here. Look at this one." He pointed to it.

It was at an abandoned building she didn't recognize. It had been taken at night and was grainy, but she spotted Dan Miller and one of the other deputies talking to a well-dressed man.

"Who do you think that is?" she asked.

"I have no idea. What's he up to with these guys?" Gavin pulled out another file, and what he saw inside was alarming. "We've got a bigger problem than we thought. Look at this." He showed her some notes written by Paxton. "Jamie, I recognize this name, Jacob Ericson. He's the head of the Southern Mafia."

She stared up at him as if trying to comprehend the significance. "Why would the Southern Mafia be involved in this unless…it's their drugs. The deputies are moving their drugs for them."

Gavin had come to the same conclusion. "That'd

be my guess, too. Looks like the Southern Mafia has bought out the local law enforcement."

He dug another file out. "Paxton sure did his homework. He has a picture of our mystery man with Ericson. I wonder what he has to do with the Southern Mafia."

Jamie grabbed a separate file and scanned it. "I don't know. What do you know about the Southern Mafia?"

While he and his team had been working a weapons smuggling case recently, the FBI had shared some intel with them. The Sothern Mafia was one of the biggest drug organization in the South.

He told her what he'd learned. "They have a stronghold in just about every Southern state, and Ericson rules the entire operation with an iron fist. You don't screw over this guy and live."

Gavin recalled something he'd heard recently about an attempt on Ericson's life that had almost worked. He told her about it. "Ericson was almost killed in a bombing. Someone rigged his car to explode when he opened the door."

His gaze locked with hers. "Just like the explosives used on your house. If you ask me, someone is trying to take over Jacob Ericson's empire, and they don't care who they kill in the process. My guess is, it's the man in the photo."

Gavin could almost read Jamie's thoughts, yet in his mind, all the information they'd uncovered so far made him even more justified in believing that what they were dealing with now had nothing to do with Charles's death.

TWELVE

"You think our mystery man is trying to take over control of the Southern Mafia?" Jamie asked in disbelief.

"That would be my guess."

Jamie pulled out another file marked Mines Purchased Recently. "Oh, no. Here's a list of all the mines that have been bought over the past few years." She recognized Paxton's handwriting next to each entry.

"Look at this." She pointed to the letter written next to each of them. "What do you think he means by I?"

Gavin stared at it for a second. "Inactive. I'm guessing these inactive mines are no longer being dug for coal. I can understand why they'd want to buy up the inactive mines. If it's private property, no one should come snooping around asking questions, but why would they want to buy the Darlan Mountain Mine? It's still semi-active. What are these guys up to?"

Jamie looked at him without answers. "Whatever it is, we have to stop them."

"The question is how? And how did our mystery guy, or the Southern Mafia, get the deputies and maybe even the sheriff to work for them? Are they all corrupt?"

In Jamie's mind, it certainly appeared so. "Maybe they're helping this guy move the drugs from mine to mine." It made sense in a way. Who better to move heroin than the people who were supposed to be keeping the county safe?

Yet none of the evidence Paxton had gathered cleared Noah's name. If she and Gavin died down here, they might never know.

With each breath, Jamie could feel their oxygen supply evaporating. "Gavin, we're running out of air," she said in alarm.

Desperate, he looked around for some way out, but the room appeared to be carved into the mountain.

He tried his cell phone. "Still nothing," he said without hope.

Whoever was behind this was willing to go to deadly extremes to keep his past deeds buried forever.

"Let's go back out to the passage and see where it takes us," Jamie said. She was trying to put on a brave front, but in truth, she was scared to death of dying in the mine.

Gavin squeezed her hand, and they left the storage room and continued down the narrow shaft.

"How do you think Paxton managed to build these tunnels by himself?" she asked, because she had to think of something to take her mind off their critical situation.

Gavin looked around. "It must have taken him years."

"If Paxton did all this, then he had to have created another way out," she said.

He looked down at her and smiled. "It makes sense to me."

She could see exhaustion in his eyes. His injury was

slowing him down, making it hard to put one foot in front of the other.

"How are you holding up?" she asked. She was worried about him. His expression drawn.

"I'm okay," he managed, but she didn't believe him. He couldn't go on much longer.

They'd walked about a quarter of a mile farther when Jamie noticed something unusual about the stone wall to her right. The coloring didn't match the rest of the wall. She knocked on it. It sounded hollow.

Gavin halted next to her. "What is it?"

"I think this is another fake wall."

Gavin tapped the wall. "You're right. It's not made of rock at all. It feels thin, like sheetrock."

"Can we break through it?"

"I'm pretty sure." He smashed the butt of his weapon against the wall. Chunks of sheetrock splintered from the site. Jamie took the shotgun and did the same. As they worked, more and more pieces fell free until there was a gaping hole in it. Nothing but darkness appeared before them.

Jamie continued to chip away at the hole until it was big enough to climb through.

"Let me go first," Gavin insisted. She wasn't surprised by his concern. He was always good at looking out for her.

"Be careful. We don't know what's on the other side." He looked deep in her eyes. There was so much more that she wanted to say, but now was not the time.

Gavin stepped through the hole and flashed the light around. "Oh, no…" But he didn't finish. Something crashed to the ground, and then the room grew dark once more.

"Gavin!" she screamed and didn't hesitate before scrambling through the hole to help him. She couldn't let anything happen to Gavin. "Gavin, are you okay?" Jamie had barely cleared the entrance when she slammed into Gavin. He'd stopped inches from the opening.

"What is it?" She had just gotten the words out when she realized why he'd stopped so suddenly. The sound of a shotgun being racked sent fear through her. They'd come this far only to die here in this dark hole without any answers.

"Don't hurt her," she heard Gavin say. "She's not part of this."

Nothing but silence followed. Jamie's hands shook. The pitch dark was broken by a light so piercing that it was blinding. Her nerves frayed.

Jamie tried a last-ditch effort to save their lives. "Please, we're trying to find my uncle. He mines this place and he's missing. We're trying to help him because we think he may be hurt."

The light in her eyes moved, and she could see again. She prayed this man wasn't connected to the deputies.

"Jamie? Is that you?" Jamie barely recognized her uncle's voice. He sounded so weak.

"Paxton!" The light dropped to the ground near the man. She realized it was the type of flashlight that miners used to mount to their safety helmets. Paxton had taken his off.

Jamie hurried to her uncle's side. Laying the shotgun down, she couldn't believe he was right there with them. It was then that she noticed the pain marring his kindly face.

"You're hurt," she exclaimed when she saw the way

his right leg was stretched out in front of him. "You've been shot."

He collapsed onto the ground, perspiration beading his forehead. "Yes, but I'll be okay. I'm not letting a couple of thugs take me down."

"I can't believe it." Jamie pulled him close again. He was alive. Thanks be to God, her uncle was still alive.

Gavin dropped down next to Jamie. "Have you been down here all along?" he asked the man in amazement.

Paxton managed a tiny nod.

Gavin took Paxton's light and shone it on the man's injured leg. It looked as if it hadn't been attended to at all. "What happened to you?"

"That deputy shot me in the leg!" Paxton exclaimed and then leaned back and closed his eyes. The very act of speaking took its toll.

Jamie shot Gavin a look. "When was this? Was it Dan Miller who shot you?"

Paxton shook his head. "No, one of the other deputies, but I think he was acting on Miller's orders. It happened the day I called you." Paxton peered up at her. "I went up to the house. I knew it was too soon for you to be there, but I wanted to make sure I was there when you arrived."

Jamie clasped his hand tight, thankful that her uncle was still alive.

"Do you know the deputy's name?" Gavin asked.

Paxton shook his head. "No, he's new to the area, but he's definitely one of Miller's goons. He demanded I leave with him, and when I tried to get away, he shot me! Then he started to drag me outside, but someone showed up at the back door and he went outside to investigate. I booked it. I managed to make it to where I'd parked the ATV in the woods some distance from the house. I never would have made it out of there on my own steam."

That explained the engine noise Gavin had heard in the woods behind Jamie's house before he ran into the man who'd attacked him.

Gavin remembered the ransacked house and trailer. Had they been looking for the drugs or something more? Perhaps the evidence?

"I was afraid he'd catch up with me before I got here, so I didn't take a direct route. When I was a little ways from here, I hid the ATV and came the rest of the way in on foot. I didn't think I'd make it." He stopped for a breath. "It took me forever to get here. When I did, I found my office torn apart. I figured they'd searched the mine by then and moved on. Miller's goons didn't know about the new additions I'd made." He stared at Jamie. "How did you find me?"

Gavin could see that Jamie was struggling with how to tell her uncle about Terry. He touched her arm. "Let me." She slowly nodded, and Gavin turned to Paxton. "There's something we need to tell you that's going to be difficult to hear. Terry's dead, Paxton. I'm guessing he was the one who showed up at your house. Miller's men probably killed him."

Paxton's mouth fell open in shock. Words wouldn't come for the longest time. "If I'd stuck around, I could have helped him," he finally managed.

"No. If you'd stayed, you'd be dead, as well," Gavin was quick to assure him. "Terry was just at the wrong place at the wrong time."

"Poor Terry." Paxton wept with grief. "He was only trying to help me. He's been helping me all along."

Jamie gathered her uncle close until he was able to talk again.

"We saw the heroin. How did it get here?" she asked.

Paxton appeared shell-shocked. It was a little bit before he could answer. "I saw where the deputies were storing it, and Terry and I took it one night. We knew we had to find a way to stop them. They just kept bringing the stuff into the county. It was killing our community and our kids. Their future. I couldn't let that happen any longer."

"How did you get all the evidence you gathered?" Gavin wanted to know.

Paxton shook his head. "I started working on that a few years ago. I figured if I stuck with it, I'd find out who was behind the drugs with Terry's help. I had no idea exactly what was going on here until recently." Paxton put his head in his hands. "Oh, Terry. I can't believe he's gone. I did this to him."

Jamie touched his shoulder. "This isn't your fault, Uncle Paxton. They're the ones who killed Terry. Not you."

"This is all because of that guy I saw them with. I found out the former sheriff and most of the deputies are dirty, and I think it's because of that guy."

From everything Gavin knew about the Southern Mafia, they were good at making witnesses disappear. How had Paxton managed to gather so much evidence without anyone realizing he was on to them until now?

"How did you make the connection? These guys are good at covering their crimes."

"It took some doing, but I followed the deputies and

got a picture of them with that one guy. The only problem is, I have no idea who he is."

Gavin had been hoping Paxton would have a clue who the man was. He was positive he'd never seen him associated with any of the Southern Mafia captains. "Did you find any evidence connecting all of this to my father's murder?" he asked hopefully.

Gavin could tell from the way Paxton didn't make eye contact that he hadn't. It was gut-wrenching. Part of him wanted to believe in Noah's innocence.

"Not yet, but I overheard Miller talking to one of his goons the day before they showed up at my place. I'd followed him because I knew he was up to no good. Miller was furious about the missing drugs and mentioned that he'd have to take care of me the way they had the last person to stand in their way. That's when I knew they had something to do with Charles's death, so I called Jamie. There's a connection between what happened to Charles and the drugs and I believe it has everything to do with the man I can't identify in the photo. He's responsible somehow."

Paxton might be convinced Miller's comments were a form of a confession, but in Gavin's mind they could mean anything. There wasn't enough evidence to prove anyone else was responsible for his father's death but Noah.

"Do you know how the current sheriff fits into the puzzle?" he asked instead of pointing out the obvious.

Paxton snorted. "Now that one, he's a slippery one. I haven't been able to tie him to any of his deputies' crimes yet. He's good at covering his tracks, but I'm sure he's dirty, just like his father."

Gavin wasn't as convinced. Andy was lots of things,

but was he a killer? Right now, the more pressing issue was getting out of the mine before they ran out of air.

Jamie seemed to read his thoughts. "None of this does us any good if we can't get out of here. Paxton, they've blocked the main entrance. Is there another way out?"

Paxton closed his eyes. "I don't know. Let me think." His voice was barely a whisper. He didn't look good.

Jamie placed her hand over Paxton's forehead. She caught Gavin's eye. "He's warm to the touch." She pointed to the blood on his jeans.

"Let me take a look at your leg. I'll need to cut away your jeans," Gavin said. Paxton didn't protest, which was alarming enough. The man didn't like people fussing over him.

Gavin pulled out his pocketknife and ripped the jeans away from the wound. Right away he could see that it was bad. The wound hadn't been treated and was showing signs of infection. "The bullet's still in there," he told Jamie. The news was frightening. "We need to bandage it to make him as comfortable as possible."

Paxton looked to his niece for reassurance. "It'll be okay," she said. "Gavin's going to dress the wound."

After staring at his niece for a long moment, Paxton agreed.

"It looks like it's not so bad," Gavin tried to reassure Paxton. He could see that the man was terrified. "I'll try to be as careful as I can."

"Just do it already," Paxton muttered.

Gavin took out some of the extra strips of cloth and wrapped them tightly around Paxton's wound. The man slumped back on the ground. He'd lost consciousness.

"Paxton!" Jamie shook her uncle with fear in her eyes.

Gavin felt for a pulse. It was weak, but steady. "He's okay. Rest is the best thing for him right now." He sat back on his haunches and tried to come up with a plan to get them out of there.

"We won't be able to stay in here for long. We're running out of air." Gavin took Paxton's light and searched around until he found his phone, then he nodded toward the entrance. "Let's talk out there."

He moved through the hole. Once they were on the other side, Jamie went a little way from it so that Paxton couldn't overhear their discussion if he woke up.

"There has to be another way out. These old mines always have another way out," Jamie said. Gavin knew that wasn't necessarily the truth, but she was hanging on to it and so would he.

"You're right." He looked inside where Paxton slept. "He's okay for the moment. Let's keep going down this passage. If we find a way out, we can come back for him."

Gavin headed down the tunnel they'd been traveling when they found Paxton. Gavin's own strength almost nonexistent. He'd taken some pain medication before they entered the mine, but he knew he couldn't handle much more.

After they'd walked for some distance, the passage suddenly ended and they were met with the stone wall of the mountainside.

They'd reached the end of the mine, and there was no way out from here.

THIRTEEN

Jamie stared at the rock before them and almost lost it. They'd come all this way only to find they were still trapped.

She turned to Gavin. Saw the same despair in his eyes and fought back tears.

"What do we do now?" She forced the words out, her voice clogged with emotion.

For the first time, the man who had been her rock through all of this had no answer. "I don't know." The desolation in his tone scared her more than anything.

"We should probably get back to Paxton." She said the first thing that came to mind because she'd never seen Gavin look so lost before. "He may have woken by now."

Together they turned and headed back to the room where they'd left her uncle. It was frustrating to realize that they were so close to finding the person behind the drug trafficking in Darlan, and yet they might not make it out alive to bring the true killer to justice.

Once they reached the hole in the wall, they went back inside. Paxton still slept fitfully, tossing and turning and mumbling to himself. Jamie sat down next to him and felt his forehead. "He's burning up."

Gavin unzipped his backpack. "The antibiotics and pain medicine. We'll need to get him awake so that he can take them, though." He looked into her eyes. "Jamie, the infection is probably spreading quickly. He needs a doctor, and soon."

Jamie couldn't think about losing Paxton now. She had to keep fighting to save his life. She shook her uncle hard. "Uncle Paxton, wake up. I need you to wake up now."

Paxton moved his head back and forth and continued to mumble. Jamie leaned closer, but couldn't make out what he was trying to say. She shook him again. "Paxton, wake up now."

Suddenly, her uncle yelled at the top of his lungs and pushed her hard. She fell backwards. Shocked, Jamie saw he appeared to be struggling to free himself from an invisible capture.

Jamie scrambled back to him and tried again. "Uncle Paxton, it's me, Jamie. I need you to wake up. You're very sick. You need medicine."

"No, no, you're not going to kill me. You're not shutting me up. I've fought too hard to clear my brother's name. I'll keep fighting until the day I do. I won't stop now."

"He's delirious," Gavin said with a weary sigh.

Jamie shook her uncle once more. He grew suddenly quiet. This was even more terrifying than the ramblings. She was so afraid she'd lose him.

Then, slowly, he opened his eyes and struggled to focus on her. "Jamie, what are you doing here?" he mumbled, slurring his words.

She motioned to Gavin to hand her the antibiotics and one of the pain pills. "Paxton, we're here to help you. I need you to take this medicine. It will make you feel better." She held it up to his lips. For a moment she was afraid he'd push it away. But then he took the pills and swallowed them. She opened the water bottle and held it up. He took a sip and then slumped back to the ground, his eyes closed.

"We can't let him die down here, Gavin," she whispered. "The antibiotics will help the infection, but he's in bad shape."

Gavin's expression was grave. "Stay here with him. I'm going to try to backtrack to the spot where the mine collapsed. Maybe we missed something that direction. It's worth a shot."

He started to get to his feet, but she reached for his hand, stopping him. "Be careful."

Regret filled his eyes. Had he been expecting more from her? She cared about him, always would, but he still believed her father responsible for taking Charles's life. They were on opposite sides of something that appeared to be about as insurmountable as the mountain surrounding them.

Gavin rose to his feet, shoving aside the remorse that tore at his heart. "I will be. Keep an eye on this guy." He grabbed his Glock and tucked it behind his back. "Keep the shotgun close. If you hear anything suspicious, shoot first, ask questions later."

She smiled at his attempt at humor. "I will."

Gavin slipped through the hole again. With one final look at Jamie, he headed back the way they'd come.

They still had no idea why the deputies were involved in smuggling drugs into Darlan. It went against everything he believed in. His gut told him Miller and the rest of his goons were committing the crime without the knowledge of their sheriff. Yet how could Andy not know what was happening right under his nose?

None of it made sense. They were missing a crucial piece of evidence, and without it, they might never figure out who was really behind the operation.

Gavin reached the point where the passageway he was on split from the original one. His side throbbed. Every breath he took became more labored. Their air supply was evaporating. He had to find a way out. There was no other option to save their lives.

The second tunnel that they hadn't explored loomed before him. He was all out of options. It was this or nothing.

Something captured his attention—what sounded like voices, just past where the mine had collapsed. He eased closer.

"This is the last of it, but there's still a whole lot more unaccounted for." Gavin recognized the voice of Dan Miller.

"You think the rest is farther in the mine?" another familiar voice asked.

"I wouldn't put it past that old coot," Miller said in disgust. "With the thing collapsed, I don't see a way to get to it."

"You're right. It will take days, if not weeks, to dig through that rubble. How are we going to explain it to him?"

Silence followed. For once it seemed as if Miller didn't have an answer. "You leave that to me," he snapped. "First thing we need to do is get this stuff to a safe location. We can't afford to lose any more product. He's coming in today, and he won't be happy with the way things have gone. That crazy old fool." The words were spat out. "Why couldn't he have left well enough alone? His brother's dead, anyway. Nothing he found out will clear his name or bring the man back."

Gavin froze. Was Miller admitting he knew something more about Charles's death?

"I need to talk to Sheriff Lawson. Find out what he wants to do here. Come on. Let's get out of here. I never did understand why someone would choose to do this for a living."

Stunned, Gavin couldn't move. Miller had just confirmed that Andy was the leader of the drug smuggling outfit. He'd been wrong. Gavin just couldn't believe it. There had to be something more he was missing.

With time running out, he eased back to the second tunnel. It was quite a bit narrower than the one they went down before. It looked much less stable, as if it had been years since anyone had been that way.

He started walking. The light from his flashlight app revealed decay all around. In several places, the rocks had slid from the walls and almost blocked the way. In spots there was barely room enough to crawl around piles of rocks.

He walked until he reached the spot where the tunnel had been boarded up, and he struggled to keep the despair away.

"Lord, I sure could use Your help now."

Gavin shone the light through the gaps in the boards. The passage didn't appear damaged beyond this spot. Why had someone boarded it up? He had to find out.

With only his hands, he yanked at the first board. It freed easily enough. The second did the same. It was almost as if someone had put them up for appearances only.

Once he'd cleared the passage, Gavin stepped over
the remaining boards and headed down the tunnel.
Nothing about it appeared any different from the way
he'd come. Was he wasting what little time he and Jamie
had left? If they were going to die down here, he wanted
every moment to count.

Something he couldn't explain urged him on. He
couldn't give up now. Jamie was counting on him.

After he'd gone a little way, he spotted more rocks
piled up and almost lost hope. Dropping to his knees
in front of the rocks, he wasn't sure how much longer
he could go on. He gathered his waning strength, and
started shoving rocks aside. Behind him, he could hear
stones falling. The passage was unstable. If it collapsed
on itself, Jamie and her uncle would be trapped inside,
and he would have no way to dig them out.

He'd moved more than a dozen large rocks, when he
felt it. Fresh air rushed in. He'd found a way out!

Gavin worked harder. When the last rock was out
of the way, he stepped out into the darkness, breathing
in clean mountain air. He had no idea where the opening let out, but it didn't matter. They had a chance. He
killed the flashlight and listened. Not a sound beyond
the normal mountain noises.

He needed to get them help right away, and at this
point there was only one person he trusted. Gavin dialed
the number for his Scorpion commander, Jase Bradford.
He didn't have to wait long.

"Hey, buddy, how are you holding up?" Before he'd
left for Darlan, Gavin had told his commander and good
friend all about his plucky grandmother, yet he'd never
been able to tell anyone, not even Emily, what had happened to his father.

"Not so good." Gavin quickly updated Jase on what they'd been through.

"Sounds like we need to get the FBI involved in this. I'll call the Louisville branch and get them on their way."

Thank You, God. Gavin's knees went weak with relief.

"I appreciate it, Jase. I should go. I need to get Jamie and Paxton out of here while we still have the chance."

"Be careful," Jase warned. "These guys are cops, and we don't know how far up the food chain the corruption goes. Get out of there before the whole thing collapses on top of you, and get some place safe. Do you have any idea where the opening is located?"

"Hang on." Gavin had an app installed on his phone that gave him the latitude and longitude coordinates. Once he had them, he gave them to Jase.

"Good. I'll pass this on to the FBI. Leave your phone where it has service. I'll have them track you from there. I'll be praying for you, my friend," Jase told him.

"Thanks." They'd need all the prayers they could get. Gavin ended the call with a small amount of hope. Someone knew where they were. He'd trust his commander to bring them help. Right now, he had to get Jamie and Paxton out of the mine before the only way out was gone.

Leaving the phone on a rock outside, Gavin hurried back through the entrance and down the unstable tunnel once more while rubble continued to fall around him. The place was in bad shape. The earlier collapse hadn't helped it much.

Please don't let it come down, Lord. It's our only

means of escape. Bring us out of this thing safely, he prayed fervently.

Once he was back in the main passage, he looked behind him. Pieces of rocks continued to fall.

With his heart in his throat, he ran back to the passage he and Jamie had taken. Picking up any speed at all was difficult, as he had to bend over the entire way. Fresh air rushed through the mine. At least they wouldn't suffocate.

What if he got them both back to this point, only to have the mine collapse? They'd be buried alive with no way out.

FOURTEEN

Gavin had been gone for almost two hours. Throughout each of those hours, Jamie's uncertainties had continued to grow. Paxton seemed to be resting a bit more peacefully, but he still hadn't regained consciousness.

Several times, she'd heard rumblings from the direction that Gavin had gone. She had no doubt in her mind that the mine was quickly becoming more unstable. There had already been one collapse; others might follow. The mine could be filling with dangerous gases. She'd never felt so helpless.

A noise coming from nearby sent her jumping to her feet. She hurried to the wall closest to the opening as footsteps grew closer. Was it Gavin? She couldn't afford to take any chances.

Someone stepped inside the room. "That's far enough," she said and pointed the shotgun at the intruder.

"Jamie, don't shoot. It's me." Gavin's husky voice had never been more welcome.

She dropped the weapon and ran into his arms. "I was so afraid the place would collapse."

He held her close for a moment then looked down at her and smiled. "I've found a way out."

Her eyes grew large. "You did? That's great."

"While I was outside, I called my commander. He's getting in touch with the FBI. Help is on the way."

There was more, she could tell. "What aren't you telling me?"

He let her go and stepped away. "The opening is located in a part of the mine that's very unstable. We don't have much time. We need to get out of here now before our only means of escape goes away."

She glanced down at Paxton. "We can't leave him behind."

He clasped her hand. "No, of course not. We'll try to wake him. Otherwise, we'll have to carry him, and I'm not sure I'm up to it or if we have that much time. Has he been awake at all?"

Jamie shook her head. "At least he's sleeping a bit more peacefully." She went over to where her uncle lay. "Paxton, wake up." She shook him hard. He winced in pain before slowly opening his eyes.

"What happened?" His voice was barely audible.

"We're getting out of here. Gavin found a way out, but the mine is unstable. Do you think you can walk?"

Paxton managed a nod and then slowly sat up, closing his eyes briefly. He put his hand up to his head. "I think I'm going to need some help."

Gavin came around to one side. With Jamie on the other, they lifted him to his feet.

"Can you put any weight on your injured leg?" Gavin asked.

Paxton tried to stand on the leg. He screamed in pain and almost dropped to the ground.

"We'll help you," Jamie assured him.

"Let me get on the other side, and I can get him through the entrance," Gavin said.

Jamie put her arm around Paxton's waist, and he leaned heavily against her as Gavin slipped through the opening.

"You're going to have to put some weight on your injured leg, but we'll make it quick," Gavin told him.

With Jamie still holding on to her uncle, he slowly put his full weight on the leg. Jamie could tell it was a struggle to keep from losing his balance. The extent of the pain was carved on his face as he eased through the opening and fell against Gavin's injured side. Gavin stumbled backward and almost lost his footing.

Jamie hurried through the opening and grabbed Paxton around the waist again, taking some of the weight off Gavin.

"Are you okay?" she asked with concern.

Gavin managed a nod, his jaw tight. She knew he was hurting.

"I think so. Let's get going. This will take a while, and I'm not sure how long we have."

With Gavin's arm touching hers, together they carried Paxton down the narrow passage. The going was slow and strenuous, forcing them to stop periodically to catch their breaths. Gavin was barely hanging on himself. She wasn't sure how much more he could handle.

"We're almost there. It's not much farther." Gavin tried to sound positive, but she could tell it was a struggle for him to put one foot in front of another.

"I heard Miller talking to one of his men. They got the drugs out of here, but they're looking for more. They think they're hidden inside the mine somewhere. I believe they'll come back here soon to look for them. We can't let them find us."

Jamie couldn't believe it. "How much drugs do you think there are? Paxton, do you have any idea?"

Her uncle was barely conscious, but he managed to answer. "There's plenty, from what I've seen. The amount of heroin they're moving into the county is massive."

Paxton's words were terrifying.

"There's more," Gavin said, and she forced herself to concentrate. "I heard Miller talking. Looks like I was wrong about Andy Lawson. He's not only involved, he's the leader."

Shocked, Jamie stared up at him. "Just how deep does this thing go?"

Gavin stopped once they reached the entrance to the shaft leading to the opening. "This is it."

Jamie peered into the decay and shivered. He couldn't blame her. Nothing about the place looked safe.

"I know it looks bad, but it's not much farther to the opening."

Jamie nodded in spite of the fact that she looked ready to drop. The three of them headed down the narrow passage. With each step they took, pieces of the wall continued to crumble away.

"Do you know where this will put us out?" Gavin asked Paxton, hoping to get Jamie's mind off the danger around them.

"I'm guessing we're on the opposite side of the mountain, not too far out of Darlan." Gavin was amazed at the older man's spunk, in spite of his physical condition.

Behind them, several large rocks split from the side

and hit the ground hard. The vibration shook the place, sending tremors down the shaft.

"Hurry, this whole place could go at any moment. Run, Jamie!" Gavin yelled and together they ran for the opening.

They'd almost cleared it when a loud rumble behind them quaked the place. Gavin lost his footing, and Paxton fell to the ground with him.

"Gavin!" Jamie screamed.

Gavin scrambled to his knees. "Help me get him outside," he managed while holding his side. The pain was unbearable.

Jamie got him to his feet. Together, they hauled Paxton up and ran as fast as they could. They barely made it out before the tunnel collapsed onto itself, and a rush of dust and debris flew past them.

Gavin dropped Paxton to the ground and fell to his knees. They'd come so close to being trapped. A few seconds more and they'd all have been dead.

Thank You for bringing us safely out. He murmured the prayer, then stared back at the tomb they'd escaped.

Jamie knelt next to him and touched his face. The tenderness in her eyes gave him strength.

"How are you holding up?" she asked.

He knew she was worried about his injury, but truth be told, he was barely keeping it together.

Gavin smiled so that she wouldn't keep worrying. "Hanging in there. We can't afford to stay here, though. Somehow or other we need to get as far away from here as we can before Miller and his people come back to look for the drugs."

He could tell she didn't believe him about being all right, but what choice did they have? If they stayed here, they'd be dead. "You're right." She turned to Paxton, who looked much worse after the harrowing journey they'd just faced. "What is the easiest way out of here?"

Paxton scrubbed a hand over his eyes and scanned the dark horizon. "There's only one way out, and it's all downhill."

Gavin dragged in a breath and prayed for the strength to finish the job. He spotted his phone where he'd left it on the rock and pocketed it. "Then we'd best get going. We have one thing working in our favor. If they come this way and see the rubble, they'll believe we're trapped inside. It might buy us time. It's something." He struggled to stand. Jamie grabbed him around the waist and helped him up.

"Deep breaths," she whispered close to his ear. "We'll take it slow. We'll be okay."

He looked down at her. Even in the darkness, he could see her reassuring smile. She was trying hard to remain positive. He needed to do the same.

He touched her face. "You're right. We will be." He turned to Paxton. "You know this mountain like the back of your hand. Keep us on the right track."

Together, he and Jamie helped Paxton to his feet.

"How are you feeling?" Gavin asked the older man.

Paxton wasn't one to look for sympathy. "Okay. You got any more of those pills you gave me earlier? I think I could use some now."

Gavin dug into the backpack and brought out the antibiotics, along with the pain medicine. "Here, take one of each of these. It'll help with the pain."

Once Paxton was finished, he handed the water bottle back to Gavin, who swallowed something for his own pain.

. "I'll need my light," Paxton told them. Gavin had no idea where the light had ended up.

"I have it." Jamie took it from her jacket pocket.

Paxton put the light on and shone it around the area. He pointed off to their right. "We'll head out that way. It should be the easiest path."

Gavin nodded. "Okay, let's get going." Gavin reached to help Paxton, but the older man pushed his hands away.

"I don't need any help. Hand me that stick over there." He pointed to a log lying close by. "I'll use it to help me along. You two need to watch your footing. It's steep through here. We don't need any more injuries."

Jamie cast a doubtful look Gavin's way. "Are you sure, Uncle Paxton?"

The older man nodded. "I'm sure. Let's head out."

"I'll take the lead," Gavin told them, half expecting Paxton to argue. Shining the light down in front of them, he could see that Paxton was right. The hike was going to be a steep downhill process.

Just put one foot in front of the other.

With Paxton between them, he and Jamie started walking. Miller's words from earlier troubled him.

His brother's dead, anyway. Nothing he found out will clear his name or bring the man back.

Had Paxton been right all along? Had Miller inadvertently let slip that there was something more going on with Charles's murder than what the sheriff's department had reported?

FIFTEEN

A rock rolled beneath her feet and Jamie almost lost her footing. Gavin rushed to her side to steady her.

"Are you okay?" he asked. The alarm on his face warmed her inside.

When her heart finally stopped thundering in her ears, she answered. "Yes, I think so. It's just hard to see where I'm going."

"It is, but Paxton was right. We can't afford another injury. Why don't you use your phone's flashlight app to watch the ground? If they're out there looking for us, they'll spot three lights just the same as they would two."

She dug her phone out of her pocket and clicked on the light.

"Ready?" he asked, and she forced a smile.

"Yes, I'm ready."

As they picked their way down the mountainside, Jamie found herself jumping at every noise around them. She didn't doubt for a moment that Miller would keep looking for them. He wouldn't be satisfied until he knew for certain they were dead. Too much was at stake. In spite of what Gavin believed, she was positive when they found their mystery man, they'd find out who really killed Charles.

Her mind went back over the things they knew so far. Making sense of it was impossible. There was no way Miller was the mastermind behind the organization. As hard as she tried, she couldn't see Andy Lawson running such a huge endeavor, either.

"Who do you think is really in charge?" she asked Gavin, voicing her doubts about Andy. Up ahead, the path widened enough so that she could walk next to Uncle Paxton. She knew he was still in a lot of pain, but using the stick as a crutch seemed to be helping.

"If you're suggesting that Andy doesn't seem capable of such a huge endeavor, I agree. Paxton, in your surveillance photos, I saw a picture with our mystery man along with Miller and some of the other deputies. It looked like it was taken in an abandoned warehouse. Do you remember what that was?"

"That's the equipment storage building for the old mine near Hallettsville. I followed Miller and his goons there one night."

Jamie recalled the photo. The man had been dressed nicely, in a suit and tie. "I'm guessing he's the real person in charge."

"That's my guess, too," Gavin told her. "We need to figure out who he is and how he's connected to all of this as soon as possible, but first we need to get out of danger."

"How soon before the FBI arrives?" Jamie wasn't sure how much more any of them could take.

Gavin shook his head. "I'm not sure. Maybe a couple of hours. It looks like we're almost at the base of the mountain." He pointed up ahead, and Jamie noticed that the ground was slowly leveling off.

"Can we stop for a moment to rest?" She was out of breath and couldn't imagine how Uncle Paxton must be feeling.

She flashed her light around and spotted a rock big enough for sitting, and helped Paxton over to it.

"Which way from here?" she asked her uncle.

He looked around the countryside he'd grown up exploring. "Best I figure, we're about five miles from town. I'd say we want to avoid that. There's an abandoned homestead not too far from here. We could hide out there until the Feds show up."

The thought of being inside sounded wonderful to Jamie. "Good idea. Hopefully, they won't look for us there."

"Let's get going then. God helps those who help themselves, I say." Paxton shuffled to his feet, and she chuckled at her uncle's bravery. In so many ways, he reminded her of her father. Always seeing the positive side of things. Never wanting to lean on anyone. Her father was a pillar of strength in her mind. Even today, she couldn't reconcile what she knew about him with the frail man he'd been before his death.

Uncle Paxton led the way. Soon, she spotted the house up ahead of them. As they headed toward it, Jamie couldn't shake the bad feeling growing inside of her. Who was the well-dressed man in the photo, and why had he met with Miller? There was something more going on here than they knew. She just had no idea what.

As they drew close to the house, Gavin stopped suddenly, as if something wasn't right.

She halted next to him. "What is it?"

He pointed to the ground. "If this place is abandoned, then why are there tire tracks here?"

Jamie had barely had time to look down when from

behind the barn, four ATVs fired their engines and headed for them at breakneck speed.

"Run for the woods behind the house," Gavin told her. Together, they grabbed Paxton around the waist and hurried for the trees. Before they'd managed even a handful of steps, one of the men began shooting at them.

"Get down." Gavin shoved her and Paxton behind an abandoned car then took out his weapon and returned fire.

Jamie eased next to him with the shotgun. All four ATVs had their lights on bright and directed right at them. He glanced behind them. The woods were close. If they could make it there, they might have a chance at getting away.

"Can you get Paxton to the woods?" Gavin asked while keeping a careful eye on the ATVs. "I can try to hold them off for a while."

Jamie peered behind them. "I think so, but I'm not leaving you behind."

He looked into her eyes. "I'll be right behind you, I promise. Head there as fast as you can. I'll see if I can get them on the retreat." Jamie hated leaving him behind. She cupped his face, holding his gaze. "Please be careful."

He covered her hand with his and smiled. "I will."

She slowly nodded, then took hold of Uncle Paxton and ran as fast as she could for the tree coverage. Behind her, Gavin opened fire.

"We're almost there," she urged her uncle, trying to sound positive. Even though just a handful of steps now separated them from the woods, it felt like miles with the firefight going on behind them.

They reached the edge of the trees. Behind them,

Jamie heard footsteps. Gavin was running their way through heavy gunfire.

Please keep him safe, she prayed. She couldn't bear the thought of something happening to Gavin.

Jamie barely made it to the first tree before she bumped into Paxton. Why had he stopped?

"Hurry, Uncle Paxton. We have to keep moving."

Paxton didn't answer. He was staring at something in front of him.

It took only a second before her eyes adjusted to the darkness and she spotted what he saw. Two men stood close with weapons aimed at them. They'd walked straight into a trap.

Gavin rushed for the trees behind the house. He spotted Jamie and Paxton right away. Something was off.

"What's wrong?" He barely got the words out when a set of flashlights clicked on, blinding him.

He recognized the first man: the former sheriff of Darlan County, Raymond Lawson. The man standing next to him Gavin had seen before, as well, in a photo. It was their mystery man.

Reality slammed into place. They'd fought so hard to get free of the mine, only to be captured by the men who put them there.

"Well, well, we have all three of you right here in one place." The mystery man stopped a few feet short of them and turned back to Lawson. "Good job, sheriff."

Who was this man? If they were going to die at his hands, Gavin had to know his true identity. "So, you're the man behind the heroin. I never did believe Miller and the rest of his men were smart enough to run an organization this size by themselves."

The mystery man looked at Gavin with admiration.

"Oh, I don't know. Sheriff Lawson here has run the operation for me quite nicely through the years. But you're right. I am the man behind the heroin. And I can see you don't know who I am."

Gavin was immediately on alert. Why would he say that? "Should I?"

A smirk followed. "Your father surely would."

The truth dawned on him slowly. "How do you know my father?" But the ball in the pit of his stomach told him he knew the answer. This was the man who'd killed Charles. The true killer. Jamie had been right all along. Reality mingled with guilt threatened to buckle his knees.

"I was the last man to see him alive, Agent Dalton."

The truth threatened to sink him. Jamie must have sensed it, because she took his hand.

He forced back rage. "You killed my father." It all became clear. This man was with the mining corporation that had wanted to buy out his father's mine.

The man smiled. "That's right. I needed the mine. He refused to sell. He had to die."

It took everything inside Gavin not to charge the man. He wanted him dead for murdering his father. "You wanted the mine because of its central location." It was a shot in the dark, but the man's expression slipped a little, confirming Gavin was right. "It's close to the other abandoned mines you've bought out, and it would allow you easy access out of town. I guess you didn't count on my grandmother not automatically selling the business to you after my father's death."

Paxton made a noise that sounded like disbelief. "You're part of Shadow Mining," he exclaimed.

The man didn't seem worried that they'd discovered his identity. He clearly wasn't planning to let them live. "Not part of it. I'm the owner of Shadow Mining. Brock Shadow."

The name didn't ring any bells for Gavin. "You had one of your goons put pressure on Paxton here to force my grandmother to sell, thinking them both easy targets. When you couldn't get Paxton to cooperate, you tried to kill him, too."

Three of the men who'd been shooting at them came up behind and started to grab them, but Shadow stopped them. "Leave them alone. We'll take care of them soon enough."

Gavin tried not to react to the threat. Would help be there in time to save them? "You won't get away with this, Shadow. I'm a CIA agent."

Shadow was unmoved. "Yes, well, mines around here collapse all the time. Especially ones like the Darlan Mountain Mine. It's been neglected for years by Paxton."

The look on Jamie's face reflected her terror. Gavin moved closer, still holding her hand. "If you kill us, how will you find the rest of the drugs?"

Shadow's gaze narrowed, suspecting a lie. "You're stalling. Get his phone," he ordered one of the men. "I want to see who he's called."

One of the men grabbed him while a second searched his pockets, came up with the cell phone and tossed it to his boss.

Shadow scrolled through the recent calls and spotted Jase's number.

"Who's this?" he demanded. "Who did you call?"

Gavin had to come up with a believable answer quickly.

"I've contacted the FBI. They're on their way here now."

Shadow's confidence slipped a little. "The FBI. It will take them hours to get boots on the ground. By then we can be out of here with our product, and you'll be dead." He motioned to the man still holding Gavin, and he shoved him away.

Shadow walked over to Paxton. "Where is the rest of my product, old man?" The anger on his face was easy to read.

Still Paxton didn't back down. "It's gone. I destroyed it. I would have done the same with the stash in the mine if I hadn't run out of time."

Shadow moved to inches from Paxton's face. "You're lying. You still have it somewhere, along with the evidence you've been sneaking around gathering."

That Shadow knew about Paxton's covert actions came as a surprise.

Shadow smiled. "You didn't think I knew? You foolish man. I've had my men keep tabs on you through the years. While you were a potential threat to my empire, everyone in the county thought you were a kook. No one believed you. You were harmless until you decided to steal my heroin. Where's the rest of the evidence? I know there's more."

Paxton's bravado faded a little. "I ain't telling you nothing."

Shadow shook his head in distaste. "It's in the mine somewhere. Get them back there. Find whatever he's been stashing and then get rid of the problem these three pose. For good, this time."

The threat was clear. They were not walking out of the mine alive. Gavin knew he had to do something to buy time for the FBI to reach them before it was too late.

Another deputy appeared behind them. "The mine's unsteady. Another tunnel has collapsed."

This was not the news Shadow wanted to hear. "Then find another way in. We need the heroin before our buyer arrives, and we can't afford to have incriminating evidence left behind for someone to find later on. Understood?"

The deputy frowned at the order. "Yes, sir." He motioned to another deputy. "You heard the man. Let's get going."

Gavin and Jamie were forced from the woods at gunpoint while two men grabbed Paxton and hauled him out, as well.

"Get the old man on one of the ATVs. The others can walk," the deputy ordered.

One of the deputies forced Paxton onto a nearby machine, got on behind him and headed back up to the mine.

A gun barrel was shoved into Gavin's back. "Move it. You two have wasted enough of our time."

Sheriff Lawson and Brock Shadow climbed on separate ATVs, as did another deputy, and followed Paxton up the mountain.

The two remaining deputies forced Gavin and Jamie to keep moving.

Gavin got as close to Jamie as he dared in an effort to protect her.

"How much longer...?" She didn't finish but he understood.

"Soon, I hope." He forced the words out. The guilt he felt at not believing her all these years gnawed at him. She'd needed him and he'd let her down. Jamie deserved someone better than him. He'd do everything in his power to get her safely out of this and then he prayed he'd be deserving of her forgiveness one day.

SIXTEEN

"No talking, you two." One of the men behind them shoved his weapon hard against Gavin's back, sending him stumbling forward. "Keep moving."

Jamie reached out to steady Gavin, who managed to catch himself before he hit the rocky ground.

"Are you okay?" she whispered.

"I said no more talking," the man growled.

Gavin nodded in answer, trying to reassure her.

Jamie grabbed his hand once more. She didn't know what the future held for them, but she was determined to make every second count. She'd hold Gavin's hand as long as she was allowed.

Up ahead, she noticed Sheriff Lawson, Shadow and the others had reached the collapsed tunnel where the three of them had escaped. They were staring at it. It would take days to dig through the rubble.

Once Jamie and Gavin reached them, she could tell Shadow was quickly losing patience.

"Don't tell me there's not another way in there. You're a tunnel rat. You know how to get into that mine. Now tell me where the entrance is."

Paxton clamped his lips together and shook his head.

"Perhaps you'll tell me if she's in enough pain?" Shadow motioned to one of the men behind Jamie. The deputy grabbed her and twisted her arm behind her back.

Right away Gavin charged the man, but the deputy behind him jammed his weapon against Gavin's injured side. He dropped to his knees in pain.

"I can have him keep going if you'd like. Break a few of her bones—or you can talk and save your niece's life."

The man holding Jamie's arm yanked it hard and she screamed.

"That's enough!" Paxton yelled. "Stop hurting her. I'll tell you where the third opening is."

Shadow smiled smugly. "That's better." He nodded to the man grasping Jamie's arm, and he eased up a little.

"Well, where is it?" Shadow demanded. "We don't have all day."

Paxton's gaze met Jamie's. She could see how bad he felt.

"It's okay, Uncle Paxton. Just tell them what they need to know," Jamie urged. She didn't want Shadow to kill him.

He slowly nodded. "It's that way. I made the opening a little while back." The direction he indicated had to be on the opposite side of the tunnel from Paxton's hiding place.

"Get him in there and find the stuff," Shadow demanded in an irritated tone.

The deputy who had ridden with Paxton hopped on the machine again and headed the ATV toward the spot Paxton had pointed out, followed by a second deputy.

"Take them there, too," Shadow told the two deputies

guarding Jamie and Gavin. Then he and the sheriff got on their machines and went after her uncle.

"You heard the boss. Get moving." The deputy let Jamie go and shoved her forward.

With Gavin sticking close to her side, they were forced up the rocky slope. Jamie could see Gavin was barely hanging on. They needed God's help now more than ever, and so she prayed with all her remaining strength for deliverance.

It felt as if it took forever to reach the place. Once she and Gavin had caught up with the ATVs, she noticed that Paxton had whittled an opening into the side of the mountain. He'd hidden it well, covering it with scrub brush.

"Get him inside and get the evidence. Find out if he's lying about the heroin. I don't trust him." Shadow gave the order. Two deputies grasped Paxton's arms and dragged him inside.

"What about these two?" Lawson asked. Jamie held her breath. Would they kill them right there?

"Not yet, sheriff. Their time will come."

Jamie's gaze clung to Gavin's. Besides the former sheriff and Shadow, there were two armed deputies standing guard. She didn't like their odds.

Gavin shook his head. The concern in his eyes told her that he agreed. If they tried to overpower the men and failed, they'd be dead before they had the chance to think about it.

As she stared at the gaping hole before them, Jamie couldn't imagine a good outcome. It broke her heart to consider what might have been. She cared for Gavin and she didn't want to lose him. Not like this. *Father, please, we need Your help. Please, don't let us die here when we're so close to the truth.*

The two deputies behind them began talking to each other. Gavin knew he had to try something to save their lives. Shadow and Lawson were watching the entrance. If they went down into that mine again, they'd probably end up with bullets in their heads.

He looked down at Jamie and pointed discreetly at Shadow and Lawson. She swallowed hard before slowly nodding.

Another quick glimpse at Shadow and Lawson proved their attention was still distracted.

Gavin placed three fingers against his chest, slowly counting them off. With his heart in his throat, he charged to where Shadow stood. Jamie did the same. With Shadow caught off guard, Gavin managed to grab the man's weapon and fire off a shot at one of the two deputy's racing at them.

Struck in the knee, he dropped to the ground, screaming in pain.

Jamie grabbed Lawson's weapon and aimed it at the remaining deputy.

"Put the weapon down on the ground. Now," Gavin ordered when the deputy standing made no move to obey.

"Take it easy. I'll do as you ask," the deputy said. He slowly lowered his weapon.

"I've got Lawson covered. Can you get their weapons?" Gavin asked and Jamie hurriedly gathered the two deputies' weapons while Gavin stood watch.

Sheriff Lawson's glare proved he was furious. "You don't know who you're dealing with, Dalton."

"Keep quiet," Gavin ordered, then addressed the standing deputy.

"Help your buddy up and over to that ATV." The man hesitated a second, then hauled the injured man over to the machine. "Now cuff him to the handlebars." Once the deputy had finished, Gavin said to Jamie, "Take the key from the ATV, and then grab the second deputy's cuffs and secure him to that tree over there." Gavin pointed the weapon at the man. "Start moving." The deputy tossed Gavin angry looks as he headed for the tree.

"Wrap your hands around it," Jamie ordered. The man seemed to realize what was happening because he didn't move.

"Do it now, or I start shooting," Gavin said and the man finally obeyed.

Jamie cuffed the man to the tree then searched him and the second deputy, taking their phones and the keys to the handcuffs. She went back over to where Gavin stood guarding the others.

"Get going." Gavin pointed his weapon at the entrance. Lawson and Shadow exchanged a look before obeying.

As they slowly headed into the mine, Shadow and Lawson whispered between themselves, no doubt scheming how to get away.

"That's enough talking," Gavin told them, and they shut up.

Jamie followed close behind Gavin. "What's the plan?" she whispered so that only he could hear.

He had no idea, only that he was doing his best to buy them time. "Just trying to keep us alive until our help arrives." He kept his voice as low as he could.

As they drew close to the place where the evidence

was stored, Gavin stopped while the men kept going. "We'll have to get the other men subdued as quickly as possible. Follow my lead."

Jamie nodded, and they caught up with Shadow and Lawson. They were close to Paxton's hiding place now. He could hear the men who had gone with Paxton talking.

"He has file cabinets filled with this stuff. He must have been collecting it for years." A file cabinet closed.

"They're out here!" Shadow yelled to alert the rest of his men.

Gavin grabbed Shadow around the neck while Jamie kept her weapon against Lawson's back. The second Gavin and Jamie entered the room, they were met with armed men drawing down on them.

"I wouldn't do that if I were you," Gavin told them and tightened his grip on Shadow. "Not if you want your boss to live."

The men hesitated, glancing at each other as if trying to decide what to do.

"Shoot them both," Shadow ordered.

"Drop your weapons if you want him to live," Gavin said in a steely tone, unlike what he felt inside. His heart pounded in his ears. They were outnumbered. He was praying the men would buy his bluff.

"Don't do it. Shoot them!" Shadow yelled.

Gavin pushed the Glock against Shadow's temple. "Tell them to lay down their arms now."

The man standing close to one of the file cabinets slowly lowered his weapon to the ground.

"Kick the weapon this way and get your hands in the air," Gavin told him.

The man obeyed. The second man shoved his gun against Paxton's side. "I'll shoot him."

Paxton was barely hanging on after the exertion of walking back through the mine. Gavin could see the fear in the older man's eyes.

"No, you won't. Drop the weapon or I'll kill your boss."

The man stared at Shadow, uncertain what to do.

"Do it now." Gavin dug the gun into Shadow's temple.

The man lowered his weapon.

"Now step away from him." He pointed his weapon toward the other man. "Over there."

The man tossed Gavin an angry look, doing as he requested.

Gavin released his hold on Shadow. "You and Lawson get over there, as well."

Shadow straightened his coat and walked over to his men.

"What do you expect to do now, Dalton?" Shadow demanded, not showing any fear.

"Now we wait for the FBI to show up and throw you and your pals in jail."

Shadow turned his anger on Paxton. "You old coot. You could have been rich beyond your wildest desire if you'd sold the mine when we came to you. None of this would be happening now if you'd stayed out of our way. And the old lady would still be alive."

"You killed Ava?" Paxton asked in disbelief.

But Gavin barely registered the shock in Paxton's voice. His legs threatened to give out beneath him. "You killed my grandmother?"

Shadow showed no emotion at all. "I didn't kill her, I simply went to visit her to try and talk some sense. Only she wouldn't listen to reason. Instead, she got herself all worked up. She figured out I was the one who had her son killed and she started screaming at me and threatening to call her grandson. Then, she just collapsed." Shadow shrugged as if it were nothing. "It was her own fault."

Gavin's thoughts fractured. Shadow might not have killed Ava, but he was the cause of her heart attack. If he'd called for help, Ava might still be alive.

"You murdered Ava because she wouldn't sell to a crook like you who's bent on destroying Darlan County," Paxton said. "You let my brother take the blame for your dirty work."

Shadow smirked in disdain at Paxton's anger, then looked behind him at his men. "What does he have on me?"

"Everything," one of the men answered. "He knows about the heroin. Your dealings with Lawson here."

Shadow turned back to Gavin. "Well, then, I'd say he doesn't know everything yet."

Gavin tried to figure out what Shadow hadn't told him. "We may not know everything, but we do know enough to put you away for a very long time."

Shadow laughed and looked at something just behind Gavin's shoulder.

Before Gavin had time to react, he heard Jamie's shocked gasp. Then someone shoved her toward Paxton. He whirled around, only to have an object slam against the side of his head. He dropped to the ground, his vision blurred, as a set of boots walked past him and kicked his weapon out of reach.

Someone stooped next to him. The last thing he was aware of was Dan Miller's face grinning down at him.

SEVENTEEN

Jamie knelt next to Gavin with tears in her eyes and hope fading.

"Get him inside. We have to gather all these files and leave here as soon as possible. I don't want to take a chance of some of this incriminating information surviving the blast." She barely registered Shadow's order before someone hauled her to her feet and shoved her over to where Paxton sat.

Still unconscious, Gavin was dragged close to them and dropped. Jamie immediately knelt next to him, cradling his head in her lap.

As she watched, the men gathered the information Uncle Paxton had stored there and headed out of the mine.

Shadow stared down at her before delivering their fate. "Make sure the rest of the drugs aren't here and then blow the mine. There's not much time. Our clients will be expecting us to fulfill our end of the deal…otherwise it won't be good for us."

Jamie had no idea what Shadow was talking about. "You're not going to get away with this. The FBI knows we're here. If we end up dead, they'll come after you."

Miller came back with explosives in his hand. "This should do the trick."

She stared at the dynamite in horror as Miller placed it close to the entrance. Jamie knew she had to try to do everything she could to postpone the explosion.

"Who are you working for, Shadow?"

At her shot-in-the-dark guess, Shadow turned back and stared at her in shock.

"What makes you think I'm working for anyone?" he demanded.

"Because there's no way you managed to get that much heroin on your own. You're working with Ericson."

Shadow stared at her for a second longer, then chuckled. "You're smart, girl, I'll give you that. I am working for someone big. Jacob Ericson and you obviously know he's the boss of the Southern Mafia. But that's all about to end. You see, Ericson has served his purpose. He got me the connections to the heroin. Supplied the means of moving it through all the right counties, thanks to having a whole lot of law enforcement on his payroll. Now it's my turn to be in charge."

Shadow watched as Miller continued to place the dynamite in several strategic locations.

"Oh, and Paxton, you should know your friend Terry sold you out. He was working for me, keeping an eye on you. He was supposed to give me something useful to get rid of you once and for all, but he failed to deliver. He had to die."

Paxton lunged for Shadow. "That's a lie. Terry wouldn't do that to me."

Shadow grinned smugly at Paxton's reaction. "He did. He would have sold his soul for the amount of money I offered him. Your friendship, well, I guess it didn't mean as much to him as you thought."

Once the explosives were in place, Shadow and his goons prepared to head out.

Shadow looked directly at Jamie. "So long, Ms. Hendricks. It's too bad you had to find out the truth like this, but at least you know your father wasn't responsible for his friend's death. That should be some comfort to you before you die."

With those chilling words, Shadow left them to their deaths.

Jamie watched Uncle Paxton. She could see how hard he was taking the news of his friend's betrayal. Yet now was not the time for emotions.

"Uncle Paxton, we have to get out of here. If those explosives go off this close, we'll die." Her words finally got through to him.

She looked down at the man lying unconscious close to her.

"Gavin, wake up. We've got to get out of here." She shook him as hard as she could, and he slowly opened his eyes, staring up at her confused.

"What happened?" he mumbled. He touched his head and winced in pain.

"They wired the place with explosives. We have to get as far away from here as we can."

Gavin stumbled to his feet with Jamie helping him. He leaned against her for a second longer, then together they grabbed hold of Paxton and hurried from the room, running as fast as they could down the dead-end tunnel.

Jamie couldn't see anything but darkness. With her heart in her throat, she kept running.

Her phone. She still had it in her pocket. She took it out, illuminating their way.

Up ahead, the end of the passage came into view. Would it be far enough away from the blast to save them?

"Hurry, we have to get as far away from the blast area as we possibly can," Gavin said, struggling to keep up. He'd been through so much over the past few days. She wasn't sure how much more he could take.

"Keep fighting, Gavin. Please, you can't give up." She tightened her grip on Uncle Paxton, trying to take some of the weight off Gavin.

They were just short of the end of the passage when the blast ripped through the tunnel behind them.

Jamie looked back. A cloud of smoke boiled toward them.

"Get down! Face away from the blast!" Gavin yelled, but there was no time.

The world around them shook like an earthquake was ripping through the area. Rocks and other debris flew past.

The blast flung them through the air. Jamie landed hard against the side of the tunnel. She screamed in pain and slid to the ground. It was a struggle to keep from passing out. The strength of the blast embedded bits of rock into her flesh.

As the world around her spun, she struggled to breathe through the dust-clogged air. Each inhalation was excruciating. And it felt as though she'd cracked a few ribs when she slammed into the stone wall.

When the world finally cleared, Jamie glanced around, trying to locate Gavin and Paxton. Her uncle was close, a few feet away. She leaned over and shook him. He moaned pitifully.

Gavin had taken the brunt of the explosion. Right before the blast, he'd pushed her and Paxton in front of him. She saw him and scrambled over. He wasn't moving.

"Gavin!" she screamed in horror and then leaned close. "Gavin, please be alright. Please don't die on me." She was in love with him and she couldn't bear the thought of having to live without him.

He could hear her calling him. She sounded so far away. His body felt glued to the ground. Somehow, he managed to move his arm. Pain ripped through his body and took his breath away. He'd cracked several ribs.

"Gavin, wake up!" Jamie still sounded far away, and yet someone was shaking him. He moaned as the agony caught up with him.

"Oh, Gavin, you're hurt." He could hear the tears in her voice, and he forced his eyes open. Jamie wasn't far away; she was leaning over him, tears spilling down her face. His heart broke. She was worried about him.

"I'm okay. Just a little banged up." He reached up and brushed the tears from her face.

She leaned down and kissed him with all her heart. "I thought I'd lost you."

Gavin pulled her closer and kissed her again. He was alive. So was she. They might not have much time left, but they were alive for now.

She held him tight. "I'm so glad you're okay," she whispered against his lips.

He smiled against her mouth. "Me, too. Now let's see if we can find a way out of here."

With her help, he managed to sit. Every move he made hurt like crazy and drained his pitiful strength.

Gavin leaned against her, and she held him close. "It's okay. Take your time," she whispered near his ear.

He closed his eyes until the world righted itself. "Is Paxton okay?"

Jamie stared behind them. "I think so."

Gavin saw the man lying on the ground, mumbling to himself. It was hard to see much in the sooty darkness. How much space did they have? If they could figure that out, they'd know how much air supply was left.

Jamie shone the phone's flashlight around. What he saw was disturbing. They were enclosed in a small space. Keeping the panic at bay was hard, but he tried, for Jamie's sake.

She clamped a hand over her mouth, seeing what he did. "Oh, Gavin, what are we going to do?"

He put his arm around her. "We wait. The FBI should be here any moment. They know we're here. It's only a matter of time before they get to us." It wasn't exactly the truth. The FBI would be expecting them to leave the area, and they'd be tracking his phone. It was with Shadow. Would the FBI turn their search that way? If so, he, Jamie and Paxton would be dead soon.

Gavin looked into her eyes and tried to be strong for her. "We just have to stay alive a little bit longer."

She forced a smile, not seeming to believe him.

Paxton stirred and sat up.

"Where are these Feds you've been talking about? Because we all know we won't make it more than a couple of hours with the air supply we have here."

"They should be here anytime." Gavin prayed they

would search the surrounding area and not give up on locating them.

"With everything that happened, I almost forgot. Shadow told me he's been working for the Southern Mafia." She recounted what Shadow had said while Gavin was unconscious.

The news settled around Gavin uncomfortably. So it was true. Shadow was planning to take over at the helm of the Southern Mafia? He remembered the recent car bombing in which Ericson's driver was killed.

"He's got to be stopped. He killed your father and was responsible for Ava's heart attack. We can't let him get away with the crimes he's committed," Jamie said.

She was right, but even if they did manage to somehow get out, how were they going to bring down Shadow when all the evidence Paxton had gathered was gone?

A thought occurred to her. "Each of us can act as a witness. He admitted killing your father to get his mine, and he told me that he worked for Ericson. That has to be enough to arrest him on those charges."

"Plus there are the backup files I left with Ava for safekeeping," Paxton announced calmly, and both Gavin and Jamie turned to stare at him.

"What did you say?" Gavin asked. He wasn't sure he'd heard Paxton correctly.

"I said I have backup files. I left them with Ava. You think I'm foolish enough not to make copies?" Paxton scoffed.

Gavin had looked through most of the stuff at his grandmother's house. He hadn't come across any files. "Do you have any idea where she put them?"

Paxton shook his head. "No, but I gave them to her on a thumb drive small enough to keep in a safe location. She told me she was going to put it someplace no one else would ever look for it. Obviously, Shadow had no idea she had the evidence otherwise he would have mentioned it."

There was only one place Gavin could think of that she'd hide the drive. But they had to get out of here in order to find it.

The air was still thick with dust particles. Every breath he took reminded him that his last one was getting close. He wasn't going to let Shadow win.

He held up Jamie's phone. "We need to make a video recording of everything that we know...just in case." He looked into her eyes and knew that she understood they might not make it out alive.

EIGHTEEN

A faint scratching noise came from somewhere above them. "Did you hear that?" she asked in amazement.

Gavin studied the ceiling. "I didn't hear anything. What did it sound like?"

Bits of dirt fell to the ground. "Like someone scratching on something."

"Or someone digging…"

Her gaze locked with his. "They're here. The FBI is here."

They had a chance. If they could stay alive long enough for the FBI to rescue them, they had a chance.

"Down here! We're down here!" she yelled as loud as she could.

A few minutes later they heard a response. "It's Sheriff Lawson. I'm going to try to dig you all out. I followed Shadow and the others and saw where they took you. Hang on, I'll see if I can get you of there."

Horror filled Jamie. "Oh, no. Gavin, it's Andy."

Gavin appeared as shocked as she was. He shook his head. "Something doesn't add up. If he's working for Shadow, why would he want to save us?"

"Unless he isn't saving us. Maybe he was sent here to make sure we're dead."

He gathered her close. "The FBI should be here soon. His digging will hopefully give us an air passage, but just in case..."

Gavin took her cell phone that held their recorded messages and hid it behind a rock.

Above them, chunks of rock broke free from the ceiling. They backed away from the spot.

"This place is unstable. It could collapse at any moment." Jamie wondered if that was the sheriff's purpose.

"Andy, hold up. The whole ceiling is about to cave in!" Gavin yelled up at the man.

The digging stopped immediately, and Jamie breathed a sigh of relief. If Andy were trying to kill them, he'd have kept on digging. "He's not working for Shadow."

Gavin nodded. "No, but if he doesn't find a way to get us out of here soon, it won't matter."

The reality of those words washed over her, and she hugged him close. "We need God's help more than ever."

"You're right. Let's pray."

Gavin took her hand. "Father, we need You to guide Andy's hands. Help him find a way out. There are bad people out there intent on hurting others. Please don't let them succeed."

With the prayer, a sense of peace slipped deep inside of her. God was in control. He wouldn't let them die; she truly believed that.

"I've called for backup. Help is on the way. Hang on down there. I'm going to see if I can dig in a different area. At least get you some fresh air coming in. Just to be safe, I need you to get as far away from this side of the tunnel as you can."

"Thanks, Andy!" Jamie called up. She and Gavin

tried to help Paxton to the area where the mine had collapsed, but he refused.

"Hang on a minute up there, Lawson." Paxton obstinately stood his ground.

"Uncle Paxton, he's trying to help. If we don't get air in here soon we'll die." She loved her uncle, but he had a stubborn streak a mile wide.

"And I'm telling you I know an easier place to dig," he announced in a gruff tone that had Jamie staring at him in surprise.

"Lawson, if you go to the north wall, there's a crack in the rock there. It should make for easier going, and I don't think the rock is that thick."

"Got it," Andy told them. Jamie could hear movement outside, and then a few minutes later the digging started again.

The oxygen level in the mine was dwindling with each breath. They had maybe another half hour's worth of air left in the small space. Any amount of exertion was an effort.

Jamie sank down to the ground. Gavin did the same. He tugged her close. She didn't want to die down here like this. Not after she and Gavin had found each other again. She wanted to have a life with him. Wanted to make up for the years they'd lost.

"How long do you think it will take him to get us free?" Jamie asked in a labored voice, because she needed something to hold on to.

"By himself…hours." Her uncle didn't mince words, and the small amount of hope Jamie was holding on to threatened to crumble. There was no way they'd make it that long. Had they come all this way, finally discovered the truth behind Charles's murder, only to take the secret with them to this dusty grave?

Gavin held her close. "But he's not going to be alone for long. The FBI is on their way here now. Don't give up hope, Jamie. We're going to get out of here, and then we're going to bring Shadow and those dirty cops to justice."

As she looked into his eyes, she believed him. She'd fight with everything inside of her to see that they all made it out of the mine alive. Then they'd bring Charles's killer to justice and break up the heroin ring that had Darlan in its grasp once and for all.

Jamie closed her eyes and leaned against his chest, her breathing shallow, like his. They were dying. As hard as Andy tried, he wouldn't be able to free them alone.

He peered around the small space, his thoughts growing fuzzy.

Outside, he heard footsteps and said a grateful prayer. Help had arrived.

Don't let them be too late...

"What are you doing here?" Andy's voice was barely audible through the solid rock.

Gavin strained to hear the answer. When he did, he almost lost all hope. It was Andy's father. "I can't let you do this, son. I can't let you free them. They have to die down there. What they know is too incriminating."

"You're going to shoot me?" Andy asked in amazement, and Jamie stared up at Gavin in horror.

Their last hope would be gone with Andy's death.

"No, you can still walk away from this. Pretend you don't know anything about it," Raymond told his son.

"I can't do that. I've lived with my suspicions about

you far too long. I won't let you and Shadow corrupt this county any longer."

The silence that followed was chilling. Then shots were exchanged, and Gavin held Jamie tighter.

When the shots ended, the silence was the most alarming.

If this is Your plan, Lord, then so be it. Gavin wasn't sure he could fight any longer.

"They're here!" Andy called out to them. "The FBI is here and they've brought reinforcements. Hang in there, guys. This is almost over."

Within minutes, heavy equipment could be heard rumbling up the mountainside.

Just the promise that the sound gave roused them.

"Take small breaths. We're going to be okay," Gavin tried to assure Jamie. Paxton was the worse for wear. Gavin noticed that his eyes were shut and he wasn't moving.

Gavin scrambled over and shook him hard. "Stay with me, Paxton. This is almost over. You can't give in yet."

The older man opened his eyes. "I ain't givin' in ever," he mumbled then closed his eyes again.

Gavin left him alone. There was nothing he could do now but keep his prayers going up to God.

He went back over to Jamie. She barely had the strength to open her eyes. "Hey, look at me. Keep looking at me. Keep fighting for me."

She briefly opened them and smiled up at him. He held on to her. He didn't want to lose her like this. Not when they were so close to freedom.

"Agent Dalton, this is Sam Wilson with the FBI. We're going to have to push the rest of the way in. Get as far away as you can from the spot and cover up. We're coming in five."

The only protection they had was a boulder that had dislodged during the explosion. He lifted Jamie in his arms and carried her behind it, then dragged Paxton over. The man mumbled to himself, and Gavin was terrified they'd lose him before they could be rescued.

Once they were all safely behind the boulder, he called out to the agent, "We're as protected as we can get!"

Within seconds, a heavy piece of equipment began pushing against the mountain. Soon, the compromised wall gave way, splintering it into chunks of rock. Fresh air rushed in, and Gavin drew in a lungful. The room around them shook and threatened to collapse. Several men poured into the space.

Gavin struggled to his feet and hauled Jamie into his arms. She wasn't moving. Was the rescue too late?

"We have to get out of here now. The place is unstable," he told one of the men. "Can you get Paxton out?"

The man nodded, and he and another agent hurried to rescue Paxton.

All Gavin could think about was the woman in his arms. He loved her. He couldn't lose her. Not like this.

Outside, the day had just begun to break. There were agents everywhere. Gavin spotted Andy Lawson kneeling next to a man on the ground. His father. Andy had been forced to take his father's life to save theirs.

An ambulance waited nearby. Gavin hurried toward it. Two EMTs raced for him with a stretcher.

He placed Jamie on it gently. "Help her. Please, don't let her die."

He loved her so much. Never stopped loving her. Now he just had to find a way to be worthy of her.

The two men placed an oxygen mask over her mouth and nose while they took her vitals.

"Her pulse is weak, but she's alive. We need to get her to the hospital right away." A few seconds later, Paxton was brought over. Both he and Jamie were loaded into the ambulance. Gavin started to get in but one of the agents joined him.

"Sam Wilson. I'm going to have some of my men follow you to the hospital as a precaution. Until Shadow and his thugs are found, you're all at risk."

"Thank you." Gavin was grateful for the protection.

"Don't thank me. Sheriff Lawson was the one who alerted us to where you were buried. If it wasn't for him, we might never have found you in time."

Gavin realized Andy was standing next to the agent. He held out his hand. "Thanks for saving us, Andy. I hate to say it, but I thought you were part of Shadow's team for a while." Gavin stared at the man lying on the ground. "I'm sorry about your father."

Andy swallowed visibly. "Thanks. I've always thought there was something wrong about him, but until I became sheriff, I had no idea how corrupt my dad and the deputies serving him truly were. When I found out the truth, I couldn't let it go on any longer. I had to do something. So I contacted the FBI and told them what I suspected. I just never envisioned this type of outcome."

"We need to go now," one of the EMTs told him, and Gavin nodded, shook Andy's hand and got into the back of the ambulance. His thoughts were fuzzy from the lack of oxygen. He'd leave everything to the FBI for now. He just wanted to be with Jamie.

NINETEEN

Jamie slowly opened her eyes. Her head ached as if someone was banging a sledgehammer inside her brain. When the world focused, she realized she was in a hospital bed. And someone held her hand.

She looked over and saw Gavin, his forehead resting on their joined fingers. He looked as if he was praying.

"Gavin?" she whispered in a croaky voice. Her throat hurt like crazy.

He lifted his head and looked at her. There were tears there. When he saw that she was awake, his face broke into a smile, then he got to his feet and enveloped her in his arms.

"You're awake. I'm so glad." His voice broke with emotion.

Jamie was happy just to be in his arms for the moment. The last thing she remembered was hiding behind the boulder in the mine.

He slowly let her go. "I was so worried about you. So afraid…" He couldn't finish, but she knew.

"I'm okay," she assured him, then she thought about her uncle. "Uncle Paxton?"

"Is fine, as well. He's resting in the next room, heavily guarded and loving every minute of the fact that he was right all along," Gavin told her with a chuckle.

She managed a smile. "When can I see him?"

"Soon. The doctor says the best thing for you now is to rest."

"What about you? How are you doing?"

He grinned down at her. "I'm fine. The doctor took a look my gunshot wound. He wants to remove the bullet, but I told him that would have to wait until this is over."

"Have they found Shadow and his men yet?" she asked.

"Not yet, but the FBI has the whole area saturated with men. All the roads are blocked. It's only a matter of time."

She could see it in his eyes. He wanted to be part of the hunt. With Shadow responsible for his father's death, she didn't blame him. He needed to bring the man down for closure.

"You should go. Bring him in. Make him pay for what he did to your father."

Gavin shook his head. "I don't want to leave you. It's too risky." He stopped and stared into her eyes with so much pain in his. Jamie believed she knew what was troubling him.

She touched his face. "It's okay. If the tables were turned, I probably wouldn't have believed you either."

His face twisted. "No, you would because that's just who you are. Jamie, I'm so sorry that I didn't do the same for you. You needed me and I let you down."

She shook her head. She didn't want his apology she wanted…his love. Would there be another chance for them?

"You didn't let me down. We were both thrown into

an impossible situation. You handled it the best you could." With tears in his eyes, he kissed her fervently and all her hopes for the future they'd once dreamed of took flight once more.

He ended the kiss, but didn't let her go. She'd give anything for this to be finished, but Shadow and his men were still out there.

"I'm safe here. I'm in a hospital room, no doubt surrounded by FBI agents. Go, bring Shadow to justice for Charles."

"Are you sure?" he asked, still reluctant to leave her side.

"I'm sure." She smiled up at him.

Gavin leaned over and kissed her once more. "I'll be back as soon as I can."

Jamie touched his cheek. "And I'll be right here waiting for you."

Gavin brought her hand up to his lips and kissed it, then, with another smile, he left her alone.

Shadow had taken things from her, as well. Her father. The life she could have had with Gavin. The years that Uncle Paxton had fought to bring Charles's true killer to justice. He deserved to pay for his crimes.

But right now, she wanted to see her uncle and thank him for all that he'd done.

Jamie sat up and put her feet on the floor. The effort left her weak. Holding on to whatever she could, she stood and then made her way to the door. Two federal agents stood guard outside.

"Ma'am, I need you to stay inside your room," one of the agents informed her.

"Not until I see my uncle." She stood up straight and didn't budge.

The second agent nodded toward the next room, where two more agents stood outside. "He's in there. Let me help you, ma'am."

The agent took her arm and slowly walked her over to the two guards. They stepped aside, and he opened the door. Once inside, the agent helped her into the chair close to Uncle Paxton's bed.

"Thank you," Jamie said gratefully. The man who'd helped her smiled and left them alone.

Paxton was resting peacefully. She clasped his hand and held it. She was so grateful to him for not giving up through the years when it would have been so easy. Everyone had doubted him, including Jamie.

"There she is." She hadn't realized that Uncle Paxton was awake until he spoke.

She smiled down at her uncle through tears. "Hey, you."

"Where's Gavin?" her uncle asked, his gaze going to the door.

"He was just here, but he left to go help with the manhunt. It's only a matter of time now before Shadow is captured, along with all the crooked deputies. Dad's name will be cleared finally, and we owe it all to you. You never gave up on proving his innocence. He would be so proud of you."

Uncle Paxton smiled up at her. "And you. I know you never doubted his innocence, either. I just wish I could have proven what really happened before he had to die in that horrible place."

Jamie squeezed his hand. "You did everything you could. You fought against so many odds to clear his name."

Her uncle lowered his head. "You and Gavin. You going to marry him?"

Jamie was surprised by the question. "If he'll have me, and I hope he will. I love him so much. I never stopped loving him."

"The feeling is mutual, Jamie. Ava used to tell me all the time that her grandson still loved you. He just couldn't let go of what he believed."

Jamie scrubbed tears from her cheeks. The damage Shadow had done to their families would take a lot of healing to move beyond.

"The past is finally finished. It's time to look toward the future now," her uncle told her. "And I have a confession to make. When I realized that Miller was intent on bringing me in, probably to kill me, I hid the rest of the heroin at the house."

Jamie stared at him. He didn't know about the house yet. "Oh, Uncle Paxton, I'm so sorry. The house... Miller and his men set it on fire. There's nothing left."

Her uncle was shocked by the news. He shook his head. "Those horrible men." He didn't say anything for a moment. "But the heroin wasn't in the house. It's in the plowed land behind the house. I buried it there."

Now Jamie understood why the area had been freshly plowed. It wasn't because Uncle Paxton planned to plant; it was because he'd been hiding evidence.

Suddenly, the lights were extinguished and the room grew dark.

"What's happening?" Jamie could hear the unease in his voice.

"I don't know. I'll check it out." She jumped to her

feet and hurried to the door. Two of the agents were still there.

"What's going on?" she asked. The entire floor was dark.

"Go back inside, ma'am. We're checking it out now. We'll figure out what's happening and let you know. Until then, stay inside." The agent pushed her back into the room. Jamie returned to her uncle, who had sat up in bed, his feet hanging over the edge.

"This is his work," he whispered in a fearful voice.

Jamie didn't have to ask who he meant, because she believed the same thing. In spite of a county-wide manhunt, Brock Shadow was coming after them to finish the job.

One of the agents standing guard had offered Gavin the use of their vehicle. He'd been updated on where the hunt for Shadow was situated—an abandoned mine that had been on the list he and Jamie had found.

As much as he hated leaving Jamie, she was right. He had to see this thing through to the end. He owed it to his father and to Noah.

Gavin drove the ten-plus miles to the mine. There were dozens of law enforcement vehicles parked down from the entrance. Gavin got out of the car and headed toward it. He spotted Andy amongst the group of men standing out front.

Andy came over.

"What's happening in there?" Gavin asked. He wondered why the agents hadn't stormed the mine.

"We tried to get in there, but they fired on us. We have no idea how many of them are in there. Wilson is letting them sweat it for a while longer, and then he's going with a flash grenade. You want to be part of that?"

"Absolutely." It amazed him how well Andy was holding up after being forced to shoot his own dad. "I really am sorry about your father, Andy. I know how hard it is to lose your dad. I can't imagine how difficult it must be under these circumstances."

Andy kept his focus on the activity in front of the mine. "It was. I still can't believe my father was the one who killed yours, acting under Shadow's orders."

Gavin stared at him. He wasn't sure he'd heard him correctly. "What do you mean?"

Andy looked heartbroken. "I learned that my dad was the one who came to your father originally with the offer. He knew your dad wouldn't accept it. Gavin, my dad went to the mine with Shadow that day. He was the one who shot your dad with a gun he'd taken from Noah's place. Then he lured Noah over to frame him for the murder."

Gavin couldn't believe what he was hearing. "How did you find this out?"

Andy looked at him with regret. "I'm sorry as all get-out about this, Gavin. I found out because one of the deputies who worked for my dad was captured trying to leave the county. I guess the rats are jumping ship. Anyway, he thought he could help himself on his sentence if he started talking."

"Unbelievable." Gavin couldn't imagine how difficult it must be for Andy to admit that not only had his father been corrupt, he was a murderer, as well.

"Looks like they're about to start," Andy told him, and they headed to the entrance.

"Once the flash grenades go off, we'll have only a

few minutes' advantage. Be prepared. They have nothing to lose," Agent Wilson told the group.

Seconds after the flash grenades were thrown into the mine, the agents stormed it.

The chaos that Gavin saw when he entered reminded him of many of the war-type situations he'd faced abroad.

Gavin spotted at least five deputies stumbling around. The grenade would make vision impossible for several seconds as well as cause ringing in the ears, disorienting the victim.

He was aware of Andy next to him. Both Gavin and Andy tucked close to the stone wall. Several of the deputies regained their vision and began shooting back at them. Gavin returned fire. He struck a man in the shoulder, causing his gun to fly out of his hand. The deputy closest to him got off several rounds and then turned and ran down the passage. Immediately, the agents, along with Andy and Gavin, charged after them.

But several of the deputies continued firing, forcing the agents to retreat for the moment. Gavin spotted Miller holding his arm. He'd been shot and was bleeding. Shadow was nowhere in sight. Was he already halfway down the passage?

Gavin didn't know the layout of the mine. Neither did the agents.

"Andy, do you have any idea where this passage leads?" Gavin asked.

"Nowhere. The mine ends in about another couple of hundred feet. They're trapped and dangerous."

"And they have nothing to lose," Gavin said. "We need to try to negotiate."

They'd gone a couple of hundred feet into the tunnel.

The deputies fired once more. Gavin and the rest of the team ducked behind the bend in the shaft.

"There's no way out for you. Give yourself up or die down here. The choice is yours," Wilson said.

More shots rang out. It didn't appear as if the men were giving up willingly.

"They'll run out of ammo soon enough," Gavin told the team.

"So we wait them out?" Wilson asked. "That could take a while."

"Let me try something." Gavin figured he had nothing to lose. He was going to try to reach out to Miller.

"Dan Miller, I know you're hurt. There's no way out of here alive. From the looks of that wound, I'd say you're losing a lot of blood. Are you ready to die for Shadow? Give him up to us, and maybe we can help you and your men with your sentences."

Silence followed, and Gavin believed he'd failed.

"He's not here to give up. He never was," Miller called out.

This piece of news scared the daylights out of Gavin. Had they been focused on the mine all this time only to allow Shadow to slip through the cracks?

"Where is he?" Gavin demanded.

"If I knew that, I'd be going after him myself. He told us to meet him here, only he never showed."

Gavin turned to Wilson. "I don't like it. Shadow is dangerous. We need to find him before he hurts someone else."

Wilson nodded. "Give yourself up, Miller. Tell your men to come out with their hands in the air."

It took only a matter of minutes before five deputies came forward with their hands held high, Miller included.

They were immediately handcuffed and taken away.

"We're going to need your offices for the interviews, sheriff," Wilson said.

Andy willingly agreed. "Whatever you need."

When Wilson got outside, his cell phone rang. Gavin could tell right away that the news was bad.

"Shadow was at the hospital. He killed the power. When two of my men went to investigate, he attacked the two agents standing guard outside of Paxton Hendricks's room. He was dressed as a doctor. That's why he was able to get close enough to inject both men with something to knock them out."

"Where's Jamie?" Gavin asked with fear in his heart.

"She's gone. Paxton's been shot. He's in critical condition. He's in surgery right now. They don't know if he's going to make it. My men are looking through video footage now to see if they can find where he took her."

Gavin turned and ran.

"Hold up, Gavin. I'm going with you," Andy told him and followed Gavin.

"Where are you going?" Wilson yelled after him.

"To find Jamie and get her away from Shadow."

"You don't know where she is. Dalton, wait up. We'll find her."

But Gavin didn't listen. He knew that if Shadow was desperate enough to shoot Paxton and take Jamie hostage, he had nothing to lose. He'd have a way out of there somehow, and there was only one place Gavin could think to look.

TWENTY

The second they exited the hospital, Shadow grabbed a handful of her hair and dragged her by it.

Jamie screamed and fought and kicked to free herself. If she got into the car with him, she believed she would soon be dead.

"Shut up!" Shadow yelled and grabbed her around the waist, clamping a hand over her mouth.

Jamie continued to kick and try to free herself, but Shadow hauled her over to a car waiting in the doctors' parking garage.

Shadow shoved her in the driver's side and got in after her. Jamie scrambled to the opposite door and grabbed the handle. Shadow snatched a handful of hair and forced her back next to him. "I don't think so. You and I have business to finish, so sit back and enjoy your last minutes here on earth."

With those words searing her heart, he put the car in gear and roared out of the parking garage while Jamie tried to control the panic growing inside of her. She had to keep a clear head if she was going to survive.

"You can't get away. Every law enforcement agency in the state is looking for you. They'll have the roads blocked. You should give yourself up while you still have the chance."

Shadow spared her an angry glare. "You think so? I'm not going to give myself up. I'd be dead before I even got to trial. You think Jacob Ericson is going to let me live when he realizes I was the one who tried to kill him?" Shadow shook his head. "No, I'm not giving myself up."

"You'll never get away. You can't hide out in the county forever."

Jamie watched as Shadow turned onto the road leading up to Darlan Mountain. Where was he going?

He caught her watching him. "I have a helicopter waiting for me at the Dalton place. Once you help me find the evidence your crazy old uncle left Ava Dalton, then I'm out of here. I know the two of them were tight. She's the only one he'd trust with it. You're going to be my insurance once I find it."

She'd be dead once Shadow was safely out of the FBI's reach. She had to find a way to stall.

When they pulled into the Dalton drive, Jamie saw a helicopter waiting behind the house.

Shadow parked the car and forced her out beside him. "Now, where would the old lady hide the evidence?"

Jamie stared at him in shock. "I have no idea what you're talking about."

Shadow's answer was to grab her arm and drag her along beside him to the chopper. The pilot hopped out when he saw them approaching.

"Did you have any problems getting up here undetected?"

The man shook his head. "Not really, but there's an awful lot of activity at the old Smithville Mine."

Shadow smiled to himself. "Good. Then they bought my diversion. By the time they take in Miller and the rest of his buffoons, we'll be long gone."

The pilot wasn't nearly as convinced. "We'd better be on our way soon. Once they figure out you're gone, they'll be watching every possible exit, and that includes the air. And there's more." He stopped long enough to look at Jamie, as if uncertain how much to say in front of her.

"Don't mind her. She'll be dead soon enough."

The reality of what Shadow had planned for her threatened to buckle her knees.

The pilot didn't seem to approve of the plan, but he knew who paid his salary. "*He's* looking for you. He knows the truth."

"How did he find out so soon?" Shadow asked, and all the color drained from his face.

"My guess is one of the buyers waiting for the supply talked. All the more reason we need to get out of here as soon as possible."

Shadow scowled at Jamie. "You heard him. Where is the evidence hidden?"

"Alright, I'll take you to it," she said and hoped she'd pulled off the lie. Shadow's eyes narrowed as if trying to decide if she was telling the truth.

The man was desperate, though, and willing to give her the chance to prove him wrong.

"Then do it. We don't have much time." Shadow still held her arm in a vice grip.

"It's in the house." Jamie had no idea where Ava might have put the thumb drive Paxton had given her, but she needed to buy herself some time and pray that Gavin and the FBI would figure out where she was.

Before Shadow realized she was taking him on a wild goose chase and he ended her life right then and there.

Gavin got into Andy's patrol car and drove up the mountain with the FBI close behind.

After spotting the chopper heading up the mountain, Gavin was convinced Shadow was going after the thumb drive containing Paxton's evidence. If they didn't reach the chopper before he found the drive and took off again, Jamie's life would be worthless to Shadow.

Andy stopped a short distance from the homestead. He didn't want to alert Shadow to their presence.

The rest of the vehicles halted behind them.

"We'll have to go the rest of the way on foot," Gavin said.

Sam nodded. "Lead on."

Gavin took point as they eased toward Ava's place.

Once they were on the edge of the property, Gavin took a second to survey his surroundings. He didn't see any movement.

"They could be inside. The chopper is still behind the house," Gavin said.

Sam indicated that four of the men should go check out the helicopter. "If the pilot's there, get him subdued and make sure that chopper isn't going anywhere. When you have him, alert me."

The men headed around back, and Sam directed a question to Gavin. "Does Jamie know where the evidence is hidden?"

"No, but if I know Jamie, she's trying to stall Shadow as long as she can."

"You think they're inside the house?" Sam asked.

"Probably."

Sam's phone vibrated and he answered it. "Good. We're storming the house." He ended the call. "They have the pilot. Let's get Shadow."

"You should know my grandmother installed monitors all around the property before she died. If they're still on, Shadow will know we're coming."

Sam nodded. "Then we'll have to be quick."

Gavin and the rest of the team eased up on the property. All the while, he prayed that Jamie was still safe.

Agents surrounded the house. When Sam gave the signal, they broke down the door and charged inside.

Gavin noticed right away that the monitors were off. He believed that was Jamie's handiwork.

They searched the house and came up empty. Gavin was scared to death he would be too late to find Jamie alive.

"The place is clear," Sam's men confirmed.

Sam turned to Gavin, frustrated. "Any idea where they might be?"

Gavin was about to say no until he remembered the old root cellar on his family's property.

"I know where they are." He told Sam about the cellar.

"Let's get going. This guy will know his only means of escape is gone. He's desperate."

Gavin's heart pounded in his chest as they slowly made their way to the cellar. Once they reached it, he could see fresh footprints.

He turned to Sam and whispered, "They're in there."

"Brock Shadow, this is the FBI," Sam announced. "We have the place surrounded. Let Jamie go and give yourself up."

"Jamie are you okay?" Gavin called out because he had to know.

"I'm okay," she confirmed. "It's dark in here but we have the chair."

Her words were cut off, but not before she'd given him a clue. They were near the single chair in the place.

Gavin told Sam what Jamie was trying to convey. "It's at the very back of the cellar."

"He's not going down without a fight. I think he'll try to kill her and himself." Sam didn't mince words, and each one sent terror through Gavin.

"We need to break down the door. Watch the floor— it's uneven and the steps are dangerous," Gavin said.

Sam knew what he was doing. He counted to five, then they breached the place. Gavin was the first man through the door. A scuffle occurred, and then Shadow fired at him. Gavin ducked as the shots barely missed him. He didn't hesitate before firing two shots into Shadow's chest. The man fell to the ground.

As the rest of the agents poured in behind him, Gavin's only thought was for Jamie.

"We need some light in here!" Gavin yelled. Immediately flashlights lit up the place. Jamie was on the floor. She wasn't moving.

Gavin hurried to her side. "Jamie!" His voice broke with fear.

And then she moved. "I'm okay," she managed and slowly sat up.

Gavin drew her close. "Are you hurt?"

She shook her head against his chest. "No, I'm not hurt. I was just so scared." She shivered against him. He lifted her in his arms and carried her out of the cellar.

"Can you stand on your own?" he asked.

She smiled up at him. "I can."

He slowly set her down beside him. "I was so afraid I'd lost you." His voice shook as he framed her face and took in everything about her lovely face.

She hugged him close. "I'm okay. He shot Uncle Paxton, though." She started to cry. He couldn't imagine how worried she was.

Gavin held her and whispered, "I know. He's in surgery."

They watched as Shadow's body was brought out of the cellar.

"He was going to kill me. He told his pilot that once he found the evidence, he was flying out of the area and he was going to kill me."

Gavin brushed back the hair from her face. "He's not going to hurt you ever again." He was so grateful that God had brought her safely through.

Sam stopped next to them. "Sorry you had to go through that, Ms. Hendricks."

She nodded. "Is there any news on my uncle?"

"There is. I just heard. He's out of surgery and holding his own. I'll have one of my men take you there."

"I can do it." Andy stepped forward.

Sam agreed. "Good. We'll be here for a while processing the scene."

They turned to go, but Jamie stopped suddenly. "I almost forgot, with everything that happened. My uncle told me that he hid the rest of the heroin behind our place. It's buried under the plowed area around back."

Gavin couldn't believe it. Paxton had been expecting something bad to happen and was prepared for it. The old guy never ceased to surprise him.

Sam nodded. "I'll have my men get to it right away."

As they left the place, Gavin marveled at all that had happened over the past few days. He took Jamie's hand in his, still amazed that they were both alive. He had her back, and he wasn't about to let anything get in their way ever again.

Once they reached the hospital, Andy went with them up to where Paxton was recovering.

Gavin and Jamie went inside, and Andy stood by the door.

Jamie saw how bad her uncle looked, and hurried to Paxton's side. She took his hand in hers, tears falling down her face.

They'd been there only a short time when the doctor came to visit them.

"Is he going to be okay?" Jamie asked, getting to her feet, anticipating the worst.

The doctor smiled kindly. "I believe he will. He's a strong man who came through the surgery well. The next few hours will be the deciding factor, but I believe he will be just fine."

Gavin touched her arm, and Jamie curled into him.

"It's going to be okay," he murmured. "Paxton's too stubborn to die."

She laughed and nodded against his chest.

Andy cleared his throat, and Gavin looked over at him.

"I think I'll head back to the station. I'll check in with you in a little while."

Gavin waved and waited until Andy was gone before he cupped Jamie's chin and tipped her head back before kissing her with all his heart.

"I love you, Jamie Hendricks, and I want to spend

the rest of my life with you in Louisville. What I do for a living doesn't matter. I just want to do it with you."

Surprised, she smiled up at him. "I love you, Gavin Dalton, but I'm ready to come home again and start our lives together in the only place that will ever be home for either of us. Let's come back home to Darlan."

EPILOGUE

One year later...

Jamie smiled up at the man who'd always had her heart, as he was sworn in as a sheriff's deputy for Darlan County. Nothing her wildest imagination could have created had prepared her for this future.

When Andy first proposed the idea of Gavin becoming his deputy and working alongside him to clean up Darlan County for good, Gavin hadn't jumped at the opportunity until he and Jamie talked it over.

She and Gavin had gotten married a few months after Paxton was released from the hospital. She was so happy to be his wife. Leaving the law firm in Louisville hadn't been as difficult as she'd feared. She'd made sure her caseload was cleared and then come back home to open her own practice in Darlan, looking out for those wrongly accused.

Gavin had known being a deputy was a tremendous opportunity for him to make something good come from what had happened to both their fathers. Charles would have been so proud. So would Noah.

With his home destroyed, Paxton was determined

to rebuild. He'd bought himself a camper trailer, and with Gavin's help, he was building a new house on the property.

Jamie and Gavin had settled into Ava's old house, and Jamie couldn't have been happier. In fact, she had a special piece of news to share with her husband and knew just the right place to tell him.

They left the ceremony and drove home. Once Gavin parked the car, Jamie got out and took her husband's hand in hers.

"I'm so proud of you, babe. Do you feel like sitting outside for a bit?"

He smiled his answer, and they headed to Ava's favorite spot: the bench behind the house.

Once they were seated, Gavin put his arm around her and tugged her close. "When I left here all those years ago, I could never have imagined being this happy again."

"Me, either." She drew in a breath. "I have some news," she said in a tiny voice and prayed he would be as happy as she was. They'd talked about having children…one day.

Gavin turned to her. "What is it?"

It took all her strength to force the words out. "I'm pregnant. We're going to have a child together." She looked into his eyes waiting for his response, her heart in her throat.

"You're pregnant?" Unexpected tears filled his eyes, and he took her in his arms and kissed her with all his heart.

"Are you happy?" she asked in between kisses.

He looked at her in wonderment. "Happy? I'm more than happy. I'm blessed beyond measure. I can't imagine living my life anywhere but here with you." He touched her stomach. "And with the child God has chosen to bless us with."

She couldn't, either.

* * * * *

**WE HOPE YOU ENJOYED
THIS BOOK FROM**

LOVE INSPIRED SUSPENSE
INSPIRATIONAL ROMANCE

Courage. Danger. Faith.

Find strength and determination in stories
of faith and love in the face of danger.

6 NEW BOOKS AVAILABLE EVERY MONTH!

SPECIAL EXCERPT FROM

LOVE INSPIRED SUSPENSE
INSPIRATIONAL ROMANCE

*A K-9 officer and a forensics specialist must work
together to solve a murder and stay alive.*

Read on for a sneak preview of
Scene of the Crime *by Sharon Dunn,*
*the next book in the True Blue K-9 Unit: Brooklyn series
available September 2020 from Love Inspired Suspense.*

Brooklyn K-9 Unit Officer Jackson Davison caught movement out of the corner of his eye: a face in the trees fading out of view. His heart beat a little faster. Was someone watching him? The hairs on the back of Jackson's neck stood at attention as a light breeze brushed his face. Even as he studied the foliage, he felt the weight of a gaze on him. The sound of Smokey's barking brought his mission back into focus.

When he caught up with his partner, the dog was sitting. The signal that he'd found something. "Good boy." Jackson tossed out the toy he carried on his belt for Smokey to play with, his reward for doing his job. The dog whipped the toy back and forth in his mouth.

"Drop," Jackson said. He picked up the toy and patted Smokey on the head. "Sit. Stay."

The body, partially covered by branches, was clothed in neutral colors and would not be easy to spot unless you were looking for it.

He keyed his radio. "Officer Davison here. I've got a body in Prospect Park. Male Caucasian under the age of forty, about two hundred yards in, just southwest of the Brooklyn Botanic Garden."

Dispatch responded, "Ten-four. Help is on the way."

He studied the trees just in time to catch the face again, barely visible, like a fading mist. He was being watched. "Did you see something?" Jackson shouted. "Did you call this in?"

The person turned and ran, disappearing into the thick brush.

Jackson took off in the direction the runner had gone. As his feet pounded the hard earth, another thought occurred to him. Was this the person who had shot the man in the chest? Sometimes criminals hung around to witness the police response to their handiwork.

His attention was drawn to a garbage can just as an object hit the back of his head with intense force. Pain radiated from the base of his skull. He crumpled to the ground and his world went black.

Don't miss
Scene of the Crime *by Sharon Dunn,*
available wherever Love Inspired Suspense books
and ebooks are sold.

LoveInspired.com

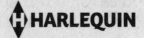

HARLEQUIN

Heartfelt or suspenseful, inspiring or passionate, Harlequin has your happily-ever-after.

With new books published every month, you are sure to find the satisfying escape you know you deserve.

HNEWS2020